"Sharon Hinck not o
once again, her comp
pages rich with imagi
challenged and encou

—JILL ELIZABETH NELSON, author of the
To CATCH A THIEF series

"Sharon Hinck weaves a magnificent tale, a collision of everyday life with the fantastical realms of the unknown. She masterfully portrays characters of no uncommon standing pitted in an epic fight to save all they hold dear. And in this is her great strength: to bring out the universal flaws of humanity while revealing that even the simplest of individuals has the innate ability to be heroic. I commend her for a series well written and well timed. Such a force is to be treasured for generations to come."

—CHRISTOPHER HOPPER, author of
Rise of The Dibor and *The Lion Vrie*

"Another thrilling adventure in the land of Lyric! Sharon Hinck not only transported me into a rich world with an epic tale of good versus evil, but through her characters she taught me truths that resonate in my soul. This is what Christian fiction is all about. Bravo to Sharon on a series every Christian should have on their shelf!"

—SUSAN MAY WARREN, award-winning author

"What a terrific adventure and what engaging characters! Who knew that a warm family drama could include swords and songkeepers, enemy treachery, and the faithfulness of the One? Thank you, Sharon Hinck, for many hours of enjoyment and inspiration."

—KATHRYN MACKEL, author of *Vanished*

"*The Restorer's Journey* has a little bit of science fiction, a little bit of fantasy, and a whole lot of suspense. A great way to wrap up a series."

—DONITA K. PAUL, author of *DragonSpell, DragonQuest,*
DragonKnight, and DragonFire

"Riveting. Enriching. Compelling. Sharon Hinck has made this third journey to Lyric as fantastic as the first."

—LOIS RICHER, author of *Healing Tides*

"Get ready for an exhilarating journey back to the world of the People of the Verses. Things have changed on the other side of the portal, and this time the price demanded of the Restorer—and his mother—may be more than either of them is able to pay. Sharon Hinck weaves a powerful tale of adventure, faith, and the victory that is found only when we truly surrender to the One."

—VIRGINIA SMITH, author of *Stuck in the Middle*,
book 1 of the SISTER-TO-SISTER series

Also by Sharon Hinck:

THE SWORD OF LYRIC (NavPress)
The Restorer
The Restorer's Son

The Secret Life of Becky Miller (Bethany House)
Renovating Becky Miller (Bethany House)
Symphony of Secrets (Bethany House)

The Restorer's Journey

THE SWORD OF LYRIC

3

Sharon Hinck

NAVPRESS

ISBN-13: 978-1-60006-133-2
ISBN-10: 1-60006-133-8

Cover design by Kirk DouPonce, www.DogEaredDesign.com
Cover photo by Stephen Gardner, www.ShootPW.com
Author photo by Ritz Camera Proex Portraits

Creative Team: Jeff Gerke, Reagen Reed, Cara Iverson, Arvid Wallen, Kathy Guist

Published in association with the literary agency of The Steve Laube Agency, LLC, 5501 N. 7th. Ave., #502, Phoenix, AZ 85013.

Library of Congress Cataloging-in-Publication Data

Hinck, Sharon.
The restorer's journey : a novel / Sharon Hinck.
p. cm. -- (The sword of lyric ; 3)
ISBN-13: 978-1-60006-133-2
ISBN-10: 1-60006-133-8
I. Title.
PS3608.I53R476 2008
813'.6--dc22

2007033177

Printed in the United States of America

1 2 3 4 5 6 7 8 9 10 / 12 11 10 09 08

to the One who is with us in even the dark places

"In every time of great need, a Restorer is sent to fight for the people and help the guardians. The Restorer is empowered with gifts to defeat our enemies and turn the people's hearts back to the Verses."

Acknowledgments

Holy One, I'm so grateful that You have wooed me from my earliest days. You've led me on paths full of joy and beauty, as well as through some dark places where doubt and pain tempted me to push against Your gentle embrace. Yet You've never let go. Thank you for guiding, comforting, and holding me during the specific challenges of writing this book. You are my strong tower.

Dearest Book Buddies, your prayers, notes, calls, blog posts, stories, efforts to spread the word about the books, and other offerings of encouragement amaze me in their timeliness and generosity. I marvel at how God's grace has poured out through many of you at key moments. You are so much more than an e-mail–update list. You are dear friends.

NavPress is absolutely full of amazing people who love Jesus and are excited to serve Him through the gift of storytelling. You have all made me laugh, spoiled me with kindness, and encouraged me along the way. Thank you for your partnership. Special gratitude to my amazing editor, Reagen Reed. You have gone above and beyond with your passion and care for this project, and getting to know you is one of my joyful bonuses in this experience.

I lean heavily on the support of wise people in the publishing world, particularly my amazing agent Steve Laube. Your wisdom and practicality bless me on this road in myriad ways. Thank you!

Warm appreciation to groups of amazing authors to learn from: Word Servants, Word Slaves, American Christian Fiction Writers, Mount Hermon Christian Writers Conference, Minnesota Christian Writers Guild, Christian Authors Network, and more.

Special thanks to critique buddies who dug into this story in progress. Sherri Sand, Jill Elizabeth Nelson, Donita K. Paul, Cheryl and Bill Bader, Camy Tang, Chawna Schroeder, Carol Oyanagi.

As I finished the last edits on this book, I enjoyed the adventure of the East Coast Fantasy Fiction Tour. Wayne Batson, Bryan Davis, and Christopher Hopper, I have deep admiration and respect for each of you, and I was honored to journey with you on our quest to share our excitement for Christian fantasy. (What day is it?)

During the writing of this book, while my mind was deep in story world, many dear friends supported me in the *real* world. "Church Ladies," you rock. You are true heroines, making a difference for Christ every day. Life Group, our family has felt supported by you all in more ways than we can express. St. Michael's, powerful times of prayer, tears, worship, and learning have happened for me inside your walls. I'm so blessed to be part of this group of the body.

Thank you to every friend who read my long e-mails or prayed with me during phone calls when I felt panic, discouragement, confusion, and fatigue along the way. It mattered.

Mom, you so often drop everything when I call, ready to

listen and encourage. Thank you.

Joel, Kaeti, Josh, and Jenni, getting to be your mom is a profound honor. And Jennelle, I'm so delighted you "married in" to our brood. You are each so tender, generous, gifted, supportive, and creative—I delight in watching God at work in each of you.

Ted, the best of every hero I write is based on you. Your constancy, strength of character, integrity, and tenderness reflect Christ to me daily. Thank you.

Chapter One

JAKE

My mom was freaking out.

She stared out the dining room window as if major-league monsters were hiding in the darkness beyond the glass. Give me a break. Our neighborhood was as boring as they come. Ridgeview Drive's square lawns and generic houses held nothing more menacing than basketball hoops and tire swings. Still, Mom's back was tight, and in the shadowed reflection on the pane, I could see her biting her lip. I didn't know what to say to make her feel better.

I ducked back into the kitchen and used a wet rag to wipe off the counters. Clumps of flour turned to paste and smeared in gunky white arcs across the surface. I shook the rag over the garbage can, the mess raining down on the other debris we'd swept up. Broken jars of pasta and rice filled the bag. Our dented toaster lay on top of the mess, looking like it had been drop-kicked across the room. I stomped it down, twist-tied the bag, and jogged it out to the trash can by the garage. Usually I hated the chore of taking out the trash. Not tonight. Maybe if I erased the signs of our intruders, Mom would relax a little.

So Cameron and Medea dropped a few things when they were looking for supplies. No biggie. Why did my folks have such a problem with those two anyway? They'd been great to me. I trudged back into the house, rubbing my forehead. Wait . . . that wasn't right. A shiver snaked through my spine. Never mind. They were probably long gone by now.

"Kitchen's done." I carried the broom into the dining room, hoping Mom had finished in there. But she was still hugging her arms and staring out the window.

She turned and looked at the china cabinet, then squeezed her eyes shut as if they were hurting. "Why?" she whispered.

One cabinet door had glass shards jutting from it, and the other hung crooked with wood splinters poking out. Broken china covered the floor. Mom and Dad had been collecting those goofy teacups ever since they got married.

I pushed the broom against the edge of the fragments, but the chinking sound made her wince, so I stopped. Dad strode past with an empty garbage bag from the hall closet and stopped to give Mom a squeeze. He nodded toward me. "Honey, Jake's alive. Nothing else matters. We all got back safe." He leaned his head against hers, and I edged toward the kitchen in case they started kissing. For an old married couple, they were a little too free with their public displays of affection.

But my mom didn't look like she was in a kissing mood — not with her lips pressed together like that. I had a sneaking suspicion she was more freaked out about what had happened to my hand than to our house. Like when I had cancer as a kid. She'd gotten really stressed about the details of a church fundraiser and cranky about everything that went wrong — stuff that wasn't even important. It gave her a place to be angry when she was trying to be brave about a bigger problem.

"It's only a piece of furniture." Dad was doing his soothing voice. When would he catch on that it only made things worse?

"Only a piece of furniture we bought as a wedding gift to each other." She swiped at some wet spots on her face. "Only twenty years' worth of poking around garage sales and thrift stores together. Don't tell me what it's only, okay?"

"Okay." Dad backed away from her prickles.

I made another ineffectual push with the broom. My folks didn't argue much, but when they did, it grated like a clutch struggling to find third gear. Typical over-responsible firstborn, I wanted to fix it but didn't know how.

Mom picked up a Delft saucer—what was left of it—and laid the pieces gently into the garbage bag. Dad folded his arms and leaned against the high back of one of the chairs. "I can repair the cabinet. That splintered door will need to be replaced, but the other one just needs new hinges. I can put in new glass." His eyes always lit up when he talked about a woodworking project. The man loved his tools.

Mom smiled at him. Her tension faded, and she got all moony-eyed, so I ducked into the kitchen just as the doorbell rang. Thank heaven. "Pizza's here!" I yelled.

Dad paid the delivery guy, and I carried the cartons into the living room. Flopping onto one end of the couch, I pried open a lid. "Hey, who ordered green peppers? Mom, you've gotta quit ruining good pizza with veggies."

That made her laugh. "We'd better save a few pieces for the other kids." She cleared the Legos off the coffee table and handed me a napkin.

I gladly surrendered the top pizza box, along with the gross green peppers, and dove into the pepperoni below. "Where is everyone?"

"Karen's spending the night at Amanda's—trying out her new driver's license. Jon and Anne are at Grandma's. But if they see the pizza boxes when they get home tomorrow . . ."

I nodded. "Yep. Pure outrage. I can hear it now: 'It's not fair. Jake always gets to have extra fun.'" I did a pretty good impression of the rug rats. What would the kids think if they found out what else they had missed? This had been the strangest Saturday the Mitchell family had ever seen.

I popped open a can of Dr Pepper. My third. Hey, I'd earned some extra caffeine. "So what do we tell the kids?"

Mom smiled and looked me up and down, probably thinking I was one of the kids. When would it sink in that I was an adult now? I guzzled a third of my pop and set it down with a thump. "We could tell them there was a burglar, but then they'd want to help the police solve the case, and they'd never stop asking questions."

"Good point." Mom licked sauce from her finger. "Jon and Anne would break out the detective kit you gave them for Christmas."

Dad tore a piece of crust from his slice of pepperoni. "If we finish cleaning everything, I don't think they'll pay much attention. The cabinet is the only obvious damage. If they ask, we'll just say it got bumped and fell."

Dad wanted us to lie? So not like him. Then again, when Kieran told me Dad wasn't originally from our world, I realized there were a lot of things he'd not been honest about. Now I was part of the family secret too.

He rested his piece of pizza on the cardboard box and looked at Mom. "Do we need to warn them?"

"Warn them?" She mumbled around a mouthful of melted cheese.

"In case Cameron and Medea come back." His voice was calm, but I suddenly had a hard time swallowing. Something cold twisted in me when he said their names. The same cold that had numbed my bones when I'd woken up in the attic. Why? They'd taken care of me. No . . . they'd threatened me. Confusing images warred inside my brain.

"You think they'll come back?" My baritone went up in pitch, and I quickly took another sip of pop.

Dad didn't answer for a moment. "It depends on why they came. If they plan to stay in our world, we need to find them—stop them. But my guess is that Cameron wants to return to Lyric with something from our world that he can use there. That means they'll be back to go through the portal."

Mom sank deeper into the couch and looked out the living room windows. At the curb, our family van shimmered beneath a streetlight.

They might be out there too. They could be watching us right this second.

"Maybe we should call the police." Mom's voice sounded thin. I'd suggested that earlier. After all, someone had broken in—well, broken out.

Dad snorted. "And tell them what?"

He had a point, but it's not like there's a rule book for dealing with visitors from other universes. Unless you attended *Star Trek* conventions.

"So what's your plan?" I asked.

"I'll get extra locks tomorrow. Maybe look into an alarm system." Dad believed every problem could be solved with his Home Depot credit card.

"And shades." Mom chewed the edge of a fingernail.

"What?"

"We need some window shades."

He nodded, then turned to me. "Can you remember more about your conversations with Cameron? What did he ask you about? What did he seem interested in?"

A shudder moved through me, and pain began pulsing behind my eyes.

Mom gave Dad a worried glance, then rested a hand on my arm. "It's okay, honey. We don't have to talk about it right now." She smoothed my hair back from my face.

"No problem." I brushed her hand away, sprawled back on the couch, and studied the ceiling. "It just seems like it was all a dream."

"What's the last thing you remember clearly?" Dad pulled his chair closer and watched me.

"Braide Wood." I closed my eyes and smiled. "It reminded me of summer camp. And I was so tired of running and hiding in caves. I finally felt safe. Tara fussed over me, and I taught Dustin and Aubrey how to play soccer. It felt like home."

I struggled to remember the rest. For some reason my memories were tangled up, like the time I had a major fever and took too much NyQuil. Mom and Dad waited.

"I went to see Morsal Plains with Tara. Brutal. The grain was all black, and it smelled weird. Tara told me about the attack—how Hazor poisoned it on purpose and how Susan the Restorer led the army to protect Braide Wood." I squinted my eyes open and looked sideways at my mom. They'd told me she had ridden into battle with a sword. "Unbelievable."

Even though she was watching me with a worried pinch to her eyes, she smiled. "I know. I lived it, and it's hard for me to believe."

"Anyway, I hiked back to Tara's house, and some guys came

to take me to Cameron. He made a big fuss over me. Said it was his job to welcome guests to the clans. Said I'd run into bad company but he'd make it up to me. He gave me something to drink, and there was this lady. She was amazing." No matter how fuzzy my memories were, Medea was easy to remember: the long curly hair, the sparkling green eyes, the dress that clung to all the right places. My cheeks heated. "I can't remember everything we talked about. She made me feel important, like I wasn't just some teenage kid. It was . . ." I sat taller and angled away from my parents, my jaw tightening. "She helped me realize that no one else had ever really understood me. I wanted to become a guardian. I had an important job to do."

"Jake." Dad's voice was sharp, and I flinched. "The woman you met was a Rhusican. They poison minds. Don't trust everything you're feeling right now."

A pulsing ache grabbed the base of my neck. I pressed the heels of my hands against my eyes. Mom's hand settled on my shoulder, and I stiffened. Weird static was messing with my head.

"Jake, they used you to find the portal. She doesn't really understand you." Mom's voice was quiet and sounded far away. I felt as if I were falling away inside myself. She squeezed my shoulder. "Remember my favorite psalm?"

I managed a tight smile. "How could I forget? You made us learn the whole thing one summer: 'O Lord, you have searched me and you know me,' blah, blah, blah."

Despite my smart-aleck tone, the words took hold, and some of the static in my brain quieted.

"What's the rest?" Dad pressed me.

What was he trying to prove? That I couldn't think straight? I could have told him that. I struggled to form the words.

"You know when I sit and when I rise; you perceive my thoughts from afar. You discern my going out and my lying down; you are familiar with all my ways." Once I got started, I rattled off the verses by rote. In some strange way, the words actually stopped the sensation of falling away inside myself.

"Sounds like there's someone who understands you a lot better than Cameron and Medea. Remember that." Dad stood up and tousled my hair. Then he yawned. "Let's get some sleep."

Mom didn't move. She was still watching me. "How's the hand?"

I rubbed my palm. "Still fine. Weird, huh?" I held it out.

A scar, faint as a white thread, marked the skin where broken glass had cut a deep gash an hour earlier. My heart gave a weird double-thump. What did it mean?

Dad shook his head. "Come on. Bedtime."

Mom hesitated but then stood and gave me a quick kiss on the forehead. "Good night, Jake. We'll talk more tomorrow."

Oh, great. She sure loved talking. I looked at Dad. His mouth twitched. "I'll get us signed up for some practice space at the fencing club."

Good. He hadn't forgotten his promise. I couldn't make sense of my trip through the portal or the sudden-healing thing, but I knew I wanted to learn to use a sword.

My parents gathered up the pizza stuff and carried it to the kitchen — out of sight but not out of earshot.

"If we hide the portal stones, Cameron and Medea won't be able to go back," Dad said over the crinkling of aluminum foil.

Someone slammed the fridge door shut hard enough to make the salad dressing bottles rattle. "We don't want them running around our world. They don't belong here." Mom sounded tense.

"I know. We have to send them back. But on our terms. Without anything that would hurt the People of the Verses. And what about Jake?"

Silence crackled, and I leaned forward from my spot on the couch.

When Mom refused to answer, Dad spoke again, so quietly that I almost couldn't hear. "We need to keep the portal available in case he's needed there. But how will we know?"

Needed there? Did he really think . . . ?

I waited for them to head back to their bedroom, then slipped down the steps from the kitchen to the basement. Most of the basement was still unfinished, except for my corner bedroom and Dad's workbench.

I hurried into my room and shut out the world behind me. Tonight everything looked different—the movie posters, the bookshelves, the soccer trophy. Smaller, foreign, unfamiliar.

I pulled a thumbtack from my bulletin board and scratched it across my thumb. A line of blood appeared, but in a microsecond the tiny scrape healed completely. I had assumed the healing power was some heebie-jeebie thing that Medea had given me or that had transferred over from my interactions with Kieran.

But now that my head had stopped throbbing, I could put the pieces together. Excitement stronger than caffeine zipped around my nerve endings. My folks thought this was more than a weird effect left over from my travels through the portal. They thought I might be the next Restorer.

Chapter Two

SUSAN

Water sprayed listlessly from the hose as I offered our geraniums a little encouragement in the August heat. The warm scent of grass clippings rose from the lawn. I used to enjoy gardening, but today my spine felt spider legs creeping up and down each nerve—the sensation of being watched.

I turned off the hose. Without rolling it up, I hurried into the kitchen and reactivated the alarm system.

Don't know why I bother. Cameron and Medea are long gone. And what good does a security system do when our family is struggling from the inside out?

Weeks had passed since our return through the portal. We'd tried to settle back into normal life, although I looked over my shoulder at the grocery store and twisted my neck scanning the crowds at Jon and Anne's summer soccer-league games. Karen was annoyed when we made an earlier curfew, and she kept setting off the new alarm system because she couldn't remember to punch in the code.

Mark and Jake joined a fencing club and talked the owner into letting them stay after class to "practice." That's when Jake's real training occurred. I joined them occasionally, borrowing a long sword from the wall. I no longer had Restorer power and speed, but my muscle memory still appreciated the feel of a balanced blade in my hand. Training gave my mind a break from the tight knot of worry that twisted and frayed inside of me.

I thought I was mentally ready for anything, but what actually happened was worse than all the scenarios I had imagined:

Nothing.

Mark hunted through our neighborhood and found no sign of Cameron and Medea. I jumped at every creak in the house, every rattle of a breeze at our windows. Each morning, my first thoughts revolved around protecting our family. I began to think my nerves would snap.

And still nothing happened.

The passing weeks had revealed a sad truth: We'd found our way back through the portal, but we couldn't find our way back to a normal life.

I rifled through the stack of mail on the counter. A postcard from North Woods Bible Camp grabbed my attention:

> *Mom, I got to canoe today and we have pop every day. But Jon's in trouble cuz his cabin threw water balloons at the counselors. I knew he wouldn't tell you, so I did.*
>
> *Love, Anne*

My smile flickered, then faded as the heavy quiet of the empty house settled around me. No children hovered nearby, forcing me to pretend everything was fine. Karen had left for her band tour, and the young ones were at camp. The summer days stretched like long pale shadows. When I most needed activity to keep me from caving in to anxiety, everything had slowed instead. I used to love these rare, empty days. Now I dreaded them.

I squeezed the bridge of my nose, my eyes tingling. I probably needed some allergy medicine. The stress of waiting for our enemies to make a move had pushed a lot of emotions close to the surface, but I refused to give in to an irrational crying jag.

On my way down the hall to the medicine cabinet, the pull-down cord for the trapdoor caught my eye. I stopped, staring at the frame that Mark had crafted in the ceiling with so much love.

For the past several weeks, I'd avoided the attic completely, but my thoughts often felt the magnetic pull of the portal. Was Kieran having success at teaching the Verses in Hazor? Had Nolan adapted to having a father and vice versa? How was Kendra feeling? Had the baby been born yet? With Cameron gone for now, were she and Tristan safer? Had the Council united in supporting the guardians and protecting the borders from Kahlarea?

The portal was bound up in the answers I was waiting for.

Time to stop hiding.

I yanked on the cord, releasing the ladder. The treads wobbled beneath my feet as I climbed the steps into the attic.

Rafters pressed in from the darkness. Black boxes crouched in the corners. I pulled the string for the overhead bulb, and the shadows retreated, but not the dark fears in my soul. I sank into the lone chair and buried my face in my hands.

"God, none of this makes sense."

I waited for a sense of soft arms to wrap around me. I craved reassurance that I had done my best and all would be well. Instead, my words ricocheted back from the dusty boxes under the eaves. Even the old dressmaker's mannequin jammed in the corner glared down at me.

I poured out my restless frustration. "We haven't found them. We're all on edge. I want to *do* something. Show me what to do."

And if I ask you to wait?

I moaned. "Then You need to help me, because I don't do patience very well."

In the dusty quiet, I sensed the Father's smile. *Yes, I know.*

I smiled too, finding some solace in His compassion. He understood me. Grace drew close and reminded me of His love. I snuggled deeper into the chair. The attic gave me a good place to practice some of that waiting that came so hard for me. I decided to stay until the chafing worry released its hold on me.

Verses drifted into the harbor of my thoughts and anchored: "Do not be anxious about anything. . . . Do not let your hearts be troubled. . . . Let the peace of Christ rule in your hearts. . . . Be strong and courageous." An armada of powerful ships, they filled the waters of my mind and blocked the encroachment of worries. I remembered how to hope.

Hours passed. The attic grew stuffy under the afternoon sun, but I wanted to stay. Needed to stay. I pulled my legs up under me and rested my cheek against the overstuffed back of the chair. An intermittent buzz and the tap of a housefly throwing itself against the tiny window came from the far end of the attic. I rubbed grit from my eyes and then let my lids drift down. I must have dozed, floating in a gentle montage of soft images.

The buzz came again. Louder. Insistent. Why was that fly so agitated?

As my eyes opened reluctantly, the buzzing built to a steady vibration. An electrical crackle teased the air. My lungs struggled for breath. Wind moaned across the chimney—at least I hoped it was the wind.

The portal couldn't be open. I didn't know where Mark had hidden the third stone, but I was sure it wasn't in the attic. Yet static prickled against my skin, and indistinct voices sounded from the eaves. My stomach flipped. I wanted to jump up and scramble down the ladder, but my body pulled deeper into the chair.

Was it possible to go back to Lyric . . . even with one of the stones missing? Maybe I should. I could go warn the People of the Verses about Cameron and Medea. Anything would be better than waiting for something to happen.

"Susan?" Mark's voice rumbled from the hallway. I hadn't heard his car pull up or the rattle of his keys as he came into the house.

"Up here." My voice was thick, so I cleared my throat. "I'm in the attic."

Mark's face appeared in the opening. Worry tightened the muscles of his forehead. "What are you doing up here?"

I bristled at his accusing tone but took a slow breath. He needed me to reassure him, not fight with him. I reached out my hand. "Just thinking . . . and praying . . . and stuff."

He clambered the rest of the way up and wedged his body into the space next to my chair. Silver-blue eyes scanned my face as he took my hand.

My heart tightened, and I looked away.

"Are you all right?" His voice rasped.

"Yes. But . . . do you feel that?" We both sat very still. The subtle buzzing and distant voices filled the air. "Why is it doing that?" I stared into his face.

"I don't know. Let's go downstairs." He tugged on my hand and shifted toward the trapdoor.

"Wait. Mark, we need to talk."

"Fine. We can talk downstairs."

I refused to budge. "When we were in Lyric, you promised that once we got home you'd tell me everything. What it was like when you came here for the first time. About the portal."

He looked at the open trapdoor.

"Mark, please. Why haven't you talked about it?"

He gave a heavy sigh and met my eyes. The harsh attic bulb created irregular glints on the waves of his hair. One curl curved against his temple, and I smoothed it back, letting it wrap around my finger. My hand slid down to run along his jaw. This late in the day, his skin was rough with stubble. I'd been so tense lately I hadn't noticed the shadows under his eyes. Or maybe it was just the overhead light.

"I love you, you know." My voice was soft.

The corner of his mouth twitched. "I love you more."

"I love you more than you love hardware stores."

He squinted in concentration for a moment. "I love you more than you love reading a book in the bathtub."

I giggled. "Good one."

"So now that we've got that settled, could we please go downstairs and away from . . . from whatever the portal is doing now?"

"And you'll tell me more about when you came here?"

"Yes. Didn't I say I would?"

He hadn't, but I decided not to argue. The moment held too much warmth and contentment to spoil it. I stood up, bending to avoid the rafters.

As if my movement had triggered it, a shrill wail burst from the rooms downstairs. I froze.

Mark recognized the sound first. "The alarm! Come on!" He scrambled down the stairs.

My heart battered against my rib cage at the same moment I heard a raised voice. I skidded around the hallway corner.

Mark stood in the living room, every muscle in his back tight and alert. I stepped closer to see why he'd frozen. Cameron stood inside our front door, looking relaxed and confident. No wonder. He had a gun in his hand.

"Turn it off," Cameron shouted over the noise.

Mark hesitated, and I glanced around the room. Medea stood near the window, looking like a New Age psychic in a flowing dress and wild auburn curls. She stared at the lengthening shadows in our front yard, her shoulders hunched. Even in profile, I could see the tension around her eyes. She seemed to be in pain.

Mark walked slowly to the keypad and punched in the code.

"The police will be here soon," he said in the sudden quiet. My ears were still ringing, and I barely heard Cameron's chuckle.

"Call them." He waved the gun in Mark's direction, but Mark didn't move. Cameron stepped closer. "You want them to die? No reason to bring others into this, is there?"

Mark was probably weighing the same options I was. Getting Cameron safely locked up might be a great solution.

Suddenly, Cameron crossed the few yards to where I hovered in the doorway and grabbed my shirt, choking me as he pulled me into the room. Cold steel pressed against my temple.

A new burst of terror hit me. I bit my lip and tasted blood.

"I'm finished being polite." Cameron's voice vibrated with

impatience. He wasn't as relaxed as he had appeared. "Call them now."

Mark's face became a blank mask, a sure barometer of the depth of his fear and rage. He stalked to the phone and called the security number. A tendon along his jaw jumped as he listened to their inevitable lecture about remembering to key in the code. He slammed the phone back into its cradle.

"Sit down." Cameron shoved me toward the couch and used his gun to wave Mark over to me. The Lyric councilmember still wore his black hair slicked back and longer than was common in our world. Arrogant ambition radiated from him, the way it had when I first met him on a transport to Lyric. But today instead of a Council tunic, he wore dress slacks, an oxford shirt, and a tie. He could pass as a slightly eccentric dot-com executive or a broker who had tossed his suit jacket aside for a moment.

The sight of this man in my living room with a gun in his hand was so bizarre and surreal I choked back a hysterical giggle.

Mark sat down next to me and took my hand but kept his eyes on Cameron.

"Better?" Cameron asked Medea.

She turned to him with a bewitching smile and rubbed her ears. "Yes. Let's go."

"I'll tie them up first to be sure they don't interfere."

A dimple deepened in her cheek. "Oh, I can take care of keeping them still."

Cameron frowned. "It'll take too long. Save your strength."

Interesting exchange. Even though I had helped free several people from Rhusican mind poison, I still didn't fully understand how it worked. I did know that Medea's power was formidable, and I prayed that they would hurry and leave. I didn't want her eyes looking into mine or her voice getting into my head.

I waited for Mark to tell them about the missing portal stone, but he didn't say anything. When I looked at him, he nodded toward two large duffel bags piled in the corner of the room. They weren't ours. That's why Mark was silent. He planned to do whatever he could to keep Cameron and Medea from taking things from our world through the portal.

Cameron ripped cords from the new blinds and tossed them to Medea. She bound Mark's hands behind him and then tied mine. Cameron kept his gun on us and stroked the top of the barrel with admiration. My stomach twisted harder than the knots around my wrists.

They forced us down to the basement, made us sit on the concrete floor, and tied us to an exposed plumbing pipe that ran up one wall. Once we were secured, Cameron rushed back toward the stairs, but Medea stood staring down at me with her head tilted. Her green eyes seemed to twirl. I thrust my chin out and glared back, defiance my only weapon against the terror that scraped chill fingernails down my spine. She took a step closer.

"Let's go." Cameron's tone was curt. Medea sighed and rolled her shoulders. She dropped her interest in me like a kitten tiring of a toy and followed Cameron up the stairs.

The door at the top slammed shut, and they slid something heavy in front of it. I exhaled slowly and sagged against the pipe.

"Are you okay?" Mark kept his voice soft, but he tugged at the ropes.

"Mark, don't you think it would have been better to tell them?"

He didn't answer for a minute.

"Here's our story," he said at last. "We don't know why they aren't able to get through. We'd be happy to help them leave, but the portal is a mystery to us. Maybe it's because they're trying to take something that isn't supposed to go through. Got it?"

The sick gnawing in my stomach must have made me grumpy. "They aren't stupid."

Mark had never fully comprehended what Cameron and Medea had done to me. At first he had been convinced that their interrogation had been a standard interview—part of Cameron's job description. It had been hard for him to believe that any councilmember could be maliciously evil. He knew better now.

"Susan, this is important. Don't tell them anything—no matter what happens." Mark's words weren't reassuring. I grappled to regain the insights I'd found during my prayer time. Mark didn't need me to argue or blame. Besides, I had just told God I'd rather do anything than wait. The waiting was over now.

"Okay. It's your call." I fidgeted until I could rest my head back against his shoulder. The position strained my arms, but it was worth it.

I longed for more comfort than that slight touch. Cameron and Medea would try to use the portal and fail. Then they'd be back.

And they'd be angry.

Chapter Three

SUSAN

We heard Cameron and Medea dragging their bags across the floor upstairs and the occasional mumble of distant voices.

"What do you think they're doing?" Rhetorical question, but if I kept talking, perhaps I wouldn't shatter from the tension. "Maybe they'll be able to get through with just the two stones. The portal was doing something strange when I was up in the attic. I know you're worried about the clans, but the One will look out for them. They have a Restorer. Unless Kieran lost his Restorer power when Jake got his, but— " I gasped. "Mark, what time is it?"

"Um, I can't really see my watch from here." Mark jerked against the ropes for emphasis.

"Very funny. When did you get home from work?"

"Well, the meeting with the development team ran late, so it was probably about six. Why?"

"Because Jake gets off work at eight."

I felt Mark's sudden stillness, but I kept babbling. "They'll capture him, too. They've controlled him before. Maybe they still can. He doesn't know where you hid the third stone, but they might hurt him. And if they see that he heals . . ." I breathed in shallow gasps between my sentences, tugging again at the ropes. "We've got to do something. I remember that when Nancy Drew got tied up, she held her wrists a certain way so she'd be able to get free. I tried, but Medea yanked the cords too tight. I can't get loose."

A strangled sound came from behind me. "Mark, are you okay?"

"Yeah," he gasped. He was shaking with his effort to stop laughing. "Nancy Drew?"

Like he was contributing any great suggestions. "What about it? Karen and Anne love those books."

"Nothing . . . it's just . . ." He coughed and another laugh escaped. "If you're going to use advice from books, couldn't you pick Tom Clancy or Ian Fleming? Nancy Drew." He barked, snorted, and finally wheezed. "Oh, honey, you're amazing."

I wanted to laugh with him. His teasing humor usually helped me find a healthy perspective on our problems. But this wasn't a frozen water pipe or a kid's bad report card. "Mark, I'm scared," I said in a small voice.

He sobered quickly. "I know. We'll be all right."

We struggled with the ropes for several minutes but couldn't get free.

"Do you hear anything?" Mark said suddenly.

I listened for a long ten seconds. The house sounded still and empty. "Maybe they've gone." I shifted to ease the pressure on my arms.

Mark gave that comment the silence it deserved.

I didn't want to let my thoughts wander back to what Cameron and Medea would do to us. "Just keep talking, okay? If you keep talking, I don't have to think."

"What should I talk about?" Mark wrestled against the ropes again, jerking against the pipe as if he could pull it free. But the solid metal dug deep into the concrete floor and didn't budge.

"Tell me about when you came here."

"Now? We were going to sit in front of a fireplace with a bowl of popcorn—"

"Mark, it's the middle of summer. We're not going to have a fire any time soon. I want to hear about it. Why do you keep avoiding this subject? Please. I'm really scared."

He didn't answer right away.

I tried again. "Maybe it will help us figure out what to do about the portal . . . if you explain it to me."

Mark sighed. "All right. Let's see . . . I've told you all about my father, and how my mother was murdered."

He had. I still couldn't imagine what it would be like to be sixteen and alone in his harsh world. I didn't want to linger on that topic. "And when the Kahlareans targeted you, the Lyric songkeeper sent you here to our world. What was that like?"

He was quiet for a moment.

"Ravon was only a few years older than me, but he excelled at his first-year guardian training and then spent a year doing advanced training in Rendor. We knew a lot of the same people. He was assigned to protect me, and we became friends."

I wanted to hurry him along, but he hadn't indulged this stream of images from his past for a long time. *Patience*. He was netting memories like fish, selecting the ones he wanted to pull out and show me before releasing them again.

"I was Jake's age back then. We'd sneak into the guardian tower to watch training matches. We found hidden doors in the Lyric walls and would slip out sometimes to explore. And we sparred every day." Mark's voice was warm with affection.

"Ravon told me that if he was going to be my bodyguard, the least he could do was train me to watch his back while he was watching mine."

I was afraid I knew where this story was going. "He sounds like a good friend," I said quietly.

"One evening after a Council session, we were coming around the curve into the main square. You know, near the tower?"

I nodded, then realized he couldn't see me. But he had already continued.

"Two guys appeared out of nowhere. We never heard them coming. Gray hoods, masks. One of them grabbed me before I could draw my sword. He had a blade to my neck and was dragging me away. Ravon was always quicker than me. He drew his sword in a flash and engaged the other guy. The attacker had only a small silver dagger. I figured the fight would be over in a second. So did Ravon. He was grinning as he swung at the guy. But then the Kahlarean threw the blade. Ravon barely winced when it hit his shoulder. He pulled it free and lunged forward to continue his attack, but he stumbled.

"I still remember his face when he turned to look at me. He was so confused. Neither of us knew anything about venblades back then. It paralyzed him fast. Some of the Lyric guardians showed up, and the assassin holding me let go. I don't know why he didn't slit my throat. Both of the Kahlareans disappeared into the twilight, and I ran over to where Ravon had collapsed onto the street and held him.

"'Sorry,' he said. His voice was so choked I could barely understand him.

"'Hey, you were great,' I told him. 'Did you see his eyes when you headed toward him with your sword? You had him scared.'

"He smiled, but then his whole body stiffened. He wheezed trying to make his lungs work. I saw the panic in his eyes and heard the gurgle in his throat, and I couldn't do anything to help him. I just held him and watched him die."

Mark fell silent.

Whose stupid idea had it been to talk about this now? My eyes welled and I blinked back tears. I tried to find Mark's fingers with my own but couldn't reach him.

He cleared his throat. "So anyway, that was when I went to talk to the eldest songkeeper of Lyric. I couldn't let anyone else die because of me. I didn't know what the prophecy meant, but I hadn't shown any signs of Restorer gifts."

He still wrestled with the choices he had made. Even with me, he felt the need to justify himself—to explain the dire events that had driven him to leave his world. The tautness in his voice told me that guilt still haunted him. I longed to reassure him.

Oh, Mark. You were just a boy. You'd watched too many people die. You've tortured yourself too long over this.

But I didn't want to interrupt.

"The songkeeper was kind of an odd guy. He was tall and so thin it looked as if he never ate. He stared into space like he was focusing on something that wasn't there. I begged him for help but wasn't even sure he was listening to me. Then he turned with a look that burned into me. His hair was sticking out all over, and those eyes—I decided coming to him had been a bad idea.

"'Yes. It's time.' He said it as if he'd been waiting for me all along. He grabbed a small bag and headed for the door. When he reached the frame, he had to duck, and he turned back and frowned at me. I was still sitting at his table.

"'Come.' That was all he said. And he started walking. I hurried along behind him. I hadn't been assigned a new bodyguard yet, so I tried to stay alert for attack as we raced through the streets. He took me out a side door in the city wall, and I didn't see anyone I knew along the way. If I'd had any clue what he was going to do, I would have insisted on talking to Jorgen, or my friends, but everything happened too fast.

"He led me to the grove, and we wove deep into the trees. He still hadn't explained anything. Then he opened the bag and shook out three stones. Gray, white, and black. Smooth and heavy. They had sliding panels with a mechanism hidden inside, something beyond any transtech gadget I'd ever seen.

"'Pay attention,' the songkeeper told me." Mark gave a short laugh. "He had my attention, all right. I was beginning to think he was totally nuts."

I twisted my head to get a glimpse of Mark. "Did I ever see him when the songkeepers led the gathering?"

"No, he never leads singing. I don't think he writes songs or teaches Verses, either. I'm not quite sure what he does. You wouldn't have met him. He's kind of reclusive." Mark stopped talking and fidgeted against the ropes.

I shouldn't have interrupted him. This was the part of the story I had been longing to know about. "So what did he do with the stones?"

"He laid them out in a pattern, told me to memorize it, then scrambled them and had me show him I could set them up correctly. We must have drilled that ten times. I still had no idea what they were for. But when they were lined up the right way, I could feel . . . a current in the air. Like the static that builds up when fabric rubs against a light wall.

"When he was sure I wouldn't forget, he put the stones back

in the bag and handed it to me.

"'Use these stones to return,' he said. His head darted from side to side, looking every direction and making me nervous. 'I'll have Jorgen tell the Council you've been sent to negotiate with the lost clans. I'm sending you through a portal. No one knows where it leads, but it is far from all the danger here. I'm the only keeper of the portal. You won't be followed. Return when you are needed.'

"I guess I thought he was leading me to a tunnel entrance that would take me to some land past Hazor. He motioned me forward, and I walked on ahead of him. I was about to ask him how I would know when I was needed, but something grabbed me.

"I stumbled forward and fell to my knees. Pain shot through my head, and I closed my eyes. When I opened them, the songkeeper had disappeared. I was still in a grove of trees, but they had changed."

"Where were you?" I couldn't stop myself from jumping in. There was so much I didn't understand about the portal, and he had never talked about this before.

Mark leaned his head back against the pipe. "I was right here. This spot. There weren't any houses here back then. I wandered out of the trees just as a cloud moved away from the sun." His voice was thick with remembered terror. "It was like an overloaded light cube about to explode. My eyes burned, and I stumbled back under cover of the nearest tree. I was sure if that light touched me I would incinerate. I'd never seen anything like it. The way the color of everything changed where the rays hit. The intense shadows. The blue sky beyond the clouds. I couldn't believe it was real. . . ." His voice trailed off again.

I ached for the frightened young man thrown into this

strange place without explanation. "What did you do when night fell?"

"Camped here. At first I was afraid to wander far from the portal. That's why years later when the new development was built, I wanted to put a bid on this house, because it was over the site where I arrived. Silly, I guess. With the stones to take me back, it shouldn't have mattered. At least I think they would work from other places. But it was my way of staying connected."

I remembered now. We had been living in a tiny apartment near Ridge Valley College. Almost overnight he had gotten all worked up about buying a place of our own—not throwing money away in rent each month. It didn't take much to convince me. We'd been saving every penny we could from both our jobs. Jake was a toddler, and I longed for him to have a backyard to play in.

"So what did you do when it sank in that you weren't in the same world as Lyric anymore?" I thought back to my confusion when I found myself in a rain-soaked street in Shamgar—pulled out of the safety of our attic into a strange world. "And why didn't you try to go back? And why, why, why didn't you ever tell me?" Mark shifted again and was about to answer when we heard something: a scraping sound at the top of the stairs.

The door flew open and crashed against the wall. My stomach swooped as if I were in an elevator that was dropping too fast. Mark stiffened, and I scrambled to remember the lie he wanted me to tell. "We don't know how it works. You can't bring things through," I muttered to myself.

Chapter Four

SUSAN

Cameron stalked down the stairs, soundless as a prowling panther. When his head came into view, I looked for seething rage, but his face was bland—almost bored. The only clue to his intent was in his eyes. They glittered black and hard.

He ignored me and walked around to face Mark. By twisting my head, I could still watch him. He pulled his gun out and made sure Mark was listening.

"Tell me how it works, or I'll kill her now."

The barrel of the gun swung in my direction.

I stopped breathing.

"It opens at midday. That's the only time you can go through." Mark's voice stayed calm and level. He was way too good at lying.

Tired of staring at the gun, I counted chips in the concrete floor.

Cameron crouched down. "You abandoned your people a long time ago." His words to Mark were low and almost caressing. "No need for heroics now. Besides, we've always been on the same side. My job is to protect Lyric."

Mark didn't bother arguing. "You'll have to come back tomorrow. The portal will open at noon."

I couldn't see Cameron's face, but I could hear his oily smile when he spoke. "How much is her life worth to you?"

Mark strained against the ropes, but he didn't speak. Cameron stood up and walked around to stare down at me. He tucked his gun into his belt, and I prayed he would accidentally shoot himself. Instead, he untied the rope that held me to the pipe. He didn't loosen the cords around my wrists as he jerked me to my feet.

I groaned as circulation returned to my back and legs. He shoved me toward the stairs, and I didn't try to fight him. I just concentrated on not falling.

"Wait," Mark shouted. "She doesn't know anything. If you have questions about the portal, ask me."

"Oh, I will. Later." Cameron's lip curled, and he pulled me the rest of the way up the stairs, ignoring Mark's yells. He slammed the door shut and thrust me into a chair.

A wash of unreality ran through me like the head rush from standing up too fast. Medea sat across from me at my kitchen table. *My* kitchen—with gingham curtains and daisies on the oven mitts. The scent of chicken still lingered in the air from supper at this table last night, when we had eaten Karen's favorite meal before she left for her band trip. I stared hard at the wooden napkin holder that Mark had made for me one Christmas. This was my home. This could not be happening.

Medea didn't say anything.

I was careful not to look in her direction. Cameron rummaged in our kitchen drawers, but the sound didn't register until he stepped in front of me. He grabbed my chin, and I had an instant to see the boning knife in his hand before he cut a methodical slit along my cheekbone. I was so shocked, it took a full two seconds to feel the stinging pain. I tried to pull away but couldn't get leverage with my arms bound behind me. My head jerked back, but Cameron tightened his bruising grip, his eyes fixed on the cut.

I stared at him in horror. Blood trickled down my face and I tugged against the ropes, wanting to reach up and wipe it away.

Cameron looked at Medea. "So it *is* true." Languidly, she drifted from the chair and came to stand beside him. She reached out and ran one fingertip along the cut, then studied the blood with mild interest.

"Has that happened before?" she asked Cameron.

"I don't know. As far as I know, all the Restorers died while they still had their powers."

Medea stretched, all supple spine and sparkling eyes. "Then the Kahlareans won't be interested in her."

Cameron sighed. "Fine. You win."

Anger churned inside me as my wrists chafed against rope. They had invaded our home, were holding us captive, had cut my face, and now were discussing me as if I were a piece of junk mail. I'd had about enough of this. "What kind of idiots are you? You both know that Kieran is the Restorer now."

Cameron released my chin with a shove and grabbed a cloth to meticulously polish the boning knife. "So you said."

"But you saw him heal. In the Council, and then when he faced Zarek. And don't get blood on my good dish towel." Somehow I had to grasp a fragment of control from this bizarre and terrifying scene.

"I had no proof you were no longer a Restorer." Cameron smiled. "Until now." He stared at the side of my face, and his smile grew. "So tell me about the portal."

I hunched up one shoulder and managed to blot the lower part of my cheek against it. My shirt would probably be hopelessly stained, but I couldn't stand the feel of blood trailing down my face. "It opens only at noon." What else had Mark said to tell them? "And you can't bring anything through. It won't work."

I stared hard at the wood table. Hadn't I heard that people looked down and to the left when they were lying? Or was that when they were flirting? There had been a television special about it—a whole report about nonverbal communication. I couldn't remember the details now, but I worked hard to stay still and not give anything away. In the silence that followed, I glanced up at Cameron.

He wasn't buying it for a second. Mark always told me my face revealed everything I was thinking. Cameron didn't bother asking me any more questions. He pulled a chair out for Medea, and she settled into it and gave me a gentle smile.

I squeezed my eyes shut, every muscle in my body tense. "Leave me alone. I know how you poison minds, so it won't work on me anymore." I didn't know that to be true, but it sounded like a good theory. Still, if my hands had been free, I'd have clamped them over my ears.

Medea's laugh was a twinkling wind chime. "Oh, but once a connection has been made, it is so much easier the next time." That surprised me enough that my eyes popped open. Her green eyes were close to mine, and my feet pushed against the floor, trying to scoot my chair back. Cameron had moved around behind me. Now he clamped his hands down onto my shoulders.

"You forget." Her voice was soothing. "I know so much

about you—how alone you are. You tried so hard to do the right thing. You only wanted to help."

Yes. She understood. That was exactly right. I had just wanted to be useful.

"And I know how much you care about Markkel." Some distant warning prickled in the back of my mind, but I couldn't call it forward. "He has no right to keep us from going back. We don't belong here. You know that. He's not even a chief council-member. He can't make those kinds of decisions."

Of course he can't. Their policy is none of our business.

"Cameron is the chief councilmember of Lyric," she said. "The clans are counting on him."

I had been taking rapid shallow breaths, but my breathing began to slow and I felt myself nodding. My head grew heavy. I was being pulled forward. Sinking. If something hadn't been holding me, I would have fallen.

"You don't want to cause trouble for Markkel," she crooned. "You can help him. You can help everyone. You like to help people, don't you?"

Oh, yes. If I could just fix this—make everyone happy. That's all that matters.

"Why didn't the portal open from this side?" Her words were smooth and liquid.

I looked up and saw our family photo on the refrigerator behind Medea, held in place with daisy magnets. I sucked a breath in and remembered who I was. "No." I tried to say the word with strength, but it came out as a whisper.

Medea shifted her position to move into my sight line again. I couldn't see past her anymore. "How do we get the portal to send us back?" Her voice was as sweet as a little girl's.

"Can't." I gasped and squeezed my eyes shut.

A flare of rage sprang up inside me. I stiffened and wrenched against the ropes. I felt a moment of confusion and then realized the burst of anger I had felt was hers. It had happened the other time she had gotten into my head. I had absorbed her feelings, not just the thoughts she had been deliberately projecting into me.

"Patience," Cameron hissed at Medea from behind me.

Medea gave a deep sigh. "I've been away from home too long." The words were so soft I almost missed them, but in a brief instant of coherence, I paid attention and filed that information away to think about later.

"Open your eyes." At first I didn't realize Cameron was talking to me. His fingers dug hard into my collarbone. I tried to shrink down into the chair but couldn't get away.

"Look," Medea said.

My eyes blinked open in reflex.

She smiled. Light seemed to pulse in her green eyes. "Yessss. We are very grateful for your help. You are saving Markkel a lot of trouble. He'll be so glad when this is over and we've left."

She was right. We could go back to normal life.

"So how do we make the portal work?"

"You need all three stones." It was a relief to say the words. The secret wasn't my responsibility anymore. The weeks and weeks of carrying around hidden knowledge were over.

"Where are the stones?" Medea's singsong continued to lull me.

"Two are still in the attic, but Mark hid one."

"Where?"

I frowned. I wanted to help them so much. "I don't know."

"It's true." Medea broke eye contact to talk to Cameron. He let go of me.

I sagged deeper into the chair. All my joints turned to liquid, and heavy fatigue weighted my entire body.

"I'll get him for you." Cameron walked toward the basement door.

Medea shook her head. "I can't. I'm tired."

I watched from under heavy lids as he veered toward her. He stroked her hair, touching her with an admiration I'd seen him show only for the weapons he liked to collect. "You rest. I'll take care of it." Cameron disappeared into the basement.

Lethargy pulled me under—mine, Medea's, or a combination—and everything faded away. I didn't know how much time had passed, but when I came to, Medea was resting her head on her arms on the kitchen table.

Cameron came back in the room from the basement. His tie was loosened, and his shirtsleeves were rolled up. His skin was flushed and damp as if he had been using a treadmill. He walked over to Medea, and she lifted her head. "Better?" he asked. She nodded. The tenderness in his voice disappeared as he grabbed my arm and yanked me to my feet. "Move."

The fog was lifting from my brain, but I was still confused and unsteady on my legs. Vaguely aware of going downstairs, my eyelids floated closed. When I opened them again, I saw Mark.

Sweet God in heaven, help him. My heart screamed the prayer in silence.

Cameron used a knife to cut away the cords on my wrists and released me to go to Mark.

I dropped to the floor, ignoring the pain in my shoulders as I brought my arms forward. Mark was unconscious, and I was glad for his sake. Jon had once fallen out of a tree, hitting several branches with his face on the way down. This was ten times worse. Swelling, bruises, gashes.

I touched his face gently and kissed the one unmarked spot I could find on his forehead. My tears splashed onto his battered face. "Mark, oh, Mark. It isn't worth it. Don't do this."

"Stubborn, isn't he? He fails to listen to reason. If you don't want me to become more . . . persuasive, you'd better convince him to talk to me." Cameron looked down at Mark with clinical detachment. "I'm giving you some time with him. Use it well." He retreated to the stairs and sat down, giving me some semblance of privacy with Mark.

Fury clawed at me, and I spared one killing glare in Cameron's direction, but he still had a gun tucked in his belt and a knife in his hand. Helping Mark was more important. I pulled a tissue from my pocket and blotted away some of the blood on his face. He stirred, and I helped him hold his head up, cushioning it so it wouldn't hit the pipe behind him.

One eye was swelling shut, but his other shone gray-blue and alert as he came to. Mark's face went ashen as he stared at me, his gaze tracking the cut on my face. "What did he do to you?" He tried to take a deep breath and winced.

"I'm fine. He just wanted to be sure I wasn't the Restorer anymore. It's nothing. Are you okay?" Inane questions were my specialty.

Mark must have been thinking the same thing, because his mouth twitched. "Just fine." Then his eyes narrowed. "As long as we can keep them from whatever they're planning, I'll stay fine."

I lowered my voice to a harsh whisper. "Mark, this is crazy. Cameron will kill you. Why are you doing this?"

He didn't answer right away. His whole body sagged, and he stared past me. "I was just thinking about Anne and her 'regrets.' Remember?"

I managed a watery smile. We'd often take walks after supper with Jon and Anne to spot the heron, box turtles, and myriad wildlife that visited the pond in our neighborhood.

One evening a few years earlier, Mark and I were lost in conversation, when Anne tugged my hand. "Mommy! The regrets flew over the pond."

I crouched beside her in confusion, puzzled by what regrets she was having at age five. Maybe she was composing a haiku. She shook her head until her curls bounced, then she pointed. I caught a glimpse of gleaming white wings as a stately egret disappeared beyond the tree line. From that moment on, whenever I saw the huge wings soaring over the pond, I prayed for my own regrets to float away with the same grace.

I glanced behind me to be sure Cameron wasn't listening. "What are you trying to tell me?" I whispered, leaning close to Mark.

"Susan, I quit training as a guardian. I fled Lyric. Then I decided to stay here even though the clans were in danger. If I can do something . . . anything . . . to stop Cameron from causing more damage, it's the least I can do."

I sat back, more afraid than before. "So that's what this is about? Regrets? Atonement?" More tears ran down my face, stinging the cut on my cheek. "Mark, we've been through this before. You are the bravest man I know. You don't need to prove anything."

He gave me a steady look and didn't speak.

My panic grew. "They aren't going to give up. How far do you plan to take this?"

He grimaced as he shifted position. "My father gave his life for our people. How could I do less?"

Cold dread twisted like an icy blade beneath my sternum. This wasn't just guilt about his past choices. Mark's whole model of what it meant to be a man was tangled up in his memories of the father he barely knew. Sacrifice, martyrdom, death. "Mark, you did what you were supposed to do. You brought restoration like the prophecy said you would. You think the only way to make a difference is to die? Please. I can't let you—"

"Hey, Mom. How come the alarm system is turned off?" Jake bellowed from the upstairs hall. I sprang to my feet.

Cameron was already racing up the steps.

"Jake, run!" I shouted, scrambling toward the stairs. Something crashed overhead. My warning had come too late.

Chapter Five

SUSAN

Cameron flourished his gun as he forced Jake into the basement. Jake looked pale, but wound up with a reckless energy, he was ready to throw himself into a confrontation. When he saw the blood on my face and shirt, his expression changed and some of his jittery vigor dissolved. This wasn't a game or an attack scenario he had practiced at the fencing club.

I stepped between Mark and Jake, wanting to protect each from the sight of the other in danger. Cameron elbowed me aside and pulled my son forward. Jake gasped when he saw his father. He stumbled and his cheeks lost their remaining color. Mark's chin dropped in weary resignation.

There was a loud click as Cameron chambered a bullet and aimed the gun at Jake's head. "I had a son once. He was Jake's age when he died." An eerie sliver of rage flickered in Cameron's eyes, and I knew with fierce certainty that he would enjoy squeezing the trigger. I looked at Mark. He had seen it too.

"I'll open the portal for you." His words were quiet, layered with shame and defeat.

Relief eased some of the cramping in my muscles. Mark

would agonize later about being forced into this decision, but he would be alive. Jake would be alive. It was the only choice.

"Untie him." Cameron wasn't smirking in triumph as I would have expected—probably disappointed he wouldn't need to do more violent "persuading."

I pried the ropes loose, and it took both Jake and me to help Mark to his feet.

"My workbench," my husband said between ragged gasps. He was having trouble standing and breathing at the same time. As soon as Cameron and Medea left, I'd drive him to the emergency room. He could come up with some explanation for all his injuries. He was great at making up stories.

We helped him to the corner of the basement where he kept all his woodworking tools. A counter attached to the wall held a bewildering assortment of bins that overflowed with nails, screws, and odd bits I couldn't even guess the purpose of. He shoved aside a couple of the boxes, pulled out a drawer, and lifted a smooth black stone from the back.

"I need to line it up with the others in the attic." His words mumbled past cut and swollen lips. Cameron nodded and gestured with his gun. We made our way slowly up the stairs.

Medea, still in the kitchen, uncoiled from her chair. "Jake. It's so good to see you again." Her voice was a low purr.

A wave of nausea gripped me. I fought it down and concentrated on helping Mark stay upright. "Don't look at her. Don't talk to her," I warned Jake.

Medea's laugh sparkled, and I found myself liking her. I ripped away that illusion and glared. She laughed again, and I stormed toward the pull-down stairs in the back hall.

The sooner we sent them on their way, the better.

The attic was stuffy and ridiculously crowded with all of us jammed into the small space. I saw the bags that Cameron had lugged upstairs earlier and hoped that somehow they wouldn't pass through the portal. Whatever they contained was sure to cause trouble for the clans.

As soon as Mark positioned the three stones, humming energy began to drone.

Cameron watched with an officious politician's smile. "Thank you. You've done a great service to the people of Lyric." It startled me to realize that Cameron still believed his own rhetoric.

"Chief Councilmember"—I forced a respectful tone that almost made me gag—"I know you want to keep Lyric safe. Whatever you're planning this time, the Verses already promise that your people will be protected. Look at the way the One delivered Braide Wood from Hazor and stopped the attack on Lyric by sending a Restorer." My voice grew impassioned. "You don't have to keep forming alliances that are forbidden or gathering weapons—"

"You are not addressing the Council now." Cameron's eyes turned cold. "You had your fun. Stirred up trouble. Inconvenienced me." He took a step toward me. Mark stood up, one of the stones in his hand. The buzzing faded and Cameron's gaze jerked toward Mark.

"Leave her alone or you'll never go back." Mark's threat wasn't diminished by the brokenness of his body. His will was a steel core that wouldn't be bent. Beside him, Jake's eyes widened in admiration.

Cameron was less impressed. "Stop wasting time. Open the portal." He swung his gun toward Jake, and Mark turned back to his work. He eyed the angle and proximity of each stone. He moved one of them about two feet farther to the side. The humming grew, and threads of electrical light crackled in the air. I looked down, biting my lip. I didn't want Cameron to read my face and notice what I had just recognized.

Mark had positioned the stones the wrong way.

He glanced at me with a grim smile that he quickly covered. I worked hard to hide my own surge of glee.

"It's working." Mark stood, stooped under the low rafters.

Cameron looked ready to start making another speech, but Medea came and rested her hand on his arm. "Don't forget what you promised me."

His gaze caressed her face. "Of course."

Jake inched closer, but Cameron's attention swung back to him. He wasn't careless enough to give any of us a chance to jump him.

"Hand me those bags."

Jake hefted one of the heavy duffel bags and looked ready to swing it at Cameron's head.

Medea must have seen it too. "Thank you for helping us, Jake. You've been very important to me. I won't forget." The soporific words leached all resistance from him, and he handed the bag to Cameron and picked up another one to give Medea.

"I wish we could take you with us," she added, her voice oversweet like vanilla icing, "but it's not in our plan right now. Perhaps we'll come back someday."

Those words sent a shiver through me. Mark put a protective arm around Jake, who was looking as dazed as when we'd pried him out of bed for Easter sunrise service. I watched them, warmed by Mark's gruff tenderness as he looked down at our son. I almost missed the movement at the edge of my vision. I turned to react. Too late.

Cameron grabbed me and pulled me into the space

between the stones at the same moment he and Medea stepped forward.

I twisted, trying to wrench away. I had one glimpse of Mark and Jake, their faces stretched in shock. Mark shouted something, but I couldn't hear it. A huge thunderstorm crashed around my head, and my ears ached from pressure as if I were on a rapidly landing airplane. Everything went black except for fragments of light—broken glass that sparkled and jabbed my skull with the pain of a migraine. I was being crushed, or expanded, or torn in two.

"Mark!" I tried to scream, but I couldn't hear my own voice. I swirled in a tornado of electrical energy that built to a frenzy and then short-circuited. I couldn't hear or see anything anymore. Stray crackles of static skittered over my skin.

Then I felt nothing.

Chapter Six

JAKE

A light flashed with a loud pop, and my mom disappeared with Cameron and Medea. My body jerked with the kind of twitch you get when you're almost asleep. I snapped awake as if windshield wipers had scraped away the confusing blur in my brain. I could think again.

My dad stumbled toward the space between the stones. He could barely walk, but he was going to throw himself into the portal.

I grabbed his arm. "Dad! Wait. We need a plan. We need swords."

He moaned and sank to his knees. "What have I done?" I could barely make out his words. Blood trickled from his swollen lips.

Panic rushed through me like it had when I'd walked into the house and Cameron had stepped around the corner with a gun aimed at my face.

"Dad, it's okay. We'll figure this out." He was the parent. He was supposed to reassure me.

He looked up at me, struggling to breathe. His face held an

expression I'd never seen before—something so hopeless that I took a step back. *What's wrong with him?* Then I blinked and the expression was gone. He was my dad again. He'd figure out what we needed to do.

"Come on. I can drive you to the doctor's. Then we'll grab some supplies and go after them."

Dad shook his head. "I don't need a doctor, but we should bring some gear." He stood up and made his way unsteadily to the opening in the floor.

We made our way down the steps. I planned to convince Dad to let me take him to the clinic, but the cooler air downstairs seemed to revive him, and he made his way to the bathroom with only a little support from the walls. Once he washed all the blood off his face, he looked better, so I decided not to press the point.

What would we need? My memory of the past hour was a little foggy, and a dull headache throbbed every time I tried to remember my conversations with Cameron and Medea. I hadn't stopped them. Had I helped them? My stomach clenched. I was afraid to ask.

Dad rummaged in the closet by the kitchen door but winced as he reached for a backpack.

"Just sit down and tell me what to pack. I'll take care of it." I yanked open our freezer and pulled out a bag of peas. One of Mom's tricks. It worked on sprained ankles, black eyes . . . all kinds of injuries that the four of us brought home.

Dad gave me a small grin that cracked open a cut on his lip again. "Ouch." He plopped the frozen peas over his swollen eye.

"I think Mom usually wraps a dish towel around it first." I looked around the kitchen and grabbed a towel from the counter. It was stained with blood. I dropped it and wiped my hands on my jeans. "Should we bring food?"

Dad's mouth twitched again. "Always thinking with your stomach."

"Hey, last time I got pretty hungry before I found help."

He stopped teasing me. "You're right. Grab our backpacks and load up as if we're going camping. And dig out the clothes we were wearing when we came back from Lyric."

I tore around the house finding everything we might need. Dad's sword was at the bottom of a bin in the attic. I didn't have one—hadn't been wearing one when Mom and Dad brought me home. I grabbed my Swiss army knife and hooked it onto my belt.

When I stopped back in the kitchen, Dad still looked bad. His eyes were closed, and his chest stuttered with each breath he took. He opened one eye. "Just some cracked ribs. I'll be fine."

I sat down next to him at the table. "Can I ask you something?"

He pulled away the bag of peas and gave me his full attention.

"When we came back, Mom said you . . . well, she was scared you were gonna die from going through the portal. She said it's gotten worse each time for you."

He didn't deny it. "I blacked out. I don't know why it affected me that way. So you need to be prepared in case it happens again."

I sat up taller. "Sure. But aren't you worried about going through right now? I mean, you're kind of a mess."

"Jake, we don't know how many hours or days are passing over there. I don't want to risk letting too much time go by. And the thought of your mom with Cameron and Medea . . ."

He couldn't say any more, and I didn't want him to. I looked at the mess of bruises on his face. He should be at the clinic, not planning a trip that could kill him. "Do we have some bandages in the first-aid kit? I could tape your ribs."

He didn't argue. "I think the first-aid kit is in Jon's room. He was using the Ace bandages to make bridges between his Lego fortresses."

I found them, hurried back to the kitchen, and started wrapping his ribs. I'd seen my coach do this once when a kid got hurt. But it was harder than it looked, and I kept fumbling the end of the bandage. "Dad, I don't think I ever told you, but when I was camping outside of Lyric, I busted up my ankle. Bad. And we needed to get to Braide Wood. So Kieran . . . he healed it. Is that something Restorers are supposed to be able to do?"

I felt weird asking him about this. He'd been teaching me how to fight and telling me the history of the Restorers from his world. But it still didn't seem very real . . . the whole thing about the signs.

He leaned forward. "I don't know. It's not the same each time. The Restorers always had the ability to heal from their injuries and had other gifts like strength and heightened senses. But they usually died in battle, and then years would go by before another one came along. Your mom didn't die. She just stopped having the gifts, and Kieran became a Restorer. And some of his gifts might have been different."

"Do you think Kieran lost his Restorer gifts when I got back here and found out I could heal fast?"

Dad looked worried. "I don't know. If that's true, I hope he figured it out before he let someone skewer him again."

"Well, just in case I can do it"—my face felt hot, and I had to swallow—"can I pray for you to be healed?"

Dad looked startled, but he nodded and bowed his head. I thought back to Kieran resting his hands on my ankle and the heat that poured through them. I put my hands over the bandages taped around Dad's ribs and closed my eyes.

"Dear God, thank You for saving us. We have to go find Mom, and Dad is in a lot of pain. Would You please heal his ribs and everything else that's hurting? And help us find Mom fast. And take care of all the clans and don't let Cameron cause too much trouble." I waited for a while but didn't feel anything special. I finally stammered an "amen" and let go of Dad, feeling stupid. His face was still beat-up, and it was obvious nothing had happened.

"Thanks, son." He wrapped an arm around my shoulders in a quick hug. "I've got a great idea."

Relieved at the change in subject, I handed him his Council tunic.

He eased it on while he talked. "When I set up the stones, I lined them up wrong. I was hoping to delay Cameron and Medea. I'm not positive where they ended up. I was hoping Shamgar, like the first time your mom went through. But what if I set the stones up the right way now? We could get to Lyric first and warn Jorgen. We can even send word to Tristan and have plenty of help in stopping whatever Cameron plans to do."

"Great! Let's go!" I handed him his sword belt.

"You wear it."

My jaw dropped open. "You mean it?"

He nodded. "I'll get one when we get to Lyric. Besides, the way I'm feeling right now, I don't think I could lift it."

I belted it on and made sure the sword rested at the right

spot against my hip. I felt about ten feet tall.

We trudged back up to the attic, and Dad put the stones in the right places. He stood up and patted his pockets the way he checked for his car keys when he left home. "I left a note for Karen."

"What?" Last time, we'd been gone for weeks, and when we got back, only an hour had passed in our world. "She won't be home for a week. You don't think . . ."

Dad gave me his "serious" look. "The point is, I don't know. I'm not sure how the time ratio works. *And* I'm not sure what will happen to us."

He was being honest about the danger, but I wished he sounded more confident. Yeah, Mom was in trouble and all, but we'd take care of it. I wouldn't have admitted it, but I was kind of excited for a chance to go back through the portal.

My desire to stay in Lyric had been planted by Medea—part of their trick to find the portal. But she had found a piece of truth to build that lie on. Deep in my bones, I felt a pull to help the People of the Verses.

And in some ways, their world made more sense to me than my own. I fit there.

"Ready?" Dad braced one hand against a dusty rafter.

I swallowed my thoughts and nodded. The portal hummed smoothly, without the wild crackling it had set off earlier. As we stepped forward, I had a moment to wonder what on earth Dad had put in the note to Karen: "Dear Karen, sorry we weren't there to pick you up from the band tour. Jake and I had to pop in to another universe to rescue your mom from a psycho chief councilmember and his mind-controlling ally. There's a chicken hot dish in the freezer. Love, Dad"?

We stepped through, and there was a flash of disorientation.

Then I recognized the trees from the grove outside Lyric. I turned to ask Dad what he really put in the note to Karen.

He wasn't there.

I stood absolutely still. Was it taking him longer to get through? I was afraid to move—to do anything that might disturb the balance of the portal or the way it worked. Had he turned back for something? No, he'd been ahead of me.

He'd passed back and forth more than the rest of us, except maybe for Mom. But that last time, he almost hadn't survived. Maybe the portal knew that and wouldn't let him through anymore.

My hair still stood up at the roots from the tingling pull of electrical current. I had better go back to the attic and make sure he was all right.

Wait. What if people had only a limited number of times they could go back and forth? I should find Mom first. I didn't want to be permanently stuck in our world. I had the signs of the Restorer, so I'd be needed here one day. Maybe even now.

I hated making decisions. Choosing what movie to go to was bad enough, or whether I wanted fries or onion rings, but this decision was serious. Dad might need my help. Mom definitely needed me, and so did the people in Lyric.

Dad, why aren't you here to tell me what to do?

What was that verse Mom kept quoting when I was trying to pick which college to go to? "If any of you lacks wisdom . . ." I couldn't remember the rest, but it probably had something to do with talking to God about it. She had drilled that into me my whole life.

I looked around the dense grove of trees. Then I did something I don't normally do: I lowered myself onto a knee.

At our house, we prayed sitting around the supper table, or

sometimes we held hands in the living room and prayed. When I was little, my mom or dad would rest a hand on my head and pray while I curled up in bed ready to sleep. But this time it felt wrong to stand around like I was placing an order at a fast-food counter. So I knelt, bowed my head, and let my hand rest on my sword hilt.

"God, it's Jake. I'm here, but I don't know where Dad is. Should I go back or should I go forward? What do You want me to do?"

I just thought about Him. I shut out my own urges and fears, my intelligent and not-so-intelligent plans. And then I waited.

It wasn't easy. At first my thoughts babbled like my sister Anne when she's had too much sugar. I kept brushing the chatter aside. After a few minutes had passed, I felt a hand settling on my shoulder. I glanced behind me, thinking it was Dad, but no one was there. Closing my eyes, I dropped my head again. My heart sped up. God was everpresent, and that knowledge had always comforted me. But knowing He was this close was a little scary, too.

It's not like I saw anything or heard a real voice like Kieran used to. That guy had freaked me out when I first met him—talking to someone I couldn't hear—until I figured out that he was praying. Well, except for the times he was cursing under his breath.

No, it was nothing that tangible. But the hand that touched me was a lot like my dad's: reassuring, affirming. And then my heart turned toward Lyric like a compass needle floating north.

"Okay. I think You want me to go forward. Let me know if I'm hearing You wrong." I waited a little longer.

This wasn't the way our youth group leader told us to make

decisions. Yeah, we were supposed to pray about it, but we were also supposed to "search the Scriptures" and "seek wise counsel." I opened my eyes and looked around the woods. Other than a few blue-feathered moths, I didn't see anyone to ask for advice.

Mom needed help. I'd been sent. That's what I had to go on right now. Dad had always looked out for our family and handled every crisis, but he wasn't here.

I drew a shaky breath, the way I used to when the doctor needed to draw bone marrow to check my platelets. That memory gave me a little courage. I'd beaten cancer. I wasn't a wimp.

Pretending confidence, with no one to appreciate it but the smooth-trunked trees, I started the short hike toward Lyric. I'd follow Dad's plan. I'd tell Jorgen what had happened and send word to Tristan.

When I stepped out of the woods, I studied the rolling hills off in the direction of Corros. A few fuzzy caradoc grazed, but otherwise the fields were deserted. We'd been back in our world for over a month. Had minutes passed here? Or years? A shiver ran through me. What if Jorgen wasn't alive anymore—or anyone else I could trust?

I looked ahead at Lyric. The worship tower gleamed in the pale gray light. Must still be early morning. I had lived here long enough to figure out the slight variations that marked the passing of each day. A thick low atmosphere always hid the sky. No one in this world had ever seen a sun or moon or stars.

I grinned as I drew closer to the marble-white city. Jon would have had a hard time building a Lego model of this place. The city was surrounded by a huge wall that rippled like a clamshell. I knew there were hidden doors in some of the scalloped curves, but I didn't have a scrambler to help me with the locks, so I circled around to the main gate. My fears left. There was something so firm and confident about this place, as if it had always been here and always would be. Tara told me it was the place where the One came to live. They believed that the One was everywhere, just like I did, but this was His special place. A surge of joy ran through me. If I'd been at home, I would have grabbed my notebook and written a song about it.

None of my friends knew about the notebook. I'd shown it to Mom once and let her read a couple pages. It made her cry, which I figured was a good sign. I never let anyone else see it. But in this place, I bet no one would laugh at a poem about the One and the way Lyric shimmered in the morning light. By the time I rounded the corner to approach the main gate, I had already come up with a few lines:

In the morning light, alone
May this tower always stand,
A tribute to Your guidance
And the comfort of Your hand.

Then I drew closer to the tunnel that led into the city and realized that something had changed. I rested my hand on my sword. There were no crowds of people milling in and out. No chatting and laughter. Just a half-dozen guardians blocking the entrance. Not Lyric guardians either—these were Council guards. Rust tunics, leather vests, grim faces. Council guards who were loyal to Cameron. I took a deep breath and approached them.

"I need to get into the city." I tried to act casual.

"No entries permitted today," one of them said with a glare.

"Okay, but I need to talk to the chief councilmember from Rendor. It's important."

That surprised a laugh from the man, and he glanced at the other soldiers. They shook their heads and grinned. I didn't see what was so funny.

"I don't know where you've been, but you'd better run home to your parents," the guard said. I would have bristled at the insult, except what he said next sapped all the nerve from my bones. "There is no Council."

Chapter Seven

SUSAN

I must have fallen forward as Cameron yanked me through the portal, because damp moss pressed against my face when I woke. My body didn't appreciate the experience of being tumbled in a huge blender. Every part of me ached and throbbed.

With tremendous effort, I pushed myself up and looked around. Cameron was stirring but must have been knocked out from the trip as well. Medea was completely limp. I couldn't be sure she was even alive, and I didn't care enough to find out.

Stupid, conniving, evil pair. They couldn't be content with Mark opening the portal? Why did they drag me through?

I stumbled to my feet and looked for landmarks. The terrain around us was barren. At first glance, we seemed to be surrounded by vast empty beaches, but instead of sand underfoot, small grey pebbles covered the ground. The air tasted like the sharp hint of mold when rain pooled in our garage. Smooth larger rocks offered the only variation in color with their clinging patches of gray-green moss. I had the uneasy feeling that all kinds of creepy crawlies might lurk beneath those rocks. Even the miles of tiny pebbles seemed to ripple occasionally as if a living current moved beneath the earth.

We weren't near Lyric. During past visits, those pearl towers had become as familiar as my own church. And the gray expanses surrounding me were nothing like the primordial forests of Braide Wood or the rolling farmland of Morsal Plains. I'd even journeyed through several different parts of Hazor, but I didn't see any sign of a place I recognized. Maybe this wasn't even the same world.

Terror shook off some of the pain in my bruised body. Wherever this was, I needed to get away from Cameron and Medea.

Lord, which way do I go?

Far in the distance, hills butted against the horizon. In the opposite direction, vast splatters of white dotted the gray land amid low, irregular mounds. The formless lumps brought back memories of burnt-marshmallow smells and deserted streets. My pulse quickened. Those distant shapes might be the crumbling homes of Shamgar. I could find my way back to the inhabited parts of the clans from there.

I staggered a few steps forward, my tennis shoes shifting under me on the loose stones. I'd covered only a short distance when heavy feet pounded from behind me. Without looking back, I tried to run, but my legs slipped out from under me as if I were trying to sprint up a down escalator. My feet couldn't get the traction they needed. Brutal hands crashed into my back and knocked me to the ground. I twisted, sitting on the pebbles and scrabbling backward.

Cameron's dark eyebrows slammed together as he confronted me. "Where are we?" He wasn't even breathing hard. How had he caught up so easily?

"I don't know."

Towering over me, he raised a threatening hand.

I rolled to the side and got my feet back under me. I came up in a crouch and faced him, wishing for my sword but determined to hold him off even without it. I'd once known how to fight. I pretended I still could.

Cameron advanced, his face twisted in a snarl. "What game is he playing, sending us here?" His chest swelled and color rose on his face, similar to the irrational fury of a two-year-old who didn't get the toy he wanted. Fists raised, I prepared to protect myself but doubted I'd last long. He reached for me and probably would have killed me then, but a hand touched his shoulder and he paused. Medea had glided up behind him.

Her skin was pale beneath her auburn curls, but she was smiling. Cameron turned to her, and the tension melted from his shoulders. His burst of temper almost seemed to refresh Medea. She sighed as if she had taken a cool drink of water.

"Thank you"—she stepped closer to him—"but you promised her to me."

He hesitated a few seconds, then nodded.

My breath escaped from tight lungs. I couldn't follow the undercurrents of their conversation, but I'd absorbed one crucial fact: Cameron wasn't going to beat me into the ground at the moment. He grabbed my arm and pulled me along as we made our way back to the bags.

"I recognize this place," Medea told him. "It's part of Hazor, but the clay fields are near. The way she was running." I felt a moment of startled pride. In spite of my poor navigational skills, I had actually set out in the right direction.

Cameron let go of my arm and I edged away, ready to run again. Medea spared a glance at me. "Your strength is gone. You can't move." Her words to me were warm with sympathetic understanding.

Suddenly, I wanted to sink to the ground. Just filling my lungs to breathe took effort.

Susan, run! You have to get away from these two and get help. But every muscle was held captive by the threads Medea had woven in my mind.

"Will you manage?" She tilted her head and watched Cameron.

He hefted one of the duffel bags and settled the strap on his shoulder. "I have what I need. You'll join me soon?"

"Of course. After a few weeks to rest."

He nodded, then looked at me with narrow eyes, perhaps regretting he hadn't had a chance to inflict more damage. "Can you control her?"

She laughed. "I'm not that tired."

Their plan began to sink in. They were splitting up. As much as I hated Cameron, the thought of being left with Medea was worse. Cameron was cruel and power hungry and believed himself above the paltry ethics of the general masses. But he was someone I could understand. Villain, yes—but a familiar villain. Corrupt politician, self-serving bureaucrat, and even schoolyard bully. He scared me, but I understood him.

Medea was a complete mystery. The Rhusicans I had encountered during my visits to the clans seemed to thrive on arbitrary pain and damage, which they caused with almost no effort.

"Cameron, wait." I swallowed, determined to choke back my panic. "I don't know what you're planning, but you can't trust her." With tremendous effort against the lethargy Medea had woven inside me, I managed one step toward him and forced myself to meet his eyes. "You know what they can do. Don't you realize? She's controlling your mind too." With his teeth bared in amusement, he listened to me for a few sentences, but then he lost patience. His hand darted forward and grabbed my throat like a striking snake.

"You should be grateful she's interested in you. Otherwise I'd leave your body here for the rizzids. It would be the least I could do to pay Markkel back for this trick."

Black spots darted along the edge of my vision as his long fingers squeezed harder.

"Don't damage her." Medea's voice was petulant. "We have a long journey."

He let go, and I doubled over, resting my hands on my knees to gulp in air. I was vaguely aware of Medea helping him sling another bag onto his shoulder. He muttered some dire curses at Mark for this inconvenience.

Medea shrugged. "There's a Hazorite outpost near the border, where you can find a lehkan. It won't take you long to reach Lyric."

I wanted to argue, wanted to rip the bags away from him and see what he had brought. Or, if I couldn't overpower them, I needed to run from them. Warn the Council. Go back to the portal and let Mark and Jake know that I was all right. But I was still lost in a swirling lassitude.

Cameron walked toward the clay fields. Maybe he'd fall into one of the pits.

Medea watched him with a soft curve to her lips. Then her face hardened. "Come with me."

She took a few steps in the opposite direction. Our path led across miles of emptiness toward the horizon. Cameron had taken all their gear. She didn't even carry a backpack.

"I don't get it." I fought the pull to walk after her. "You go to our world and help him bring back . . . whatever he was collecting, and you don't get anything." I was still hoping to stir up conflict between Medea and Cameron. It worked in all the action movies. Get the bad guys mad at each other. "He's just using you. Can't you see that? What do you get out of it?"

She stopped and turned toward me. This time when she smiled, her eyes lit with anticipation. "You."

She resumed walking, and I found myself trudging along beside her. Each step was a tremendous effort. Because of the commands she had planted earlier, my muscles were still convinced they were too weak to function.

She threw me a sideways glance and seemed to find my struggle with the conflicting mental commands amusing.

"So nice of you to be concerned that I'm being treated fairly. Since he can't barter you to the Kahlareans anymore, he said I could have you. I've gotten some of what I've wanted. Later there will be much more." She ran her hands through her hair and lifted her face to the sky. A soft drizzle was just beginning to fall. Early afternoon. The thought of all the hours until nightfall made me want to cry, but I kept walking as she talked. "Cameron and I have found a number of ways to benefit each other."

I should have asked more questions to uncover their plans, but conversation took too much effort.

I shuddered at the endless expanse in front of us. Fatigue made each stride a battle. My feet scuffed through the pebbles, then slipped on them as they grew wet from rain. I fell to my knees more than once. Medea ignored me and strode forward, unconcerned. The next time I fell, I marshaled all my will and stayed down, trying to regain mental control. I focused on the cool drizzle that had soaked my clothes and made my socks squish inside my tennis shoes. I grabbed a fistful of the rain-slicked pebbles. Nothing would force me back to my feet. Medea couldn't compel me to take one more step.

She turned back and noticed me. "Get up," she said with casual annoyance.

I closed my eyes and channeled every effort into refusing. I used her earlier mental suggestion to bolster my efforts. *My muscles are weak. I can't move. I won't move.*

Stones crunched. She stood over me, but I kept my eyes closed.

"Clever"—she studied me for a minute—"but do you really want to anger me?" Her voice hardened, and I glanced up at her. Irrational rage distorted her face as it had in the second before she plunged a knife into my heart in the Council chamber.

"Have you forgotten already?" Her tone was soothing again, and I blinked, confused. "I know you so well. Let's go. We have a long way to travel and no time for games."

My body shifted, ready to stand up, but I closed my eyes and fought her words again. My fingers dug deep into the pebbles, and I held fast.

She laughed. "Interesting. Don't say I didn't give you fair warning." She crouched near me, her words whispering sweetly near my ear. "You're all alone here. Your god abandoned you again. And it's no wonder. You gave Cameron the information that Markkel could open the portal." I knew where her words were leading me, but it was too late to hold them back. Despair swirled into me in a torrent.

Stop. No. Pebbles fell from my hands as I reached up to cover my ears. Still, her words bored into my mind.

"Cameron wouldn't have beaten Markkel if you hadn't told him about the portal stones. It was all your fault." She sighed. "So many things have been your fault. Should we review them?"

"No . . ." The plea wrenched from my throat, but it was too late. She kept talking—listing all the people I had let down, the damage my choices had caused. I barely heard the words. I was already in a dark place surrounded by fog. Emptiness called to me—a deep abyss that would make the pain stop.

I had been in this place before. Once, Linette had called me back with the strength of her songs. Another time Mark had found verses from our own world to fight the poison and draw me out of the darkness. Recognizing this place should have made it easier to fight.

God, I know You're here—even in this dark place.

The fog continued to swirl and images lashed me. Coherent thought was impossible, and my attempted prayers scattered. I saw faces of the people who had died because I led them into battle. Then the picture shifted to my own world: the pain I had caused Mark, and not just by telling Cameron about the portal stones, but all the ways I had let him down over the years.

No. It's forgiven. Don't listen.

The mental pictures wouldn't stop. I'd never been the wife he needed. Selfish, withdrawn, needy—the words struck me like a fist, and I couldn't fight them. Then it continued to the children: the danger Jake was facing, the conflicts that Karen and I wrestled with, my crankiness with the younger children. I was a terrible mother. Impatient, inconsistent . . .

Suddenly, the black fog of torment disappeared, and I was kneeling on smooth stones, shivering in rain-soaked clothes, and sobbing. Medea watched me impassively. She had called me back somehow, with the same strange ability she had to send me. I could have kissed her feet in gratitude for snatching me back from that evil place.

I tried to remind myself that she was the one who had caused the mental torture, but my mind was so wounded I gave up on reason.

"Let's go."

Direction. A simple goal. Step forward. Again. And again. No need to think.

The rain eased to a soft mist and then stopped. Medea kept stalking forward with fierce energy, yet the hills on the horizon didn't seem any closer. I began to believe that I had always been stumbling over this pebbled ground. My entire existence had been years of trudging forward through an unchanged landscape, moving toward nowhere. There had never been anything but gray skies, gray stones, gray hills in the distance that we would never reach.

We stopped a few times to drink from small creeks that trickled across our path, hidden among the flat, pebbled ground. After miles of quiet walking, my brain began to recover from her assault.

Lord, show me how to fight this thing. Why aren't You stopping her? I drew a steadying breath. *Help me hang on to truth.*

The next time I glanced up, the hills seemed closer. It was hard to tell, as the sky was deepening to charcoal. Soon we wouldn't be able to see the horizon at all.

She didn't intend to walk all night, did she? I looked around the vast emptiness. There was nothing to use for shelter. How far did we still have to travel, and what would we do for supplies? Could Medea's kind use their mental powers to protect themselves from the night scavengers that were such a danger in this world? I was afraid to say anything. I was terrified of setting her off, after her brutal reminder of what she could do to me.

"It's almost dark," I ventured at last.

She turned, her eyebrows lifting in surprise as if she had

forgotten me.

"Yes, it is." She continued walking. "I know this area. We'll reach shelter soon."

I didn't delude myself that she cared about reassuring me, but she seemed to be in the mood for conversation. "This is the longest I've ever been away," she said. "I can't wait to be home."

The mention of home stirred a pang of longing in me.

She looked at me. "Yes, you understand, don't you?"

Understand? Her? Not likely. Hours ago she'd tormented me and mocked me. Now she was chatting with me as if we were school chums.

"Of course, I came home for a while after the Restorer caused so much trouble. We all came home then."

Goose bumps prickled along the back of my neck. Had she really forgotten that I was the Restorer that had caused all her people to be banished from the clans? Or had she just forgotten I was walking alongside her?

"But as soon as the trouble died down, Cameron sent a messenger. I probably should have stayed in Rhus longer. This last trip was more difficult than I'd expected. What an interesting place—your world." She giggled. "And it's so nice of you to join me on my trip home. We'll have so much fun."

Dear God, she's completely insane.

I'd known she was erratic and unpredictable. Her motives, her plans—they had been a complete puzzle to me. But she seemed even more unstable and arbitrary than before. How would I protect myself? How could I keep her calm when I couldn't understand her?

"Here we are." She suddenly raced forward, her voice bright.

I squinted into the darkness and realized that what I had thought was a stream up ahead was really a thin gash in the rocky ground. Steps carved into the side led down into the dark cavern. I followed her, my hand braced along the rock face for support as we picked our way down. At the foot of the stairs was a narrow opening. She reached inside to shift a lever, and a pale glow lit the entry. A tunnel stretched ahead for what looked like miles of stone light walls. The glow of illumination seemed to come from deep inside the smooth rock surfaces—one constant, unvaried tube of pale light.

She headed directly onward.

"Wait. Aren't we going to rest here for the night?" My voice croaked with exhaustion.

Her laughter echoed from the rock walls. "Not now! We're almost home. If we hurry, we can be there by morning."

I stared at her, aghast. My back and legs ached. My head throbbed. I couldn't remember when I'd last eaten.

She looked at me, and a sneer of disdain chased away her good humor. "Don't slow me down. Understand?"

I drew an unsteady breath, and a shiver ghosted through me.

She gestured for me to go ahead of her.

I hadn't been able to break free from her control earlier and had even less energy now.

Just stay alive. You'll find a way out later. I walked forward. At least the tunnel floor was smoother than loose pebbles and uneven rocks. When I glanced back over my shoulder, Medea's green eyes seemed to be twirling in the glow of the light panels. Beyond her the dark entrance receded.

Mark would come to save me. I'd told myself that from the second I woke up with my face pressed against a moss-covered rock. In all the fear and despair I'd felt today, the knowledge had hummed like a calming bass line beneath a chaotic melody.

But how would he ever find me here? The deep, reassuring tone of hope faded as I walked farther into the tunnel. Medea had used twisted thoughts to torture me earlier, but she based her poison on fragments of truth.

I was very alone.

Chapter Eight

SUSAN

The long passage stretched into a forever of lines diminishing to a point in the future that could never be reached. Dozing on my feet, I barely managed to avoid crashing against the light walls. Medea didn't care how much I stumbled, as long as I kept moving. Even when I was awake for stretches of time, my mind was too battered and exhausted to be aware of much. Again the monotony of weary steps consumed me, along with the growing belief that my whole life had been nothing but this pale tunnel that would never end.

Hours later we reached a stone staircase weaving several stories upward. I stared at it, confused, but Medea bounded up the first steps. I trudged behind her, vertigo dancing through my brain like a fever. When I swayed for a moment, I almost gave in to the loss of balance. It would have been such a relief to simply fall down to the crushing rock floor and be done with this, but I caught myself against the wall and forced myself onward until, at last, we emerged into an open courtyard.

The pale light of the morning sky rubbed a sheen on the white stone archways. We'd walked all night.

A man in an azure tunic lounged on a marble bench. His face had the soft lines of a Raphael painting, with red-gold curls teasing his temples—similar to the Rhusican I had killed in Braide Wood. When he saw us, he jumped to his feet.

"Medea!" His face lit, and he ran toward her, ignoring me.

"Nicco. Were you watching for me?" She reached a hand toward him. "I made it home." Then with a sigh she wilted onto the ground, as pale as the marble pillars in the courtyard.

Medea's fierce intensity to reach her home had propelled me. Now the link broke like an electrical plug pulled from a socket. My knees buckled; I sank to the ground, freed from the trance-like compulsion to walk. I wanted to curl up and fall asleep right there in the courtyard.

Nicco gathered Medea into his arms. "Rest now. We've been worried."

She opened her eyes, dull sage in color and no longer twirling with emerald light. "Take her to the conservatory," she whispered. "Keep the others away from her."

His angelic face clouded for a moment. "Now? When she's new? That's no fun."

Her hand drifted up to stroke his cheek. "I'll share later. I promise." Then her arm floated down and she closed her eyes. He lifted her with almost no effort and carried her through one of the archways.

My mind struggled to absorb the new surroundings and make sense of the fragments of conversation. I hadn't felt this kind of deep fatigue and confusion since being stranded at an airport gate during a blizzard. Two days and nights without sleep—with fluorescent lights glaring and the constant jabbering of the public address announcements—had produced this same sense of floating outside of reality.

One fact gradually formed into a coherent thought: I was free. For the first time since facing Medea at our kitchen table, she wasn't twisting around in my brain. And what was more, the courtyard was empty. The chance I'd been waiting for.

I stumbled to my feet. There were several directions open to me. Archways beckoned in a semicircle around the courtyard, but the only sure way back to the clans, to the portal, and to Mark was the tunnel. I shuddered at the thought of facing that interminable passage again but forced my feet to move. Again dizziness hit me on the steep stairs, but I scrabbled down and reached the bottom safely. The Rhusicans seemed to have short attention spans. Maybe Nicco would forget all about me. By the time Medea was aware again, I would be gone.

God, give me strength.

The Rhusicans were good at mind games, but I'd use my own bit of mental trickery to help me endure this. When I was Karen's age, I had run track in school. I pictured the cinder track stretching before me and imagined that I was young and strong. I loped forward, blocking out my pain. I promised myself I would slow to a walk after I'd put some distance between Medea and myself.

One hundred steps. Just count off one hundred, and then you can rest.

I kept losing count.

All the better. Start over. One hundred strides, then you can rest.

Laughter and voices suddenly bounced around the tunnel walls. I couldn't be sure whether they came from behind me or in front of me, but I kept moving. Nothing could make me turn back now. The voices rang in the air like those of children in our neighborhood back home. Playful shrieks, sporadic giggles.

Adrenaline fed my blood and I ran faster.

I didn't hear their footsteps over the sound of my gasps for breath, but when I glanced back over my shoulder, I saw them: two boys and a girl. They could have been Jon and Anne with a friend. They whooped when they saw me look back, and the girl gave a little skip. My panic eased.

Then one of them called in a sweet, high voice, "Look out for the rizzids." The others laughed, as if she'd made the best joke in the world. I ignored them, but as my gaze swept the tunnel ahead, something moved.

A red-furred body the shape of a salamander and the size of a large squirrel slithered down from the wall, its fangs bared.

I pulled to a halt. Could I get around it? A rizzid's bite could be deadly, but if I just slipped around the side . . .

Two more rizzids squirmed down the wall across from the first. Where were they coming from?

The children had stopped running and were gamboling toward me now.

"Stay back," I warned them. That triggered peals of laughter.

One of the boys stopped a few paces from me and tilted his head, studying me. Then he nudged his friend. "How about a bear?"

"Yes." The other boy smirked. "Be careful. It'll tear you to pieces."

I looked forward into the passage, past the growing group of rizzids, and saw a huge bear. It rose onto its hind legs, its head almost brushing the tunnel's roof as it roared.

My arms thrust out in the universal protective-mom gesture as I took a few steps back. This sent the children into more hysterical laughter.

"I told you just to stop her. No games. This one is Medea's." Nicco strode up behind the children. His stern words were undercut by the grin he flashed toward the children. Their disappointed protests sounded exactly like my children when they were told there was no ice cream for dessert.

Didn't any of them care about the huge beast in our path? The bear dropped to all fours and lumbered our direction. I spared a quick glance at the tall Rhusican, but it was all he needed. Nicco's eyes flickered with malevolence even though his smile never faded. "Come here."

I stumbled toward him. "But the bear . . ." I looked back over my shoulder to see a long, empty tunnel glowing with gray light. No rizzids. No bear.

The little girl jumped up and down, clapping. Nicco put a hand on her shoulder and nudged her back up the tunnel toward the stairs. "Off with you. Thanks for helping. Next time follow directions."

The three young Rhusicans ran ahead, chattering like normal children. I shuddered. Nothing here was normal.

He sent children to stop me. My escape was a sorry joke. Bitterness curled under my ribs, and I turned to run from him down the now-empty corridor.

"Don't move." The words held me in a fist.

Where Medea had twined her way into vulnerable places in my brain and gradually asserted control, Nicco's link was as sudden and lethal as a snake's strike.

I stood frozen, straining against an invisible force.

How can they have this much power? God, where are You? Stop this.

Nicco walked to stand in front of me, studying me as if I were a statue on display in a museum. He used one finger to tilt my chin up.

I tried to pull away but couldn't make even that small movement, and I found myself staring into rain-forest green eyes.

"You're just like the rest." His tone was slightly puzzled. Then he shrugged, losing interest. "I'm sure she'll explain later. Follow me."

Unable to do anything else, I followed him along the passage: up the stairs, through the courtyard, under marble arches, past a garden I would have admired if I weren't seeing it as a captive. He didn't say a word, and I was too confused to speak. He led me to a long two-story building of smooth gray stone. Curved windows interrupted the monotony of the first level. The second floor exterior was solid stone. We entered the building through an open arch. No doors. I noticed stray details, but my normal curiosity was muted by bone-weary exhaustion. We climbed wide stairs and walked a long hall that looked like the tunnel, complete with light walls glowing a pale gray. Unlike the walls of the tunnel, thin seams indicated doorways evenly spaced along both sides of the hall. Pale crosshatched symbols marked each one.

As we passed one of the doors, something scratched from within and then thudded against the barrier. From farther down the hall, a muffled wail rose up and then changed into maniacal laughter. Finally, Nicco stopped and touched a recessed lever. The door in front of us slid upward and disappeared into the wall above. Cold dread overcame my lethargy. There was something very final about crossing the threshold into the small ten-foot-square room. I held back with the last bit of will I had.

Nicco grinned down at me, then closed his eyes and took a deep breath as if savoring my terror. Spinning away, I ran back down the hall. I tripped over my own feet and fell, sprawling, against the gleaming floor. Nicco grabbed my shoulders and hauled me to my feet, then let go of me abruptly, as if irritated he had been forced to touch me. His eyes flared but quickly shuttered again.

"You'll never leave here." His bland words were simple, but they gripped my soul in iron manacles. "You can struggle. You can fight us." He cocked his head and smiled in anticipation. "I hope you will." Then the smile disappeared, and he spit out each syllable. "But you will never leave."

The words overpowered me like blows from a club. I barely noticed as he led me back to the room. Some part of me registered that it looked like a sterile hospital room or an empty college dorm. A low pallet stretched along one wall, and two chairs and a table filled the space along another. A sliding panel hid some plumbing fixtures. Nicco slid aside another panel to reveal a closet.

"I'll send someone with clothes for you." His voice seemed far away. "Medea will feel better in a few days. She'll see you then." He said it as if those words would make sense to me. I sank into one of the chairs, my hand shielding my eyes from the painful white glow of the light walls. I barely noticed Nicco leave, realizing only after he was gone that I was free from his mental control. I summoned enough energy to throw myself at the door, clawing at the tight seam where it met the floor, scrabbling for any means of escape. I searched for any indent to give me a grip. When nothing budged, I flung my shoulder against the door, pounded, and yelled until exhaustion defeated me. I made my way to the pallet and curled into a tight ball, too tired to even cry. My broken mind shut down, and I slept.

Mornings are for opening things—opening eyes, opening window shades, opening the door and stepping out into a new day of possibilities.

Here, in this place, I opened my eyes each morning and saw the same stark light walls, the same windowless room, and the same door that would not let me out. I wasn't only imprisoned in Rhus; the isolation held my mind captive and shriveled away my inner strength. Even without Medea's or Nicco's interference, my thoughts battered me, circling around and around like a carnival ride. I had even taken to talking to myself.

The first morning, when a young Rhusican girl delivered some clean, dry clothes, I asked her questions, but she ignored me. After she left, I changed into the loose tunic and shapeless pants, both as colorless as the room. When the door slid up slightly so a tray of food could be pushed inside, I had pressed my face to the gap and called to the person that must be outside. No one responded.

I searched every inch of my cell for anything that I could use to escape but came up empty. Each morning, I stretched and worked through the training forms I had learned from the guardians. After two or three days, that resolve faded. Apathy held me immobile with more power than chains ever could. Nothing made any difference, so why bother going through the motions?

"The funny thing is, there is something familiar about this feeling." I stood up to pace the room one day, in what I guessed was the afternoon. "What was I talking about? Oh, yes. This feels familiar. And why is that? It's not like the prison in Hazor. It's not like the holding cells underneath the Council offices where Cameron stashed me once."

My mind was diverted by the curious fact that in my short

visits to this world, this was the third type of prison I'd had the chance to experience.

"Remind me to complain to my travel agent. Not exactly the kind of tour package you want when you're visiting a new country."

Now, what had I been thinking about? I almost didn't bring my thoughts back to it. Focusing was difficult—too much effort.

"Why does this feel familiar? When have I been here before?"

It wasn't Rhusican poison that I was recognizing. Since Nicco left me here, I'd barely seen any of them, and no one had further tampered with my thoughts, as far as I could tell. Medea still hadn't put in an appearance. More than a few days had passed, although I had lost track of exactly how many.

"Come on, Susan. Think. You can still do that." I paced the two steps across to the other wall and slid the panel back. The slide of a lever released water into a basin, and I splashed some on my face. The cut on my cheek was healing, but my fingers traced the scar that was forming. Not hairline thin like the Restorer wounds that had once healed instantly; this scar itched and felt rough and uneven.

I moved to the small table, lowered myself onto a chair, and rested my head in my arms. Alone, abandoned, day following day with no useful purpose.

That's it! Those were the same words I had used when I talked to our pastor.

The month before Mark built the attic pull-down, I had been slipping into a smothering cloud of depression. The simplest tasks took tremendous effort and brought no sense of pleasure—even things I used to love. The feeling became so frightening that I went to talk with my pastor. I never told Mark about that visit. He'd always been frustrated by anything he couldn't fix with a new set of drill bits or his table saw. Besides, he wouldn't believe that it wasn't his fault. He would think there should be some way he could make me happy. He didn't need to take on that burden.

Pastor Nathan had been both compassionate and practical. He talked with me about the complex web of causes for depression and helped me assemble a collection of tools—physical, spiritual, relational—to help me battle it.

I hadn't made much progress before the portal wrenched me away and into Shamgar.

"Okay, that's important," I said loudly. "Being here is a lot like the depression last spring. And you know ways to fight it. What do you remember?"

I tried to picture the perky brochure Pastor Nathan had given me. It had a silly title like "You and Your Depression," as if the illness were some unruly pet I was learning to train. But there had been that list of tips.

Social contact.

Hmmm. That was going to be a bit difficult. I was already talking to myself. Unless I began developing other personalities, I was a little short on a social circle right now.

Talk with a trusted counselor.

Ditto on that one.

Exercise, sunlight, regular sleep schedule. I started laughing, then scared myself with the sound of my laughter in the empty room.

I took a steadying breath.

"This is the human mind left to itself." Fragile, confused, dark. Then like a blaze of the sun I hadn't seen in days, a new thought gleamed.

"I'm not left to myself." I jumped up and paced. "Not then, not now." I settled back into the chair and rested my forehead against folded hands. "God, I don't know how to fight these people. I can't even think clearly. I don't know how to find my way back." My voice choked. That last sentence was exactly what I had prayed while deep in depression. "I'm lost here, but I know You're with me. You know the way out. Thank You for holding my hand." Tears poured down my face unrestrained as I continued to pray. For the first time in days, I could grab hold of passages of Scripture that had been lost in my memory. "The Lord is my light and my salvation—whom shall I fear? The Lord is the stronghold of my life—of whom shall I be afraid?" Old verses took on new meanings. Words that had once been pretty poetry became my lifeline.

Hope thrummed deep within me for the first time since stepping into the tunnel with Medea. Maybe her dark thoughts had lingered more than I'd realized. Wiping my eyes, I began to recite another psalm.

A whisper sounded from the door as it lifted.

I watched it rise. It wasn't time for supper yet, was it? My only sense of time came from the meals that arrived at what I assumed were morning and evening.

The door continued slipping upward. Nicco stepped into the room. I looked past him to the hallway. There was nothing to see, but my eyes longed to focus on something beyond the four walls of my room, if only for a few seconds.

"Medea is still recovering. She was away far too long." He stepped forward, and the door slid closed behind him. "She said I could come and talk to you." He crossed his arms and watched me.

"Why?" I still had no clue what Medea wanted from me.

"Why?" He still looked exactly like an angel in a Renaissance painting, and his voice was warm. He pulled up the other chair and sat down. "So you won't go to waste." A smile grew across his flawless face, and a new wave of fear crashed against my fragile courage.

Chapter Nine

SUSAN

"Will you explain what she wants from me? Please." After so many days in complete isolation, words tumbled from my lips as if Nicco were a caring person who would converse with me. "Why did she bring me here? Why were your people in Lyric and Braide Wood? What do you want from the clans? If there's something they can help you with, there must a way to do that without tampering with people's minds. Do you even understand what you were doing to the people there? How many people you hurt?"

He yawned and settled more comfortably into his chair. "How have you been feeling?"

"Fine." If he ignored my questions, I didn't plan to bare my soul to him.

His face darkened, and he leaned forward, resting his elbows on the table. I was careful not to meet his eyes.

"No," he said in a voice as rich and smooth as cream. "Tell me what it is like to be trapped . . . alone . . . hopeless."

Each of his words conjured my feelings to the surface. Refusing him the voyeuristic satisfaction of seeing my struggle,

I sprang out of my chair and paced the few steps toward the door, letting anger well up inside me.

"Just how do you think it feels?" I forced the words through clenched teeth. "I don't belong here. I'm worried about— "

Don't talk about Mark and the children. He didn't need ammunition. I was vulnerable enough already.

"I'm furious." My skin heated with the first real energy I had felt in days. "Cameron hurt my husband, and your friend Medea is helping him. You're holding me here, and you have no right. I was dragged on some death march and then locked up with no explanation. I don't know what you want." I spun and glared at him. "You won't get away with this."

Nicco watched me with a satisfied smile. "I'm beginning to understand."

My voice grew in volume. "What? That you can't just kidnap people and lock them away?"

He laughed. "No. Why Medea bothered to bring you all this way."

"So explain it to me!"

He shook his head. "You don't need to know. Just do what you're told and try to stay alive for a while. She went to a lot of trouble for you."

The instincts I'd developed riding with an army and crossing swords in battle flared to life. In one smooth motion, I advanced on Nicco, grabbed my chair, and lifted it to swing at his head. I was much more of a middle-American homemaker than a mythic Restorer, but I wouldn't give up without a fight.

Crushing pain burst through my chest, and the chair fell from my hands. My vision sparkled; I couldn't breathe. I felt myself collapsing and knew I was headed for the floor.

Mercifully, I blacked out before I hit.

When I came to, Nicco crouched near me, watching. As soon as he saw my eyes open, he leaned closer.

He didn't touch me. He didn't have to. His eyes grabbed me.

"Ground rules." His voice rumbled with menace. "I can make you feel anything . . . anything you've ever felt. Any pain in your memory. Don't ever"—another stab of pain made me gasp—"attack me again."

He thumbed a remote on his belt to open the door, stepped out, and chatted with someone in the hall, the words inaudible through the moans coming from my own throat. The door slid back down, and I crawled toward the pallet. It had taken a long time to get over the pain I'd felt when Cameron's drugs had damaged my heart. Or the searing ache of the knife that Medea had plunged into me in the Council session. I had just relived that torment in full—every nuance, every screaming nerve ending. I curled into a ball and whimpered.

I slowly realized the pain had been a Rhusican illusion. Nicco hadn't done any real physical damage. The agony faded rapidly, but my helpless dread didn't.

Why did You let him hurt me?

All I could do was cry out to God and beg Him to make this all go away.

Then a quiet memory nudged its way forward: my friend Ruthie sitting across from me at our favorite restaurant. Months earlier, her husband had been killed in a car accident. Loaves of banana bread and flowers proved inadequate support, so after the funeral, I began to take her out for lunch each Wednesday. We talked a lot about evil—senseless evil that raised questions and rattled faith. Each week I listened to her pain expressed in soul-wrenching honesty. I reassured Ruthie it was normal to ask "why?"

But one day she faced me with a firm chin. It was hot that day, and she fanned herself with the menu and pressed her iced tea glass against her forehead. "I know it's okay for me to vent. And thanks for letting me sort it out. But if I get stuck forever shouting all my 'why' questions, I could get trapped in my own frustration."

I pushed aside my salad plate and leaned forward. "I don't think God minds our questions."

"I know. But there are some things God may not choose to explain to us on this side of heaven." She gave me a wry smile. "That's a hard truth, but He's God and we're not."

What else had she said? The sounds of the restaurant flooded back into my memory. The smell of cashew chicken. The texture of the paper napkin wadded in my hand.

Her eyes were brighter than I'd seen them in months. "I'm trying something new. When I'm confronted with something unfair, hurtful, unjust . . . a crime I read about in the newspaper, or someone who's rude to me in the checkout line, or . . ." She swallowed. "Or the empty side of my bed. Instead of asking 'why?' I'm asking God, 'how?'"

"Huh?"

She grinned. "No. 'How.' How do You want me to respond? How are You planning to work good even through this tragedy? How can I be part of the grace You want to bring in this situation?"

I had soaked in every word. Ruthie had faced pain I couldn't even comprehend.

Now, as if she were sitting in my cell with me, her words rose up to challenge me.

I groaned and hugged the blanket against my chest, curling up tighter. She hadn't meant this circumstance. She hadn't meant being kidnapped by mind-controlling Rhusicans. Still, the words had lodged in my memory for a reason.

"Okay, Lord. How? How do You want me to respond?" The question felt stiff, but I continued. "I really mean it. Show me what to do. I'm overwhelmed here. This is beyond anything I have the strength to fight."

There was real relief in admitting my need, and my death grip on the blanket loosened. "What are You planning? And if You can't show me that, just show me what You need from me today. . . ."

My voice trailed off. I felt a little better, though I didn't really expect an answer.

Pray for them.

"What? Sure. I'll pray." I began to go through my nightly prayers, asking God to protect and bless Mark and each of my children, and—

Pray for Medea. For Nicco. For the Rhusican people.

I froze. "God, I can't be hearing You right. They're evil. Haven't You seen what they've been doing? And not just to me."

How many times in my life had I done this dance with God? Asking Him for direction, then promptly arguing when I sensed His guidance. I sighed.

"Fine. God, destroy this evil place. Stop their plans. Crush them."

The silence in the room stopped my words.

Then verses stirred in my memory. Unwelcome at the moment, but persistent. "Love your enemies. . . . Pray for those who mistreat you. . . . Do not be overcome by evil, but overcome evil with good. . . ."

I pulled the blanket over my head, but it didn't shut out the call. Warm love wrapped me in tender arms and dared me to let that love work through me.

"And I thought learning to use a sword was hard work," I muttered.

Praying for my captors didn't come easily. Over the next several days, I fought my feelings of repulsion and niggling rebellion and began to pray. Little by little, my thoughts shifted during those times of prayer.

"God, draw close to Medea. If she is so conscienceless, she must be very empty inside. She needs You. Stir in her heart—if she has one." My prayers were sincere, but I couldn't resist an occasional side comment. "Make her hungry for You. Bring Your light to these people. Help me to understand them—to find ways to share truth with them. And bless Nicco." The words almost choked me, and I stopped to cough. "He seems to have an important role here. Thank You for his curiosity about me. Turn it into a curiosity about You. Show him that there is more to life than hurting others for enjoyment."

They hadn't brought food in a long time. It was hard to guess how much time had passed, since the glaring light never changed. As well as I could determine, several days had come and gone. The small sink provided water but that was all.

Had they forgotten me? Or was Nicco making a point? Maybe he wanted me weaker before he talked to me again.

I pushed the questions aside and kept praying. Strangely, my mind grew clearer during this involuntary time of fasting. I experienced brief glimpses through Other eyes, something that had happened several times when I was the Restorer. The One's love for the people of Rhus began to empower my prayers.

One day I was sitting at the table playing a game of tic-tac-toe, using a grid made from threads I'd pulled out of the blanket. I was trying to remember whose turn it was, when the door slid open. Nicco stood in the doorway. A frisson of fear ran through me, but it was followed by a wave of peace that came from outside myself. I swallowed hard and started praying.

He sauntered into the room and pulled up a chair. "How are you?"

I'd planned how to respond if he started this way again. *Okay, Susan. Stay calm.* "I'm fine." I sat up taller. "I know I'm not alone. The One is with me." I let the peace well in me, hoping Nicco would sense it, hoping I would shake his arrogance.

He tilted back his chair and studied me through half-closed lids.

"You really are like all the rest." He sounded disappointed. "They all go through this phase. They thrash around for a while. Then they turn to their gods." He sounded bored. "It doesn't last long."

I shifted on the chair, clenching my fists. Then something he said snagged my attention.

"What others?" I knew I wasn't the only person imprisoned in their "conservatory," but I understood almost nothing about this place.

He grinned and seemed to weigh my question. His chair dropped forward with a bang. "All right. We have special gifts."

I wouldn't call twisting and tormenting other people's minds a gift, but I held my tongue.

"And we bring guests here to help us develop and strengthen our gifts." He rubbed the back of his neck. "It's a bother, of course, and they never last as long as we would like, but"—he shrugged—"it serves our purpose."

His eyes targeted mine. "Now"—his voice was a whiplash in the small room—"let's talk about your fears."

When he left much later, my clothes were soaked with cold sweat, and I was shaking and nauseated. He, however, strode out with an energetic bounce, as if refreshed by a good night's sleep. I crept to my pallet, pulled the blanket around myself, and wept.

After I'd slept and recovered from his latest assault, I scoured every inch of the room again, looking for something to use as a weapon or a means of escape. The material that formed the light walls might be translucent enough to conduct light, but it was hard as steel. Even when I swung a chair into it, my efforts didn't leave a dent. The seam where the door met the floor was so tight that even if I'd had a tool, I wouldn't have been able to wedge it in as a lever. I broke my fingernails trying.

"God, get me out of here. Show me what to do."

Pray for them.

Resentment throbbed in my head. "Were You even here? Did You see what he did?" I punched the unyielding door until my knuckles bled. Drops of red stained the white floor and my white tunic. Blood.

Holy, precious blood.

"Holy, precious blood, and innocent suffering and death." The phrase from my childhood catechism splattered across my mind. Christ had bled for me. Now He was asking one thing of me. One simple thing. One impossible thing.

If I surrendered to the hatred and terror that battled for

supremacy in my heart, I'd be lost.

Instead, I knelt in the center of the small room, folded my hands, and bowed my head. When I couldn't dredge up words of petition for my captors, I used Scripture to help me. "Lord, You are a shepherd. The Rhusicans don't know You, but they need You. You can restore their souls. I'm not sure they even remember what it means to have a soul, but You can restore them."

Hours passed in sleep, prayer, pacing the room, inventing games to keep my mind from chaos. They gave me food again. Apparently, Nicco decided he'd made his point and didn't need to starve me.

The next time the door opened, it was harder to grab hold of peace, but I shot out silent prayers like a quiver's worth of arrows. This time, Nicco was accompanied by Medea.

In a strange way, it felt good to see a familiar face. I forgot myself and greeted her as if she were the old friend she sometimes pretended to be. She didn't seem to mind. She made her way to a chair with her usual grace, but there was a heaviness around her shoulders and dark shadows under her eyes.

"Nicco tells me he's enjoyed visiting with you. I'm sorry I missed it. The early days here, our guests are so . . . stimulating."

"You shouldn't have stayed away so long. Everyone knows how strong you are. You didn't need to show off." Nicco's words were teasing, and he rested a hand on her shoulder as he took a place beside her.

She turned her head to show him a pout. "I wasn't showing off. I didn't know it would take Cameron so long to find everything."

I was fascinated by their conversation. What exactly was

their relationship? Medea used flirtation with everyone, so that could mean anything or nothing. I cataloged the few facts I could collect from this interchange.

"Go ahead. I'm curious to see what you've found so far," she said to him.

He gave her an affectionate smile, and they both turned to me. My mouth went dry, and I tried to brace myself.

And the peace of God, which transcends all understanding, will guard your hearts and your minds . . .

I was trying to finish the thought, when Nicco reached past Medea and grabbed my chin. He turned my head to look at the scar on my cheek. "What did you feel when Cameron did this?" I didn't remember telling him that it had been Cameron. I tried to resist the pull toward that memory, but it flared up in blinding Technicolor—the physical sting, the shock, and then the anger.

Nicco let go of me and stood behind Medea. "Yes, tell me about your anger."

One by one, he led me through other incidents in my memory. Petty annoyances and blinding furies. He strung them out like violent red beads on a string. My body shook, and my pulse pounded behind my forehead. I closed my eyes but couldn't shut out his gaze, his words, his power to stir all of this.

I hated what I was feeling, hated being caught in a maelstrom of rage, hated the way he twisted memories to create fury well beyond what had ever occurred. He wouldn't stop. I tried to focus the anger on him, but he just savored it for a moment and then diverted it to the next image he triggered. My heart raced, I breathed hard, and every muscle tightened.

"Enough." His word released me.

I slumped against the back of the chair, barely able to stay upright. My pulse slowed, and I reeled from the places he had taken me.

Medea giggled. "That was quite good." She sprang up and gave a cat-like stretch.

He grinned. "I know you prefer guilt and despair, but I thought this might help more."

She slid her hand along his back. "You've always known what I need."

He laughed but didn't seem to take her seriously. "I don't mind helping anytime. Even when you're stronger." They left arm in arm, Medea obviously feeling much better. They never even glanced back.

The door slid down behind them, and I wished for strength to throw myself against it, but I could only brace myself against the chair and move a few wobbly feet to collapse onto the pallet.

My mind was still numb from the aftermath of Nicco's invasion, but I stubbornly folded my hands and closed my eyes.

"Dear God, help me survive this. Find an opening to let them see Your love. Help the people in the other rooms in this building. Deliver us from evil." A shudder ran through me. How many more visits like this would I have to endure?

So much time had passed. There didn't seem to be any hope that Mark would find me. Had he at least stopped Cameron from whatever he had planned for Lyric and the People of the Verses?

After all this time, what was happening in my own world? Was Karen still on her band tour? Were Jon and Anne wondering why they weren't getting postcards at camp from me? Was Jake holding down the fort at home? Or did Mark let Jake come with him through the portal to save me? He wouldn't have, would he? We hadn't talked much about Jake's Restorer signs, but Mark would know that it was too dangerous for Jake to come through, especially with Cameron running the show. I tried to guess what they were all doing, but then my mind went as flaccid as my body. Sleep rolled over me, and the pain retreated.

Chapter Ten

JAKE

I stared at the Council guards, my mouth hanging open. Why would they tell me a lie like that? Of course there was a Council. For Pete's sake, these were *Council* guards.

They tired of me gaping at them. "Head back to the transport." One of the muscle-bound soldiers waved me toward the road. Arguments wouldn't get me anywhere. And I didn't bother explaining I hadn't arrived on a transport. No need to raise suspicions.

Technically, these were supposed to be the good guys, although I was a little fuzzy on that issue. Kieran had despised the Council and didn't trust any of their guards, but Dad had been a councilmember.

I followed the road they had indicated. Last time I was here, some Council guards had escorted me from Braide Wood to Lyric. Maybe I could retrace the route to Braide Wood and find Tristan. He would know what to do. Both Mom and Dad trusted him. He was a head guardian. Even though he was a little grim sometimes, I liked him. I used to read lots of books about Arthur and Camelot when I was a kid. Tristan could have been any knight off those pages.

Yep. Good plan. I jogged along the road to the transport station but slowed when it came into view.

Before, there had been people everywhere. Today it was deserted. The silence gave me the creeps.

I once showed up for college entrance exams on the wrong day. I ran through a classroom building, afraid I was late. Every room was dark and empty. My footsteps echoed in the halls, and panic tore around in my head as I wondered where everyone was. I felt the same way now.

I slumped on a bench. I had planned to ask someone for directions. It wasn't like I could study a map or read a list of hubs like at a bus stop back home. The people here didn't use a written language. They just knew stuff—which was fine if you lived here all the time, but not so great when you were a stranger.

I remembered the direction I'd come from when we pulled into the Lyric station, so I waited until an automated transport pulled up heading that direction. When the sleek metal door slid up, I stepped on and sat on one of the molded plastic benches that ran along the sides of the compartment. The transport pulled out with me as the only passenger. It was a lonely feeling.

After a while, the transport stopped at another deserted station that I knew wasn't Braide Wood. But I remembered going near another town on the ride with the guards, so maybe I was heading the right direction.

The terrain began to change. The bare rolling hills gave way to trees with smooth twisting branches and then steeper cliffs with tall pine trees. This felt familiar, and when the transport stopped again, I jumped out. As I remembered it, the trail to

Braide Wood was an hour of aggressive hiking. I muttered about the transportation system in this world. Tara had once explained that each clan kept the transport stations some distance from their villages as a barrier of time and space. Convenience and speed weren't a high priority among most of the People of the Verses.

I rummaged in my pack and was relieved to find my water bottle. As I straightened, a plop of water hit my head. Must be early afternoon already. I groaned and pulled out a rain poncho from my hiking supplies, settling it over me and my pack before starting up the trail. I heard rustling sounds deep in the woods and made sure the poncho didn't get in the way of my sword hilt.

It would have been a nice walk if I hadn't been wondering where Mom was, what was wrong with Lyric, and whether something dangerous would jump out at me around the next bend. I jogged some of the way, slowing when the path angled upward. I wasn't 100 percent positive this was the right trail, but I was committed now. If I didn't find Braide Wood within a few hours, I would hike back to the transport.

I had brought some food along and could have stopped for lunch along the trail, but urgency drove me to find Tristan. He had pledged friendship to our family. He'd help me rescue Mom.

The rocks grew slippery, and as I reached a high ridgeline, nothing looked particularly familiar. Trees were trees. The rain felt cold as a few drops hit my nose, and I shivered. I might be completely lost. As I rounded a curve, the roofs of Braide Wood spread out below me.

Kieran and I had approached from a different direction the first time I had come here. I hadn't appreciated how big the village was. It took me a moment to get my bearings, but I figured out which house was Tristan's and worked my way down the path toward it.

The first thing I noticed was the silence. The afternoon rain was letting up, so I expected to see children running between the log homes, laughing and distracting themselves from chores. The last time I was here, several people left their doors open or called to each other from their porches. Lots of the men and women were probably working down at Morsal Plains, planting or harvesting, or trying to restore the poisoned land. Yet there should have been some activity.

Every door was closed. Cold bumps rose on my arms.

Our city zoo had a prairie dog exhibit that boasted a whole town full of hills and tunnels. On one of my visits, the zoo volunteer demonstrated how some of the prairie dogs stayed on guard and then when they sensed danger, warned the others. She pulled a fake hawk across the ceiling of the exhibit. As the shadow fell, a whistle went up and all the prairie dogs disappeared into their burrows with a flash of brown fur. The resulting emptiness was exactly how Braide Wood felt to me.

I found Tristan's house and tapped on the door. I had to knock a couple of times before a small crack appeared. Eyes peered out at me and then the door swung wide.

"Jake! What are you doing here?" Tara pulled me in and quickly closed the door. She gathered me in a hug, then pulled back to stare at me like she couldn't believe her eyes.

Her white hair swirled around her head, and her smile was warm, but she looked older than I remembered. "Are you alone?" she asked.

I nodded. "I just came from Lyric. They wouldn't let me into the town. What's going on? Is Tristan around? I need to talk to him."

A shadow crossed her face—the hawk passing over the prairie dog town again. "Tristan and Kendra had to leave."

My stomach felt like lead. "Where did they go?"

Tara helped me out of my wet poncho. She shook it out with a snap and draped it over a chair. "They couldn't tell me. It's safer that way." She looked up at me with misery in her eyes.

I sank into a chair, afraid to find out more but desperate for information. "Do you know where my mom is?"

Her eyes widened, and she pulled out a chair for herself. "Why? Didn't she go back to your world?"

"Yes, but then Cameron and Medea came and took her. They beat up my dad, and they're planning something bad." My voice got louder. "They were bringing some bags of stuff back with them."

Tara shushed me and looked around like there were enemies hiding in the closets. "Jake, be careful what you say."

My head was starting to hurt. I should have stopped to eat lunch on the trail. Tara hadn't offered me anything. Things must be really bad.

She looked down. "Don't speak against the king."

"King? What are you talking about? And why did the guards in Lyric tell me there's no more Council? How much time has gone by since we left?"

Tara leaned forward and spoke in a low voice. "Only two seasons. Two long, dark seasons for the People of the Verses."

I struggled to work out the math. If I remembered right, a season was about sixty days, the length of time it took for their major grain crop to mature. The equivalent of four months had passed.

"But we came through the portal within an hour after they took her."

"Your father is here?" Tara's eyes flashed with hope.

I shook my head. "He didn't make it through. I'm not sure why. His plan was for us to get to Lyric before Cameron and find help to stop him. Please tell me what's happened. And where is my mom?"

Tara reached forward and took one of my hands in hers. She answered the important question first. "I'm sorry, Jake. I haven't heard any news of your mother. Tristan came back from Lyric and told me that your family had left. He told me about how Kieran stopped Zarek's army and that Kieran was going back to Hazor with a few of the songkeepers. We could hardly believe that Hazor wasn't going to be a threat anymore. We had a huge celebration." She smiled sadly. "That was the last time we've had a reason to celebrate."

I shivered. She offered to make me some hot clavo, but I shook my head.

"It wasn't long after that—a few days I think—that the announcement came. They sent messengers to all the clans. Cameron had discovered some old Records that had been lost and gave them to the songkeepers. The clans were called to listen to them, even though it wasn't quite season-end."

Tara's shoulders seemed to grow heavier as she talked. "The Records told of a time when two Restorers would rise up in one generation and mark the end of the line of Restorers. The new Verses said that it was the sign of a new era for our people. We were to disband the Council and instead become a people strong and secure like the nations around us by honoring one king to lead us. The leader of the city where the One dwells was to be king."

"Cameron," I said, feeling sick.

She nodded. "It all happened very fast. What could we do?

We could oppose a law we thought was unjust or a plan we believed was wrong, but we couldn't oppose the holy Records. Cameron disbanded the guardians—just kept the Council guards who were loyal to him. He called all the transtechs to Lyric to produce weapons. Kahlarea had attacked the outpost again, and there was a threat of war along the River Borders. Cameron said he would lead the people to safety when the time was right. In the meantime, he . . ." She swallowed and looked away. "He gave Rendor to the Kahlareans to appease them."

I sagged back. "Rendor? That's my father's clan." When Dad and I fenced together, he told me about his clan. It was a part of me.

Tara nodded and pursed her lips. "Tristan and Kendra had to run. Kieran had warned them what Cameron would do to them if it were ever in his power. Now everything is in his power."

"This is crazy!" I jumped to my feet and paced. "Cameron is lying. Somehow he's got everyone convinced he's supposed to be king, but this is all wrong. We've got to stop him."

Tara pulled me back down and leaned forward. "Jake, be quiet. Don't speak against the appointed king. I don't like it either, but we can't disobey the Records." Her voice was quiet but intense.

I ran a hand through my hair. "What am I going to do? I've got to find out what Cameron did with my mom. And I can prove he's lying." I was about to tell her about the Restorer signs that I had but stopped myself. Maybe this wasn't the time.

"Grandma? Can we come out now?" Aubrey's voice chirped from the hallway, and then Dustin's head popped around the corner.

His big eyes grew even wider. "Jake!" He launched himself across the room at me, Aubrey close behind him. I laughed as they tumbled into me, almost knocking me from the chair. They were thin, and their faces were drawn and pale. I glanced at Tara, and she saw my reaction.

"Food has been short. Repairing the damage to Morsal Plains wasn't one of the king's priorities."

I reached for my backpack and pulled out granola bars for the kids. I had to show them how to rip open the wrappers. "Will you play soccer with us?" Dustin asked with his mouth full.

I tried to smile but couldn't. "Sorry, I have some things to take care of. Maybe another time." Tara shooed them out of the room, and it worried me to see how little energy they had to protest. Back home, Jon squirmed through dinner and Anne chattered nonstop. They drove me crazy half the time, but that's how kids were supposed to act. Seeing Dustin and Aubrey that subdued scared me.

"What am I going to do?" I asked again.

Tara studied me for a minute. She leaned forward and spoke in a whisper. "There are some men, former guardians, who are avoiding the king's mandates. They aren't opposing him directly, but they've gathered and are staying hidden. Mind you, I don't approve."

Yeah, yeah. She'd made the point and then some. "I understand. Can you tell me how to find them?"

She hesitated and then sighed. "Yes. I'll take you now." I grabbed my gear, and she led me down a path and directed me to a trail leading up to a ridgeline. "There are caves up there. The men all rode with Tristan. You can trust them. I just don't know what any of you can do now. Maybe when the hostilities with the Kahlareans are over, you can petition to see Cameron and ask him about your mother."

I took a deep breath and drew myself up. I wouldn't add to her fears by arguing with her about Cameron. "Thank you for your help." She nodded and hurried back to her house.

I trudged up the trail. Kieran had needed to stay hidden when we were in Braide Wood together, and he had talked about staying at some caves. Maybe this was the same place. My breath labored in my lungs by the time I reached the top of the steep climb. I pushed forward through the underbrush to step into the clearing.

Something hard crashed into the back of my head and knocked me forward. I tucked a shoulder and rolled to come up fast, drawing my sword. Dad's training was paying off, but my head throbbed, and I didn't like the looks of the man facing me. He was built like an action hero, with a mane of dark hair and a confident sneer. His own sword was out, and he didn't stop to ask me who I was. He just swung at me.

I skittered back, then planted myself and blocked and parried.

His eyebrows lifted, but then he brushed my sword aside like it was a toy and attacked again.

This time my countermove wasn't as clean, and his blade scraped my shoulder. Pain stung, but from a distance. Adrenaline is a great anesthetic. The wound tingled as it began to heal, and I ignored that as well. I danced around the man, trying to hold him off long enough to introduce myself.

He was too fast. A few more clashes and he moved past my guard and grabbed my arm. He crashed his hilt against my forearm. My sword fell to the ground, clattering. His foot swept behind me, and I hit the ground with a thud.

I looked up the length of his sword, which was pointed directly over my heart.

A ring of faces moved in to join his, and none of them looked very happy to see me.

Chapter Eleven

JAKE

"Who is he?" one of the men asked.

"I don't know," said the black-haired warrior who pinned me. "He has a bit of skill with a sword, for such a young pup."

"Stand aside."

A couple of the bodies moved apart, and another rough, bearded face joined the circle, although his beard was a mere scraggle compared to beards of the other men. He frowned down at me, a bear of a man, only a few years older than me.

I ignored the sword aimed at me and braced myself on my elbows to glare up at him.

His eyes held a glint of humor. "Who are you?"

"My name's Jake."

That wasn't the answer he wanted. "Your clan, boy. What clan are you?"

It took me a second to figure out how to answer that. I decided to claim my father's clan. "Rendor."

That worked. There were instant murmurs of sympathy from several of the men, and the sword was pulled back. I was helped to my feet, but before I could say another word, an arm grabbed me from behind, and the cold blade of a boot knife pressed against my throat.

"He's lying, Wade. I've never seen him before."

My guess was that the man holding me was from Rendor. The man called Wade stepped closer. Whatever humor I'd seen in his face was gone.

I swallowed and my Adam's apple pressed against the blade. "I didn't live in Rendor." My voice squeaked, and I wished I could clear my throat without risking a major artery.

"I'll kill him and get rid of the body. If the king's guard sends another, they'll never find him."

Bloodthirsty much? Man, the guy behind me was way too eager. If Wade didn't turn out to be a little more rational than my captor, I was toast.

"Who sent you?" Wade's tone was weary.

"I came to find you—"

The man holding me growled and twisted my arm behind me. "What did I tell you? They're hunting us already." Anger and suspicion spun around the clearing, rumbling like approaching thunder.

I couldn't breathe. They'd slit my throat in the next second. "Wait. Please. I came to find you to ask for your help. And I *am* from Rendor clan."

Wade stepped closer. The man holding me didn't loosen his grip or move the dagger from my throat. "You're mixing up your lies now, friend. Care to try the truth?"

I groaned in frustration. "My father is from Rendor."

Wade seemed to reach a decision. "Let him go, Ian." The man called Ian withdrew his knife from my throat and released my arm, though it still stung. "Who's your father?"

I tried to remember what my dad had taught me. I faced

Wade squarely and offered him my sword arm. "I'm the son of Markkel, councilmember of Rendor. My mom is Susan of . . . I'm not sure which clan, really."

The effect was dramatic. Wade's mouth dropped open, but then he grabbed my forearm in a fierce grip. "Well met, Jake. I'm Wade of Braide Wood." He turned to the men around the clearing. "Put away your swords. I'm pledged to protect his house." He drew me aside and sat me on a fallen log while the other men backed off. Some grumbled. Others stared with blatant curiosity, but they gave Wade space. "Are your parents here?"

Finally, an ally. I sighed and focused on Wade. "Cameron dragged my mom here. Dad and I tried to come through to rescue her, but Dad didn't make it. I didn't know what to do. I was going to ask Tristan for help."

Wade looked bleak for a moment. "Never thought the finest of the guardians would be run out of the clans like a criminal."

"So how can I find Tristan? Can you send him word?"

"We'll see." Wade shook himself out of his dour mood and grinned. "So you've had some training with a sword?"

I shrugged. "I trained with the guardians in Lyric when I was here before. After we got home, my dad started teaching me."

Wade nodded. "Glad to hear it. I trained your mom, you know." My stunned expression made him laugh—a loud belly laugh that pushed away dire problems and made me believe that everything would be okay.

I wanted to hear more, but I glanced around the clearing and my answering smile faded. Most of the men ignored me, but several glowered in my direction.

Wade followed my gaze. "Some of them think that if the Restorer hadn't left, none of this would have happened. They won't all respect you for being Susan's son."

"But she wasn't a Restorer anymore. Don't they know that?"

He shifted his weight. "There's what you know, and then there's what you feel. But you don't need to fear them. I'm your house protector. They won't touch you."

"Are you making plans to attack Cameron?"

Wade frowned. "Lower your voice." Then his easy grin returned. "We can talk plans tomorrow. Time for some supper and rest. You look like you've had a long day."

I'd worked a full day at Harvey's before arriving home to find Cameron in our living room. Then another day of traveling in this world. I stifled a yawn, and Wade chuckled.

I emptied the food from my pack and shared it all around, which went a long way in winning a grudging acceptance from the men. They gave me some watery stew from a large bowl warming on a heat trivet. Ian watched me through narrowed eyes. He was about Dad's age, battle-hardened, with hair as light as my own but an expression dark with cynicism. I shivered. There was something about the way his eyes followed me that made me resolve to sleep with my sword close.

Most of the men drifted into conversations and simply shut me out. Arland, the dark-haired man who'd attacked me when I entered the clearing, gave me a nod of thanks as I tore apart a peanut butter sandwich from my pack and offered him half. He pried it open, curious, but then wolfed it down. Obviously, these men had the same shortages of food as the village. Definitely bad news. I'd rather cross swords with Cameron than go hungry.

As the gray light faded, men broke away from the group and disappeared into various caves surrounding the clearing. I fought back a yawn.

"There's room in our cave," Wade said.

I groaned. "I thought I'd seen every cave between here and Lyric when I traveled with Kieran."

Wade's warm manner suddenly chilled. "Kieran?"

"Yeah, he found me when I was lost here the last time. He brought me to Braide Wood, but there were some assassins chasing us." I shuddered, remembering those days of running and hiding. I looked at Wade's face. "What's wrong?"

He gave a snort of harsh laughter. "We've had our differences." Wade refused to explain more, but I felt I'd lost some ground with my only ally.

This was more complicated than the web of relationships in high school. I looked around the clearing once more before following Wade into a cave. Swords and daggers glinted in the reflected glow from the heat trivets.

More complex, and a lot more dangerous.

The ground was hard and several of the men snored, but I had no problem sleeping. My mind was as exhausted as my body. Too many things to absorb. Too many surprises. I didn't even bother pulling off my boots. I removed my sword belt and then held the sword in my arms.

I'd never had trouble sleeping in strange places, but I wondered about Jon and Anne and how they were doing at their camp. Anne hadn't been away overnight before, except to our grandparents'. Was she hugging the stuffed octopus I'd given her in case she got homesick in her bunk at night? Was Jon tipping over canoes and generally wreaking havoc? Probably.

I breathed a quick prayer for them before I fell asleep.

It was barely first light when Wade shook my shoulder. I jolted up, confused by the hairy grinning face towering over me and by the musty smell of the cave. He gestured for me to follow him. The rest of the camp wasn't stirring yet, except for a few men who were on guard in the clearing.

We didn't stop for breakfast. Wade led me down the trail toward the village. "If Cameron has your mom, I can guess where he's keeping her. I'll need a scrambler to get into Lyric. Skyler's gone—called up with the rest of the transtechs. I'm sure he wouldn't mind us borrowing a few things."

Wade was enjoying himself. I couldn't shake off my nerves. We slipped from home to home, ducking and hiding, until Wade opened the door of one small cabin off by itself and we hurried inside. The room was a dream. Pieces of inventions that I couldn't even guess the purpose of—every gadget and gizmo I'd seen in this world—covered all the surfaces of chairs, tables, and the floor. We picked our way among the chaos.

"Who is this guy?" I asked, staring around the cabin. I picked up a strange cube but dropped it when it started to hum.

"Kieran and Kendra's father. He went a bit . . . off . . . when his wife died. Keeps to himself." Wade rifled through a pile of fragile-looking equipment, then tossed a few pieces over his shoulder. I caught them and set them down gently. "Ah, here we go." Wade held up a scrambler. Kieran had used one to get us in and out of a hidden door in the Lyric wall. "Find some magchips, will you?"

I moved around the room, bewildered.

"Um, Wade? What are magchips?"

He stopped rummaging and turned to look at me. His eyes squinted over his round cheeks when he smiled. "You're a lot like her, you know? Although I see your father in you too. He's a good man. It'd kill him to know what's happened to his clan."

"Tara said Cameron 'gave' Rendor to the Kahlareans. What does that mean?"

Wade stilled, then swooped up some more gear. He bundled it into a bag. "Let's go."

"Wade?"

He wouldn't look at me. "Jake, you have enough to think about."

I decided not to press him. "I want to stop in and talk to Tara again."

"Better to leave her out of this."

"But I— "

Wade gave me a level stare. "The men can't afford to trust anyone. Now's not the time to be visiting old friends."

I swallowed and nodded. If Wade had sworn to protect my family, I'd better follow his lead, especially while loyalties were shifting and uncertain. He clapped a huge paw against my back. "Maybe when I get back, we can go talk to her."

I followed him outside and waited until we were under the canopy of trees before talking again.

"When *you* get back? But I'm coming with you."

"Jake, Lyric is the last place for you to go right now. Trust me. If your mother is there, I'll find her. And I'll get her out." He peeked at the jumble of equipment he had grabbed from Skyler's cabin. "I hope one of the men can teach me how to use a scrambler."

I brightened. "I know how. Kieran taught me."

Wade rolled his eyes. "He would. Well, like they say, 'Even a ground-crawler feeds the earth.'"

I had the feeling Kieran had just been insulted, but I didn't comment. My own view of Kieran was a bit confused anyway. When I'd been in this world the first time, he'd ambushed me, stuck a knife in me, and scared me more than once. But he'd also healed my busted ankle, led me to Braide Wood, and, from what Mom and Dad told me, helped them get me safely home. I had assumed he was some sort of criminal, but he was also a Restorer and had given himself to Hazor to stop a war.

I wished there were simple-to-categorize good guys and bad guys here. I wished it again as we entered the clearing by the caves and I saw the hostile eyes of the men.

"Arland," Wade called cheerfully, "I have to leave for a few days." Wade's arm circled my shoulders and he nudged me forward. "Work with the boy while I'm gone. We'll need every strong sword arm we can muster."

One of the men muttered something and spat, but Arland exchanged a serious look with Wade and nodded. Then he turned to me. "No time like the present!"

I didn't like the glint in his eyes.

"I need Jake's help first." Wade said the words loudly, and some of the movement around the camp stilled. "So Jake, could you show me how this thing works?"

He was as subtle as a train wreck, but I appreciated what he was doing. My value to these outlawed guardians rose another degree. We sat down, and I showed him how to use the scrambler to get past magnetic locks. I shared every transtech trick Kieran had taught me, and several men drifted over to watch. By the time Wade rose to leave, I felt a little less threatened. These were grim and dangerous men, but I finally believed what Wade had told me. I'd be safe here. For now.

I tried once more to convince him to let me accompany him to Lyric, but he was adamant.

"Train with the men. Win their respect. You can trust Arland." Wade puffed out his ample chest. "I'll bring her back, Jake." He brimmed with confidence. I squared my shoulders and nodded, hiding my nervousness at being left with these men who didn't trust me, resented my mom, and had very sharp swords.

"All right, men. We'll train on the plateau today." Arland gave brisk orders, and men scrambled off to stand watch, saddle the few lehkan that were left at Braide Wood, or pair off for some sword work. "You're with me," Arland said. I followed him from the clearing. He held back, letting the other men go ahead, and I kept pace with him. He glanced at the bloody tear on my tunic sleeve. "We should wrap that cut. Don't want it to get infected."

"Oh. Um, it's fine. It was just a scratch."

Arland gave me a sideways look. Let him think I was being a bit of a braggart. I didn't want him to see the healed skin.

But I was supposed to train with him. How would I explain if he saw a cut or bruise disappear? It wasn't like these guys were huge fans of the Restorer. This didn't seem like a good time to let them know I had the signs.

I'd just have to keep him from making contact.

I glanced again at his broad shoulders and powerful arms. Yeah, that was gonna happen. I sighed.

Arland made sure everyone was busy before leading me to a level area of grassland and squaring off. Although the other men were training, they still managed to glance our way frequently. I ignored them and paid attention to Arland.

Dad's sword felt heavy in my hand, but Arland was methodical, taking me through familiar patterns. I began to relax and let my reflexes kick in.

"Good," he said as I parried a fast strike. "Try it again from the other direction. Watch your footwork. No, keep your blade up. Look." He demonstrated the opening I had left by repeating his attack in slow motion. Then he showed me how to fix it. We went through the movements again and again until I mastered them at full speed. Sword work was a lot like playing tennis. Total concentration focused onto one thing, and worries were forced to disappear. There was no room for them. My mind went clear, and my body strained and sweat. I began to enjoy myself.

Something odd began to happen as we sparred. I knew I should be tired, that my arms should ache from the effort of blocking his powerful blows. Instead, I felt stronger. Mom had described how she began to simply *know* how to fight as her Restorer gifts developed. I could feel it happening. I'd had some training but not enough to keep up with a warrior like Arland, who was ten years my senior and outweighed me by half.

Yet the longer we fought, the more my skills rose to match his. He was noticing it too. His teacher demeanor disappeared. Something hardened in his eyes, and his jaw tightened. Using a move I'd never seen before, he knocked my blade aside. His own whistled through the air and stopped a hairsbreadth from my neck. I froze and looked at him in panic.

He stepped in closer, the edge of his blade unmoved.

"Now," he said, breathing hard. "Why don't you tell me what you're really doing here."

I studied his face, looking for a sign that this was just part of his training. He didn't blink. He was dead serious. I had a feeling that if I didn't come up with an answer fast, I'd be seriously dead.

Chapter Twelve

JAKE

Arland's fierce eyes locked with mine, but I held my ground. "I told Wade everything. He'll tell you what he wants you to know."

He didn't relax his sword arm, and steel bit my skin. "Wade's not here, and I'm asking *you*."

More decisions. It hadn't been this way in the stories I used to love. Dragon threatens village. Knight slays dragon. Huzzah!

"I came to rescue my mom." My anger toward Cameron churned to the surface. Surprisingly, Arland pulled his sword away. He glanced around to be sure the others weren't within earshot.

"The Restorer?"

"Yes. I mean, no. She's not anymore."

"She's here?"

"Somewhere." I sighed and rubbed my neck. "Cameron came to our . . ." I was about to say "world" but didn't want to get into an explanation about that. "He came to our home. He was with a Rhusican named Medea. He beat up my dad and grabbed my mom and brought her back here. I came to find her."

"And Wade?"

"He's going to Lyric to look for her."

Arland swore and thrust his sword into the ground. "And if he finds her, will she help us?"

I blinked. "Well, she needs to go home. She doesn't belong here." Arland seemed to be growing angrier, so I talked fast. "You know she doesn't have any gifts anymore, don't you? Kieran became the Restorer."

Arland speared me with his eyes. "And Kieran went to help Hazor instead of serving his own people. And now Wade is distracted by this worthless errand."

"It's not worthless." My anger rose another notch. "She fought for Braide Wood. She's in danger. He wasn't about to leave her with Cameron, even if the rest of you are too scared to oppose him."

Arland went very still and white around the mouth. Too late to pull back my words, I pulled myself back instead, stumbling a few steps away. His black eyes assessed me like a crow approaching carrion. He unsheathed his sword from the earth and lifted it in my direction. I brought my own weapon up in defense.

"Whoa . . . wait. I only . . ." Nothing I could say would make things better now.

Arland bared his teeth and kept coming. His blade swung straight for my head.

I blocked, and the vibration jarred all the way up my arms. This sparring session was about to get a whole lot scarier.

I pushed down my panic and tried to focus. He didn't give me time to recover but swept his sword in a wide swath that could have cut me in two. I jumped back and countered with a lunge of my own. Our blades clashed again and again. My breathing grew ragged, and I watched his face for any sign that he didn't intend to kill me. I couldn't find it.

"Easy for you to call us cowards." He followed his words with three lightning-fast strokes.

"I didn't mean—"

He didn't let me finish but moved under my guard, and his blade scraped across my belly. "We need help, and what are we given? The One says there will be no more Restorers."

"That's a lie!" I jumped back, trying to gain some time. I needed to explain that Cameron's new Records were fake.

No. More pressing goal.

I needed to keep his sword from hacking off my limbs.

Arland's eyes were wild as he jabbed forward. I blocked with a two-handed grip and tried to twist his blade away. He pulled back to disengage and swung again. "What choices do we have?" The rage poured from his words in harmony with his relentless attacks. "The One insists we follow a king who's destroying our people."

"But He didn't . . ." I couldn't breathe and couldn't see through the sweat stinging my eyes.

Arland wasn't listening. He was mad at a whole lot of things besides me. Unfortunately, I was the one in front of him at the moment. I shut out his words and stopped trying to answer him. My world became the glint of his sword, the flurry of movement between us, and the shock of blows that reverberated up my arms. From somewhere, strength flowed into me. I kept my footing and answered each attack. He pulled back for a heartbeat and then came at me like a berserker. His wild attack left him vulnerable, and I took the opening and spun in, ramming my shoulder into his massive chest and slamming the flat of my blade against his arm. His sword dropped, and I turned and held my blade to his throat.

Ha! He hadn't seen that coming. I would have loved to gloat, but this wasn't the time. Shock snapped across his face, and his eyes cleared of the blind rage he'd been indulging at my expense.

When I saw I had his attention, I snarled, "Would you stop trying to slice me to pieces and just listen?"

His eyes narrowed, but he nodded. I pulled my sword back. We were both breathing hard, trembling with fatigue. I glanced around and was surprised to see that no one was paying any attention to the confrontation that had gotten too real. Still, I kept my voice low.

"Number one, Cameron is lying. I'm not sure how he did it, but those new 'old Records' are fake. I'm going to find out what he did and prove it."

I didn't realize that it was true until I said it. My initial plan hadn't gone beyond finding Tristan and getting help to rescue Mom. Now I knew that I had to let Tara and these guardians and everyone else know they were being tricked.

"Number two, we can't trust Cameron to hold back the Kahlareans, and we need to get Rendor back." Arland's eyes widened. I glanced at the band of men stretched across the plateau. A few dozen at best. "We need to gather more allies."

"We?" Why had I said that?

Those words had come from somewhere outside of myself, yet they felt completely right. I may be a mixed-up mess, but the One had a clear direction in mind.

I took a deep breath and swiped at the sweat on my forehead, pushing my hair out of my face. I glared back at Arland. "Number three, saving my mom is not a worthless errand. It's why I'm here. She may not be able to lead your people into battle anymore, but she's my mom. I'm going to make sure she gets home."

The corner of Arland's mouth twitched, and he took a steadying breath. "So the pup has heart." He retrieved his sword and wiped it down with the edge of his tunic. "Good. You'll need that and more if you believe you can go up against the king."

What had Wade told me to do? Train and win their respect. Arland seemed like a decent guy when he wasn't furious with me. And if I didn't make any more stupid comments implying they were all cowards, we might get along.

"So what have you been planning? You're not hiding in caves and training for the fun of it."

Arland shook his head. "We'll talk when Wade gets back. Maybe. Right now we'll see what you can do—besides talk. How's your riding?"

I looked over at the lehkans and blew a silent whistle through pursed lips. They were huge animals and looked vaguely like elk, although they had long thick hair like llamas. The cuddly impression ended with their razor-sharp antlers. I watched two of the men nudge their mounts with their knees and launch them into a galloping charge. Hooves tore up clods of dirt and sent them scattering.

Arland chuckled at the awe in my face. "Well, you've had enough sword work for this morning. Ian!" He waved. Ian rode near, purposely careening too close before pulling his mount to a halt. He had blond wavy hair like my dad's—though much longer—and the same strong jawline that I knew I shared. With a jolt, I realized that if Ian was from Rendor, we might be distant cousins. Now wasn't the time to explore family connections, however. Ian's distrust and hostility radiated from him in waves.

"Let's see if the boy can ride," Arland said.

Ian leapt from the lehkan and gestured to me with a sneer. Arland showed me how to mount but had a wicked glint in his eye.

After an hour of trying to stay on the fidgety creature, I decided Arland had planned a new way to kill me. The crazy animal kept bolting sideways, springing like a deer and throwing me the opposite direction. My legs ached from trying to stay with him, and my ego was more bruised than my backside. Ian and Arland were having a good laugh, and I gritted my teeth as I clambered on for the twentieth time. I finally got a feel for the leg commands and managed to walk my lehkan the length of the plateau. I was feeling pretty proud of that accomplishment when I turned back at the far edge. Ian and Arland were several soccer-field lengths away. But before I could savor my record time in the saddle, Ian let out a piercing whistle. My animal's muscles tightened, and I dug in like a tick just in time. The lehkan shot forward and galloped along the plateau, the wind stinging my eyes.

If I were at a theme park, this would be the ride where they take your picture just as the roller coaster hits the scariest drop. Hair flying, mouth open in a scream, eyes wide.

Even though my stomach stayed somewhere behind, I held on and made it to the end of the plateau. When the lehkan skidded to a stop, I slid off onto wobbly legs, grinning like my brother, Jon, with a new video game. Ian gave a grudging nod.

Arland clapped me on the back. "Lunchtime."

Best words I'd heard in a long time. I limped beside Arland back to the campsite. The bruises and aches were quickly healing, but I was bone tired. When we reached the clearing by the caves, Arland held me back until the men had all gone ahead.

"Jake, first rule of combat: Stay in control. Don't lose your temper." He nodded toward the cut across my tunic. I'd forgotten about that wound to my stomach. "I'm sorry about that. Shouldn't have taken it out on you."

I scuffed my foot and lifted a shoulder. "No problem. I know you didn't mean it."

Arland unwrapped a strip of fabric wound around one sleeve of his tunic. Before I realized what he was doing, he pushed my tunic aside to check on the cut he'd given me during our swordplay—the cut that had completely disappeared. He studied the blood on my tunic, the slit in the fabric, and my whole, unmarked skin. His gaze traveled up to my face, and his jaw tightened.

My hand reached for my sword hilt, but Arland's fingers closed over my wrist. I tried to back away, only to find a tree pressed against my spine after a few steps. Arland's free hand twisted into the front of my tunic.

"Care to explain that?" His voice was dangerously calm.

"Promise me you won't tell them yet." I was pleading, but protecting my pride didn't seem like an important issue right now.

His voice was as sharp as his blade. "I'll make you no promises. What does it mean?"

But he already knew. I saw it in his face.

I squeezed my eyes shut. "Yes. I'm the new . . . that is, we think . . . I have the signs."

He released me as though it burned his hands to touch me, but I didn't go for my sword. He stared at me with a weird mix of horror and anger—and maybe a little hope.

"I'm sorry. I didn't know who to tell. It's how I know Cameron's new Records are a lie. The era of Restorers can't be over." His silence frightened me. "Please don't say anything to the others yet."

He finally shook himself. "Have you told Wade?"

"No. I will. I'm just trying to figure out the right timing."

Arland paced a few steps, tangling his hand in his hair. "In every time of great need, a Restorer is sent to fight for the people and help the guardians." His voice was soft. He was reciting to himself. I knew the words because Mom and Dad had explained them to me. "The Restorer is empowered with gifts to defeat our enemies and turn the people's hearts back to the Verses." Arland faced me. "But you want to go against the Verses."

"Not the real Verses. Just these new Records. They're a lie. And I don't know if I'm supposed to fight for the people yet. I've had the signs for only a month or so."

Arland stalked back toward me. I lifted my hands. "If I'm supposed to help, I will. But first I need to make sure my mom is okay." He ignored my words and grabbed my arm with his left hand. His other hand slid a dagger from his boot sheath. Before I could pull away, he sliced down my forearm. I winced and tugged against him, but his grip was a manacle. He kept his eyes on the skin every second as if he expected me to play a magic trick. When it healed, he let his eyes lift, and for a moment, when they met mine, he let me see his confusion.

"Please," I tried again. "Just let me stay here and train. At least until Wade comes back."

"Whose side are you on?" His brows canted down in a hard line.

Complex question. I lifted my chin. "I serve the One."

I couldn't read his face. Maybe that wasn't the smartest answer to give. Arland and all the men were angry with the One. In their view, they'd been deserted and even betrayed by the Records. Cameron was claiming that he was the One's chosen king.

He twisted my arm and looked at it again, shaking his head. "Come on." His words gave nothing away. He shoved me ahead of him toward the clearing.

My stomach twisted at the thought of the men's response. I stopped and looked back at Arland. His face was grim, and he didn't meet my eyes.

Chapter Thirteen

JAKE

The men were tearing into some hard bread loaves, and Ian handed me a piece as I limped into the clearing. Sinking onto a boulder near the edge of the woods, I looked out over the rooftops of Braide Wood and thought how I'd rather be in Tara's home, sipping clavo and talking to Tristan—letting him make a plan. Or even Kieran. He would have known what to do. My lips twisted. Shoot, even little Dustin and Aubrey probably would be handling this better than me.

I kept a wary eye on Arland, but he just grabbed some food and sprawled near his men. When he didn't look like he planned to make any proclamation to the group, I relaxed a bit but still didn't have much appetite. He looked angry—well, angrier.

All the men carried a layer of frustration as pervasive as the smell of sweat and wet leather. These men were guardians who had pledged faithfulness to the Verses and protection to the clans. Now they didn't know how to fulfill the second without betraying the first.

I sympathized. The One had been stirring something in me. He wanted me to stop Cameron, but just like the men here, I didn't know how. I closed my eyes and prayed for guidance. When I opened my eyes and looked at Braide Wood, I knew part of my answer was there. I'd have to convince Arland to let me talk to Tara.

Just as I resolved that, Arland sprang to his feet and I tensed. "All right," he said in a loud voice. "Break camp."

Relief flashed over me — and faded just as quickly. We were leaving? I elbowed my way through the activity in the clearing. "Arland, don't we need to wait here for Wade?"

Arland frowned at me like he was having second thoughts about keeping my secret. "Too risky to stay in one place. Wade will catch up." He tugged a strap on his pack and shoved it to one side.

I swallowed and stepped in front of him. "I think I should stay here."

He pulled himself up to his full height and stared me down. Back home, with three younger siblings and fresh from my senior year, eighteen felt mature, strong, and capable. Here in this clearing full of trained warriors in their twenties and thirties, I looked and felt like a scrawny kid. I didn't like the sensation. I also couldn't go skulking around the countryside with them and miss Wade's return with my mom.

"Are you heading closer to Lyric?"

Arland gave me a hard look. "Blue Knoll."

"Then I'm staying here."

He grabbed my arm and cast a quick glance around. The other men were busy packing and covering signs of the camp's presence. "Don't push me, Jake. You're coming with us." His voice was quiet but as threatening as if he had shouted the words.

I kept my voice low too. "If you believe me, even a little bit, then you know I've got to take orders from the One. I need to wait here."

He cursed and let me go. "Do you have any idea how it will look if you leave now? They'll be sure you're going to betray them."

I forced myself to meet his eyes. "Do you believe that?"

Arland rubbed the back of his neck and sighed. "No. I'm inclined to think you mean well. Heaven knows why. Still too attached to the old myths I guess." He frowned. "That doesn't mean I think you have much to offer. Keep quiet and stay out of trouble."

"I don't want to cause trouble, but I'm staying here. Wade will come back to Braide Wood first, won't he?"

Arland nodded.

"Then I want to be here. I'll come with him to join you later. Please."

A low growl rumbled in his throat. His eyes traveled to my arm, where he had watched a cut heal.

"Fine," he snapped. "Head down to the village now. When they notice, I'll tell them I sent you on an errand. They won't like it, but I'll manage."

I offered Arland my sword arm. He scowled at it but then gripped my forearm. "Thank you," I said. "And I promise I'll find a way to help."

He raised one eyebrow. "Right." The sarcasm didn't exactly warm my heart, but I scampered down the trail before he could change his mind.

Weight eased from my shoulders as I got farther from the campsite. The barely veiled animosity and distrust had been hard to deal with. People almost always liked me. I hadn't felt so much suspicion since—well, since Kieran caught me following him outside of Lyric. Not that I blamed these guys, but still, I was glad to get away.

I slipped into Tara's house without knocking, not wanting to risk being seen outside her door. She looked up from the common-room table with a nervous start. She wasn't alone. My stomach did a funny flip.

It was *her*. Linette. I had met her briefly the last time I was here and thought of her often since then. Her white-blonde hair was pulled into a long braid, but I imagined the hair in a soft curtain around her shoulders. I bit the inside of my lip and stopped myself from imagining anything else as I took in her graceful form.

She had startled at the sound of the door opening, but now her eyes softened as she smiled. "Jake, I didn't know you were here." It was obvious she was a songkeeper. Her voice was like music. I'd happily learn Verses from her all day long.

"Close the door, Jake." Tara's chiding hid a thread of amusement. I had been frozen and staring, like the first time I'd met Linette. I blinked and forced myself to move.

"The men are heading to a new site." I pulled the door closed and walked toward them. "I need to stay in Braide Wood until Wade gets back. He went to find my mom."

"She's here?" Linette's eyes brightened.

"Does he know where she is?" Tara asked at the same time.

I sank into a chair at the end of the table and focused on Linette. "She's here, but Cameron forced her to come. He must be holding her somewhere in Lyric." I sat up taller and cleared my throat. "I came to rescue her."

"And Wade went to get her?" Tara ladled clavo from a bowl on the table and passed a mug to me.

My skin heated. "He wouldn't let me go with him."

"That was wise," Linette said quickly. "It sounds like Lyric is a dangerous place right now. Kieran sent me to find out what I could about what's happening in the clans."

"From Hazor? Isn't that a rough trip?" What was Kieran thinking, using her as a messenger?

She laughed. "You sound like him. He wasn't thrilled about it. Insisted on sending a dozen of Zarek's soldiers to escort me to the pass. I slipped across to Morsal Plains this morning. They'll wait for me just over the mountain."

Her smile faded. Afternoon rain pattered on the roof like drumming fingers.

"And why didn't Kieran come himself?" Disapproval colored Tara's voice. Seemed the guardians weren't the only ones angry that the Restorer had apparently deserted them.

Linette turned her soft eyes to Tara and patted her hand. "It was his first impulse—to ride straight to Lyric. He was furious when he heard Cameron had been declared king. He came up with a dozen counterplans. Zarek gave his blessing too. Of course, Kieran would have found a way to come even if Zarek had locked him up."

"So where is he? Why didn't he do anything?" I drained my cup and set it down on the table.

Linette's finger traced a pattern of whorls in the wood. "That night, the One came and talked to Kieran. Told him to stay in Hazor and keep doing the work he was called to." She shook her head in rueful affection. "He hasn't been very happy about it." She looked up at me. "Still seems to argue with the One a lot. But he's been doing great work in Hazor."

The admiration in her voice was clear, and for some reason I didn't like it. I shifted in my chair. Then a flash of rational thought finally broke through the haze that took over whenever I was around her.

"Tara, could I talk to Linette alone?" My ears grew warm, and I hoped I wasn't blushing.

Tara didn't tease me. "Of course." She stood slowly, letting her old joints readjust before leaving the room.

Linette watched her and sighed. "Things are even worse here than we were told."

"Told by whom?" I asked.

Her eyes brushed over me and away. "Oh, you know. Messengers."

She was hiding something. Would she tell me the truth about other things?

"Linette . . ." I liked saying her name.

Jake, focus.

"Linette, has Kieran lost his Restorer gifts?"

I hadn't planned to be that blunt, but I didn't know how to ease into this topic. Her eyes widened and she leaned across the table.

"Why would you ask me that?" Her voice dropped to a wary whisper. Great. More distrust.

I jumped up and retrieved a small knife from the kitchen. A quick slice across my index finger drew a thin line of blood and a gasp from Linette.

When she saw it heal, she sagged back against her chair, studying me with a blend of equal parts wonder and sadness. "Oh, Jake."

"So does Kieran know? Or is he still a Restorer too? What am I supposed to do?"

She considered for a long minute, then sighed. "Yes, he knows. After we got to Sidian, he got a bruised rib from sparring with Zarek. It didn't heal fast. He's kept the knowledge hidden because he's not sure how Zarek will react. The whole reason Hazor didn't destroy Lyric was because Kieran offered them a Restorer."

Her pale forehead wrinkled. "He still hears the One, and he's been able to heal other people sometimes, but he doesn't have the Restorer signs anymore."

Now it was my turn to slump against my chair. I had hoped he was still a Restorer, that my time hadn't come yet. Or that there would be two Restorers at the same time—even if the Verses didn't record that happening before.

Linette slid her chair closer and rested a hand on my shoulder. "Jake, if the One has called you to be the new Restorer, He'll show you what to do." Her words rang with so much strength and fire that I managed not to think about how close she was to me. "When your mother came here, she didn't even know what a Restorer was. The One brought people to help her and equipped her for her role. She saved Braide Wood and the Council. And when Kieran was called by the One . . ." Linette's lips curved. "Well, it wasn't easy for him, either. But he stopped the entire army of Hazor from destroying Lyric."

"But people don't even believe in Restorers anymore, thanks to Cameron's lies." I wanted to act confident and courageous in front of Linette but couldn't help being honest with her. Fear churned inside me. "Things are a mess."

She squeezed my shoulder. "Yes, they are. You aren't going to be able to do this by your own power. That's what your mother learned. It's what Kieran is still learning."

She stood up suddenly.

"I could use a little encouragement myself," she said with a shy smile. "Come on, I'd like you to meet someone."

I liked sitting at Tara's table with Linette. I was tired of meeting new people and guessing who to trust and how much to reveal. "Does this someone have a sword?"

She looked bewildered. "No. He's Braide Wood's eldest songkeeper."

"All right." I pushed myself to my feet without much enthusiasm.

My rain poncho would look too out of place, so I borrowed a cloak from the pegs by the door. Our feet squished on the wet paths along the edge of the village to a small home under a tall spice tree. Linette's gentle tap garnered a hoarse invitation to enter.

We shook the rain from our cloaks, and then she took my hand to lead me into the cabin. A tingle traveled through my arm and fluttered in my lungs. The sensation stopped when Linette dropped my hand to hang up her cape.

"Jake, this is Lukyan."

The old man gave us both a warm smile from his chair but didn't rise.

"Linette, what a treat for these tired eyes. And welcome, young Jake."

Lukyan's eyes were blue, clouded by age. Veined hands rested in his lap, and he seemed so frail that I was afraid if he took a deep breath, his bones would snap. Linette waved me to pull up a chair near him, and she settled gracefully to the floor near his feet, tucking her legs under her.

"Have you finished your work in Hazor?" He reached out with one trembling hand. She took it in both of hers and held it for a moment against her cheek.

"No. But we're making progress. I'll tell you all about it later. Jake needs your help."

Lukyan turned his rheumy eyes in my direction and studied me. He began to nod, but I wasn't sure if it was age tremors or intentional.

"Go ahead," Linette urged.

I looked at her.

"Jake, you can tell him everything. He helped your mother. He even took a dagger in the back that was meant for her."

My eyes widened, impressed. He *was* the eldest songkeeper of Braide Wood. What better place to start in my desire to prove Cameron's new Record was a sham? I poured out my story, with occasional help from Linette. By the time I had reviewed everything that had happened and the huge dangers facing all of us, my throat felt raw.

"So where do I start? How do we stop Cameron and save Rendor? How do we let everyone know the Records are fake?" I noticed my foot tapping, and I stopped it with effort.

Lukyan hadn't taken his eyes from me while I talked. Now he turned to Linette. "I can help, of course. But you see the greater danger, don't you?"

Linette looked up at her teacher and frowned in concentration.

Greater danger? Things weren't bad enough?

"Linette, think. What will happen when Jake makes this known?" His voice wasn't as frail as the rest of him.

She shook her head once, still puzzled. Then something clicked; color washed from her face.

Lukyan nodded and turned back to me. His shoulders caved and his eyes drooped. "Jake, your course could destroy our People."

I pushed my chair backward and launched to my feet. "How did I become the bad guy in this? How could telling people the truth destroy them?" I turned a pleading gaze toward Linette, but she shook her head and studied the floor.

I looked at Lukyan again. Why wasn't he happy? I'd just let him know that the People had a new Restorer.

"Sit down, Jake." His voice was weary. "If this is what the One has called you to do, we'll both help you. But you must understand: the problem is much worse than you realize."

"So explain it to me." I gave him my full attention, wishing I could stick my fingers in my ears instead.

Chapter Fourteen

JAKE

Lukyan stood up slowly, waving away Linette's offer of help. He hobbled over to a wall cubby and pulled out a wooden case. Made from the twisted golden branches of the strange spice trees that grew throughout the clans, it was worn smooth. When he brought it to his table, Linette and I gathered close. He lifted the lid and folded back a layer of forest green cloth.

"A few days after Hazor's army retreated, Cameron called all the songkeepers to Lyric. We assumed it was to show support for the new Restorer or to celebrate the victory of the One."

"Hold on." I rubbed my temples. "A few days? Cameron and Medea came into our world the same day that Kieran made his deal with Zarek. They were in our world for over a month." Lukyan and Linette gave me blank looks. I'd forgotten that with no visible moon, they didn't measure by months. "I mean half a season. This doesn't make sense. Does he have a twin?"

"Jake." Linette's mellow voice held off the headache that kicked against the inside of my forehead. "I knew your father slightly when we were both studying in Lyric. He was a Council apprentice. I was a new songkeeper. We were both eighteen then."

That was too weird to follow. She smiled at my face. "I know, I was confused too when I met him again. He had been gone for two years. Now I'm twenty, and he's forty. Time flows differently between the two worlds."

"And when Cameron dragged my mom here," I said slowly, "I came an hour later, but two seasons had passed already." I shook my head. "It's not fair."

Lukyan frowned, his hands gripping the table edge for support. "For anyone to use a portal between worlds and survive is beyond what is fair. I told the Lyric songkeeper it was not our place, but he chose to send your father through the portal, and look what has happened." His face was dark.

"Okay, so after Kieran left, Cameron called the songkeepers together. Then what?"

Lukyan drew a long shaky breath, and Linette pulled a chair close to the table for him. He sank into it with a grateful smile. "He told us of a visitation of the One, who came and spoke to him in the tower. We were skeptical, of course. Cameron has never supported our efforts to stay close to the Verses or to trust the One for our protection. But he gave each of us one of the new Records that were given to him by the One."

With trembling hands, Lukyan lifted an object from the box. He laid it on the table reverently, and Linette's eyes shone as she stared at it.

I burst into laughter.

Lukyan's grizzled eyebrows drew together, and Linette stared at me like I'd lost my mind.

"This?" I sputtered. "Cameron gave you this? It's just a jacked-up MP3 player." I reached out to hit Play, but Lukyan slapped my hand away. I pulled myself together and took a deep breath. "I'm sorry. Can we listen to it?"

Linette's eyes were huge as she looked at Lukyan. His white hair fell across his face as he bowed his head. After a long pause, he nodded and activated the recording. I had to admit it was impressive. Cameron had accomplished a lot in a month: learning the technology, getting someone to mix these recordings, gathering everything he would need.

A powerful voice intoned a message about the new generation and the prophecy of the king who would make the People of the Verses secure.

I reached over and shut it off, causing gasps of shock from Lukyan and Linette.

I didn't feel like laughing anymore. Dad had told me about the real Records. They were the audible voice of the One, carefully listened to at each season-end gathering. They were the touchstone of the Verses, making sure the oral traditions didn't slip and introduce any errors. He couldn't even talk about them without his voice dropping to a whisper of awe. This trick was pure evil.

"I assume that the voice is similar to the one in the real Records?"

Lukyan nodded, watching me closely.

I folded my arms. "It's a fake. In my world, these kinds of audio records are common. Does it look like your other Records?"

Lukyan lifted out another object, taking care to keep it protected with cloth. It was a short metallic tube, sort of like a thick stack of CDs. There were no visible buttons, but like much of the technology on this world, there were probably hidden levers or panels. "These Records have guided our people for hundreds of generations," Lukyan said with quiet dignity.

I nodded. "I understand. This other thing won't play for

generations. The batteries—um, magchips—will wear out in a few seasons. But we can't wait that long to prove they're fake." I paced a few steps away, rubbing my hands together. "I could record over the voice or change the recording to show how it works, but I don't have any equipment. Maybe there's something from Skyler's house that I could use. Or would it be enough for me to explain that I know how these are made?"

"Jake." Lukyan was grave and stopped me in my tracks. He glanced at Linette, and she gave me a worried look.

They were doing it again. They were looking at me like I was nothing but trouble. "What?"

"Do you understand what might happen when you reveal that these holy Records, personally given to Cameron by the One and listened to by each of the twelve clans, are simply a man-made creation?"

"Yeah! They'll know not to believe Cameron, and they'll reinstate the Council."

"Or?" Lukyan sat back and watched me patiently. What was he getting at?

Finally, Linette helped me out. "Jake, there have always been some among our people who doubt the truth and worth of the Records. The *real* Records."

I might be slow sometimes, but I'm not stupid. "You mean if they find out these are fake . . ."

Lukyan nodded sadly. "It may be all that is needed to destroy generations of faith in the true words of the One."

I fumbled for a chair and dropped into it.

Linette came to stand behind me and rested a comforting hand on my shoulder.

I couldn't even enjoy her touch. Stripped of all my impatience and cockiness, I looked at Lukyan. "What should we do?" The words felt raw and scratchy in my throat.

His grim demeanor eased and a starburst of wrinkles deepened around his eyes. "What can we do when we don't know which road to choose?"

A grin twitched into place. "Ask the One."

He nodded and bowed his head.

Much later, Linette and I returned to Tara's house. Lukyan's time of prayer had rattled me around, emptied me out, and filled me with something new and strong. Even with the risk involved, after our prayer time, we all believed that the people needed to learn the truth. Lukyan agreed to send word to the other songkeepers about what I'd told him and demonstrate how the technology worked, if that would help. We hoped he could reveal how Cameron created false Records but avoid revealing that the new technology came from another world. We didn't need more people to find out about the portal. Since Hazor was always developing new advancements, the songkeepers might assume it was a new invention from Hazor.

Tara had soup simmering on a heat trivet, and Dustin and Aubrey had enough energy to tackle me as I came in. Tara noticed me looking around the large table at the many empty places. "Payton went with Gareth and Talia to do some hunting. They'll be back in a few days. Tristan and Kendra . . ." She turned away and wiped a hand over her face. Then she turned to Linette with a desperate look. "The baby is due soon."

Mom and Dad had told me that after years of waiting, Kendra was expecting her first baby. What a time to have to run for their lives. Linette hurried to Tara's side in the kitchen alcove and gave her a hug. She whispered something in her ear, and I realized I was able to hear it. I didn't mean to eavesdrop but was fascinated by how easily their quiet conversation carried. Feeling a little guilty—but not guilty enough to interrupt them—I continued to listen.

"I told you; she's doing great. We'll send a messenger as soon as the baby is born. Kieran is taking care of all three of them."

I busied myself by removing my sword belt and propping my gear against the wall. Keen hearing was one of the Restorer gifts, but I hadn't noticed it before now. Of course, I hadn't been paying attention, either.

So that was what Linette hadn't wanted to talk about earlier. She and Kieran and the other songkeepers in Hazor had heard all the accounts of what happened—not from a messenger but from Tristan and Kendra. Good thing they were safe and not sleeping in caves like the renegade guardians were. I put on a deadpan face before joining Tara and Linette at the table.

"Can we play soccer?" Dustin tossed a small bread loaf from hand to hand.

I laughed. Tara shook her head. "When we ran out of gourds, they tried using stones and smashed a window and nearly broke their toes."

"Stones? No, no, no. I have a better idea." I dug into my pack for my extra hiking socks and waved them in the air. "A sock ball will work great."

Tara rolled her eyes. "Not until after supper." She tried to frown, but a dimple flickered in her lined face.

The next morning at first light, Linette tied a cloak around her shoulders, preparing to return to the pass over the mountains by

Morsal Plains. I worked up my nerve and gave her a quick hug, urging her to be careful. For her part, she rested a hand on my head and spoke a blessing over me. I soaked in her words like my skin soaked in the baking sun on a day at the beach in August.

"Give your mother my love." She opened the door. "Let her know that the shrines have been closed down in Hazor and many people are learning to know the One." I promised to pass along her message, and then she slipped out like a goldfinch flitting from tree to tree.

Tara fed me some breakfast, and I grabbed my gear and hiked back up to the caves. I didn't want to risk staying in the village any longer and figured that Wade would come here first. Since the clearing was empty, I drew my sword and practiced the forms that Dad had taught me, as well as the new moves Arland had shown me yesterday. After a good workout, I retreated into one of the caves and took a nap.

As I drifted into sleep, my mind retreated to the comfort of the familiar. I was at Harvey's helping a man find spark plugs for his pickup. We walked down the cramped aisle to the cash register, and the man moved around behind the counter.

"Hey, wait," I said. "Customers aren't allowed back there." I used my best customer-service smile, but the man started scanning in the spark plugs, ringing up the price over and over. The amount kept climbing, and I didn't have the money to pay for them. I told myself that I wasn't the one buying, but then the man looked up, and he wasn't a man anymore. He was Medea. She smiled, and I took a step back, crashing against the rack of pine-tree air fresheners.

"Poor Jake. You really don't understand the cost, do you?" Her words slithered into me, and goose bumps rose on my arms.

I managed to turn away, but the store was gone, and I was in a small white room. Someone rested her head on a table, sobbing. The pain of those cries tore me apart. "Lord, let me help." I reached out to touch her but realized my sword was in my hand. The room dissolved into walls of hooded figures. Gray cloth masks obscured their faces and they moved toward me on silent feet.

"Don't let them pass, Jake!" a voice shouted from behind me.

I glanced back and saw Kieran. His tunic was burned from syncbeam fire, and blood darkened the fabric from a sword wound that should have killed him. His eyes were wild, and he shouted my name again. Why didn't he draw his sword and help me fight?

"Jake, you have to stop them. Jake!"

A hand grasped my arm, and I jolted awake.

Wade's jovial face was shadowed by the cave walls. "Jake, you need to sleep light if you don't have anyone to watch your back." He turned and ducked under the low stone of the entry to leave the cave.

I followed him into the clearing, rubbing my face and trying to shake off the dreams. "Where is she?" I looked around, wondering if Wade's bulky form was blocking her from view. "Where's my mom?"

He stopped me with a hand on my shoulder. "I'm sorry. She wasn't there."

My mouth opened, but I couldn't speak.

"I looked everywhere. Had a run-in with a few of the king's guards, too. Whatever Cameron did with her, she's not in Lyric."

He saw my shock and gave my shoulder an awkward pat.

"Maybe she already went back home."

I jerked away. "No. I have to be sure. I'll go myself."

"And accomplish what? Get yourself captured? Jake, I'm telling you, she's not there. Now, grab your gear. We have to go warn the men. Cameron knows they've been gathering, and he's sending a regiment against them. Somehow he found out they were headed to Blue Knoll." Wade tossed me my sword.

I belted it on but shook my head. "Wade, I can't go galloping around the countryside with the guardians. I have to find my mom."

"You don't have any choices right now."

Choices. Lukyan's words echoed in my head: *What can we do when we don't know which road to choose?* "Wade, wait. Let me stop to talk to Lukyan. If he agrees I should go with you, I will."

He scratched his head. "You want to go visit a songkeeper? Didn't you hear me? The men are in danger." He turned and started toward the path.

"It'll only take a minute." I ran to block him. "Hey, you swore to protect my dad's house. Help me with this. For the sake of your oath."

His teeth clenched, and for a second I thought he'd shove me aside and continue on his way. Then he snorted out a breath like an angry bull. "All right, but we have to hurry."

I nodded and threw my pack over one shoulder. I tore ahead of him down the trail and went straight to Lukyan's cabin.

Lukyan showed no surprise when his door crashed open, and Wade and I raced inside.

I told him the latest news. "So what am I supposed to do?" I was still breathing hard from the run. "The One showed me I'm supposed to expose the false Records and help reclaim Rendor."

A grunt of surprise came from Wade, but I kept talking to Lukyan. "But first I have to save my mom."

"Do you?" Lukyan seemed to lean forward on his chair without moving.

"Of course I do. That's why I came."

"That's what pulled you to come. But what is the One's purpose for you?"

Wade shifted his weight side to side and scratched his arm. He glanced toward the door and back.

Lukyan turned his watery eyes on Wade. "What is the role of the Restorer?"

Wade blinked in confusion but decided to humor the old man. "In every time of great need, a Restorer is sent to fight for the people and help the guardians. The Restorer is empowered with gifts to defeat our enemies and turn the people's hearts back to the Verses." He rattled off the rote speech in the machine-gun cadence of a little kid reciting the Pledge of Allegiance.

Inside me, the words hummed with power like an engine revving. I stared at Lukyan.

Past the cloudiness of age in his irises, I saw an answering fire. He nodded once. "You will hear many calls. There are hundreds of places where your help could be of value. But you cannot be His tool for each. Trust the One. No need will go unanswered. Follow His task for you today. What you cannot do, be assured the One will send another to do."

I grabbed at that promise, as the decision tore me in two. Wade cleared his throat and shuffled his feet. No more time.

"Thank you." My voice was a hoarse whisper around the lump in my throat.

Lukyan raised one trembling hand. "Go with the One."

Wade and I stepped outside. "What's with the songkeeper

double-talk?" he asked.

"I'll explain later." My hand found the hilt of my sword and drew strength from it. "Now, which way to Blue Knoll?"

Chapter Fifteen

SUSAN

"You once called me to surrender." I prayed out loud while pacing in circles around the small room. My mind could no longer focus if I prayed silently. I had lost count of how many weeks I'd been here or how many times Medea, and sometimes Nicco, had visited to burrow into my thoughts. But I could measure the toll on my mind. I couldn't concentrate, couldn't remember things—sometimes didn't even know what was real and what wasn't.

"I give up. I can't fight this anymore. It's what You want, isn't it? I surrender."

No.

The word was so resonant in my heart that I stopped circling.

Surrender your life into My hands. Don't surrender your mind to these lies.

"But I can't keep fighting this. I'm so tired." I sank into a chair. A tear, and then another, slid down my face. I touched my cheek. I hadn't thought there were any left in me.

My head drooped against the small table, the metal surface

cool against my forehead. "Help me." They were the only words I had left to pray.

The door slid upward with a swish like an elevator gasping open. They were back. A deep tremor shook me, but I didn't look up. Maybe if I kept my eyes closed, they wouldn't see me and they'd leave.

"She won't last much longer." Nicco's bland voice came from the doorway.

"I'm bored with her anyway." Medea sounded like a petulant child.

Nicco laughed. "If you ever learned to focus on anything for more than a day, you could develop amazing powers."

Medea yawned. "I have what I need. Why bother?"

"Because your plans are going to take strength, and they're important to all of us." Nicco's usual affectionate tolerance for Medea disappeared; his voice held a hard edge.

Her laughter sparkled. "What do you know about it? You've never crossed our borders." Then she sighed. "Stop being so moody, Nicco. Cameron just sent a bunch of new ones. Want to come see them?" Now her voice was playful and wheedling.

"And her?"

"I don't need her anymore. You can have her."

Holy God in heaven, no. Medea had been keeping me as some kind of pet, but she didn't like to expend much energy. She preferred to tap into my surface weaknesses and savor the things she found: guilt, loneliness, regret, despair. It was misery, but a comfortable misery that kept one foot in reality. I had sensed her growing stronger in these past weeks, but she didn't direct that new strength toward tormenting me. She was storing it up for some other purpose.

Nicco seemed less concerned with preserving his own

mental power. He could take one small thought and twist it into a raging lie that drowned my rational mind. He didn't do it to gain strength. Often he'd even seemed drained after a brutal campaign through my thoughts. I wasn't sure what his purpose was. Maybe, like Medea, he was just easily bored. Whatever his reasons, he didn't bother with emotions that were easy to access. The few times Medea let him delve into my thoughts, he dug for small threads of irrational terror or savage anger. Greed, rage, vicious cynicism. I knew all humans had the root of every sin trapped in their fiber, but these were less common battles for me, and I didn't know how to fight them.

A hand rested lightly on my head. "So much chaos." Nicco's voice was right above me and dripped with false sympathy.

I squeezed my eyes more tightly closed.

"Well, if you're sure you don't want her anymore," he called to Medea.

"She's yours." Her voice was already fading as she moved down the hall.

I couldn't stop the shudder that ran through me.

"Giving up already? This is too easy," he sneered. The hand lifted from my head. "Pull yourself together. I'll be back later."

I followed the sounds of his footsteps, the clatter of something falling, and the hiss of the door closing. After several deep breaths, I gathered the courage to look up to see if he really had left.

The relief of being alone again lasted only a few minutes. He'd be back. That knowledge propelled me to my feet to pace and pray. During my second circuit of the small room, I noticed an object on the floor. I blinked a few times, then crouched down, afraid to touch it. It took huge effort to dredge up a memory of where I'd seen it before.

The remote to activate the door. Nicco wore it on his belt.

I collapsed to my knees, gasping in air.

He had dropped it when he left. He'd notice soon. No time to formulate a plan. I needed to take advantage of this miracle and run.

I snatched up the small device and stumbled over to press my ear against the door but couldn't tell if the hallway was empty. My thumb hit the remote, and I was out of the room before the door finished sliding up. There was no one in sight. Which way were the stairs? I chose a direction and ran, passing door after door. Then I skidded to a halt. How could I leave everyone else trapped in these rooms?

Kieran's words from when we'd escaped the prison in Sidian floated up from my memories: "You can't help them all."

Maybe not, but at least I could give these captives the same chance I had.

Despite my frantic attempts, the remote wouldn't work on any other doors. Throwing glances over my shoulder, I studied the panel outside one of the rooms and slid recessed levers until the door began moving. I ran to the next door and did the same.

A few people stumbled out into the hallway. Many cowered in their cells—men, women, even some children—each alone, each with haunted eyes and unsteady movements. Some had the distinctive angular cheekbones and dark hair of Hazorites. Others looked like they could be Mark's distant cousins, with strong jaws and long wavy hair.

I didn't stop to coax them but raced to open each door as I made my way toward the stairs at the end of the hall. When I poked my head around the corner, the stairway appeared empty. I listened for sounds below, but all I could hear was the rush of blood in my ears.

No time for caution. I ran down the stairs, my foot missing a step in my panic but then catching the next with a jolt. I was through the archways and into the open air in seconds. One of the paths must lead to the tunnel, but every direction looked the same. The long underground passage probably wasn't the best way to escape, anyway. If I could hide for a while, maybe I could find some other way out of Rhus.

Aiming for the shelter of trees, my heart pounded with elation as well as fear. Freedom was an explosion of flavor, like biting into a dark chocolate filled with cherry liqueur. As I slipped into the deeper shadows of the woods, I heard raised voices by the conservatory. Those sounds faded quickly as I kept running. When my lungs burned from exertion, I stopped to rest a hand against a tree and wheeze in more air. The trees here were as smooth as green tapers, stretching dozens of feet upward before sending out narrow shoots of jade leaves from the top of the willowy trunk. Nothing gave me a clue about where to run next. I turned a slow circle, peering between the columns of deep green. Each direction looked identical.

Fear screamed at me to keep running. Rational thought urged me to make a plan. Necessity forced the two to compromise. I turned Nicco's remote in my hand. The clasp on one end had a sharp edge. Gouging it across one of the trunks, I was able to create a mark. A scent of mint hit my nose.

I'll be able to keep from going in circles. No, no—they'll see the marks and use them to follow me.

Arguments pounded back and forth with the rhythm of my breaths. I ignored them and ran forward, scraping another symbol into green bark. Minutes passed. The slender trunks were getting closer together. After battling claustrophobia while weaving through the narrow gaps, I was forced to accept that I couldn't go farther. The trees drew even nearer to each other, as dense and impenetrable as a hedgerow. I backtracked in frustration and set off in a direction perpendicular to my first course.

I'm free. That's what matters. Just keep moving.

Soon my path was blocked again, and I chose a new direction. I no longer bothered to scratch a mark in the trees. I was lost in a confusion of green pillars and the cloying scent of wintergreen. The bark was as smooth as bamboo—and impossible to climb—so I couldn't get my bearings from a better vantage. At least there was no sound of pursuit. Perhaps a mile farther, when I paused to listen again, I heard flowing water. Desperate for a sign that there was an end to this forest, I aimed toward what I hoped was a river.

The clearing appeared so suddenly that I stumbled into it before I realized the wall of trees had parted. A fountain sent water cascading over double perpendicular arches into a pool contained by a ring of white marble. Although a constant wall of atmosphere shrouded the sky, the effect of breaking out of the woods was almost like stepping into glaring sunlight. I inched forward, drawn by the promise of a cool drink. My head swiveled in all directions as I made sure that I was alone before plunging both hands into the fountain. The water tasted as good as I had imagined it would. After drinking my fill, I splashed my face. As I shook droplets off my eyelashes, I looked down into the still depths and saw my own reflection for the first time since my arrival in Rhus. My face was gaunt and pale, although that might have been an effect of the white marble beneath the water.

Suddenly, as a ripple passed over the surface, two other faces appeared near mine in the water: Medea and Nicco. I spun around and shrieked. They stood on either side of me. I hadn't heard them approach, or maybe they had been there all the time but clouded my mind so I couldn't see them.

Medea's laughter sparkled like the clear water. "You're right, Nicco. That was fun. Although the others won't be happy about the effort it took to put everyone back."

He shrugged. "All right, I admit I didn't expect that." He turned to me with a smirk. "I'll take that back now."

Lifting my hand, I realized I was still clutching his remote. He pried it from my fingers and frowned at the green shreds of bark still clinging to the clasp.

"You left it on purpose?" My voice was hoarse with despair. "Why?"

"Entertainment," Medea answered for him. She smiled at Nicco. "But now I need to go. I leave tomorrow and have things to take care of." She turned and stepped away.

"Medea, are you sure you're done with her?"

Her silvery laughter floated past. "Yes, yes. I told you. Do whatever you like." He watched her stroll around the fountain and disappear into the trees. I edged silently backward, hoping to reach the shelter of the other side of the clearing. I'd made it only a few yards when Nicco turned his attention back to me. I froze, and his teeth appeared in a feral smile.

"Come here," he said quietly. I held my ground for a moment, testing the control of his words. It surprised me to discover he wasn't compelling me forward but had simply asked. I looked toward the trees. How far could I get before he set loose the physical pain he was capable of creating? Instead of running away, I walked toward him, my stomach roiling.

Nicco sank onto the low wall around the fountain and dangled a hand into the depths, lifting it to watch the water run through his fingers. My eyes followed the droplets as they slipped back into the safety of the pool. His fingers tightened into a fist, which he then braced against the low wall. He pulled his eyes away from the water and turned to study me.

"I'd like you to explain." His tone was mild, which scared me. I didn't feel an intrusion into my psyche yet and couldn't read his mood. The times he had visited me in the past, he had been the most brutal when his expression was most bland.

I swallowed hard. "Explain what?" My nerve endings tightened. He could attack my mind at any second. His momentary restraint chilled me.

His tongue flicked over his lips as if he could taste my fear. "You had your opportunity to run, but you risked it by stopping to open other doors. Why?"

I struggled to figure out what he wanted to hear, still reeling from the knowledge that this had all been another Rhusican game and my moments of freedom had been a lie. When I didn't answer quickly, his face clouded. "You made a lot of colleagues angry at me." His voice turned silky and dangerous. "Was it to cause chaos? Slow down the search?"

I drew a shaky breath. "No. I just couldn't leave them." My voice dropped to a miserable whisper. I stared at the spray of water in the center of the fountain. "No one should live like that. I had to try to help."

Nicco stood, and I shifted my focus to watch him. He took a step closer, and I flinched.

He's going to kill me. Should I try to run, only to have him enjoy crushing me? Or should I summon the last fragment of courage in me and face this directly?

"Look at me." His soothing tone and false smile reminded me of Medea. My eyes met his. His irises glimmered like the water under the fountain. My heart lurched, and I couldn't breathe.

God, take care of Mark. Help him with the children when I don't come back. Keep them—

"No." His word cracked.

I blinked.

He gentled his voice with effort. "You're safe. I won't hurt you."

While a corner of my rational mind clamored in protest, my body obeyed his suggestion and my muscles relaxed. I hadn't realized I had been trembling until it stopped. The terror leached away, and I listened to the calming sound of water splashing nearby and sweet notes in the trees. Bird song? I sighed again.

"Now," Nicco said, "show me what you felt when you escaped."

Immediately the memory of fleeing my room played out. The blood-pumping panic welled back up, but I felt as if a hand pressed it aside. I relived the fumbling moments in the hallway, working to open the doors. Compassion burned as I worked my way down the hall, throwing levers. The hours of prayer for the unknown people who suffered in their cells had built a core of love in me.

Faces swirled past, each one precious. The sense of seeing with Other eyes hit me, and I knew they were each cherished and would not be forgotten.

Nicco turned away with a strangled sound, and the vivid memory stream jolted to a stop. I stumbled a few steps back, confused. His hold over my emotions slipped, and fear raced back into the front seat as he stared at the fountain and rubbed the back of his neck. I wasn't sure what had just happened, but he wasn't paying attention to me and seemed weakened.

I ran. Adrenaline charged through me as I expected pain to grab me at any second. Instead, I reached the edge of the woods. Not daring to look back, I sprinted hard, dodging between narrow trunks, until everything was a blur of green. When the trees grew close, I switched direction but kept running. It didn't matter where I was going, as long as it was away. My throat ached from panting, but when my legs threatened to give out, I pushed harder. Spotting a gap in the trees, I surged forward . . .

. . . and into the clearing again. Nicco lounged against the fountain wall, arms crossed, looking bored. I stumbled to a stop as my burning muscles gave out, and I fell to my knees. Doubled over, breathing hard, I was powerless to run or fight anymore. I lifted my head with effort and glared at Nicco.

"Is this all an illusion? The woods? The clearing?"

He gave an amused shrug. "Not all. It's a simple matter to steer you here." He gave a hopeful grin. "Care to try again?"

A snarl broke from my throat, and I tried to will myself to rise, only to fail. Nicco pushed off from the low wall around the fountain and walked toward me with his head tilted. He was soaking in the rush of my panicked flight and the kindling rage that I felt now. Just to spite him, I took a calming breath and murmured a prayer. But as I refused to indulge my anger, I realized that the only thing left was fear. Nicco read it too, and his smile grew as he stood over me.

"No?" he mocked. "You're sure you don't want to run again?"

Bitterness gagged me like a deep breath of smoke. I shook my head, unable to speak around the taste of ashes in my mouth.

"Well, I don't have time to look after Medea's playthings, now that she's done with you." He pulled a cloth pouch from a pocket and slid it back to reveal a short-handled gold blade. I had forgotten that in spite of their mental powers, Rhusicans used more tangible weapons as well. The Rhusican that Tristan fought had been skilled with a sword. And I knew firsthand how lethal Medea was with a dagger.

"You've been very entertaining." Nicco's eyes traveled over me, assessing targets. I imagined I saw something like sympathy when he glanced at my face. "I won't drag this out," he said with what I suppose he meant to be kindness. I couldn't manage to feel gratitude.

He crouched down, grabbed my hair in his fist, and pulled my head back. I looked at him and saw my death. But in that moment, a liquid peace filled me from within. Beyond this enemy, his weapon, and the promise of death, I saw life. I knew its truth in my marrow.

The knife flashed as Nicco lifted it. I looked up at the sky. *Holy One, I'm going to see You face-to-face very soon.* Then I closed my eyes and let the peace hold me.

Chapter Sixteen

SUSAN

Some part of me was aware of the drizzle that began to fall, brushing my closed eyelids like soft tears. It must be afternoon. Serenity protected my heart like gauze. The struggle would be over soon. Alongside peace, poignant sorrow played out a montage of my family. I hated thinking that they would never know what had happened to me. I saw images of Mark with sawdust adorning his flannel shirt, grinning as he showed off a new set of shelves. Jake racing down the field after a soccer ball. Karen's wry smile among the piles of free-form laundry sculpture in her room. Jon building Legos, and Anne skipping toward me. All their dear faces around the supper table. I could hear the laughter and the clink of silverware and smell the lasagna and garlic bread.

Thank You, Lord. You blessed me with so much. Give me courage now.

The memories and prayers flashed through me in seconds. Gratitude, love, longing, and loss swirled together, and still the peace held me. Nicco's hand twisted harder in my hair and my eyes stung. I held my breath and waited. He drew in a sharp breath as he prepared to strike. Did he plan to slit my throat, or stab me in the heart the way Medea had done?

Suddenly, he released me with a shove that knocked me sideways to the ground. My eyes opened and I stared up at him, confused.

"What was that?" Nicco's face twisted with fury. He backed up a few paces but then stepped close again, waving his dagger while his other hand raked through his hair. He towered over me, stormed away a few yards, and then came striding back. "Get up."

I didn't move fast enough, and a vise like a migraine pierced through my temples. He hadn't touched me, but the pain was as fierce as any physical attack. I grabbed my head and moaned.

"Get up!"

I'd never heard him shout before, and the force of his words along with the physical torment he projected shook my whole body. A strangled scream echoed from somewhere far away; then I realized it was mine.

The pain cut out as abruptly as it had hit. My hands pressed against the damp ground, seeking a touchstone to reality, to sanity. I stumbled to my feet. Nausea rocked me, and I staggered toward the fountain, sinking onto the wall. I doubled over, hugged my stomach, and waited for the vertigo to pass. When I could finally open my eyes again, Nicco was sitting near me. He was completely calm now, but his burst of temper had been real. Something had upset him.

Good.

He put his weapon away in its cloth sheath. The rain fell in earnest now, creating competing ripples in the pool of the fountain. Nicco's hair was matted, and he seemed oblivious to his wet clothes.

He frowned at me. "Let's go."

No explanation. He had been about to kill me, and now all he said was, "Let's go"? He could at least ask if I were able to move yet—which I highly doubted. I felt as weak as if I'd had a bout of food poisoning; I didn't trust that my legs would hold me.

Resentment hummed in my gut. "You weren't going to kill me? It was just another game?"

"Not a game," he said coldly but gave no further indication of why I still lived or what he planned now. The peace that had protected me was gone, a soft bubble that had evaporated when it was no longer needed. I tried to conjure it back, but it eluded me.

Nicco led me across the clearing and through the woods a short distance. We stepped out into the open terraces in front of the conservatory building. I thought I had traveled miles in my wild run, but in reality I hadn't gotten anywhere. As I followed him up the stairs, my shoulders sagged at the futility of my escape. I crossed the threshold of my cell without protest. The last glimpse I had of the world beyond my tiny room was Nicco's face. His expression unreadable, he stared at me until the door slid down and hid him from view.

Capture should have devastated me. Instead, all I felt was tired relief. The heart-pounding terror of being hunted, the stress of trying to make a plan—I was glad it was over. Several times as a girl, I had snuck a book from my dad's collection of World War II prisoner escape stories. I remember being surprised by how often Allied soldiers talked about a powerful compulsion to surrender themselves. Standing on a German train platform with carefully forged papers, some men would be so overwhelmed by the fear of discovery that they wanted to walk up to a soldier, hands raised, and announce their identity. It never had made sense to me until now. I sank onto a chair, drained, and forced myself to look away from the door.

Now what? Did he still plan to kill me? Was it something in my memory or emotions that had interrupted his plans? Maybe the One had stayed his hand. But what would he do now? What could *I* do?

Pray for the people of Rhus.

My teeth ground together at the familiar prompting.

"I have," I said into the emptiness. "And what about me?" But the habit of obeying that call was strong. I pushed my wet hair back from my face and grabbed the blanket off my pallet to wrap around my shoulders. Sitting at the bare table, I bowed my head and returned to my prayers.

The brief time in open air—connecting to a world beyond my cell—had cleared my mind. It was as if the smell of wet earth, the sight of lofty trees towering overhead, even the texture of moss under my hands when I fell awakened me. I prayed for Rhus and tried again to develop a framework for understanding Nicco or Medea or the rest of the Rhusicans. What drove them?

Considering the conversations I had overheard, Medea and Nicco barely regarded me as a person. To them I was an experiment or an unwanted pet or a source of energy. They ignored any of my questions or attempts to converse as an equal. But I'd still been able to collect jigsawed pieces of information. As I prayed, the bits of knowledge shuffled around, revealing some cohesive clues. Hoping the ideas were inspired by the One, I began to formulate a plan.

My meal that night tasted odd. Maybe they planned to poison me. I didn't eat much of the lumpy gruel, and I lay awake for hours afterward, waiting for some unknown drug to take effect. Nothing happened. Eventually I slept, dreaming of a smooth green road and the scent of wintergreen.

The next day, I wasn't surprised when, shortly after morning rations, the door opened again.

Nicco prowled the small room, conducting a cursory search as if I could be manufacturing and hiding weapons. I generally did all I could to avoid drawing his attention, but today I had a plan.

"What's wrong?" I asked, startling myself with my boldness.

Nicco half turned, eyebrows lifted in mild surprise.

"Did you get in trouble for letting me out?" I added when he didn't respond. I bit my lip as I realized how taunting that sounded. He could still change his mind and kill me. I needed to be careful.

He just grinned. "Why?" He turned the other chair and straddled it, crossing his arms across the back. "Worried about me? How considerate."

I returned his gaze calmly. His eyes narrowed. In a second he would be burrowing into my mind, igniting disturbing pictures and twisting memories. Soon I'd be left with no capacity for rational thought. He rested his chin on his arms, and his eyes took on the illusion of spinning light. I didn't have much time.

"Wait." I held up my hands as though they could shield me from his mind and talked fast. "You asked me a question yesterday. I know you were curious. Maybe I can explain."

Only a hint of interest flickered across his face. I took a quick breath. "You've been digging around in my memories, triggering emotions, looking for . . . something. I promise you there are things you've missed. I'll show you."

He lifted his head, and a skeptical smile glided upward. "Your point?" After all, so far I'd found no real way to resist his intrusions into my mind. Offering to cooperate was rather moot.

"You don't know where to look." I met his eyes. "There is more. You asked what was happening, back at the fountain when you . . ." I couldn't force myself to talk calmly about my own execution and looked down at my hands. This was a far too dangerous game. My plans of last night now seemed silly.

"Assuming you're right—that there are things I haven't found yet—why would you want to show them to me?" He sat with a new level of stillness that made the rest of the room seem to twitch.

I'd caught his interest. My plan was working. The intensity of his focus made it hard to breathe, but I had prepared for this.

"I want something in return." My voice was quiet, but at least I didn't stutter.

"Freedom? I've been offered more interesting things in trade from other guests wanting freedom."

I shook my head. "I know you won't let me go. I only want an exchange of information." His forehead wrinkled, and I hurried on before he could say anything. "Let's just say I'm curious. I want to understand your people."

It was the truth, as far as it went. I leaned back. "What do you have to be afraid of? Think of it as a dare . . . a challenge to your courage. Will you let me show you real truth? And will you tell me about Rhus?"

"I've already seen the truth of what's inside of you." He watched me, unmoving.

"No. You twist things and— "

"And I have no interest in your opinion of my courage or lack of it."

Sweat prickled my skin. I'd played my best card, and I'd only delayed the inevitable. He'd invade my thoughts, control and torment me until he lost interest and killed what was left of me. My problem was, I didn't have enough to offer him.

I slid my chair forward and gave him my best "double-dare" look. "But you are curious, aren't you? You want to know what happened inside of me when I was facing death. You wonder if there are doors you haven't found."

"All right. Explain what you were seeing. Tell me what you felt. What was it?"

My head felt heavy, and I realized he was slipping a compelling force into his words. I fought the cloudiness.

"I will. But tell me about your people. Your families."

"Irrelevant." He glared at a point on my forehead, and it began to throb.

"No it's not. It's important to understanding." The pain grew, and I gasped. "Nicco, just try to have a normal conversation."

His eyes flared wide, seeming shocked at my use of his name. It broke his concentration, and the pain stopped drilling into my head. I know how to be earnest. That's why I did a great job fund-raising for the school library. Mark always said my basset-hound eyes were lethal to anyone trying to say "no" to me. I used every bit of my sincerity now.

"I saw two things when I was about to die. First, I remembered my family. I can't show you what those feelings mean until I know what you feel about family. Medea told the Council in Lyric about her husband—how he was the Rhusican that Tristan killed. It helped me understand . . ."

My words trailed off because Nicco threw back his head and laughed.

I waited for him to calm down.

"Fine. I'll explain that much. He wasn't Medea's husband. We don't have bonds like the people of the clans."

"But she told them . . . Why would she lie?"

He smiled. "Why would she tell the truth? She needed their sympathy. She knew how important links like that were to them."

I struggled to stay on track. "So you don't marry? But you have children. I've seen them. Who cares for them?"

He shrugged. "Everyone, no one."

"But how do they learn love, compassion, commitment?"

Nicco was amused at my dismay. "Why wouldn't they feel loved? Everyone in Rhus accepts everyone else. We would never banish someone the way the clans do or drive them to run away like some of the Hazorites we've taken in." He shifted his chair, growing bored with this conversation.

"We look at family life a little differently," I said slowly. "Mark and I committed our lives to each other. Wait." I lifted a hand when he was about to interrupt. "It's important for you to understand. Our children know that no matter what happens to them or to us, we love them. That's why I was thinking of them in that moment."

Nicco's small store of patience was gone. "Show me." His eyes grabbed mine, a deep vibration beneath his words.

I resisted for a second. "You don't have to do that. Let me concentrate." I closed my eyes and took my mind back to the images I had seen in the clearing by the fountain. I let my feelings well up again—sweet emotions of love and longing. I lingered on the scene of our family at supper. Then I deliberately steered my memory to another scene from four years earlier. Mark's arm wrapped my shoulders as we leaned against the familiar couch cushions. Anne's head rested in my lap, and one of her blonde curls encircled my finger. Jake sat across from us, looking earnest. Karen stared into the distance. She was only about twelve back then but already had compassionate eyes. Jon sat on the floor by Mark's feet, and Mark rested a hand on his shoulder.

"The best thing we can do is pray for her," Mark said. We bowed our heads and awkwardly joined hands. Anne spoke first, lifting her head an inch off my lap.

"Please make Grandma better," her words lisped through baby teeth, and she settled back down with the satisfaction of prayer well prayed. I felt the sweetness of the moment again as each of us spoke. We'd spent a grueling evening outside the ICU, and when the doctors had my mom stabilized, we came home reeling with fear and questions. As had become our habit when life's concerns overwhelmed us, we huddled together in this circle of support.

I opened my eyes and looked at Nicco. His head angled in concentration and confusion. That had been my plan: to shake his complacency, let him see beyond the strange emotional torrents that he and Medea played in; to show him truth; if nothing else, to keep him curious and gain more time.

He took a slow breath, and his eyes came back into focus.

"All right. Let's look at your family some more."

And suddenly, with the same skill as Medea, he found memories behind barricaded doors. Exhausted days of chasing toddlers with my voice raised in aggravation. Mark's revelation that his past had been a lie and my shock and betrayal. Children quarrelling, Karen's disdainful turning away when I asked her about her day. Painful snapshots of the worst moments of family life shuffled past at lightning speed as I tried to stop them, explain them. Then they began to twist. The pictures distorted. The arguments and petty rages built and covered over all other memories. Soon all I felt was repulsion for the entwining bonds that forced these six humans to live together, interact, and hurt each other over and over. It was Sartre's "No Exit" in a suburban family. Eternal misunderstandings, eternal irritation, eternal prison.

"No!" I fought what Nicco was doing but couldn't push him away from my mind. "You're lying. You're changing it." I could barely gasp out the words. The worst agony was in knowing I had invited him to see this part of my heart. I thought truth, beauty, and goodness would have the power to make him question—search for meaning in his own strange, capricious life. But it was just another toy for him.

He rummaged through my mind, a thief upending drawers and tossing family treasures over his shoulder in utter carelessness. "Stop!" I pressed my hands against the sides of my head and tried to shut out the images he was creating. At some point, I slipped to the floor, my muscles incapable of holding me in the chair anymore. I curled into a ball, distantly aware of tears, of my shoulders shaking with sobs. I couldn't form words anymore—couldn't even think coherently enough to pray anything beyond a desperate "Help me!"

At last he lost interest and stopped his assault. The churning of my thoughts died down like a lake after a storm has blown over. I was numb, broken, empty.

Nicco stood up and pushed his chair against the table with a scrape. "I'll be back tomorrow." He sounded positively happy. My plan was in shambles. I couldn't take more of this, and it hadn't changed him at all. "Tomorrow you can show me the second thing."

What was he talking about? My battered mind struggled to remember. I had told him there were two things that I saw when I was about to die. The first was my family and their love. He'd so poisoned that, I couldn't even think about them without shuddering. I lifted my head and focused bleary eyes on Nicco's back as he left. The door slammed down.

Tomorrow he'd be back to destroy what was left. The second thing I had seen beyond the specter of my own death.

The face of the One.

Chapter Seventeen

JAKE

Wade might have the bulk of a linebacker, but he moved with the speed of a wide receiver, charging through brush and around any obstacle between him and the band of guardians camped at Blue Knoll. We wouldn't rest there, either. After this blitz, I'd have another long hike to look forward to as we fled Blue Knoll and the threat of ambush by Cameron's guards. I looked up at the tall pines so prevalent outside of Braide Wood and tripped on one of the rocks that dotted the trail.

Wade finally took pity on me and stopped near a stream so we could drink and I could catch my breath. "Thanks for letting me see Lukyan before we left." I wiped my sleeve across my mouth. "He and Linette are—"

"Linette? She was in Braide Wood?" Wade sat up straighter. "Why didn't you tell me? Was she staying with her family? How did she look?"

I blinked at the onslaught of questions. Wade ducked his head with a shrug. "She was engaged to Dylan. He was a good friend. I've tried to look out for her since he was killed."

My mouth tasted sour, as if I'd bitten into a Lemonhead.

"She seemed okay. She wasn't planning to stay. Just wanted to find out what was happening in the clans."

Wade nodded. "Good. I wasn't happy when I got back from the River Borders and found out she'd left for Hazor. But it's safer than Braide Wood right now." Wade swooped up a large pinecone and tossed it at a low-hanging branch. "Did she still seem . . . you know . . . sad?" He was staring at the stream, and his voice grew quieter. "Do you think she's getting over Dylan?"

I jumped to my feet, my face turning warm. I did *not* want to be having this conversation. "I wouldn't know."

He hefted himself to his feet and slapped a heavy hand against my back. "Not your concern, boy. I was just thinking out loud."

"I'm not a boy." I shouldered past him toward the trail. "I'm almost nineteen."

"Really?" Wade's voice was friendly, oblivious to my mood. "You look a lot younger. Must be your size."

I hunched my shoulders and stormed ahead on the path.

A few miles farther, the rocky terrain began to level out. We emerged from a climb through a thick growth of spice trees to see a cluster of log buildings spread out on rolling hills.

"Blue Knoll." Wade pointed ahead. Waves of blue ferns rimmed the forests like the wide circle of one of Anne's chalk drawings on our driveway. The fronds bobbed as rain hit them. The mid-afternoon downpour was beginning, and we'd never even stopped for lunch. I adjusted the hood of my cloak and followed Wade as he skirted the edge of the clearing. We moved back under cover of the trees, and Wade pulled up short.

"Jake, about what you said to Lukyan." He fidgeted with the ties of his pack, careful not to look at me. "Do you really think the One told you those things?"

I bristled. He sounded like he thought I was a crackpot who claimed to be Napoleon. Then again, if Wade had made the same claims, would I have believed him?

"I know it sounds crazy, but yes, the One wants me to tell people that Cameron's new Records are a fraud. Lukyan is already contacting the other songkeepers."

Wade's head snapped around. "He agreed to that?" I didn't like the horror in Wade's expression. "Do you have any idea what kind of trouble that will cause? And what Cameron will do?"

Cold cleats tromped up and down my spine as I thought of Lukyan. Was he in danger now too?

I drew myself up. "Yes, he agreed. And the One also showed me we need to reclaim Rendor."

Now Wade thudded his meaty hand onto my shoulder. "Jake, I know you mean well. I'm sure you have a good heart, like your mother." His face drew closer. "I've sworn to protect your father's house, but I can't protect you if you make claims like that."

And he hadn't even heard my most outrageous claim: that I had Restorer signs, at a time when the new Records declared there would be no more Restorers. I sputtered a protest, but he squeezed my shoulder. "Listen"—he was whispering as if the feathered moths and ground-crawlers would eavesdrop—"I'm not saying that things won't head that way in time. I'd like to get Rendor back more than anyone. I was at the River Borders when we held back the Kahlareans. But for now you've got to promise me you'll keep your mouth shut about the One talking to you, all right?" Another squeeze.

He took my silence for assent and gave me a wide smile. He

released me with a last hearty thump and lumbered forward. I followed, massaging my sore shoulder.

Deeper into the woods, Wade stopped and cupped his hands by his mouth to make a chirping sound, something halfway between chipmunk and tree frog. We listened in silence, and then a call answered. Two cheeps, a pause, and then a third. Wade nodded and led me forward.

It took some maneuvering and a clamber under thick brambles to reach the hidden clearing. The size of the group had grown—more than a few dozen now—or else the numbers seemed larger because the space was smaller. Men sat in tight knots, speaking very little. Some whittled with boot knives, others stitched repairs into gear, and a few were engaged in a game with black and white stones spread in obscure patterns on the packed earth. I spotted Arland right away. He turned from a low-voiced argument with a young guardian and saw us. Relief lit his face for a second, but he masked it and stood to make his way toward Wade. Scanning for other familiar faces, I noticed Ian scowling in my direction. I jerked my gaze away.

Arland joined Wade with feigned casualness. Barely moving his mouth, he asked, "What word?"

"Council guard on the way," Wade answered him in the same undertone.

"Do we stand now?"

Wade shook his head. "I say we move out. Gather more forces."

Arland gave a sharp nod and turned to issue quiet orders. A murmur rippled through the clearing. Soundless as ghosts, the men morphed from bored campers at rest to an army ready to move. Game stones were kicked aside, gear was gathered, and camp broken. Arland led the men out through the same small break in the bracken where we had entered. Wade waited until the clearing was empty, scanned it a last time, and signaled me to head out.

The column of men wove along the blue band of foliage at the edge of the clearing, vague shapes against the thick trees. I looked at the distant homes on the knoll, wondering if the families in Blue Knoll were facing the same struggles as the people in Braide Wood.

A sharp crack rang through the air. Someone must be shooting bear or other wildlife. Tara had mentioned that her husband was out on a hunting party. The men in front of me twisted their heads, squinting in all directions. It took me two full seconds to remember there weren't guns in this world.

Or at least there hadn't been before Cameron's visit to our world.

Another shot split the air. "Get down!" I shouted, my voice sounding shrill in my own ears.

Wade grabbed my arm. "What is it?"

"Weapons." I wrenched away from him and ran forward, waving to the men. "Down! Take cover!"

A sharp tear sounded as a bullet ripped through leaves and branches just over our heads. I ducked in reflex. The men closest to me finally grasped what I was shouting. They pulled deeper into the woods, using trees for protection. I jumped up to run forward and warn the others but was tackled from behind.

"Jake, stay down." Wade's bulk crushed the air from my lungs and the argument from my will. He jumped up and raced along the line of men. I lifted my head just enough to watch his progress. A volley of shots crackled, and my heart raced. One man jerked and fell. I scrambled to my feet to run toward him but was grabbed and pulled back.

"Those aren't syncbeams." Ian's fierce growl came inches from my ear.

"No." I shoved against him, but his grip didn't loosen. "They're guns. From my home. Let me go—I have to help."

"Wade told you to stay down." Ian didn't care about protecting me. He just enjoyed hampering my efforts.

I craned my head around, searching for our attackers. My vision telescoped. Another Restorer gift. I squinted and spotted a flash of rust tunics. We were being fired on from the buildings on the edge of Blue Knoll.

More explosive pops filled the air, stirring memories of firecrackers in July.

"Take cover!" I shouted, straining to get my head above the underbrush before Ian pulled me back. "They're behind the buildings!" Arland turned in my direction. He jerked, then stumbled back. He'd been hit too. Panic surged through me, and I wrestled against Ian. Wade guided Arland deeper into the woods in a bent-over sprint.

Ian stayed in a crouch as he dragged me back. I lurched to the side, frantic to run to the aid of the man who had fallen, but Ian grabbed me again with a curse. Wade burst from the trees and dove into the deep ferns. He threw the fallen guardian's arms over his shoulder and dragged him to the relative safety of the woods.

"Pull back." Wade's deep voice resonated through the confusion of trees and underbrush. I couldn't see Wade, but Ian guided me away from the clearing.

"Where are we going?" I panted.

"Just follow me. Can you do that much?" Ian's voice was thick with disgust.

I was too shaken to respond in kind. "Yes. Go ahead."

He turned and sprinted deeper into the woods, and I tore after him. Even supporting the wounded, these guys moved fast. I could have used them on my soccer team last year. I struggled to keep Ian in sight. Most of the men were stretched out far ahead of us somewhere. There was no trail. A twig whipped across my eyes, leaving a stinging scratch that began to heal even as I dodged the next tree.

I felt a presence loom up alongside me and glanced over, leading to another collision with a low branch. I shook it off and pushed my hood back so I could see better. Wade was matching my strides.

"You all right?" He was breathing hard.

"Yeah." I jumped over a fallen tree. "How's the guy"—I sucked in oxygen—"who got shot?"

"We've got him." Not much information, but this wasn't a great time for a discussion.

"Wade, the weapons." I slowed without realizing it, and Wade nudged me to pick up the pace. "They're . . . from my . . . world." The words came out in gasps as I pushed back into a sprint.

"You can explain later. Run."

I dug in and ran.

The terrain grew more rugged. The men's pace eventually slowed, but we kept traveling until it was nearly dark. Wade stayed close to me, although he jogged ahead a few times to confer with Arland. Two men dropped back to watch for signs of pursuit, but there were no further attacks.

"Where are we?" I asked Wade when rocky cliffs loomed over us.

He rubbed a tired hand over his dirt-streaked forehead. "Along the Hazor border. I doubt they'll follow us here."

Ian passed near us. "Why would they bother, when someone can keep them informed of where we are?" He shot me a dark look.

"Hey, I didn't tell anyone—"

"Cameron already knew," Wade said firmly. "I found out in Lyric. Jake had nothing to do with this."

Arland called a halt and directed the men upward. It took some scrambling, but eventually we were all safely hidden in a large cave.

Wade signaled for me to follow him deeper into the cave. When I glanced back, Ian was talking to a cluster of men. Their eyes tracked me as I walked across the cave.

Farther back into the shelter, Arland crouched near the young guardian who had been most seriously wounded. Arland's own sleeve was soaked in blood, but he ignored his injuries, working to stop the unconscious guardian's bleeding.

The boy's skin had the same pale translucence as the heat trivets scattered throughout our hiding place. His eyes were closed, his breathing ragged.

"Jake, you said the Council guard used weapons from your world. How do we help him?" Wade's voice was quiet, but the words shook me.

"I . . . I don't know."

Arland glanced up, his eyes narrowed. "What caused this?"

I stammered an explanation about bullets and the damage they could cause. "If it's still in there, we should try to get it out."

Arland didn't seem happy with that suggestion. He lifted the wad of cloth pressed to the boy's chest, exposing an angry, gaping tear. Blood pooled thick and black, revealing glimpses of exposed muscle. Nothing like the small neat hole I would have expected. I pushed down the bile rising in my throat.

Wade knelt and stroked the boy's hair back from his face, making crooning sounds. Before Arland could ask me any more questions, the gasping breaths stopped. The body gave a shudder, sagged, became still. I looked away. Wade's arm slipped around my shoulders, and he steered me out of the cave.

I huddled on a boulder and wrapped my arms around myself, still fighting back nausea.

Arland emerged from the cave and walked over to join us.

I looked up at him. "You just left him?"

"The men will take care of it." Arland met my eyes, unflinching and cold, but I sensed the fierce sorrow and anger behind his words. I sensed it because I felt it too. I'd never seen someone die before. Everything inside me screamed that it was wrong. Senseless, a mistake, wrong, wrong, wrong. And I hadn't even known his name.

"I tried to get to him. Ian wouldn't let me." It seemed desperately important to explain.

"I told you to stay down. Ian was following orders." Wade was matter-of-fact.

"But—"

"Jake, we need to make plans. Arland seems to think we should include you in this discussion." I heard Wade's thoughts behind his simple words: *Don't lose it now, Jake. Hold it together a little longer.*

I took a deep breath and nodded. "Okay." My voice sounded small, but it didn't quaver.

Arland settled heavily onto a large stone, bracing his injured arm against his chest. "Can we spare a messenger tomorrow?"

Wade nodded. "Should we set up a base here until we get word back?"

"It's as good a place as any."

I struggled to stay focused and follow the conversation but realized I was confused about something.

"Wade? Who's in command of this . . . well, whatever this group is now?"

He didn't answer me but exchanged looks with Arland.

"Wade is giving the orders." A crooked smile softened the grim planes of Arland's face. "But I don't blame you for being confused. He's not much older than you, is he?"

Wade made a low sound in his chest in protest. "Arland is the leader of the guardians. Or what's left of us."

"But Wade has been bringing us orders from one of the head guardians—the one who kept us together when the guardians were disbanded. The man that these men are here to follow," Arland said.

It began to make sense. "Tristan?"

"Told you he's smarter than he looks." Arland shifted his weight and looked at Wade. "Do you think we'll go ahead with the plan?"

Wade shrugged. "I don't see any other choice. Once Tristan rejoins us and we build our force, we'll have at least a chance." Wade cuffed my shoulder. "Every sword arm helps, right, Jake?"

Arland's eyes narrowed as he watched me. He was waiting for me to tell Wade that I was more than one spare sword arm—that I was the Restorer. I couldn't do it. Wade didn't have a bit of guile in him and would never keep my secret. The thought of the men's response to my claim paralyzed me. I hadn't been of any use at all in this first skirmish. How on earth was I going to win their trust and convince them to fight for Rendor? Wade had already warned me not to talk about hearing from the One, and he didn't know the worst of it.

I gave a small shake of my head, and Arland frowned.

"So," Wade said, "a messenger tomorrow to Tristan. We'll send out what word we can and keep gathering men." Wade paced the hard-packed earth with an eager energy that amazed me. "Let's get some rest."

"We'll be along in a minute," Arland said smoothly. "Jake, will you help me tie up this scratch?" I winced at the amount of blood soaking his tunic sleeve but nodded. Wade called an easy "good night" and headed back toward the cave.

Arland watched him stride away with affection on his face. "I think even when he's old, he'll still be young." Then he turned his attention to me, and the temperature of his gaze dropped twenty degrees. "You, on the other hand—who are you really, Jake?"

His eyes were full of angry questions. A shiver ran through me. I'd told him the truth outside the caves at Braide Wood. I didn't have any other answers.

Chapter Eighteen

JAKE

"Am I really supposed to believe that you're the Restorer?" Arland muttered the words to himself. A bitter smile twisted his face. "Another hero to desert us?"

I didn't try to answer. So far he'd kept my secret, but he wasn't happy about it. My best plan was to bind his arm and then stay out of his way.

He shrugged out of his leather vest, grimacing as he moved his shoulder.

I helped him peel his tunic away from the clotted wound on his arm. He handed me the small gourd from his belt, and I used the liquid to blot away some of the blood.

A pungent smell of alcohol hit my nose. "This isn't water."

"No, it's better. Save some for where it'll do more good." He grabbed it back from me and took a long swallow, then offered it to me.

I shook my head and returned to my examination of his wound. As far as I could tell, the bullet had only grazed him. I wasn't about to suggest poking around for any sign of it lodged in his flesh, so I wrapped his upper arm with a fresh strip of cloth.

He didn't flinch as I tied it off, but I looked up to see him studying me through hooded eyes. "Too bad I can't use your little trick," he said. "Must be handy. Instant healing of battle wounds."

The cold glint in his eyes scared me. I handed him his tunic and backed toward the cave, muttering something about letting me know if he needed help changing the dressing tomorrow. I made it only a few steps.

"Jake"—there was nothing of Wade's genial manner in the man—"come here and sit down."

Why had I been confused about the true leader of this group? Wade might act as Tristan's proxy, but Arland carried the confidence of experience and keen alertness to everything around him. His face was forged into a mask of grim determination that reminded me of Tristan. But instead of Tristan's staunch faith, Arland lived in a vortex of angry desperation.

"Not experienced at obeying orders yet, are you." No inflection.

Was he thinking of my attempts to help outside of Blue Knoll? I dragged my feet back toward him and slumped onto a boulder nearby. "I know that Wade told me to stay down when the shooting started." I braced one foot on the rock and hugged my knee. "But I wanted to help. You know what I am. I wouldn't have been permanently injured."

"And Wade doesn't know that." Now Arland's voice was silky. "You said you would tell him. I thought you had by now."

I swallowed hard. "I . . . I told Lukyan. He's helping me. But I—"

"A songkeeper? I'm sure that will be a huge help."

I winced but didn't argue.

"And in the meantime, if Wade had known the truth, he

wouldn't have ordered you to stay down." His voice was harsher now. "Maybe you could have saved Denniel."

"Who?"

Arland pushed to his feet and towered over me. "The boy who was killed. The boy we carried through a half-day's march and watched die."

His words impaled me. I sucked in a breath and felt dizzy. Was he right? Was it my fault someone had died today?

He leaned close enough for me to smell the alcohol on his breath and see the hard lines of his face in the deepening twilight. "Did you tell the king's guard where we were heading?"

My stomach lurched. "No! Wade told you— "

"Wade is only interested in protecting you."

"Not if he thought I'd betray you. He knows he can trust me."

Arland's face twisted in a snarl. "But he doesn't know everything, does he?" His look lashed me, his voice scathing. "So this is what the One sends us now."

I leaned back, reeling from his accusations.

He laughed, an ugly sound. "I thought the One had forgotten us, but it seems the truth is worse: He's mocking us."

"No. He cares about you— "

"Like your mother cared about us. But where is she now?"

Yes, where was she? Worry distracted me from Arland's tirade. If Wade was right and Cameron didn't have her in Lyric, what had happened to her? How would I find her? I'd need help from these men.

"Or Kieran?" Arland demanded. "Deserted us just like the One has."

My eyes burned, and I blinked fiercely. I could barely choke my words out. "You're wrong. Mikkel, my mom, Kieran—they were sent to help, and they did. But they're only human. Mikkel died, my mom had to go home, Kieran was sent to Hazor. They did what the One asked of them."

Arland pulled back. "So now He sends you?"

I stared at the ground. It *was* ridiculous. I saw myself in his eyes: a scrawny kid who barely knew any of the history of this world and was too timid to tell anyone about the Restorer signs. "If I tell Wade, he'll tell the rest of the men." I hated the weakness in my voice. "They still think the new Records are true and there can't be any more Restorers. Is this the best time to tell them? Will it help?" I looked up at Arland. "Tell me what you want me to do. I'll do it."

He frowned down at me, judging my sincerity, sorting out his anger toward the One and his frustration with me. Finally, he shook his head. "I don't know." The tension in his muscles softened a fraction. He turned away, and a long silence stretched between us. "I rode with her, you know."

My jaw dropped open. "At the battle of Morsal Plains?"

He nodded. "Most of these men followed her against Hazor." He gazed toward the cave, his voice growing quiet, edged with awe. "The things that happened that day . . ."

I wanted to hear more but didn't dare break into his thoughts.

He drew a slow deep breath. "We haven't forgotten. But so much has gone wrong since then." He adjusted the bandage on his arm and turned back to me. "Tomorrow I want to hear everything you can tell me about Cameron's new weapons." His tone was brisk, and I felt as though a shadow had passed by. "Go get some rest."

Relieved to have survived the conversation, I scrambled to my feet and started past him to the cave entrance. His hand snaked out and grabbed my arm. "Oh, and Jake . . ." His fingers dug into my bicep as he jerked me to face him. "If I find out you betrayed us, I'll cut you into so many pieces that no Restorer power will be able to put you back together."

The adrenaline that shot through me left me tossing for hours on the hard cave floor.

A haunting melody woke me the next day. I rubbed sand-crusted eyes and looked around the cave. I was alone. No one had bothered to rouse me from where I had huddled under my blanket against the far wall of the cavern. So much for winning the trust of this group. A plaintive tenor voice warbled from outside. The minor key and the flickering phrase endings reminded me of an Appalachian folk song we learned in chorus my senior year.

I rolled to my feet, dusted grit from my clothes, and cautiously ducked out into the morning light. More voices had joined the first. I followed the sound to an open area around the side of the cave.

Most of the men focused inward, gathered in an uneven circle. Only a few stood apart, alert and on guard. But even they joined the singing. I eased my way toward the circle. The men on watch tracked me with their eyes but didn't wave me back.

Was it their custom to have a morning worship time? If so, it was a somber start to the day. I could follow the words of the song now.

In the gray of our despair,
The One will bring a light,
When our battle ends,
And we face our longest night.

Sweet life or bitter death,
He yet remains our Tower,
Facing our last journey
Held by His love and power.

I stepped into a gap between two of the guardians and caught my breath.

Denniel's body was on the ground, still garbed in a blood-soaked tunic, skin white and empty of life. His hands had been crossed over his heart. During my childhood battle with cancer, I'd shared a hospital room with boys who had looked almost this pale. Yet even then, the breath of struggle and fire of life animated their bodies.

This was like seeing a crumpled wrapper tossed aside, useless. I wanted to turn away. Arland's accusation replayed in my mind. Was this man dead because of me? Was there anything I could have done differently? I forced myself to stay, letting the melancholy tune twist pain deep into my heart.

As the song finished, heavy, uneven voices joined in a creed I recognized from the Verses.

Awesome in majesty
Is the One eternal.
Perfect in His might and power,
The only truth and only source,
He made all that is and loves all He made;
His works are beyond our understanding.

Arland stepped forward with a small cloth-wrapped bundle and handed it to one of the younger men. "Safe journey to the Gray Hills. Let his family know we honored him in life and death." Arland's jaw shifted, and I thought he was going to say more, but he gave a terse nod, and the boy left immediately. Another of the men handed something to Arland. It was a small white block, similar to the light cubes some of the men from Rendor used. Arland crouched down and placed it under Denniel's hands.

I shuddered as I watched him touching the lifeless shell of a man who had been sharpening his dagger, joking with friends, and tramping confidently through the ferns just yesterday.

Arland slid a lever on the side of the cube. "Go with the One," he said. He pushed himself heavily to his feet and stepped back into the circle. A low hum rose from the object.

The buzzing reminded me of the portal, and panic flashed through me. I glanced around the circle of men.

They waited with somber faces, gazes fixed on Denniel. Light grew in the cube, from a soft glow to a blaze that seared my retinas. The humming built to a sharp crack.

I threw my arm over my face and turned my head away. When I squinted back to the clearing, all that was left was a small oval of ashes. No one else showed any surprise. One by one, men slipped away from the circle.

I stood frozen, staring at the gray dust, empty and shaken.

The sounds of morning chores and murmuring voices drifted from behind me.

Verses from my own world spun in my head. "To me, to live is Christ and to die is gain." Brave words that I thought I'd always believed. After all, few of my friends had come as close to death as I had as a child. Cancer had forced me to do a lot of thinking about life and death, and I'd quoted those words many times, believing I understood them better than most. Now I tasted my own dread.

I wanted to beg one of the men to lead me to Lyric so I could find the portal and go home. Dad and I would formulate a new plan to find Mom, and the One could send someone else to fight Cameron and save Rendor.

Do You really want me here, God?

The clearing was silent and the morning air chill.

I took a shuddering breath and tore my eyes away from the bed of ashes.

Arland stood across the clearing from me, waiting. Everyone else had gone, but he watched me, arms crossed, expression shuttered. "Ready?"

I wanted to snarl at him, *No, I'm not ready. I'm not ready to face the things that are happening. I'm not ready to fulfill this role.* Instead, I nodded and turned to leave the clearing.

"Come with me." Arland's expression gave nothing away. "Keep quiet and pay attention." I blinked at him, confused.

He stepped closer, impatience twitching his face. "Can you do that?" He studied my face. "Have you eaten?"

The thought of food made my stomach lurch. "No, thank you," I managed.

I stuck close to Arland as he wound his way among the men.

"Any sign we're being tracked?" he asked one of the guardians who had lagged behind to scout yesterday. At the negative reply, he sent the man back out to watch for any approaching trouble. "How are supplies?" he asked another.

"Low, as always," came the curt answer.

Arland nodded. "Take three of the men with you to hunt, but don't go near any villages."

The man jumped up.

One by one, Arland interacted with each of the men,

collecting information, issuing orders, even dispensing a quiet word of encouragement to some.

I shadowed him, flinching under curious stares and trying to absorb all I could.

"Wade, Ian," he called at last. "With me." Arland led us up the rocky ridgeline to a point where we could watch the campsite.

Wade's genial energy was subdued this morning, but he gave me a smile and asked how I'd slept.

Ian scowled at me. "Do you think it's wise discussing anything in front of the boy? He's the one who knew where we were. A convenient ambush if you ask me."

"I told you; he was with me." Wade adjusted his bulk on a rock ledge and glared at Ian. "He means you no harm. You could just as well accuse *me* of telling Cameron where you were."

Arland watched the argument, then shot a knowing look in my direction. "Ian, I understand your concerns. But right now"—he paused on the word—"he's useful. The weapons the king's guard were using came from his home."

"Do they work like syncbeams?" Wade jumped in. He looked at Ian. "We could build a disrupter like Skyler did at Morsal Plains."

Three faces turned to me: one eager, one speculative, and one suspicious.

I cleared my throat. "I don't think you can build a field like that. They aren't like syncbeams. They work with a different kind of energy." I floundered, doing my best to describe guns and how they worked. The three men were surprisingly patient with me. "What I don't understand is how they have so many of them," I said when they ran out of questions I could answer. "Cameron brought only a few bags of gear through the—that is . . ." I kicked at a pebble. "He couldn't have that many. And he'll run out of ammunition soon."

"Unless that's part of what he has all the transtechs doing," Ian said. "I say we attack Cameron in Lyric now, before he can create more weapons."

Wade shook his head. "We need to gather more men and wait for orders."

Arland turned to me. "And what do you think, Jake?"

To Ian and Wade it sounded like an innocuous question. They didn't recognize the challenge underneath his words. I wasn't going to let Arland twist me in knots any longer. I sat up tall. "Wade, Tristan is going to meet us soon, right?"

Ian's brows drew together, but Wade nodded. "We should get word by tomorrow."

I faced Arland squarely. "So let's wait for Tristan." Tristan would help me find my mom. He'd tell me how and when to declare myself as the Restorer. He wouldn't let Arland blame me for things that weren't my fault.

The rugged guardian tipped his head in acknowledgement, but his eyes were hard. "A sound plan."

"Unless he's trying to keep us here so Cameron's men can find us again," Ian said.

Wade stiffened, ready to take up that argument.

"Ian," Arland interrupted. "I've heard Jake has some transtech skills. I'm assigning him to assist you. You can keep an eye on him, and he can help you with repairs you're making. And later today you can do some more sword training with him."

My eyes widened. What was he thinking? Bad idea.

"I can work with the boy." Wade rose.

I sighed with relief. Having a house protector came in handy sometimes.

"No, I need your help with something else. Ian will take care of him." Arland's voice was bland, but satisfaction gleamed in his eyes. He nudged his chin in the direction of the path. "Head back to camp."

Ian nodded at Arland, and then his eyes raked me. "Come on."

Wade's voice faded into grumbling noise as I followed Ian back down the ridge. He ignored the few guardians still busy around the clearing, led me into the cave, and overturned a large pack at my feet. A confusing array of gadgets and parts littered the hard ground. He sank to his knees and rummaged in a pouch for tools. "Get busy, Jake."

I looked at the cave entrance, wondering how long a walk it was to Lyric.

"You aren't going anywhere." Ian's tight voice did little to mask the seething anger he felt toward me.

All I could do for now was make myself useful. I sank to the cave floor and picked up a smooth white cylinder with a clip like a carabiner on one end. "What's this?"

"It's a signaler," Ian said just as my finger found a recessed lever.

Instantly, a blaring shriek filled the cavern. Ian launched himself at me, knocking me to the ground.

The shock of the noise and the collision of my skull against rock left me stunned.

Ian pried the gadget from my hand and turned it off. He hauled me up by the front of my tunic as several men charged into the cave, swords drawn.

I squinted against the throbbing in my head.

Arland shouldered his way through the men. "What's going on?"

Ian gave me a shake and turned to Arland. "He couldn't get away to tell Cameron where we are, so he found another way to reveal our location." Disgust dripped from his words, but the look he turned on the men was triumphant. "I told you we couldn't trust him."

Chapter Nineteen

JAKE

A semicircle of hardened faces stared at me with open animosity.

I searched past the ring of men for Wade but didn't see him. Not a single ally in the group. This was not good.

Ian slid a dagger from his boot sheath, and his eyes glinted with the same sheen as the metal. A rumbling sound rose from the men like the growl of a hungry tiger. They were out for blood.

I wrenched free from Ian's grip and darted past him, diving for the entrance to the cave.

Sinewy hands grabbed me with the same power they used when wielding swords and threw me back toward Ian.

"No!" I shouted. "It was an accident. He—"

Ian twisted my arm behind me and forced me to my knees. Arland braced one hand on the cave wall and watched impassively.

"Where's Wade?" I writhed to untangle myself from Ian's grip.

"Gag him," Ian ordered.

"No. Just listen to me. I was only—"

Ian wrenched my arm harder.

I gasped, pain spiking through my shoulder.

One of the men pulled a strip of cloth over my mouth, the knot tangling in my hair as he jerked it tight. Ian bound my wrists behind me with a leather cord. Arland didn't move as he watched my struggle. "I sent Wade to meet Tristan and bring him here." Expressionless, he pushed away from the cave wall. "But now we won't be able to wait for them. Break camp." His calm order stirred instant activity as the men scattered. Ian's blade pressed cold against my throat.

My wild pulse beat against the steel as if my artery were jumping out to meet it. I strained away, but Ian had a firm grip on my arm. My neck couldn't bend any further.

The light from the entrance dimmed as Arland sauntered forward to stand over me, blocking the sight of the world beyond this cave.

"Don't do this. You know it's not true." Those were the words I tried to speak, but only a muffled groan made it past the gag. What were they thinking? Ian had heard me ask what the signaler was. He knew I didn't mean to set it off. Why was he doing this? And was Arland going to let Ian slit my throat? Gray static flickered around the edge of my vision, and I tried to draw in more air through my nose. This wasn't fair.

"We can leave his body here," Ian said. "A message for Cameron's men when they show up."

I screamed against the fabric in my mouth.

Arland cuffed me with an almost casual blow, knocking me to the ground and away from Ian's knife. "No, he knew about the long-range weapons. He may know more about Cameron's plans. Bring him."

Ian hissed a protest but yanked me to my feet.

My own aggravation matched Ian's and then some. Arland had just admitted I'd told them everything I knew about the weapons Cameron was using. Didn't that prove I was trying to help them? Ian might believe I was a king's spy, but Arland had to know better. He knew who I really was. Why wasn't he defending me? Was he still trying to force my hand?

Ian shoved me out of the cave. Hunting parties and scouts raced into the clearing. They'd heard the signal and thought it was a call to arms. Arland explained what had happened and the necessity for another fast relocation. Most of the men jumped into urgent preparations to hit the trail again, but more bitter glares were directed at me. If I could just explain the truth.

I tugged frantically at the binding on my wrist and bucked against Ian's grip on my arms, almost breaking free from him.

He shifted his hold and punched me square in the stomach.

I doubled over, choking for breath against the gag.

Arland turned from jamming gear into a pack and watched my struggle with Ian. He strode over to us and grabbed a fistful of my hair, pulling my head up so his bleak eyes could meet mine. "You had your chance to tell the truth." His voice was soft, but veins pulsed at his temples.

We both knew it was an excuse. It wouldn't have mattered if I'd told all the men about my Restorer signs earlier—my very existence infuriated Arland. Why? I wasn't much, but the One had sent me. Why couldn't he take that as a sign of hope?

He didn't flinch from the desperation in my eyes. "Keep him alive," he told Ian. "That shouldn't be too hard," he added in a sour undertone meant for only my ears. Then he called to the men. "Move out."

Ian seemed to take delight in watching me struggle on the

rugged climb down from the camp. Without my hands for support, I skidded several times on the steep terrain, my body coming down hard against rocks with no way to break my fall. Things didn't improve as we began a fast-paced hike through jagged canyons. Every time my steps lagged, Ian shoved me hard enough to crash me to my knees. I considered trying to break away and run, but he was looking for excuses to hurt me. Too many more injuries, and it would become obvious I was healing.

I used to love watching police dramas on television. I'd sympathize with the cop on the side of justice who went a bit far in roughing up a criminal. After all, he knew the guy was guilty as sin and deserved much worse, and he was only trying to solve the crime. I suddenly felt a new sympathy for the bad guys.

We stopped for a brief rest, and Ian pulled the gag down long enough to give me some water.

"Thank you," I rasped.

He started to tug the fabric back into place.

"Why do you hate me so much?" I blurted out. "If you're from Rendor, you had to have known my dad."

He tightened the gag with unnecessary force. "Oh, yes. I knew your father well. Though how he has a child your age . . ." He swigged from his water gourd. "He was your age when he disappeared from Lyric. That was three years ago."

I mumbled against the cloth in my mouth and bobbed my head.

He ignored my gestured offer to explain. Since Arland wasn't calling everyone forward yet, Ian pulled his dagger from its sheath and grabbed a twig to whittle. He peeled long strips away with the blade. It seemed to soothe him.

At least he wasn't releasing his stress by testing his knife on me.

"Has your father told you about Ravon?"

I searched my memory. I couldn't place the name. Was it a clan? A city? I gave a tentative shake of my head.

Ian dug a deep gouge from the wood, jaw clenched. "When your father ran from his guardian training and went to apprentice with the Council in Rendor, he was assigned a house protector. Kahlareans had been after him for years."

Okay, I knew some of the story.

"Ravon was a good man. My sister met him when he did his second-year training in Rendor. I'd never seen her so happy. They were planning to wed, but first Ravon needed to finish his assignment in Lyric." Ian paused to look at me. "Guarding your father."

Eyes wide, I leaned forward. For the first time, I could see beyond the bitter anger and disgust Ian constantly directed toward me. There was a festering injury fueling it.

"Ravon never returned. He was killed by a Kahlarean venblade that was meant for your father. My sister still grieves for him."

I listened, helpless. With the stupid gag in place, I couldn't even tell him how sorry I was.

He snapped the remains of the twig and tossed it aside. "Next we heard, Markkel had disappeared. Run away somewhere. It was all for nothing." He sheathed his boot knife and launched to his feet. He hoisted me up by my arms. They screamed in protest, strained and numb from being tied so long. "And now you come along claiming to be his son."

I made a sound in my throat and nodded my head.

Ian snorted. "Yeah, Wade explained it. Even if it's true, forgive me for not being thrilled to have you turn up." His tone darkened. "I have a score to settle with your father. Since the coward's not here, I'll have to make due with his son."

Outrage wrenched through me, and common sense snapped like a thread. My father was no coward. I roared and drove my head into Ian's chest with all the force I could muster, sending him crashing backward. I landed on top of him and slammed my head against his.

He flung me onto my back, my own weight crushing my tied arms. His knife was in his hand again. "Fine, then we'll settle it now." His words were a strangled knot of fury. "For Ravon and Ailyn and the life they'll never have together." His hand drew back.

I braced for the strike of the blade.

"Hold." Arland's quiet command froze us in a lethal tableau.

Ian turned his head slowly and looked up at his commander, the blood haze clearing from his eyes. Arland offered him a hand and helped him to his feet. "I need him alive for now." There was no rebuke, only sympathetic understanding. "I'll watch him for this next leg of the march." Ian gave me one more killing glare and fell in with the men who were moving out.

Arland stared down at me. "You can't stay out of trouble, can you?"

The injustice of that comment drove another muffled yell from my throat.

He lifted his dark eyebrows, unimpressed with my indignation. "On your feet."

He offered no assistance as I rolled to my side and struggled to get my legs under me and stagger upright. Once I was standing, I glared at him, breathing hard through my nose.

"Any more tantrums, and I'll let Ian practice his carving skills on you." Arland's mouth quirked in speculation. "What do you think he'll do when he sees you heal?"

Horror washed through me again. They wouldn't kill a Restorer, would they? I watched the men marching out, their frustration as ever-present as the heavy gray sky. Ian might. He was angry enough. And how long would it take to kill me? I remembered the stories about my grandfather Mikkel. They claimed he was stabbed fifty times or more.

My head drooped forward as I set out after the column of men. Arland followed close at my heels. At least he didn't shove me like Ian had.

Drizzle began to waft down, and I savored the cool touch against all the aching scrapes and bruises that hadn't finished healing. Soon the rain fell hard, and I struggled to keep my footing on slick rocks and hard-packed mud. My mind slipped along in a path as unforgiving as the landscape.

Nothing was going the way I'd planned. I still didn't know if my mom had gotten away from Cameron and was safe at home. And what response was Lukyan getting as he sent out word that the new Records were fakes? Was he all right? Had Linette made it safely back to Sidian? My mind dwelt on her for several bright minutes. I heard her words again. *Jake, if the One has called you to be the new Restorer, He'll show you what to do.*

Show me. Please show me.

Tristan and Wade would join us soon. I needed to stay alive until then. They'd listen to me. We'd come up with a plan to stop Cameron and reclaim Rendor from the Kahlareans. I thought about Ian's bitter anger. It was the Kahlareans who killed Ravon and my grandfather. We were all on the same side: Ian, the guardians, and I. Tristan would show Ian who the real enemy was. He'd convince Arland to trust the One.

Show me Your plan. Be with me.

Rain weighted my eyelashes, and I blinked against the cloud of water beating down in front of us. It seemed thicker than a normal downpour. I couldn't see the other men up ahead. A fog began to swirl around my feet; the trail disappeared, and I slowed, confused. Mist welled up around me. I expected Arland to bark an order or jostle me onward, but he had vanished as well.

The mist wrapped around me like my favorite sweatshirt. I couldn't step forward—didn't know where forward was anymore. A sense of peace arrived with a soft pressure that drove me to my knees. I sank to the ground. This was the same holy presence I'd sensed in the grove outside of Lyric. I forgot my bound wrists, my bruises, the unjust anger that had lacerated me. My awareness filled with the One: the same One who inspired the awkward poems in my notebook at home; the One who breathed comfort into my heart those many nights in a hospital bed when I was a child; the One who was calling me to be a Restorer for my father's people in this world.

I didn't hear an audible voice, but He spoke anyway. As I thought about my mother, a stilling hand calmed my mind with an impression that it wasn't my task. Instead, urgency pulsed through me to spread the news that Cameron's Records were a lie. This time more direction unfolded.

Rendor appeared like a photo in the mist—the clan I had never seen. Tall buildings of wood and clear windows rose up near a wide river. Homes stood empty. Kahlareans sauntered through the streets. Compelling purpose welled up inside me. The clan had to be rescued. No space remained in my thoughts for doubt. This was why He'd brought me here.

Deep breaths pulled the mist into my body until I was saturated with peace. Time stopped. Love wrapped around me and shut out all my confusion and fear.

The visions in the mist disappeared first; then the tufts of fog swirled away. I was kneeling on a rock-strewn trail again, rugged cliffs boxing me in from each side. Arland circled from behind and crouched down to face me.

I lifted my head, hoping he would think the moisture on my face was rain.

His cheeks were bloodless, eyes wide. "What was that? What happened?"

I could only shake my head, my own body still trembling with the awe of the One drawing close in a tangible way.

Arland pulled the gag away. I tried to answer him, but my throat was dry. He pulled out his canteen and guided some water into my mouth.

"Thank you." I didn't want to try to explain. I didn't want his sneering rebukes to spoil the peace I still felt in my very lungs. "He was here. The One."

Arland's voice was barely above a whisper. "What did He show you?"

So much. So little that I could explain. I tried to shrug but winced at the pain in my shoulders. "Different things. But I know I'm meant to help Rendor."

Arland studied me with a clenched jaw. "How?"

The edge of my mouth pulled up. "I don't know."

Weary lines added heaviness to Arland's face. He was a guardian who had sworn to follow the Verses and protect his people. He had ridden with my mother to defeat Hazor. He was a good man baffled by the inexplicable disasters that had come in the past several seasons—not sure whom to trust. I got that.

"The One is with you." I felt the steel of truth in my voice.

Arland sucked in a sharp breath as if I'd punched him. Then

he reached forward, slid the gag back in place, and pulled me to my feet. "Come on. We're falling behind." But there was no harshness in his manner. I wondered if he could feel the peace that still beat inside my pulse.

After another hour, the rain stopped. The effects of my encounter began to lift, and I wished I could pull back the happy daze I'd experienced. I was hungry and exhausted, and my arms ached from their unnatural position. The terrain gave me no clue of where we were hiking.

Striding alongside me in grim silence, Arland had gone back to regarding me as a troublesome piece of cargo and finally left me in Ian's care again. The last vestiges of my peace fled under Ian's shoves and grumbled insults.

As the glow of reassurance from the One faded, I thought of Arland's question: "How?" The One had confirmed that He was present and had given me a sense of His purpose for me. But why couldn't He give me some specifics to work with?

I still didn't know when to declare myself as the Restorer. I didn't know how to convince the men to take a stand against the Kahlareans. I didn't know where my mother was, and the One's reassurance that He was caring for her suddenly didn't feel like enough.

Ian gave me a vicious jab, sending me stumbling forward again.

How? How exactly was I supposed to accomplish any grand purpose? I was bound and gagged and surrounded by men who believed I'd betrayed them—or hated me for other reasons.

I concentrated on putting one foot in front of the other, shutting out Ian's comments with one firm thought.

Stay alive until Wade and Tristan catch up. Everything will be fine then.

Chapter Twenty

JAKE

Arland relented enough to untie me at supper, keeping me separated from the rest of the men. He stood over me, sword drawn, as I choked down some stew and bread. My arms burned as circulation returned to them, but I fought to hide the pain.

"Does Wade know where to find us?" I asked in a hoarse whisper.

Arland buffed an invisible smudge on his sword and then studied me. The crease in his forehead deepened. Finally he gave a small nod. "He knew where we'd head next. They should meet us here tomorrow."

Hope revved up my pulse. "Where are we?"

Again, Arland considered before answering. "Near Corros."

"Where Hazor rode out to attack Lyric?" My parents had filled me in on that event. I'd been in Lyric at the time, but couldn't remember much because of Medea's control over my mind during those days.

Arland nodded.

So we were close to Lyric. Maybe the guardians planned to follow Ian's suggestion and attack Cameron in the capital.

Despite divulging that much information, Arland hadn't softened toward me. He made sure the leather cords were firmly in place when he cinched me to a tree.

I spent a miserable night sitting braced against the trunk, dozing for a few seconds at a time before my head would bob forward and wake me again. It was worse than sleeping on the school bus during the cross-country drive to a youth group camping trip. My back cramped with pain. Ian had everyone convinced that I'd do all I could to call attention to our hiding place, so the wretched gag stayed in place, leaving my mouth pasty with a dry taste like burlap.

When the makeshift camp stirred to life the next morning, the hostile glares and threatening glowers fired my direction hit me with the sting of paintballs. I had assumed Arland kept me apart from the rest of the men so I couldn't win their support or trust. But maybe he was just trying to keep me alive.

I hadn't been particularly popular in high school. Not much of an athlete, except for using my speed and agility in soccer. Too straight-laced to fit with the fringe crowd. Too awkward by half. But, though I sometimes felt alienated or ignored, I'd never been despised by everyone around me like this.

They don't know the truth about me. Their opinions don't matter.

Still, their scorn made me shrink inside.

Arland's mud-spattered boots planted themselves in my line of vision, and I forced my head up. He looked as grumpy as ever, but I was glad to see him. Sure, his power over my fate was a constant threat. But twice now he'd stopped Ian from killing me. Maybe he wasn't as ready to write off the promised Restorer as he tried to be.

He untied me and led me through the woods that

surrounded the camp to a stream, where he stood guard while I drank deeply and splashed a few layers of grime off my face and arms. He stayed alert, as if expecting me to attack or run. He had a lot more faith in my strength than I did.

I had no weapons, and my legs barely supported me. With the cords removed, ligature marks on my arms began to heal, but my muscles were slower to recover from the long, painful night.

Arland perched on a tree stump, spine relaxed, but eyes watchful. "We'll stay here today to wait for Wade and Tristan."

I was wary of how to respond. I shook wet hair back from my face and straightened, kneading a fist into my lower back. "Sounds good."

He frowned. "I don't know. Yesterday the men were distracted with the hike. But a few dozen angry guardians who feel betrayed and have time on their hands . . ."

It didn't take much imagination to follow his thoughts. The cold water in my stomach hardened to ice. I looked at him more closely.

Hollow eyes burned in their sockets as if his sleep had been as poor as mine last night. He acknowledged my worry with a brief nod. "I'll do what I can to keep you out of sight."

That small hint of support thawed some of the chill in my gut.

True to his word, Arland positioned me deep under a wide-branched tree away from most of the activity in the improvised guardian base. When he tied me, he left a little more play in the cord. Then he held up the gag. I couldn't restrain a moan.

He ignored that and pushed my head forward, knotting the fabric firmly in place. "Don't do anything to draw attention to yourself, understand?"

I could only nod.

Arland stalked away to organize the morning's activities. He sent most of the men out foraging or patrolling but stayed within sight.

I whiled away time by experimenting with some of my heightened senses. I watched the progress of a shiny beetle deep in the woods on the far side of the clearing. Next I focused on quiet conversations I shouldn't have been able to hear. At first, the jumble of voices made my head ache, but I kept practicing, directing my focus and learning to shut out extraneous sounds.

"I've family in Lyric," one grizzled man was saying. "Hard to think of being this near to them."

"Are we really that close?" Ian asked. He was reassembling a heat trivet, tools spread out around him on the ground. I'd been making it a point to keep track of Ian, relieved that so far he hadn't even glanced in my direction.

"Mm-hmm." The old man handed a long, metal-tipped tool to Ian. "Just over that ridge you'd see the open plains of Corros Fields."

When I tired of eavesdropping on random conversations, I closed my eyes and talked to the One. I composed more verses to the poem I'd begun about Lyric. While I was wrestling with a phrase that wasn't quite right, the earth vibrated with the pounding of approaching hooves.

Arland turned from a conversation with one of the men and drew his sword, running out to meet whoever was approaching. Ian left his gear to watch Arland's back. They left the clearing and my line of sight, but I closed my eyes and focused on the sounds. A lehkan skittered as it was reined in, and the thud of heavy feet hit the ground.

"Wade. Well met. Where's Tristan?" Arland's voice.

An exasperated sigh. "Not coming. Zarek has Sidian sealed up tight—nervous about what's happening in the clans. Tristan got a messenger out to tell me, but he didn't dare leave Kendra in Zarek's power, and she can't travel. Where's Jake?"

Someone growled. Probably Ian.

Arland cut in smoothly. "I'll fill you in. But first, what word did he send?"

"He appoints the command of the guardians to your care." My imagination filled in the picture of Wade thrusting his shoulders back in respect. "He recommends going ahead with the plan, but leaves it to your discretion."

"And you'll follow me?" Arland asked in a measured tone.

"Of course." Wade sounded confused. "Now where's Jake?"

"Dead if I had my way," Ian said. "We know he's working for Cameron." He gave a twisted account of what had happened yesterday, along with all his speculations of my intent to lead the king's guards to them. Wade interrupted with questions.

Arland spoke low, and I strained to the limit of my hearing to catch his words. "I know you swore to protect his house. But your first loyalty is to our people. I can't let Jake keep us from our plans." The fact that there was genuine regret in Arland's voice didn't comfort me at all. He might shed a tear at my funeral, but I'd still be dead. "He's a danger we can't afford. I'm sorry."

Come on, Wade. Tell him off. Remind him of everything my parents did for the clans. Or at least offer to take me away from here if they refuse to trust me.

Instead I heard a heavy sigh and Wade's voice, subdued and weary: "I understand."

My hope crumpled like a pop can crushed in an angry fist.

"Should I kill him now?" That was Ian.

"Or we could trade him to Cameron." Arland's voice was

matter of fact. "Might buy us something we need. I have to think Cameron would pay well for the return of his ally. Might get him off our back for a time while we build our strength."

The shock broke my concentration, and I lost my link to the voices. But I'd heard enough.

I worked frantically at the cords around my wrists, scraping them against the bark and scouring layers of skin off my hands at the same time. I barely felt the pain, aware of nothing but the snap as one of the bindings broke. In seconds I scrambled free and ripped the gag from my mouth. I was deep enough in the shadows to avoid notice. The few men in the clearing hadn't looked my way.

Darting from tree to tree, I skirted the camp. The old guardian who had been talking with Ian earlier had wandered away, so I risked a few steps forward to grab Ian's pack. When he had dumped his pile of gadgets yesterday, a scrambler had rested in the mix of broken gear. Could come in handy. I threw the pack over one shoulder and headed for the ridge that was supposed to offer a view of Corros Fields.

Using my heightened senses, I slipped past two of the men patrolling the perimeter. As soon as I was far enough not to worry about silence, I flew into a desperate sprint. I had meant to pace myself, but I was too terrified for that.

The old guardian had been right. From the top of the ridge I could see the open fields and gray-green rolling hills of Corros. Far in the distance, the towers of Lyric pierced the horizon line.

With a mountain bike I could cut straight across and get there in a few hours. But I didn't have my bike, and I didn't dare venture into the open. Wade had a lehkan. I'd never be able to outrun him if I was spotted. And who knew what kind of patrols Cameron had on watch near Lyric?

I stayed along the forest's edge and ran harder than I'd ever run in my life. When I couldn't draw enough breath and my legs trembled, I paused to listen for sounds of pursuit. There were soft rustles in the underbrush, too distant and scattered to sort out. I tried to stretch my hearing further, but the sounds all blended into a mess of ambient noise. They could be right behind me, or might still be at the camp.

I staggered back up into a lurching jog. Brambles tore at me, and at times I felt as though I were swimming through the tall grasses and ferns. Since I couldn't risk the open plains, I finally cut deeper into the woods where the undergrowth wasn't as thick. Then I grew frightened of losing my way and edged back toward the fields.

Sheer exertion finally burned away some of my terror, although my heart raced into hyperdrive with each cracking twig or unidentified sound. Rain fell in a hazy wall across the fields. I lifted my face, mouth open, and caught a little moisture, which only made me thirstier. No time to rifle Ian's pack looking for a canteen. Not yet.

Lyric seemed to draw further into the distance in the afternoon rain, and I longed to sink to the ground and give up. But I settled into a rhythm of running until my ribs ached, then trudging just long enough to catch my breath and get my bearings. By the time the rain eased, I was approaching the thick forests along the side of Lyric. Kieran had camped here when he was hiding from the Kahlareans. I'd followed him to his campsite then. I wondered if I could find the spot again.

My calves strained as I cut upward into the hills. I found the clearing where Kieran had first jumped me. A small stream still tumbled past exactly where I had remembered it, and I whispered a prayer of thanks as I drank all I could. Next I gathered a wall of bracken and wedged my body under an overhang, pulling the brush around me as a shield. This is where I'd slept the night when I'd hurt my ankle, with Kieran keeping watch in a tree nearby.

He had been a strange and frightening companion, but I wished he were here now. Or my dad. This would have gone so differently if Dad had made it through the portal with me. That thought started such a deep ache that I distracted myself by digging into the pack I'd stolen from Ian. There was a cloak rolled into a tight sausage in the bottom. I wrapped it around myself and curled into a ball as night lowered onto the woods.

Now that I wasn't running, wounding feelings of betrayal caught up to me.

Ian had a grudge against my dad. He had either set me up, or really believed that I was trying to give away their position to Cameron. It was unfair, but I could almost understand him. Of course it wasn't easy to justify anyone who cheerfully volunteered to kill me.

Wade's refusal to defend me stung much worse. I had a basic understanding of the vows of house protector. His return to the guardian camp was supposed to fix everything. But apparently his loyalty to the guardians came before protecting me.

Arland—hearing him casually suggest bartering me to Cameron—that wound gouged the deepest. He was the only guardian who knew about my Restorer signs. He'd seen them himself. He had even been with me when the One gathered me into visions in the mist. Still I was only a bargaining chip to him. My life had no value to any of them.

Black despair settled on me along with the darkened sky.

One more thought stirred, feeding the bitterness in my

heart. I'd only come here to rescue Mom. But the One had called me to do more. And it was for their sakes. For people like Ian, and Wade, and Arland. I was supposed to be their Restorer. And I'd just overheard them calmly discussing whether to kill me themselves or let Cameron do it.

A small rock dug into my shoulder, and I shifted my weight.

Tomorrow, I'd make my way to the grove outside of Lyric and find the portal entrance. I was sick of having my prayers answered with vague impressions and visions—fed up following guidance that led me into more danger. I didn't care about these people and their politics. What did it matter if Cameron was king, or the Kahlareans encroached on the clans? I had proven over and over that I was the wrong person for this job.

I was going home.

Chapter Twenty-One

JAKE

Hoods and masks obscured their faces, but I could still make out dark, bulbous eyes against the unnatural whiteness of their skin. Kahlarean assassins. Dad had told me about them, and I'd thought they sounded like characters from a bad sci-fi movie. Now five of them floated toward me in complete silence.

Terror twisted my throat. How had they found me? Where was the underbrush that had covered my hiding place? I pressed back against the rock face behind me.

In unison, like some demented drill team, they each lifted one arm toward me. Loose sleeves shifted to reveal white-knobbed knuckles. Their hands clutched twisted daggers. Venblades.

I willed myself to charge past them, but fear held me paralyzed as if their lethal blades had already scored my skin. "What do you want?" My voice was a strangled croak.

They moved closer, and I realized there was no ridge behind me. I was standing in a mountain pass. The roar of a waterfall drowned out my panting breaths. I stumbled back a step, throwing my arms in front of me. My right hand moved heavily, and I realized it was clutching a sword. I stared at the weapon in confusion as—almost of its own volition—it sliced the air, holding the assassins at bay.

Strength raced from the rocky ground and into my spine. "You cannot have them!" I shouted. My voice had gained power along with my muscles. Somehow I knew that behind me were the forests of Rendor and I was meant to stand in this gap and hold back the destroyers of the clans.

The eyes of the lead Kahlarean squinted, and his head shook slightly. He made a strange hissing sound. Laughter. His hand lifted and snapped forward. The venblade spun through the air. My eyes tracked its movements as it whirled past my defenses and into my heart.

The pain was bruising instead of sharp.

I jerked into wakefulness, my hand moving toward the painful place on my chest. It was only a sharp stone that I had rolled onto in my sleep. I shuddered and curled into a tight ball, pulling Ian's cloak over my head, too weary to wake fully and think about the disturbing dream.

Other than the nightmare, I slept hard through the night. There's a lot to be said for not being tied to a tree. In the morning light I jolted awake, surprised to be safe and free. But once I fully remembered where I was, the weight of the choices I faced crashed down on me with new force. Should I stick with my decision to return home? Maybe I should reconsider. Then I pictured the grim faces of the outlawed guardians. Wade was unwilling to defend me. Arland barely hid his unreasoning anger toward me for not being more than I was. Cold resentment spread through me like frost on a car's windshield. I shook sleep from my head and left my nest. No more agonizing over decisions. I was going home.

In the clearing, I upended Ian's pack and studied the assortment of gadgets. Dad had boasted that Rendor enjoyed technology more than any other clan and produced more transtechs than even the capital city of Lyric. I recognized light cubes and a heat trivet. Most of the objects hadn't yet been repaired, but there was a working scrambler.

I turned it in my hands, and my heart beat more quickly. I could slip into Lyric. I knew the location of at least one hidden door. I could find out what was happening about the Records and Cameron and Rendor. My skin tingled with that inner urging again. I had a flash of vision—the feel of a sword in my hand, the roar of a waterfall, masked faces advancing through a rocky pass.

I jammed everything back into the pack. Must be remnants of my nightmare. Rendor meant nothing to me. This world would do nothing but hurt me. I shouldered the pack. Mom and Dad might enjoy seeing the contents. I didn't let myself think about the possibility that Mom hadn't found her way back yet.

The nudge hummed inside me again.

Use the scrambler; slip into Lyric. Tell people the truth. You can make a difference.

Slamming the door on those thoughts, I made my way down through the woods. Lyric glistened in the morning light. The tallest tower stood firm, visible above the walls.

You are here for a purpose.

I turned away from the city and ran across open land to the grove that sheltered the portal. Had it been only a few days ago that I knelt here and asked for direction? My conscience prickled. I rolled my shoulders and shrugged it off. I had followed the guidance I'd received then and every day since. And everything had gone wrong.

Time to make my own decisions.

As I wound my way through the dense branches, the hunger to be home drowned out every other thought, including caution. The narrow gap in the trees came into view, and a huge grin spread across my face. I bounded forward.

An obstacle swung out of nowhere and slammed into my stomach.

I doubled over, fighting for air. Polished boots swam into my vision. My gaze traveled upward. Black trousers, a rust-colored tunic, a wide array of weapons, and the hard, expressionless face of a king's guard blocked my view of the portal.

Another guard grabbed my arms from behind and wrenched the pack from my shoulder. The electrical tingle of the portal's field crawled on my skin like a thousand daddy longlegs. Didn't they feel it? It was so close.

I tugged against the man holding me, straining to draw a ragged breath.

"Who are you, and why are you here?" the guard in front of me asked.

He had no idea how complex that question was. I struggled to formulate an answer.

The guard tossed my pack to his companion, who pawed through it with interest. He looked at me again. "Are you a transtech? What are you doing outside of Lyric?"

My head spun. Cameron had gathered transtechs from all the clans to work for him. The guard's guess made sense and was less dangerous than the truth.

I concentrated on looking harmless—not much of a

stretch. I was unarmed, scrawny, and hunched over my bruised diaphragm. "I just wanted to go for a walk."

"We should take him back to the king's crew. Let them deal with him." The voice behind me sounded bored. Standing around a deserted grove must not be elite guard duty.

"No." The man in front of me frowned. His tunic was unwrinkled, his hair shorter than the norm, and there was something familiar about his stiff posture.

I finally made the connection. Substitute a gray suit for the uniform and add a notebook in hand, and he would easily fit in on an FBI television drama. He studied me now as if comparing my face to a "Most Wanted" poster.

"Remember what happened the last time the grove was left unguarded? No one knows where those guards were reassigned," he said.

"But this isn't the one the king is watching for." The man behind me shoved me forward a step for emphasis.

Who *were* they watching for? My mom? She had to have made it back across by now. My dad? If he found a way to get the portal to let him pass, I hoped he would arrive well armed. A low hum vibrated in my ears. Fine hairs rose on my arms. One step closer to the portal. To home. To an end to this horrible misadventure.

"You can let me go. I'll go straight back to Lyric so you don't have to leave your post," I promised.

Two seconds. That's all it would take me to leap forward and through the portal. *Just let go and give me two seconds.*

Mr. Toe-the-line wasn't buying it. "Escort him back to Lyric. I'll wait here for the next patrol."

I was so close. Just a few feet from home. Safety, comfort, pizza. I wrenched hard against the guard's grip but couldn't budge him.

He pulled me away, toward Lyric. The buzzing vibration of the portal faded.

I couldn't let this happen. Panic added strength to my struggles. When I couldn't break free, I dropped into a dead weight, stopping our progress.

The guard kept one hand manacled on my arm but let go with his other.

I pried at his fingers with my free hand and pushed against the earth with my feet, desperate to gain a few inches back toward the portal. The wall of energy bent the air, although the guards seemed oblivious to it.

A gray metal shape swung into focus a foot from my face. A gun.

I froze.

"Good. I see you know what this is, tech-boy. Your crew hasn't made enough yet, but the ones we have work very well." He let go of me and kept me in place with a casual gesture of the weapon. Mr. Toe-the-line crossed his arms and watched, impassive.

Helpless rage raced through my veins. It was the same fear and frustration I had felt when Cameron held a gun on me and forced our family to let him through the portal. Would a Restorer heal from a gunshot? I wondered if I should risk it. Could I make it to the portal if he shot me? I stared up at the dull barrel in the guard's steady hand. Even knowing I might heal, I couldn't stomach the thought of a bullet plowing a hole between my eyes.

Gun Guy stared at my forehead as if he were picturing the same thing. "Up," he said, sounding a little less bored.

I eased to my feet. He steered me out of the grove and back toward Lyric. With every step I took, I swallowed back shrieking frustration. I'd missed my chance. All I wanted was to get away from this insane place. Maybe I could still break free.

I glanced sideways at the guard, but he kept one hand clamped around my arm and his gun aimed at me. Shame sucked the last of the fight out of me. What kind of Restorer was I? I wasn't brave or heroic. I didn't want to risk being shot. I'd spent most of my days here feeling confused and scared.

And now that I knew how ill-equipped I was to help these people, I couldn't even get away.

As we drew closer to the city, I squared my shoulders. At least this king's guard didn't shove me or tie me or gag me—or pull a sword on me and insult my parents. I might be a prisoner again, but my escort acted like an aloof professional with no personal animosity. The outlawed guardians were grubby, surly, and mean. I managed to take some comfort in being away from them as the king's guard marched me around the city and toward the main entry. I didn't try to talk to him because any conversation would quickly reveal I wasn't one of the transtechs gathered in Lyric.

A few other king's guards rode past on lehkan, patrolling the hills between Lyric and Corros Fields. What were Arland and his merry men doing on the other side of those fields? What would Cameron do if he knew they were that close? It was silly to worry about them after the way they had treated me, but my thoughts kept straying their direction. Wade, Arland, and the rest of the former guardians had been quick to turn on me, but I didn't want them to fall under a barrage of bullets.

We strode through the crystal-lit tunnel and into the central square of Lyric. As much as I wanted to go home, a thrill caught in my lungs like a gasp of winter air. The worship tower stood sentinel over the middle of the city, its shining white walls the place where the One so often chose to meet His people. My mom had described being touched by Him under its clear-paneled roof, and Dad had told me how holy mist settled on the people who sang there on season-end Feast days.

Through one of the tower's huge open archways, I saw stacks of lumber, piles of dead leaves, and other signs of neglect. My heart sank at the proof that the true Verses were being forgotten. The last time I had been here, even the marble floors gleamed with the kind of care given to the finest of cathedrals. How could things change so fast?

Uniformed guards patrolled the streets, and the few civilians we passed kept their gazes down, their faces pinched. My escort steered me toward the guardians' training tower.

Anticipation surged through me. I had spent many happy days training as an apprentice guardian the last time I was here. The feel of a sword in my hand became more natural than a soccer ball against my knee. I had belonged, had a purpose, and excelled. Of course, my parents had warned me that much of what I felt had been influenced by Medea's mind control. There were gaps in my memory and a vague sense of having no desire to see my parents once they had found me. And I could remember a powerful loyalty toward Cameron, which baffled me now. But in spite of the confusion in my memories, entering the training tower felt a little like coming home.

Until I saw the changes there as well.

A polished black desk blocked the first hall. A guard stood up as we approached. "What are you doing back from your patrol already?" His frown and the authority in his stance gave me a clue to his higher rank.

"It's all right, Case. The grove is still protected." My escort nudged me forward. "The transtechs misplaced one of their apprentices. We caught him wandering around outside the city."

Hard eyes raked and dismissed me. "The crews are upstairs. Go see where he belongs."

Gun Guy waved me to the stairs along the tower wall. Trudging upward, I struggled to absorb all the differences in the building. I should be thinking about escape or what I was going to do when the guard found out I wasn't a transtech, but I was distracted by all the changes. The training halls we passed had been converted. No guardian apprentices were sparring today. The new king's guards had taken over this tower, and from one balcony we passed, I saw them training—not with swords but with handguns and rifles and syncbeams. A shudder ran through me.

We arrived at a section of the second floor that had once been barracks. Noise, smoke, and the smell of burnt plastic poured from the doorway. Gun Guy yanked my arm and pulled me inside.

Dozens of people worked with frantic energy, pounding, twisting, and assembling things. I rubbed my eyes.

"Who's missing an apprentice?" the guard shouted over the sounds of hissing, clanging, and loud arguments. Some of the noise died down as the men near the doorway noticed the interruption and turned to look at us.

Over the racket in the rest of the room, I heard a familiar voice.

"I told you they aren't producing these fast enough. I need you to give them some energy. Make them understand how important this is."

My eyes scanned the huge room and spotted the man who stood apart from all the activity. His back was to me, but I had no trouble recognizing him, or the woman beside him.

"I can't do everything," Medea whined. "Make up your mind. Do you want me to control the songkeepers or help these men with their toys?" In a blink, her face shifted into a sneer. "You've become weak. You can't manage anything without me."

Cameron stepped closer to her. His jaw barely moved, and his words were a tight whisper, but I focused past the clamor in the room and heard him.

"Could someone weak have taken control of all the clans? Don't forget who I am."

Her malice flickered out of hiding. "Don't forget who put you here."

"Hey!" Gun Guy shouted again to the room at large. I jumped and tried again to pull away. "Who does this boy belong to? Next time we find someone wandering outside the city, we won't bother bringing him back."

The room quieted. I couldn't hear anything beyond the rushing in my ears.

As if in slow motion, Cameron and Medea turned toward the guard bellowing in the doorway. Then they zeroed in on me. Cameron's eyes widened, and he paced toward us. Slithering along in his wake, Medea laughed a light sparkling trill that made my stomach clench like I'd been sucker punched again.

The guard holding me stiffened to attention. "S-sorry to . . . to interrupt . . ."

A slow smile spread across Cameron's face. "No need to apologize. I know exactly where he belongs. We'll take care of him."

Gun Guy released me and nodded, backing out the door in a rush.

I tried to step back too but couldn't move. Sick dread churned in my stomach.

"This is a very . . . timely surprise," Cameron said softly.

Medea tilted her head. "We've had a few problems that were unexpected. The songkeepers suddenly began to debate the new Records."

"And progress on the new defenses hasn't been fast enough." Cameron rubbed his temple before slicking back his hair.

Maybe his rise to power was giving him headaches. I could only hope.

Medea stepped closer to me. "But now the king will have a son to help him." Her voice was sweet and comforting. Cameron chuckled, but the sound seemed to come from far away. All I heard clearly was Medea's voice. All I saw were her eyes. "This is better than we could have hoped. Everything is falling into place."

I frowned and shook my head.

Medea's gaze traveled over me. Then she met my eyes again. "Poor Jake. So confused. So weary. What has been happening to you?"

Her sympathy was a balm. She understood. I hadn't asked for any of this. I'd tried to help, and no one had appreciated it.

Her smile filled me with warmth. "I'm sure you'll tell us all about it. But it doesn't matter. The important thing is that you've found your way home."

I nodded. I was here to help. This was where I belonged. Some voice inside me called a warning, but I brushed it aside.

Cameron rested a hand on my shoulder. "Come. We have new plans to make, son."

Plans? What was he talking about? Memory threads darted across my thoughts. I was trying to find something . . . someone.

"Let it go, Jake." Medea's voice soothed. "The king is your father now. He needs your help. We're glad you've come. There's so much to do."

They needed me. They were glad I was here. Eagerness welled up. "How can I help?"

Cameron and Medea both laughed. "So many ways," Medea promised.

Oceans of contentment bathed me. I followed them from the room. No more doubts, no more struggle. I floated down the hall, leaving behind the questions and conflicts that had tortured me. This was so much easier. I'd found my purpose. I was here to help the king. He had chosen me to be his son.

Chapter Twenty-Two

SUSAN

Nothing in the stark cell had changed, but when Nicco settled into the chair across the table from me, a higher level of tension filled the room. His fingers flexed as though they were eager to wrap around someone's throat. "You offered to show me secrets," he said without preamble.

I swallowed hard. "I offered to exchange information. Truth for truth. I want to understand your people and why you . . ." My words trailed off. I couldn't find a tactful way to phrase it. ". . . why you twist people's minds."

Nicco tilted his chair back onto two legs and stared at me through hooded lids.

Cold seeped from the bare cell floor through my feet. I pulled my blanket around my shoulders. I'd had a rough night since my last encounter with Nicco, haunted by nightmares and confusion. My only comfort was that he didn't look too great either. His eyes were dark-ringed, and his usual control was fraying.

He crossed his arms and glared at me. "Show me the things I haven't found yet."

My time was running out. I cleared my throat. "Have you come across other people who have your mental . . . skills? Can the Kahlareans do what you do? Have your people always had these powers?" I just wanted to get him talking, keep him calm.

The angry lines across his forehead eased. He watched me thoughtfully for a moment and leaned farther back. "I don't know. We have some stories, passed down by the ones who came before. But it's hard to know how much is true. As our people near the end of life, they become . . . confused."

I leaned forward, intrigued in spite of my fear.

Nicco stared at the ceiling. "Those with the greatest power become the most disturbed. We lose so much of what they've experienced."

"Medea?"

"She's the strongest." Affection and admiration wrapped his words, but he sighed. "And growing more erratic."

A hint of pity bloomed inside me. The emotion startled me. Maybe it was another of Nicco's manipulations.

They are so lost.

The whispered thought wasn't Nicco's or my own.

I studied him more closely, sadness thickening my throat. "You don't know the truth about your people—your world."

His chair crashed forward, and his face twisted in a growl.

I tensed, compassion quickly smothered by fear.

Nicco took a deep breath. Like the flip of a switch, the anger left and his voice was casual when he spoke. "We create truth." A confident smile spread across his face. He leaned on the table, chin braced on one hand. "That's far better."

"Is it?" I met his eyes. Some stray pool of courage fed my nerves. "What purpose does your life have if nothing in it is real?"

His eyes widened, and the smile disappeared.

I bit my lip. I'd pushed him too far.

Just then a chime sounded outside in the hall. He pressed the remote and stalked to the door before it finished rising. A Rhusican woman in a vibrant magenta tunic waited in the hall.

"I'm sorry to disturb you, Nicco." She dropped her chin. Deference or unease? I barely heard her next words. "We've lost two more."

He rubbed the back of his neck and nodded.

The woman threw a curious glance in my direction before hurrying down the corridor.

I ran to the door. "Lost two more? Two more prisoners? Nicco, you can't do this to people. Torturing their minds. Isolating them. They'll all die."

He squared off and locked eyes with mine, harsh angles etched into his face. "She was talking about *our* people." He bit the words out and took a step toward me.

Backing away, I collided with the cell wall.

Nicco moved one step closer and thumbed the remote. The door slid down, and suddenly there was no air in the room. "There's some reality for you," he said slowly, letting his rage cool into a much more dangerous malice. "There's some of the truth you've pestered me for."

I couldn't answer. Couldn't look away.

He loomed over me. "Maybe you're right. Someone should understand us."

I closed my eyes. My muscles clenched in reflex, preparing for his invasion of my mind.

A chair scraped across the floor.

My eyes flew open.

Nicco was slouched against the table, a grim smile curving his mouth. "Sit down." He gestured to the chair.

I couldn't bring myself to walk closer to him.

"You know," he drawled the words, "you are so jumpy, it's impossible to have a conversation with you."

That statement was so unfair that my mouth hung open while I tried to find a response.

Light from the walls sparked in his eyes. "I won't hurt you." The now-familiar intrusion of compulsion entered my mind. Years ago, a nurse had injected something into my IV right before a minor surgery. A strange chemical calm had infused my body in seconds. I felt the same way now. A part of my mind knew the sense of peace was artificial, but it was such a relief to be free from terror, I didn't care.

I floated to the chair and sank down, strangely detached from my own body.

Frowning, Nicco studied me, and the soothing tranquility in my mind withdrew slightly.

"Are you paying attention?" he asked.

I nodded with effort and struggled to remember what we had been talking about. "Truth," I whispered.

He gave a short laugh. "Yes, and why we're able to create our own." He shifted his weight to sit on the edge of the table. "We haven't found others like us—not that we've been able to search very far. We learned early on that our skills fail and our minds begin to break if we are away from Rhus too long."

The sluggishness in my mind eased, and I could concentrate again. "Is it something in the air? In the water? Or is it that you need each other?"

Nicco shrugged. "We've never found out. One of our guests said it must be the gods' way of keeping us from venturing too far. Few of us dare leave Rhus. Medea has sacrificed more than anyone else to help our people."

His fondness for her resonated through the link he held to my mind.

I shuddered, hoping he couldn't read my wave of disgust. Medea was beyond irrational, but it made sense if the travels had affected her mind. The other Rhusican who had attacked me in Braide Wood had turned on me with a crazed roar and lunged into my sword. Maybe he had also been away from Rhus too long. But then Nicco wasn't particularly levelheaded, either.

"Have you done a lot of traveling?" I asked.

He glanced down at me. "No. I've never wanted to leave."

"But you seem to be . . ." I hesitated. "You're a lot like Medea."

His eyebrows lifted.

A frisson of anxiety tried to assert itself but was pressed back by imposed serenity. My breathing remained steady, and I waited.

Nicco pushed to his feet and paced across the room and back. "Our people don't live long. As our mental strengths develop, we find our emotions also are more intense, harder to control. Those with little creative powers live longer. Those of us with greater gifts . . ." He sank into the chair across from me and sighed.

"Maybe if you stopped messing with people's minds. Maybe if you stopped creating your own realities." A flare of hope ignited in the gray emptiness of my spirit. "Maybe that's why I'm here. To help you find truth."

Nicco leaned forward, his face mirroring my earnestness for a second, absorbing and tasting my desire to help. Then he threw himself back and laughed long and hard, until he had to wipe tears from his eyes.

I sank down into my chair, defeated.

"No"—he choked on another burst of laughter—"you're here because we live for fresh experiences, and Medea found something new in you. You provided fuel for her work. You're still alive because, and only because, there are a few things I haven't finished exploring." His eyes narrowed. "Now. Fair exchange of information. That's what you wanted, isn't it? It's your turn."

I pressed against the hard back of the chair.

A muscle jumped along Nicco's jaw, and then he went very still, eyes riveted on me. "When you were about to die, you saw something. Show me."

I didn't want to relive that moment near the fountain, but I couldn't push him out of my mind. The feelings rushed back. The desperate attempt to escape. The brief sputters of hope. The crushing despair when I knew I had failed. The knowledge that my life was going to end. The yearning to connect one more time with Mark and the children. I closed my eyes, gripping the edges of my chair for support.

Then it happened again. Beyond Nicco's snarling face and raised dagger, I saw Life. The One. A presence wrapped in light and mist, radiating welcome and comfort. Even the memory of that moment stirred deep feelings of awe and trust. I followed that thread to other encounters. The fiery blast of assurance right before the battle of Morsal Plains. The tender wooing of my heart in the Lyric tower by One who asked permission to heal me. The powerful words that called me back from Medea's poison as Mark recited, "He restores my soul."

Moment after moment unwrapped and played across my thoughts like spools of film. Overlaid above the images of my own story was the glow of the Source. It was His goodness, His compassion, His hand that spun the reels and allowed my life to play out. For a second, I could almost understand the way He had steered and shaped my existence to touch something far beyond the confines of the film. I lifted my focus from the scenes of my life to His face, basking in His love. Time stopped.

Slowly, I remembered where I was. Long minutes had passed, maybe hours. Where had Nicco gone? I didn't feel him twisting, controlling, or even observing my feelings. I opened my eyes.

Nicco's face was white, his eyes wide with horror. His shoulders moved raggedly with each panted breath he took. "What . . . who . . . ?" He skidded his chair and backed away from me.

"It's all right. It's what I've tried to explain to you."

He grabbed fistfuls of his hair and doubled over, hands pressed against his head. When he looked up, his eyes were wild. "How did you do that?" The words rang against the walls of the small room.

I flinched.

Nicco backed away toward the door, his muscles tensed so tightly he shook. "Tell me."

"I didn't do anything. It's the One. Nicco, your people have been so busy creating realities, you've never been willing to see Him. If you want experiences that won't bore you in moments, try real truth." Let him mock my earnestness again. I didn't care. It might be the last chance I would have to tell him this.

He was still breathing hard, but hunger and cunning replaced his fear. "How do you control that power?" A dark smile twisted his lips.

I shook my head with a moan of frustration. "It's not

something I control or that anyone can control. The One . . ." I floundered for an explanation and remembered the creed I had first learned in Braide Wood:

Awesome in majesty
Is the One eternal.
Perfect in His might and power,
The only truth and only source,
He made all that is and loves all He made;
His works are beyond our understanding.

Nicco stood very still, as if analyzing every syllable. He seemed to be searching for a trick somewhere.

I met his eyes with complete openness. "You've learned to control a lot of things—even the minds of other people—but you're not the source of power." Strength welled up in me and lifted me to my feet as the truth of those words sank into my own heart.

Nicco's chest lifted and he sneered at me. "Do you want me to remind you how much power I have?"

"I haven't forgotten." For once fear didn't race through me at his threats. "But you know the truth now. There is One with much more power than you."

"I can fill your mind. I can make you feel pain beyond imagining." Nicco pulled his dagger from a deep pocket and slipped it out of the fabric cover. He ran a finger along the edge of the blade. "I can take your life."

I squared my shoulders. "Yes. But after, there is One who will meet me, and you have no power over Him."

Nicco reached out and traced the raised scar on my cheek. His hand slid lower to rest against my throat.

My pulse pounded against his fingers. He had rarely physically touched me, for which I had been incredibly grateful. Now I was afraid to move.

"So little life left," he mused. "And you boast about power."

"Not mine." I choked the words out. "His. Are you ready to face Him again?"

I hadn't meant the words as a challenge. I only wanted him to understand.

His hand tightened, cutting off my air.

Gray glitter moved in from the edges of my vision. He snorted and shoved me away with so much force I collided with the wall.

My knees buckled and I sank to the floor. I brought a hand up and felt tears on my face. I couldn't make him understand, and it tore me apart. "He wants you to know Him."

"You think I should try to know this One, whom I can't control? You're insane." He reached for the remote on his belt, and the door slid open. Sneering down at me, he put his dagger away. "You were right. There were some things I hadn't found before. But I've seen enough now. You bought yourself today. Tomorrow I'll need this room for new arrivals." He stalked out of the room, and the door slid down.

For a moment, I had really believed truth was breaking through to him, but he wouldn't hear it. Grief pressed the breath out of me. I had given up on being rescued weeks ago. I'd let go of ambitions to escape. I'd resigned myself that I wouldn't get out of here alive.

Still, through each long day, one hope refused to be crushed. I had held on to a spark of faith that my being here would have a purpose—make a difference somehow. The spark dimmed now. Maybe nothing could make these people change.

I hugged my shins. The wall behind me felt cold in spite of the light emanating from it.

"Lord, I can't see a way. I'll be coming to meet You tomorrow, and I think I failed at bringing truth to this place. But I know You." My voice clogged with tears. The bare ceiling blurred as I looked straight up and smiled. "You have purposes better than anything I can guess at. Come in power. Come in love. Fulfill Your plans, whatever they are."

I dropped my forehead to my knees and closed my eyes. "And please give me strength for one more day."

Chapter Twenty-Three

JAKE

"Let's go for a picnic." Medea's voice wheedled. Then she leaned across Cameron's desk and giggled.

Cameron. The king. My father. He insisted I call him Father, but I still thought of him as Cameron. Sometimes late at night, strange images tangled in my mind and made my head throb. Most of the time, I ignored the questions and pictures. They only stirred painful confusion. It was easier not to fight. Cameron was my father now. When stray fragments of my past resurrected, I buried them.

Medea was always quick to remind me how important I was to her. I was special. Her affirmation filled me with purpose. She was powerful, beautiful, and breathtakingly good. The People of the Verses would have fallen apart without her help. Cameron couldn't have managed his struggles as the new king without her. The thought that she cared about me made my heart race each time she looked at me.

Now she dipped her fingers into a mug on the desk and flicked water at Cameron. "Come on. It's a beautiful day."

I glanced out the window. Rain sheeted down in a gray curtain.

Cameron watched her as if she were a broken toy that he had once adored but couldn't glue back together. "I need you to go to the tower. A handful of songkeepers are meeting again. Every time they do this, it incites trouble."

"Songkeepers give me a headache," Medea whined. Then she laughed, a high shrieking cackle. "Or I give them one. I forget."

Cameron pressed his fists against the onyx desktop and shot to his feet. "Pull yourself together or go back to Rhus. You're no good to me like this."

They were fighting again. I wished they wouldn't. It jarred the edges of the happy family picture wavering in my mind. I wanted to help them, but their conflicts escalated daily. I hunched my shoulders and concentrated on the electronic components on the table in front of me.

Cameron had assigned transtechs to develop magnetic power sources for the MP3 players he'd brought from my old world. He assumed I'd be able to help, but so far I'd done nothing but short out and fry equipment. I pushed the hair back from my face and sighed.

"Oooh," Medea crooned. "You've upset the boy again." She strolled around the large desk and danced her fingers over one of the swords mounted on a wall bracket. Her hand reached for a silver venblade.

Cameron swatted her arm away. He scowled in my direction. "He's been no good to me, either."

Shame twisted my stomach, and I stared at the floor. I had wanted to help him so much—to earn the honor he'd given me by taking me in as a son. "I told you where Tristan is hiding."

"Beyond my reach." He pounded his fist on the desk in one sharp blow.

I couldn't face his scorn. "I told you where the guardians were camped."

"And they were gone when my men arrived. How could you not know where they were heading?"

"They didn't tell me. They didn't trust me." We'd been over this at least a dozen times. "I'm sorry." My voice cracked.

Cameron pushed Medea out of his way and came around from behind his desk. He raised a hand toward my head.

I flinched.

Instead of hitting me, he ruffled my hair. "I'm sorry. I know you're trying to help. You have to understand the pressure I'm under. It's my job to keep Lyric safe."

I nodded eagerly. I did understand. He was fending off the Kahlarean threat, building up an army, creating weapons—important tasks. And yet foolish people opposed him. The songkeepers were stirring unrest everywhere with their call to stay true to the original Records. The outlawed guardians dodged from clan to clan, growing in strength. I met his dark eyes. "You know I'll do anything I can to help."

A slow smile grew across his face. My heart warmed under his approval.

"It's about to get easier for us." Cameron smoothed a nonexistent wrinkle from his rust tunic. "One of my patrols sent word that the guardians are back in Braide Wood. I'll be sending in my army to wipe them out once and for all."

Medea made a howling sound from behind the desk. "You promised them to me!" Fury sparked in her eyes, and anger leapt inside me, driven by my link with her.

Cameron stalked over to her. "Now who's upsetting the boy? Let's discuss this somewhere else." He reached toward her arm but then pulled his hand back.

She tossed her head and stormed through the door into an inner room.

"I need to explain some things to her, son." Cameron stared after her. "You keep working." His face was hard as he followed Medea through the door and closed it.

I shivered. Without thinking, I stretched my hearing to listen. They still didn't know I could do that. I kept forgetting to ask Medea about the special power I had and whether it could help them somehow. It was easier to just answer their questions and do whatever they asked.

"I'm not going back to Rhus empty-handed." Medea's feet made soft scuffing sounds as she paced.

"You're welcome to take some of the songkeepers and get them out of my hair."

She made a sound like a snarling tiger. "They're more trouble than they're worth. I wanted the guardians."

"The guardians have become too much of a threat." Cameron's voice turned soothing. "There are too many of them. I can't risk letting them live any longer."

There was a long silence. I wondered if he was stroking her hair. She didn't usually like for anyone to touch her. "And I'm worried about you." The words were muffled. "Let me take care of this problem, and then I'll be sure you get back to Rhus."

"Coward!" she shrieked.

I heard a gasp and a scuffle.

Something snapped in my mind, and my spine jolted. Mental blinders vanished. Outside control had guided my thoughts in carefully constructed channels. Now memory exploded open in sparks that seared the insides of my skull. My gaze swept the room and I noticed a wall bracket was empty. One of Cameron's daggers was missing.

Stretching my hearing again, I heard Cameron's low moan. "No. Noooo."

I lurched to my feet, disoriented.

Think, Jake. Think.

They'd been controlling my mind for days, maybe weeks. This whole time, I'd forgotten who I was—why I was here. Nausea washed over me and I staggered to lean against Cameron's desk. My insides felt coated in an oily evil. I gagged and then swallowed hard. Shame welled up, but I shoved it down. No time to deal with it now. I had to get away before they realized my mind had broken free. My heart raced as I glanced around the room.

One of the swords hanging on the wall was a good size for me. I grabbed it and wedged it into my belt. I worked the lever and slid the outer door aside.

Crash! The inner office door slammed open and Cameron staggered out. "Jake, run and get the healer. Medea . . . she's . . ." He groaned and looked at his hands. They were covered with blood.

Shock enabled me to keep a blank stare on my face. I nodded and shot out the door. The guards outside didn't move. No one would hinder me. They may not be used to seeing me on my own—in the past weeks I had been with Cameron or Medea all the time—but everyone knew me as Cameron's son.

My face twisted as I ran through the central square. May as well take advantage of that hideous role now and leave the city while I could.

What had happened in Cameron's inner office? Was Medea dead? Did she attack Cameron in a fit of rage, or did he decide he'd had enough of her? Did he try to kill her and then regret it? If she lived, would she be able to regain control of my mind?

Fear pulsed through me with every stride.

I glanced through the arches of the worship tower. A few songkeepers huddled in the center of the cavernous space. I wished I had time to talk to them, but a more urgent need drove me. Whether Medea was dead or alive, I had to get as far from her and Cameron as possible. Next, I had to warn Arland and the other guardians that Cameron was about to send his army to attack them.

Tossing a brisk salute to more of the king's guards, I jogged through the wide tunnel and out of Lyric. Praying that the automated train-things were still running during these days of chaos, I sprinted toward the station.

I leapt onto the first transport pointed in the direction of Braide Wood. The long ride in the deserted car gave me time to catalog my memories. My mind worked its way back to the days before Cameron and Medea found me.

When I thought of my choice to go home—to reject the call to be a Restorer—my skin flushed hot. If only I could blame that on Medea's mind control, but that resentful decision had been all mine. I hadn't accomplished anything I'd come here to do. In fact, I'd made things worse.

Medea and Cameron had never mentioned my mom, so I still had no idea if she were safely home. Humiliation burned my skin as I realized I'd forgotten about her the whole time I was living in Lyric. Cameron and Medea had been my family. A shudder coursed through me. How could I have let them use me that way?

Yes, the guardians had gotten away from Corros Plains before Cameron's men attacked, but they would know I had betrayed them. I needed to gather a force to hold back the Kahlareans. How would I win the guardians' trust now? If they knew I'd been living as the king's son, they would hate me. I'd never convince them to help me.

At least the songkeepers were challenging the false Records. Lukyan had set that resistance into motion.

The transport slowed to a stop at the trailhead to Braide Wood. The door rolled upward, and the engine powered down. As the hum died away, I stepped outside.

The murky sky warned me that evening was approaching. These wild lands were dangerous after dark. Bears, mountain cats, poisonous rizzids, and lethal ground-crawlers owned the night. I drew my sword and took stock. I had no gear, no lights. The safe plan would be to stay with the transport until morning and then hike to Braide Wood.

Stabbing my sword into the ground, I dropped to my knees, keeping one hand on the hilt. Verses from the true Records spun in my head. My throat felt thick, but I forced myself to speak. "Awesome in majesty is the One eternal. Perfect in His might and power, the only truth and only source." My voice broke. "Holy One of all worlds, I'm so sorry."

My head hung forward. "I thought it would be cool to be some sort of hero. I figured I'd be a great Restorer. Better than Kieran was. He didn't even believe in You." For the first time, I saw the pride that had snaked its way into my thinking since the Restorer signs appeared. "I didn't know how confusing things would get. And then I quit listening."

Something rustled deep within the wall of trees. I shivered. "Show me the way to go."

No mist encircled me. No voice nudged me. In sudden horror, I wondered if the One had chosen a different Restorer. I opened my fist. With a swift pull, I cut open my palm on the edge of the sword still planted in the dirt. I lifted my hand, looking up at the deepening sky. "I'm Yours. If You still want me."

Even as I said the words, I heard their foolishness. He had never threatened to withdraw His love for me. I was the one with the unsteady heart, not Him.

I tilted my face up further. "Whether I'm a Restorer or not, I want to follow You. Please give me the strength."

I closed my eyes and let His love touch me, even though part of me wanted to crawl away in shame. I didn't deserve His understanding, His forgiveness. But that was kind of the point of grace.

"My dreams of coming through for You . . . I thought I'd somehow deserve Your affection—that I'd be on even footing." A laugh that was half sob burst from me. "I was so dumb. Use me. Don't use me. I don't care anymore. That's up to You."

I lowered my arm and opened my eyes, afraid to look at my hand. I expected to see the deep gash unchanged. Warm tingles danced over my skin. I rubbed away the blood on my pant leg and stared. The wound was healed.

Gratitude and relief swept through me. "Thank You." My breathing grew so ragged I couldn't speak anymore. I bowed my head in silence, admitting, receiving, and finally seeking. "Show me what to do."

Follow.

Such a simple word. It was all He had ever asked of me. One simple thing. But instead, I'd bounded ahead, detoured aside, and even run directly away. "What about the guardians? How can I warn them without being killed? And what should I do about Cameron? And how can I find out what happened to my mom?" I could have spun in a gyroscope of questions all night.

Follow. The voice was as soft as a breath.

My worries quieted until there was nothing in my heart but a whispered answer. "Yes."

The night lowered over the forests. No moon or stars broke the expanse of darkness. I might have stayed kneeling on the ground for hours, but my legs grew stiff, and my shoulders shook from the damp cold. With a sigh that was half exhaustion and half peace, I leaned on the sword and hauled myself to my feet.

A mournful howl sounded from a ridge in the woods far above me. The shell of the transport was a vague shadow behind me. The trail was invisible in the darkness. Which way?

In the past my prayers had been, "Show me the path to take so that I can save the day and make You proud." Or, although I wouldn't have admitted it, "I don't like this path; show me a different one. I've got a better idea." But now I consciously set aside all my agendas, my desire for importance, my desire for ease. It was a new and awkward prayer for me. "I'm here. What should I do?"

Wisps of fog played around my ankles and then drifted forward, away from the transport. It was odd that I could even make out the tendrils in the dark. Slowly, I realized that the cloud itself was glowing with a soft light.

Follow.

The call was clear. My thoughts jabbered in rapid rebellion. *What if I followed the mist and it deserted me in the middle of the dangerous trail? What if I reached the caves above Braide Wood and the guardians were there? They'd imprison me or kill me.*

With a deep breath and quiet will, I steered those thoughts aside and stepped forward into the tiny part of the path I could see. The vapor cast a pale glow, only enough to move forward one step at a time.

The hike was slow, and I carried my sword at the ready. Since I couldn't see down the trail behind me in order to estimate how much ground I'd covered, I lost all sense of distance and time. Fear lapped at the edges of darkness, but I kept watching the patch of fog as it drew me forward and upward. A sheen of sweat coated my skin as I climbed. Whatever dangers were ahead, I was determined to follow—not to show the One how much greater I was than anyone else but because it was the only place I wanted to be.

The path leveled out for a time, but the darkness was impenetrable. No sign of Braide Wood. I had hoped for some glimpse of the homes' light walls—illumination slipping under doors or past window shades. If the town rested in a clearing somewhere below, I couldn't see it.

The trail wound upward again. I strained my hearing, hoping to have some warning that the band of guardians was close. My eyes ached as they squinted beyond the wispy light around me and into the darkness. The rough texture of branches under my grasping fingers was reassuring. I was still part of the physical world.

When my hands didn't find trees for several paces, I realized that something had changed. The mist was fading. I tensed and took another cautious step forward.

Suddenly, a heavy form exploded from behind me and knocked me to the ground. My sword flew from my hand.

"Who are you?" A fierce growl rumbled in my ear as his bulk pinned me flat.

I knew that voice. "Ian? Thank the One I found you." I spit some sand out of my mouth and tried to lift my head.

Rough hands flipped me over, and a light flared and burned my eyes. Ian's long hair and angry face loomed behind the light cube. A dagger glinted in his free hand. He crouched above me, a bundle of unrestrained fury.

"Jake?" Shock warred with rage in his voice.

"I have important news. Please take me to Arland."

"I'll take your body to him—and he'll thank me for it."

I had no time to absorb his words, no time to react.

His dagger sliced down into my chest and jammed upward. I could swear I heard a pop as my lung collapsed. A second later I felt the pain. My body thrashed and struggled like a fish being gutted. I tried to say something but choked on blood. My brain screamed in protest. Then blackness crushed me like a boot grinding me into the ground.

Chapter Twenty-Four

JAKE

It hurt. More than puking my guts out after chemo when I was kid. More than the time Gary Rundle head-butted me after a bad call during a soccer game in seventh grade. Fighting my way back from the black nothingness was no picnic.

I had no clue how long I'd been out or who might be around. I could play dead. It might buy me some time. Good theory, but I couldn't stifle the gurgling cough that erupted as soon as I drew my first deep breath.

"I was beginning to wonder if you'd come back." That was Arland's dry voice.

My eyes flew open. His face was shadowed, but a heat trivet somewhere behind him splattered color on the cave walls.

Pushing up onto one elbow, I looked around.

We were alone.

I sagged back to the ground, relieved but wary. "How long?"

"Almost two watches through the night. It's near morning." Arland slumped against a boulder. He shifted and some light reached his features. It struck me that he was everything that polished, poised Cameron wasn't. His face grooved from caring, Arland was unshaven, smudged—real. Thoughts of the Velveteen Rabbit hopped into my head. I decided my brain must be starved for oxygen.

Time for another cautious attempt at a deep breath. This one hurt a bit less. "Was I . . . ?"

"Dead?" Arland nodded. "As a skewered rizzid."

I couldn't tell if he was relieved or sorry about my recovery. It didn't matter. I had to tell him what I knew and somehow take my place as the Restorer. I'd wasted too much time already. "I came to warn you. Cameron knows you're here. He's sending an army. We've got to move."

His eyebrow lifted at the word "we," but otherwise his expression was grim, closed. "Answer one question."

I opened my mouth, but he held up his hand.

"One question. The truth. Did you tell Cameron we were camped near Corros Fields?"

I sat up and struggled to take a deeper breath. Coughs racked my chest. "Let me . . . explain. There's so much—"

Arland's hand slammed into my throat, pressing my head back against the cave wall. He held me in place with little effort. "Yes or no, Jake."

"Yes." I choked out the word.

He snatched his hand back and wiped it on his tunic, as if touching me had polluted him.

My own feelings of betrayal rose to meet his. "Don't look at me like that." I rubbed my throat. "I heard you."

Arland's disgust faltered for a second. "Heard me?"

My hand felt for the wound Ian had given me and came away sticky from the blood on my clothes. The gash in my tunic was a vivid reminder of Ian's killing stroke, but the pain was almost gone now. I glared at the head guardian. "Yes. It's one of the Restorer gifts. I could hear you when Wade got to camp. Ian wanted to kill me." My fingers played with the damp fabric again. "And you were going to turn me over to Cameron. Even Wade didn't try to protect me. So don't go all righteous and indignant on me. You would have run too."

Arland kneaded his shoulder and scowled. "I was trying to gauge where their loyalties were. If you had stuck around, you'd have heard Wade argue us into the ground trying to defend you. You've got a stubborn house protector there, and he doesn't even know what you are."

"No, but you do. And you were going to trade me—for what? A few lehkan or Cameron's promise not to hunt you if you stayed far from the central clans?"

Arland looked toward the cave opening and didn't answer.

My anger faded quickly. I couldn't blame him for not trusting me. In his place, I'd have done the same. I sighed heavily and was glad to find I could breathe easily again. "Do they know?"

The guardian looked back at me sharply. "That you're a Restorer?" He shook his head. "No, but they'll be expecting a funeral at first light." His eyes glinted, and his hand rested casually on his sword hilt on the ground near his side. "Maybe that's not such a bad idea. Of course, they won't feel much sentiment in committing your soul to the One, but it would solve a lot of headaches."

I thought of the funeral of the boy who had been shot—the light cube that burst into a nova and left nothing but ashes. Restorer healing wouldn't bring me back from that.

Somehow, dying once already tonight had used up my capacity for fear. "You'd do that? You'd kill me and turn me into toast? Destroy a promised Restorer without even telling them who I am?"

His face went hard, and he didn't answer.

I studied his eyes and tried to convince myself that he couldn't do it. "Look, I don't blame you. I was too scared to tell everyone what I am. But there's something worse." To have any chance of gaining Arland's help, I needed to be honest. "I was going to leave. Go back to my home. Give up on being the Restorer." My voice grew quieter with each phrase. "Cameron's men found me."

He snorted. The sneer on his face made it clear he despised me. "Sure, Jake. And you sent him after us the same day. Oh, and we've heard you were very comfortable in Lyric. Living like a prince."

"They poisoned my mind." Sickness welled up inside me. I spit the words out. "They controlled me. Medea . . . she's a Rhusican. They were using me."

He leaned back and quirked his brows as if he were indulging a teller of fairy tales.

I pushed myself to my feet, crouching to avoid hitting my head on the low ceiling of the cave. "Fine. Believe what you want. But we do have to get out of here before Cameron's army comes." I took a deep breath. "And it's time for me to tell the guardians who I am."

Arland gave a bark of laughter. He sprang to his feet and gestured toward the cave entrance with a mocking bow. "Be my guest."

He didn't think I would do it. And he wasn't going to make this any easier. No problem. I was following the One who had called me to this role. If He could bring me back from death and guide me along dark trails to find the guardians, I could trust Him to help me now.

I ducked under the rock of the cave entrance and stepped

into the clearing. Pale half-light revealed lumpy forms everywhere I turned. At first I thought I wasn't above Braide Wood after all. Everything looked unfamiliar until I spotted the entrance to the large cave where I had slept one night waiting for Wade. Slowly, the confusing shapes coalesced into sleeping men.

Back in Lyric, I'd overheard agitated conversations about the growing number of renegade guardians. When Cameron had first come to power, some of the guardians simply faded into the wild. They didn't want to serve him but wouldn't risk opposing him when the new Records said he was destined to be their king. But as the Kahlareans threatened to move farther into the clans and word spread that the new Records might be fakes, more men joined Arland every day. Cameron had raged at leaders of the king's guard, demanding they track down and eliminate this threat.

But those snatches of conversations hadn't prepared me for the size of the guardian band now. There had to be more than a hundred men piled in snoring heaps around the clearing. And who knew how many were in the large cave or sheltered under the trees.

My resolve bled away. What was my next move? I took a few steps forward and then looked back.

Arland leaned against the rock face near the small cave entrance. His eyes burned into me, the way Mr. Weldman's once did in honors lit when he was about to make me read my essay to the class.

"Hey! Did you get here yesterday?" The friendly voice belonged to a wiry man only a few years older than me. He stepped around a huddle of sleeping bodies as he made his way across the clearing toward me.

I shook my head. "I came in last night." I didn't recognize him from when I'd last camped with this group.

"You traveled at night?" His voice jumped in volume, and several men muttered in complaint. Others stirred and looked around. Dawn was peeling darkness off the clearing.

At least he didn't assume I was an enemy. I was warmed by his acceptance of me as another guardian coming to join their cause. "I had to. I had urgent news for you."

"It's Jake!" One of the men across the clearing scrambled to his feet. He lurched toward me. "Traitor!" In moments the whole camp was stirring.

The hundred men looked like twice that as some of them rose from their blankets.

I squared my shoulders and raised my voice. "I've come to warn you. Cameron is sending his army after you."

"So you led him to us again?"

"When did you get here?"

"Where were you hiding?"

Angry voices advanced on me, along with some of the men.

I glanced back at Arland. Arms crossed, expressionless, he did nothing but watch. No help there. I drew myself up. "I hiked from the transport in the middle of the night."

"Impossible." One of the older men spat on the ground.

"He must have been hiding in the village. Kill him before he can get word out to the king." The men who had met me earlier continued to spew helpful comments, while the newer members of the group nudged each other and murmured questions.

Fear pushed at me, but I pushed back. "Ian knows when I arrived."

Someone called for him, and he elbowed his way through a tangle of men. "What's going on? I was on watch half the night. Can't you let a man get some sleep?" He stepped forward and spotted me. His muscles locked up, and his chest caught mid-breath.

"Is it true?" One of the men asked Ian. "Did he arrive last night?"

Ian didn't answer. His gaze tracked over the blood on my tunic, the rip in the fabric.

I stepped closer to him. I didn't like moving farther into the middle of the clearing, surrounded by hostile glares, but Ian wasn't moving, so I got close enough for him to smell the blood on my clothes. "Tell them."

"Jake?" The hard anger that usually furrowed his face was washed away by shock.

In that moment, I was startled again by his resemblance to my dad. The thought was disorienting. "Yes. Tell them."

The men shuffled, and some edged forward, nudging each other and murmuring. Several men looked over to Arland, but he refused to react.

Ian cleared his throat. "Jake stumbled into our camp during the first watch."

A mumble of questions and comments welled up, then died back.

I met Ian's eyes. "Tell them the rest."

His gaze flicked over me again, and he pulled out his boot knife as if to check that it was still real. "I killed him." There was no apology in his voice, only shock.

Stunned silence held the clearing for a few heartbeats. Then an explosion of mutters, questions, and debate erupted as all of the men demanded explanations at once.

"Ian, can I borrow your dagger?" I asked.

He hesitated, then handed the blade to me and shuffled back several paces.

I held the blade above my head until the noise in the clearing died down. Tired, grubby, bewildered faces focused on me.

It was time to speak. "In every time of great need, a Restorer is sent to fight for the people and help the guardians. The Restorer is empowered with gifts to defeat our enemies and turn the people's hearts back to the Verses." They weren't an easy audience. I'd better make this good. Gritting my teeth, I held up my free hand and sliced deeply across my palm with Ian's knife.

Blood ran down my arm; some dripped onto the hard-packed dirt. I turned slowly, letting them all see the wound. The entire clearing held its breath.

I wiped my hand against my tunic and held it up again. The long gash was gone.

"The One has sent me to help you. To return the clans to the true Verses. To rescue Rendor and push back the Kahlareans. Some of you know me already. I'm Jake, son of Markkel, son of Mikkel of Rendor. I'm a Restorer."

Relief surged through me as I spoke. They'd believe me, or they wouldn't. They'd fight alongside me, or they'd kill me. At least I had done what I was supposed to do.

Silence weighted the air.

"How can you be?" A grizzled warrior, older than my parents, limped forward. "The new Records say there will be no more Restorers."

"The new Records are a lie. Cameron created them to deceive you." I held up my hand again. "Look at the sign."

Ian tossed his head back. "You all know that when I leave an enemy dead, he's dead. I don't know what we should do about him," he growled, "but it's true that he came back."

"Then he must be a Restorer." Wade's deep-chested voice

rang through the clearing. Others stepped aside as he came forward to stand beside me. "I guarded the house of his parents. I knew his mother. I rode with his father." He rested a hand on his sword hilt. "And I'll defend him. But I didn't know he was a Restorer until now." A measure of hurt muted his voice.

"You betrayed us to the king's guard!" someone shouted. Murmuring and rancor bubbled up like lava. Wade stepped closer to me.

"No. They twisted my mind." I pushed my hair back. "Cameron and his guard are no friends of mine. I want to stop them from corrupting the Verses."

A young eager-looking guardian had been watching, chin in hand. He jumped to his feet. "Then you'll lead us in attacking Lyric. Time to kill the king!"

Other excited voices joined his, chanting for Cameron's death.

At least they weren't calling for mine. It would be easy to be swept into their enthusiasm. For this second, they were united and willing to accept me.

The men had been glancing over at Arland, but he had held back, letting them come to their own conclusions. Now he pushed away from the rock wall and looked at his men.

"We're going to ride against Lyric. Breach the walls, use the secret doors, charge the tunnel." His voice was low and compelling and grew in force as he spoke. "Cameron and the king's guards are like a nest of stinging beetles inside a tree. We need to crush them before they destroy the whole trunk from the inside."

The men cheered.

Follow Me.

The quiet reminder breathed into my mind. I saw the gap

at Cauldron Falls. I saw the central city of Rendor that had haunted my dreams. From my first hour through the portal, the One had urged me in that direction. I bit my lip, scared again by what I was about to say. I took a slow breath.

"No."

Only a few men nearby heard me and turned to stare.

I tried again, louder. "No. You can't attack Lyric." The vibration of their frustration rumbled like the low growl of an angry pit bull. "It would lead to civil war."

"You support Cameron as king?" The shrill voice of a boy my age piped from the back of the pack.

I shook my head. "He had no right to become king. He lied about the Records. But he was one of your Council. It's the job of the guardians to serve the Council. Let the One take care of Cameron. He won't be able to hold on to power much longer."

If only I could get them to trust, to understand. I turned to Arland, holding a hand out in a plea. "The One sent me to help you, and I have to follow Him."

The planes on Arland's face were stiff, immovable. He didn't care about any direction I had from the One. He saw only a challenge to his control. I wanted his understanding. I needed his support. The men needed his leadership.

I forced myself to meet his eyes—to hide nothing. "We have to save Rendor." I didn't understand the passion that welled up inside me. I didn't know where the feeling was coming from, but I let it pour out. "You have enough men. The One has sent you a Restorer. Let's push the Kahlareans back across Cauldron Falls."

"Have you ever faced a Kahlarean in battle? Do you know anything about their weapons?" A voice called out the challenge behind me, but I kept looking at Arland. He met my stare, resisting me, resisting the One who sent me.

Another of the men called out with a sneer: "If you've been sent to help us, then ride with us to Lyric. Lure Cameron out. From what we've heard, he trusts you."

I shook my head, frustration growing.

Holy One, speak to these men.

My eyes drifted to Wade. He had a spare blade strapped in a sheath on his back: my father's sword.

Wade saw my glance. Planting his legs wide, he reached back, drew the sword, and offered it to me hilt first.

I raised the sword and faced the men. "My grandfather died at Cauldron Falls, and the Kahlareans were defeated. He was a Restorer and glad to give his life for the People of the Verses. So am I. I want to fight with you, in the power of the One, and free Rendor. We can drive the Kahlareans back across the River Borders. But if you won't go with me"—I pivoted slowly, looked hard at all of the men, and finished by staring deep into Arland's eyes—"I'll go alone. I'll fight them with every breath in my body, because that's what the One has asked me to do."

Then I braced myself and waited to see what Arland would decide.

Chapter Twenty-Five

JAKE

The strength of my own words startled me. Hard to believe this pledge had come from my mouth. I didn't even know how to get to Rendor. Yet fire burned in my bones, directing the words. I felt their power. I saw their impact.

Men who had been lounging on the ground rose to their feet. Others shifted uneasily and looked away. Sneers transformed into cautious attention. Their faces showed the transition in their thoughts: *Is it possible? If the One has sent a Restorer, maybe we can dare to hope again.*

They waited for Arland to answer me. Scores of eyes darted between us, measuring, weighing.

A grumbling voice piped up from behind me. "High time someone did something for Rendor."

I whirled to stare at Ian. Talk about an unlikely ally.

He shrugged gloomily. "After all, what difference will it make whether we die by the king's new guns or by Kahlarean syncbeams and venblades?"

At that cheerful assessment, the men began to mutter and argue again.

Arland shot an annoyed glare at Ian, then stepped forward. "Prepare to move out." He didn't enter the debate, didn't give any clue which destination he would choose. Every guardian in the clearing leapt into action.

I watched the organized chaos with admiration.

Arland grabbed my arm and pulled me off to one side of the clearing. Although he'd been stoic as he spoke to the men, his eyes blazed into me now. "This is your plan? Stir up mutiny? Cause the men to debate the best of hopeless options?"

"No! Arland, I'm just telling you what the One has called me to do."

He jerked my arm. "What if you're hearing wrong? You'll ride to Rendor and die. Your death would be a waste." His eyes burned, not with anger but with his passion to protect every life: the People, the guardians, even the Restorer.

I faced him with absolute conviction. "I belong to the One. My life is His to waste."

He made a harsh sound in his throat and let go of me, then paced a few steps away. When he turned back, frustration drew his hand by instinct over the grip of his sword.

My fingers tightened around my own sword, but I was careful not to lift it even an inch. "Please, Arland. The men will follow you anywhere. Can't we at least try? You have enough guardians now to make a difference. If we follow Him, the One will protect us."

He walked back to me, his words low and intense. "How? What is His plan?"

A reasonable question. I was begging Arland to lead his men into danger based on my word as a Restorer. Trouble was, I didn't have the answers he wanted. "I don't know. He'll show us in His time. All I know is that we need to follow Him."

Arland rubbed his shoulder and moved it stiffly—the same shoulder I had once bandaged for him. Wade had hovered near, pretending not to listen. Now he shuffled forward and ducked his chin, approaching Arland like a puppy expecting to be swatted in the nose. "What would it hurt? It would have been part of the plan eventually. We haven't had word out of Rendor in weeks. We could at least scout the area—find out what's happened to the families that were left."

Arland gave Wade a level look. My house protector stepped back a pace and added quickly, "Of course, it's up to you. You're the head guardian."

"Yes"—Arland jabbed his chin in my direction—"and he's the Restorer." Was that bitterness in Arland's voice?

He still didn't know what to do with me. I still didn't know how to convince him. "Please," I said simply. "I'd rather fight by your side than alone."

He absorbed that and raked a hand through his hair. "Wade, I want you sticking to him like brambles to lehkan fur. Understood?"

Wade snapped to attention and nodded eagerly.

"And you." Arland pressed his lips together and shook his head, already showing regret for his decision. "I want you to keep me informed of anything the One tells you. No taking off without explanation. No throwing yourself into situations you don't understand."

My head bounced, and I grinned until my face hurt. He believed me. We were finally heading onto the road that the One had nudged me toward since I arrived. And I wouldn't have to face the Kahlareans in battle alone.

Arland gave a short whistle. Ian and several other clan captains made their way to him. In a low voice, he issued new orders. I had expected him to shout to the whole clearing, "We ride to Rendor," but Wade quietly reminded me that the guardians' only defense these days was secrecy. Each group of men would be told the minimum, and only when necessary.

I had also expected we'd mount lehkan and charge across the plateau toward the River Borders, like the cavalry in a Wild West movie. Instead, the guardian band split into units. Most would hike to a transport stop beyond the lehkan plateau. We couldn't use the nearest station because we'd run smack into Cameron's guards on their way from Lyric. After a long hike, we'd board the automated cars in shifts, twenty-five men to a car. A second, smaller group would take the remaining lehkan pastured near Braide Wood, planning to arrive a day after the rest to patrol the land outside the city and provide a secondary defense if we were forced to retreat. The piecemeal procedure quelled some of my naïve visions of riding at the head of a vast army.

Arland gave terse orders but still took time to speak with each captain about his supplies, the status of any injuries, and the morale of his men. A young messenger drew close and listened to Arland's orders to one captain. He stepped forward. "I want to volunteer. I'll take word into Hazor and let Tristan know our plans."

Arland clapped a hand against the boy's back and smiled. "It's a rough journey these days. Zarek isn't making it easy to get a message into Sidian. But if Tristan does find a way to join us, it will be vital that he hears the plans. Go with the One."

The boy nodded and turned to leave.

A sudden warning shrieked in my head—inaudible, but as insistent as the burglar alarm Dad had installed in our home. "Wait!"

Wade looked at me, eyes wide. Arland fired a frown in my direction.

The impression of danger flared into a physical pain in my skull, and I winced. My mom had told me about seeing and knowing strange things when she was the Restorer. I thought she meant the enhanced hearing and vision, but this was a different kind of gift. I struggled to explain it to the impatient head guardian. "Something's not right."

Arland rolled his eyes. "Wade, why don't you take the boy and get him geared up."

"Wait." I rubbed my temples. I didn't want to irritate Arland now, when he was just beginning to support me, but something needed to be confronted. "Cameron knew you were at Blue Knoll, and it wasn't from me. He found out you were camped here. I heard him talk about sending his army. Someone has been bringing him information."

The messenger was sidling away.

I looked at him and knew. Beyond my ability to know, I was sure of how Cameron kept finding the guardians. "Wade, stop him."

Wade wrinkled his forehead but clamped a hand around the boy's arm. Arland looked at the messenger and then back at me. He shook his head. "No, it's not possible. I've known Evon all his life."

Evon gave Arland a wide-eyed stare. "What's this about? I need to be on my way to cross the mountains before night."

I stepped in front of him. "Look me in the eyes and tell me the truth."

Childhood words. Words my mom used to say, with the claim she could always tell if I lied. When I was five and my new red tricycle disappeared from our garage, I ran three houses down the alley and confronted Troy Abernathy in his backyard. "Did you take my trike?"

He shook his head and calmly pushed his Tonka truck deeper into his sandbox.

I pulled myself to my full kindergarten height and used the magic words with all the righteous indignation in my soul. "Look me in the eyes and tell me the truth."

Troy's lip quivered. He jumped out of his sandbox, frightened by the fierceness of my gaze and the mystical power of those words. "Okay, I borrowed it. I hid it in my garage."

I was a Restorer now. In a mysterious way, my demand for the truth had compelling strength—at least I believed it did. The messenger believed it too. His chest began pumping like a bellows, and his eyes locked into mine. Deep in the pupils, I saw shifting images. Deceit wove strands that I recognized as Medea's dark skills. It was the last thing I wanted to see. I felt like I was choking.

"Jake?" Wade's concerned voice reminded me to breathe, but I didn't look away from the boy.

"What was the song you sang at Denniel's funeral?" I whispered the words to Wade. The messenger stood frozen, expressionless, eyes still bound to mine.

Wade cleared his throat and chanted the first lines, self-conscious: "In the gray of our despair, the One will bring a light."

"That's the one. It's from the Verses?"

Wade nodded, a blur on the edge of my vision. I stared into the dark web of Rhusican poison in the boy's eyes. "Sing the words with us."

His mouth drooped open, lifeless. I could just as well be ordering one of my sister's stuffed animals to sing.

Wade began again, and Arland's strong voice supported the melody.

"In the gray of our despair, the One will bring a light."

I joined my voice with theirs, the Verses seared into my memory from the funeral. "When our battle ends, and we face our longest night." *Holy One, free this boy.*

Evon's mouth began to move, barely mouthing the words. "Sweet life or bitter death, He yet remains our Tower."

I sang gently. It was like breathing on tinder, coaxing a flame from a rumor of a spark.

Dangerous threads writhed and knotted in his eyes. I didn't let myself marvel at the odd images. All my focus was needed to pull him out of their control. "Facing our last journey held by His love and power." Coherence glimmered in his face.

"The creed. Say the creed with us." My parents had once used those words as a test and tool to find councilmembers who were influenced by Rhusican poison. I struggled to remember how it started.

Behind me, Arland sighed at my floundering. "Awesome in majesty," the guardian said quietly, then paused.

"Is the One eternal." The messenger gritted the words out, tendons throbbing on the sides of his neck. Wade felt the tension and stepped behind him, still gripping the boy's arm, more to support him than confine him.

"Perfect in His might and power"—Arland stood like a wall at my back, guiding the boy in front of us through the words—"the only truth and only source."

The boy's eyes rolled back, and his whole body stiffened. He had been whispering the creed, but now a howl burst from his throat. He went limp and Wade eased him to the ground. Behind us, I heard the activity freeze and questions fly. Arland ordered the men back to their preparations and turned to help me again.

I was afraid Evon had died, but his chest was still moving. In fact, his whole body trembled. I crouched beside him and rested a hand on his head. "It's all right. She can't control you anymore. Say the words." I spared a quick glance at Arland.

He lowered to one knee beside me. "He made all that is and loves all He made; His works are beyond our understanding."

The boy's eyes flew open, filled with panic, confusion, and a growing awareness. He groaned, beginning to understand.

I remembered my own feelings of shame and horror as the fog of Medea's poison had faded. I had felt so slimy I wanted to find a cave and pull the entrance in after me. "It's all right," I said again.

Arland took the boy's hand. "Say the creed with us."

The messenger stared at his captain and saw no repulsion, only concern. By force of habit, he followed Arland's orders. He spoke the words from the Verses with us, and the shaking in his limbs eased. His breathing calmed. When we finished, he sat up and moaned again, rubbing the side of his head as if trying to erase the lies that had held him. "It was me. Arland, each time you sent me out, I went straight to Lyric instead." His face bunched up with the pressure of the remorse that tore at him.

Suddenly, he grabbed a dagger from his boot sheath. Wade, Arland, and I tensed.

The boy turned the weapon and offered it hilt first to Arland. "I've betrayed the guardians."

Justice in this world was unforgiving. I knew firsthand how little mercy these men would show someone they thought was a traitor. I opened my mouth to plead with Arland.

"Jake!" Wade said sharply. He gave a small shake of his head. It wasn't my place to tell Arland what to do, especially when we had just formed an uneasy alliance.

Arland turned the dagger in his hands, lost in thought. He sighed and handed the knife back to the messenger. "I don't want your death. At least not here where it won't do our cause any good."

Evon curled in on himself, the answer making him feel even more defeated. Arland stood up, and Wade helped the boy to his feet.

I rose and then wobbled from sudden light-headedness. The encounter had drained me.

Arland looked behind us at the men, who were assembling and waiting for his orders. He turned back to the boy. "If you want to pay for your betrayal with your life, then spend it fighting Kahlareans, where it will do some good."

The boy's head lifted and took in the words. He straightened. Despair gave way to determined purpose.

"Go on, join your group." Arland waved him away.

The boy thanked him in a choked voice and hurried off. Gratitude chased away my fatigue. "Thank you. You did the right thing. I'm sure—"

Arland snapped his head toward me. "Jake. Enough."

I sagged and stepped back. I had kind of hoped he would thank me for finding out something so vital. Why wasn't he happy that we had been able to free the messenger from enemy mind control?

The guardian checked his sword belt, adjusted his sheath, and set aside his temper with effort. "I thought we'd agreed you'd check with me before doing crazy Restorer things." But the side of his mouth twitched.

Before I could answer, a man raced into the clearing, panting for air. He spotted Arland and jogged over. "The scouts say the first transport has arrived from Lyric. Twenty of the king's guards, with the weapons they used at Blue Knoll."

Arland gave a terse nod. "And there will be more to come." He dismissed the man and turned to me. "We have no way of knowing who else in our band is controlled by Cameron. And now we have no time to find out."

No wonder he hadn't been thrilled with our one little victory. I looked at the large group of men. Any of them could be traitors. We were about to set out to battle a powerful enemy nation, and Arland didn't know who he could trust.

The head guardian gave his orders, and the men moved out. Arland looked at me one more time, then turned to Wade. "This isn't a game of Perish. Keep an eye on him." Then he charged out of the clearing to join the first group of men, leaving Wade and me to fall in behind.

I'd felt exhilaration when Arland made the decision to come with me to Rendor. I'd been awed at the powerful experience of watching poison's hold break away from the messenger. Now reality crashed in.

We were on the run again—running from Cameron's army and heading straight into a battle with the Kahlareans, who had killed my Restorer grandfather and had tried to kill every Restorer since then. My brave words came back to haunt me, and I whispered them again to give me courage. "I serve the One. My life is His to waste."

Chapter Twenty-Six

JAKE

"Hurry up!" I called to Wade. The weakness caused by fighting Rhusican poison had faded, and I was determined to join the first transport for Rendor.

Wade labored along behind me. A few weeks earlier, I'd had a hard time keeping up with him. Today, Restorer strength propelled me. We passed other guardians, jogging along the narrow trail away from Braide Wood and toward the River Borders. By the time Cameron's soldiers reached the clearing above Braide Wood, they'd find nothing but empty caves and stray pinecones.

When we caught up to Arland, he frowned and exchanged looks with Wade. My house protector shrugged his large shoulders. "He wants to ride in the first transport."

Arland's eyes flicked over me, cataloging all my flaws with the sharp skill of a military analyst. "Of course he does. All right. We'll fit you in."

We loped along for miles. Among the cliffs and forests, the narrow path was rough with roots and stones. Soon Arland led us off the path and straight through dense underbrush to scramble down a towering ridge. We reached a paved road and picked up the pace again.

"Will Cameron send some of his men past the Braide Wood transport stop once he finds out we're not at the clearing?" I puffed out the question, keeping pace with Arland.

The dark-maned guardian didn't bother to look at me. "He might."

"What would we do then?"

Wade laughed and patted my shoulder without breaking stride. "Then we fight."

"Shouldn't we stay off the road? We're an easy target out in the open."

Arland stopped so suddenly, I was two paces past him before I caught myself. I turned back to confront hard eyes and muscles clamped into angry stillness.

"Jake, we're heading toward Rendor because we had to go somewhere. I decided we aren't ready to face Cameron in Lyric." He flexed his large hand.

I remembered those fingers crushing my throat and swallowed hard.

He took a step closer and glared down at me. "Just because we're going the direction you wanted to go doesn't mean I plan to listen to your bright ideas every time I turn around." His fist closed over the hilt of his sword. "Unless you plan to take over leading these men?"

Wade stepped between us. "Of course he doesn't. The Restorer is sent to help the guardians, not rule them. Arland, he's only trying to help."

Arland turned a hard-edged face toward Wade. "Then keep him out of my way." He growled the words with the fierceness of a wolf caught in a steel-jawed trap, then brushed past us to resume his steady run.

I stepped back, shaken by his hostility. "I'm just trying . . . I only . . ."

Wade pulled me aside as a few dozen men jogged past. "I know. Let him do his job."

We fell in to the back of the group. As my feet tore up the pavement, I had ample time to see Arland's point of view. Weeks ago, when I had first blundered into their campsite, Arland had disarmed me in seconds. Since then, I hadn't done much to make a better impression. His ongoing annoyance toward me stung, and I determined to keep my mouth shut and follow his lead. But what would I do if another Restorer insight hit me?

Worry chewed at my heels as I ran.

Arland let Wade and me join the first group of about two dozen guardians crammed into the transport. Someone's sword hilt jammed into my hip, and bodies crushed against each other so tightly it was hard to breathe. I was near the back but could focus my hearing and hone in on Ian's guttural bass as he argued softly with Arland.

"They'll have soldiers watching the transport station. They'll incinerate us before we can get off."

Arland answered him with more patience than he'd ever shown me. "The Kahlareans are secure in their treaty with Cameron. I'm thinking the station won't be heavily guarded. Just be ready to move out fast."

"Hey, I've seen what their syncbeams can do. If they're waiting, we won't have time to move out."

Anxiety bubbled inside me like soda in a can. I shifted my weight. "Wade, how far is it?"

He yawned, stretching his shoulders with a popping sound. He was so large that even small movements forced the men near us to shift back a few inches. For a little while, it was easier to breathe. "We'll arrive before nightfall."

I wished again that this world had maps. A picture at the transport station with a big red arrow saying, "You are here" would have been helpful. I had no idea it would take all day to reach the River Borders.

We switched transports at one point, the only relief from the cramped space. Wade explained that instead of heading toward the central clans, we were now moving in the direction of the River Borders. Rain fell for a few hours, then eased away. My legs ached. I'd much rather run, or even ride a skittish lehkan, than stand still in this tin can that felt more and more like an overcrowded elevator.

Wade didn't need to tell me when we were drawing closer to Rendor. Soft conversations faded away, and I could taste the rising tension. The scratched plastic windows were fogged over, so the trees flying past outside were only vague shadows. On this leg of the trip, I was closer to the front and managed to lean toward Arland, who hadn't spoken to me since the road outside Braide Wood.

I chewed the edge of my lip and cleared my throat. "Let me get off first."

His head swiveled, and his eyebrows jabbed down.

I braced myself against the subtly shifting floor of the transport. "When Kieran was the Restorer, he took a direct syncbeam hit and survived. Let me go first. Please."

The transport slowed. The only sign of Arland's indecision was his glance toward Wade.

Before Wade could jump in with an opinion, I wedged myself into a small gap closer to the door. "Please. It's what I'm here for." A Restorer was a valuable resource, even one as untried as me. Wade's instinct was to protect me. While it would have been much more comfortable—for both of us—to let him do that, I was here for a reason, and letting other people risk death in my place wasn't right.

Arland's stance projected confidence, but the eyes he turned toward me held shades of worry. "Are you sure?"

Of course not. I was terrified of the Kahlareans. They'd been haunting my nightmares since I came here. But it was time I started doing the things a Restorer is supposed to do. I nodded.

"All right. Wade, stay with him." He hadn't needed to give my protector that reminder. Wade had stayed so close all day, he'd stepped on my feet more than once.

I elbowed my way closer to the entrance.

Arland angled to face his men. "Jake, Wade, and I will head out first. Wait for my signal before you join us." The transport rolled to a stop.

I faced the door, preparing to dash out and confront whatever enemy waited for us. I bounced on the balls of my feet a few times.

"Jake"—Arland's voice was dry—"you'll need your sword."

Startled, I glanced back. Arland and Wade both had their weapons in their hands. How had they managed that? Clumsily, I drew my sword in the cramped space.

The curved door slid upward into the roof of the transport.

I lurched forward, my legs taking a few seconds to unlock after standing still for so long. I ran, dodging side to side like the cops on television dramas always did. Walls of trees rose on both sides of the road. An enclosed shelter hugged the edge of the woods like the hut at an entrance to a campground. Still weaving, I aimed in that direction. The setting triggered a flashback to family hiking trips, and I almost expected a ranger to step out and check our state park permit. Something moved near the open door.

A Kahlarean soldier. Oversized black eyes swam in skin white as the belly of a catfish, just like my nightmares.

A yell broke from my throat. I stopped zigzagging and raced forward.

The soldier charged from the shelter. His sword swung toward me.

Jake, you've got a sword too. Use it.

I remembered to block a heartbeat before his blade would have reached my neck. Time slowed. It registered in a back pocket of my mind that other Kahlareans had poured from the shelter. Wade and Arland were fighting nearby, but my universe became my opponent's sword and mine. His lips parted as he scythed a powerful swing at my head. I was close enough to see that he didn't seem to have teeth.

Too close. I ducked, parried, skittered back. Then my clumsiness melted away, and my muscles remembered well-rehearsed patterns. My weapon flew, created an opening. His arm swung wide in defense. I spun in. My arm jarred as my sword connected with his metal breastplate. He fell back a few paces, and I followed through with a slice that caught him beneath the armor. He doubled over. I watched him sink to the ground, frozen in horror at what I'd done.

I had just killed a man.

"Jake!" Wade's shout broke through my daze. He was holding his own with another soldier. "The shelter!" He blocked an overhead blow and deflected the blade. "Syncbeams!"

A hum rose into the air. In the doorway of the shelter, one

of the Kahlareans held a black half-sphere in an awkward grip. The sound grew, and the soldier lifted his hand. Light seared the ground near my feet.

I roared and ran toward him, the smell of burnt hair in my nose. The syncbeam flared again, this time hitting somewhere behind me. Someone gave a rasping scream, but it was part of the fog of background that my mind couldn't absorb. The soldier looked down to adjust something on the weapon. I was only a few yards away.

Pain scorched across my thigh. I stumbled but still drove my sword downward at the Kahlarean. The strike almost severed his arm and knocked the weapon from his hand. He backed into the shelter, and I limped after him.

"Jake, hold!" Arland managed to shout the words, even while gasping for breath.

I turned, confused. Arland ran toward me. Soot marks scored his side, and his gait was lopsided. But he shoved me to one side of the shelter's open doorway.

Why had he stopped me? Fury exploded through my chest as I struggled to keep my feet under me.

A blast of syncbeam fire seared through the doorway—a direct hit to the empty space where I had stood a second earlier.

Arland watched the angle of the blasts and crouched low, charging into the shelter. I peered around the door frame in time to see him slice the sphere from a second soldier's hands and then calmly kill both the men inside. He hurtled past me and back into the clearing.

Wade jogged over to meet him. "Is that all of them?"

Arland snapped his gaze around the clearing, then finally released his tight shoulders with a slow breath and nodded. "For now."

A grim smile tugged at the side of Wade's mouth, and he wiped sweat off his forehead with the back of his hand, smearing a track of stray blood. "Good thing it takes them some time to get those syncbeams powered up. You all right, Jake?"

The men both looked at me, and all I could do was swallow. During the adrenaline of the last frantic minutes, I hadn't had time to indulge fear or shock. Now I could hardly breathe. Arland tossed his sword to Wade and stepped closer to rest a hand on my shoulder.

"What were you thinking? Don't ever follow an enemy alone into a potential ambush. You didn't know how many were inside or what kind of weapons they had ready."

The familiar sound of his gruff scolding helped my world stop spinning. My nose wrinkled against the scorched smells again, and my eyes traveled to Arland's tunic.

"You were hit."

He looked skyward in exasperation at my grasp of the obvious. Then his hand went heavier on my shoulder and he staggered.

I called out in panic. "Wade!"

My house protector closed the space and grabbed Arland, helping me lower him to the ground. Wade signaled the men who had waited in the transport, and they poured out, scattering around the station. I envied their confidence. Everyone seemed to know what to do. Some headed into the woods to patrol; others unloaded supplies. One man tossed a pack to Wade.

"Come on, chief. Not a great time for a nap." Wade rifled through the gear. I unsheathed my boot knife and cut the seam of Arland's tunic, carefully folding back the scorched fabric. It stuck to his skin where it had melted into the burns.

I turned worried eyes to Wade. "Shouldn't we find a doctor?"

He ignored that and pulled out a gourd. Water spilled over the wound. "Hold his head."

I shifted to support Arland's head. His eyes were still closed. Wade lifted the gourd to Arland's lips.

I shoved his hand away. "You aren't supposed to give him something to drink if he's unconscious."

"So you're a healer now too?" Arland's eyes snapped open. "Jake, you have to be the expert on everything, don't you?" But he gave me a crooked grin.

I tried to come up with a flippant response, but I was too worried. Wade poked at Arland's wound, and the head guardian's lips pressed together, white with pain. "How bad is it?" I asked Wade.

"Just grazed me," Arland answered for him. He turned dark eyes to Wade. "What did I miss? Help me up." He braced his elbows and tried to prop himself up.

Wade pressed a meaty fist into his chest. "Take it easy and let me bandage this first. We don't want you keeling over again." Arland grumbled but didn't fight. Wade assured him the men were setting up a perimeter and the second group wasn't due to arrive for a while yet.

Arland curled his head up, trying to get a look at the burns, but then thought better of it and twisted his head away. "Ian," he barked.

The fair-haired guardian had been hovering near and rushed over to crouch down across from Wade.

Arland twisted and pushed up on one arm. "You know Rendor better than anyone. I want you to get close to the city. Find out what you can."

Ian's chin came up. "Glad to."

Arland gave him a rare grin of appreciation. "By the time

we've got all the men gathered, we'll know how to plan our next step." He sucked in his breath as Wade tightened a bandage. "Watch yourself."

Ian smirked. "Look who's telling me to be careful. I'm not the one who walked into a syncbeam."

"I was distracting the other Kahlarean," Arland protested. "It was strategy."

"Right." Ian jumped to his feet. "I'll be back soon."

"What are you laughing at?" Arland growled in Wade's direction. The younger man choked back his chuckles and helped Arland sit up. The head guardian scanned the station. I followed his perusal of the activity to find that someone had already moved the bodies of the dead Kahlareans.

When I tried to stand up, I found my leg bones had turned to taffy. I wobbled and rested a hand against the shelter wall for support.

"First real fight?" Wade asked quietly. I nodded and used a shaky hand to push hair out of my face. He handed me a canteen of water. "Don't think about it now. We need to focus. You'll have time to think later."

I tried to take his advice, but I kept seeing the Kahlarean's face. The bug eyes and gummy grimace and the body that fell into the dirt. Alive one minute, dead the next—by my hand.

Wade stayed with me as activity whirled around us. He set me to work clearing rocks and twigs from a wide patch of earth under the trees, preparing a smooth surface for blankets and travel pallets. By the time the next group of men arrived, we had set up camp and thrown together a cold supper, which Wade insisted I eat despite my lack of appetite. A scout returned to report that they had found a few more Kahlareans on patrol outside Rendor and one of our men had been injured in the resulting skirmish. Arland listened to this and other reports as he moved around the station stiffly, waving off any concern about his burns.

Ian didn't return until after the third group of men arrived and the sky had deepened to the shade of dark granite. As he marched into the clearing, I had a wild flare of hope that my dad had found a way through the portal and come to join us. Same wavy hair, same mannerism of leading with his chin. Ian scanned the group, eyes darting, hand raking through his hair, and the resemblance to Dad faded.

I reached him the same time Arland did. The head guardian demanded rapid answers. "What did you find? How many hold the city?"

Ian glanced around. "We need to speak in private." His voice was as tight as his muscles.

Arland's eyes narrowed, but he nodded and led Ian to the shelter. I followed the men inside. Ian glared at me, but Arland didn't send me away.

"They're gone." Ian blurted the words as if they would make sense.

Arland frowned. "The Kahlareans?"

Ian swore and spat into the dirt. "No, the families. Rendor clan. There's no one left but the Kahlarean army."

It took a moment for that to sink in. I piped up. "Did they escape? Flee to other clans?"

Arland's impatience flared. "No, Jake. That's not what it means." He walked out of the shelter, his gait stiff.

I followed him, needing an explanation.

Arland stopped and turned to face me. "Use your head, Jake." The bleakness in his eyes slipped past his military control.

The implications of Ian's report came into focus in my tired brain.

They'd all been carried off into Kahlarea.

Or were dead.

We were too late.

Chapter Twenty-Seven

JAKE

Arland gathered his captains. I hovered near, and when he gestured me over to join them, I sprang forward. "Our job just got easier," he told the men. "Apparently, the Kahlareans have moved all the civilians from Rendor, so we have a clear field for attack."

He didn't comment on the possibility that the entire Rendor clan was dead. The men's jaws clenched. Unlike me, they instantly grasped the truth. But discipline held them in check. Would I ever learn to compartmentalize that way?

Focus on the job at hand.

Arland began sketching out a plan for the next morning's attack.

Were they all dead? All my father's clan? All the distant cousins I had hoped to meet one day? Mothers, children, old men. Was it my fault we hadn't come here sooner?

"We'll hope Jake can find out," Arland was saying.

"What?" I blinked and focused.

He took a deep breath, then winced and guarded his ribs with one arm. "I *said* we need to capture a few alive so you can get the truth from them—find out what they did with all the families in Rendor."

"Me?" The word came out like a squeak.

Arland gave me a warning look, then dismissed the men. After they scattered, he turned to me. "Jake, you're the one who spotted the messenger who was betraying us to Cameron."

"But that just happened. It's not like I can read people's minds or anything."

Arland sank onto a bench. Sweat beaded his face. I didn't know much about first aid, but clearly he was in a lot of pain. Strangely, it made him less brusque with me than usual. "Jake, I know you're a little . . . unsure of yourself. There isn't a Council anymore, so I can't take you to them to confirm your claim as the Restorer, but we've all seen what you can do. You said the One sent you to rescue Rendor. Right now there's nothing to rescue."

Was he going to back out of the plan now? I opened my mouth.

Arland raised his hand. "I'm willing to attack the Kahlareans. We all know, even if Cameron is too foolish to see it, that this is just their first step. If we don't push them back, they'll take over all the clans. But if we ever needed a Restorer, it's now."

I took a deep breath and nodded. "I'll do whatever I can."

"I know you will." Arland leaned back and looked up at the black emptiness overhead. "And I lied to you earlier."

"What? When?" He'd said a lot of things.

"My decision to come here. It wasn't just because it was as good a place as any." He pushed to his feet. "Go get some rest. You'll need it tomorrow."

He limped away, and his words sank in and warmed me. He was beginning to believe that the One had a purpose in all this.

Knowing that helped me believe it again too.

I expected to have trouble sleeping after the violence and bad news of the day, but I curled up under a cloak with my knapsack as a pillow and drifted off to the soft rumbles of Wade's snores.

I was sitting by the pond near our house, playing guitar. The chords flowed in an awesome progression. Some part of my mind was aware enough to think, *Man, you've got to remember these chords when you wake up. They're brilliant.* Then I lost myself in the melody. The poem I had written about Lyric had music now and I sang to the green-capped mallards bobbling on the smooth water.

Another voice joined mine, high and sweet. Linette stood on the green grass. Gold hair whispered around her face in the breeze. Her lips shaped the notes, and the song lifted around us. We sang verses of trust in the One, a chorus of praise for His love and mercy. When the last tones faded into the wind, I laid down my guitar and jumped to my feet. I hugged her with no awkwardness, spinning her around in a moment of shared joy.

She laughed when I released her. "I didn't know you wrote music, too. You could be a songkeeper."

"But I'm the Restorer." My shoulders sagged under the weight of the role. "There are battles I have to fight."

Her eyes glowed with the same liquid light as the sunny pond. "You can do both."

The gentle words flooded me with eagerness. I grabbed her hands. "We could write songs together. When this war is done. We could be songkeepers together."

Her hands slipped from mine, and somehow she was across the pond. The water between us grew murky as clouds grayed the sky. "Wait!" I called. The pond grew larger and her figure shrank, disappearing into the distance. She waved and called something, but I couldn't make out the words. Helpless, I watched her vanish.

I stepped to the edge of the pond and looked down. My reflection wavered on the surface. Was I really that pale? Two other faces appeared, reflecting beside mine in the water. One was a curly-haired man I didn't recognize. The other I knew too well. I glanced around, but there was no one near me. I looked back into the pond.

Medea smiled up at me from beneath the water. "The cost is too high, Jake." The words were surprisingly clear. "He asks too much from the ones who follow Him. Haven't you learned that yet? It's not too late. You can turn back."

"No." I meant the word to be firm, but it came out as a whimper. I backed away and searched for a glimpse of Linette across the pond, which had become an ocean. She was gone, but the sweetness of her voice still echoed. I ran toward it, along the edge of the water and away from Medea's face. I kept running past troubled fragments of images throughout the lingering hours of dreams.

I woke long before first light and stared up into the vast darkness overhead. I didn't want to disturb Wade or the sentries who quietly paced the edges of the station, but anxiety tossed me from side to side. Part of me wanted to run screaming from the day ahead.

"God, why did You call us here? Is this really what You want from me?" I mouthed my prayers in silence and heard silence in return. My dad had always told me that having courage didn't mean you weren't afraid. It meant you felt fear but did what you had to do anyway. The One had heard my fears when I slept alone in a hospital bed ten years ago knowing my odds of beating cancer weren't great. He'd given me the strength to tell the guardians who I was. And He heard my heart now as I spread my fears out at His feet. "I need You. I can't do this alone. I can't do this at all. Work through me today. I give You my life."

I sniffled and wiped my eyes, grateful for the darkness. No one would know how alone and uncertain I felt. Eventually, I eased away from Wade and picked my way to the edge of the station. The muted glow of a light trivet helped me avoid tripping over sleeping guardians. I murmured a few words to the sentry and sank onto the bench near the transport shelter. Resting my head in my hands, I prayed again. My thoughts ricocheted from fear to hope to doubt to faith like a pinball game. When a hand rested on my shoulder, I assumed it was the One and sighed with a reassurance of peace.

"Jake?" It was Arland.

I lifted my head. When had morning arrived? The forms in the clearing were becoming more visible. Arland wore an expression of steely resolve. "Will you speak to the men before we move out?"

I hid my surprise and gave him a firm nod.

I had figured we'd get up, strap on our swords, and march into Rendor to fight. But men had to eat, injuries had to be looked at, weapons sharpened, inexplicable preparations made.

The men prepared for battle in a way that reminded me of play practices in high school. Actors hurried into place in the wings, where they cooled their heels while lighting technicians changed a gel or refocused a Fresnel. Stage managers moved around positioning props and set pieces. Musicians fussed with their instruments and argued about tempos. Somehow all the parts wove together when the curtain went up.

Arland directed the confusing range of activities like it was second nature. He fed confidence and courage to the men.

The frenzy stopped suddenly, and Arland appeared by my side. Scores of faces looked in my direction.

My stomach knotted. "Now?"

Arland rubbed his mouth. He looked as though he were going to speak, but then he just nodded and stepped back.

God, help me. Give me Your words for these men.

I cleared my throat. "From the time I arrived in Braide Wood, the One put Rendor on my mind." My voice grew stronger. I stepped up onto the bench so I could see everyone. "I didn't understand it, but I knew there was a purpose. When I came here, the One asked two things of me: to let people know Cameron's new Records were a lie, and to rescue Rendor."

The men's faces were impassive. They were listening, but they weren't with me yet.

"My parents always taught me that if the One calls you to do something, He will give you what you need. You aren't here today because it was my idea, or Tristan's plan, or Arland's strategy. You're here because the *One* has asked us to free Rendor."

A light began to kindle in some of the men who watched me. The young messenger stood to one side, anguish and fervor burning equally in his eyes. Wade pulled himself up taller and nodded. Ian rubbed the back of his neck and studied the ground.

"That's where your strength is today. Look at me. I'm just a guy without skill or experience, but I'm going to fight in the name of the One. No one can stand against Him." The words rang through the group, carrying a power beyond my own voice. Faith burst to life inside me like a light that chased each cringing corner of doubt away. The same earnest trust glowed in the faces around me. I took a deep breath, savoring the power of the One's presence.

Arland stepped up beside me. "Awesome in majesty, perfect in power!"

"One to deliver us, He is our tower!" roared the men in response.

And just like that, we headed out to fight.

Moving was better than waiting. Marching along moss-covered footpaths, I could pretend for brief seconds that I was back at the adventure camp I'd gone to my freshman year of high school. But we weren't heading forward to navigate a ropes course, play paintball, or scale a rock wall.

On his orders, I stayed as near to Arland as I could on the short march. Wade stuck so close behind me that at times I could feel his breath on my neck. I wondered if my face held the same set expression as the men around me. I rubbed my jaw, realizing my molars throbbed from how tightly I was clenching my teeth.

We covered the path from the station to Rendor in only a few minutes.

My first glimpse of the city raised goose bumps on my skin. The images I'd seen in my dreams had been accurate. Tall wooden towers generously inlaid with huge windows rose from the tumultuous river and out toward the forests and cliffs. There was no city wall—just the gentle defense of thick forest and underbrush.

As we drew close to the outer buildings, Kahlarean soldiers swarmed out to meet us. Like the soldiers at the transport stop, deep, remorseless eyes glared out of pale, chinless faces that reminded me of frogs. And like an Egyptian plague, they poured out of every building and gap in the trees.

A man next to me spat out a curse and lifted his sword.

"Ugly monsters, aren't they?" Wade clapped my shoulder. "Don't worry, I've fought 'em before, and the ugly doesn't give them any advantage."

Another guardian snorted in amusement, even as he braced himself for the coming attack.

A syncbeam flared and a chunk of bark exploded from the tree to my right. Wade pushed me behind a different trunk. I crouched and looked around wildly.

All the men had scattered and ducked. I drew in a steadying breath and smelled ozone and burnt resin.

Another beam crackled.

Every impulse in my body screamed for me to retreat—to run away from the searing weapons and the hoards of enemy soldiers.

But Wade charged a few yards up and took cover behind a rock. He beckoned to me.

I took a deep breath and dove forward to join him. Around us, every guardian was doing the same.

Syncbeams fired from multiple points ahead, a dangerous grid of resistance. Far to my left, someone yelped and crashed down into the underbrush.

I shuddered. *Pull it together, Jake.*

Using the cover of trees, we maneuvered closer without all being mowed down.

Move fast. Engage them before they can do more damage to our advancing guardians.

Stay low. Dash forward. Watch Wade's back. Follow.

Then the next wave of Kahlarean soldiers was on us. Those with the syncbeams stayed back near the buildings but stopped shooting as their own men filled the firing line. Our guardians scattered into a chaos of sword-to-sword combat. I raised my blade and ran forward, zeroing in on one soldier. A loud clash rang out to my right. Wade blocked an attack that would have impaled me from the side.

I stumbled. *Pay attention.*

The surrounding noises unnerved me. I'd never heard anything like the shouting, clanging, and screeching of scores of men battling. Then the Kahlarean I'd targeted was in front of me. Time to fight.

He swung his blade toward my neck, and I sidestepped and countered. Clumsiness vanished, and I followed his next move. Our swords clashed over and over. I retreated, drawing him deeper into the trees. Arland wanted a Kahlarean alive. I needed to stay on my feet while capturing one of the enemy. I anticipated his next move, slipped past his guard, and landed a slice into his collarbone, near his neck. His sword dropped and he tumbled back. I ran to crouch beside him.

"Where are the people of Rendor?" I shook his shoulders, staring into his froggy eyes. The bulging orbs were lifeless. I'd cut him deeper than I'd intended. Sickening guilt wrenched my gut, but I dropped him and stood up, scanning the chaos.

Arland dragged a Kahlarean away from the line of battle and toward me. This soldier was still alive, twisting against Arland's grip even though the guardian pressed his boot knife under the man's ear.

I ran toward them, again forgetting to pay attention to what was happening around us. Arland's shout alerted me. I turned and swung wildly at a Kahlarean who leapt at me from behind. This time I didn't try to wound him. A few quick strokes and he was dead on the ground.

Arland retreated farther with his prisoner, and I caught up to them.

"The people from the clan." I was gasping for breath. "What did you do with them?"

The Kahlarean ignored me, still struggling with Arland. The guardian pulled his dagger away, then clocked his prisoner on the side of the head with the pommel. The man's head lolled forward, and he stopped fighting. We dragged him behind a large trunk and out of sight of the battle. Wade followed, watching our backs.

Arland braced the semiconscious man against the tree, still on his feet. "Come on, Jake."

I stepped closer and stared into the enemy's face. "Tell us. Where are the people who were left in Rendor?"

The Kahlarean lifted his head heavily and squinted in my direction. As coherence returned to his face, his lips curled in a sneer. He turned toward Arland. "Your people are so desperate, they're sending out boys to fight?"

Arland shifted his grip on the soldier's hand where he held it against the tree. There was a snap, like a breaking twig, and the man gasped, sweat beading onto his pasty face. He sagged, and Arland used his forearm under the guy's neck to brace him against the tree. "Answer him," Arland said through clenched teeth.

I heard another grinding pop, drowned out by the prisoner's animal howl.

I stepped back and stared at Arland. What was he thinking? He was breaking the Kahlarean's fingers. Stubby digits with knobby joints, they hadn't looked great in the first place. Now the hand pressed against bark was twisted at a grotesque angle. Bile rose in my throat. Arland was the closest thing to a role model I had in this place, and he was calmly torturing someone. It wasn't supposed to be like this.

"Jake!" Arland snapped at me.

If I wanted this to stop, I needed to get an answer. "Where are they?" My voice leaked desperation, but I didn't care.

The Kahlarean's focus pulled out of his place of pain with difficulty, but he met my eyes. "We took them across the river."

It would have been my first guess. It sounded plausible. But a shadow wavered in his oversized pupils.

"You're lying."

Arland drew back and smashed the man's mangled hand against the tree.

"Stop that!" I yelled. Arland looked at me with surprise but adjusted his grip and simply held the man up.

The soldier's whole body twitched, and he breathed in ragged gasps.

"Tell me the truth." My eyes claimed his, and I saw the first flicker of fear that he'd shown. I pressed my advantage. "Where are they?"

There was power in the words. Some part of me recognized it. I wasn't surprised when he told the truth this time.

"It was part of our deal with your king. We turned them over to that witch of his. She sent them to her country." His sneer returned, though with less energy. "We don't have need of barbarian slaves. Apparently they do."

Cameron's witch? *Medea.* I stepped back, stunned. What did she want with them? Where were they now?

"Is he lying?" Arland asked. "Jake, is it true?"

I sagged, suddenly bone weary as the surge of Restorer power faded. "It's true." I took a few more steps away and rubbed my face.

From Arland's position by the tree, a blur of movement startled me.

I looked back. The Kahlarean sank to the ground with a line of dark blood at his throat. Arland wiped off his dagger and slipped it back into his boot sheath. My mouth rounded in horror.

Glancing up, Arland saw my expression. "Jake, I know it isn't good news, but we'll deal with it later. Right now the battle is that way. Let's go." He drew his sword and headed back toward Rendor.

He'd misunderstood my dismay, but I didn't bother explaining. Arland was supposed to be one of the good guys, yet he'd just tortured and killed a guy in cold blood. My stomach lurched. I took a few unsteady steps toward where Wade waited for me.

"Jake, don't think right now. Time enough for that later. The men need your help."

Wade was right. I had convinced them to fight this battle. No time for wavering. I pushed away my thoughts for later and charged after Arland, ready to take out my frustration on the first enemy soldier I could find.

Chapter Twenty-Eight

SUSAN

The light walls never stopped glowing. Pallet, floor, and ceiling were all white, as were my tunic and drawstring pants. Yet this was the darkest place I had ever known.

"*There were some things I hadn't found before. But I've seen enough now. You bought yourself today. Tomorrow I'll need this room for new arrivals.*"

Nicco's words invaded my attempts to sleep. I had told myself that death would be a relief, yet my mind screamed in rebellion. I didn't want to die. Dreams chased me. Regrets hounded me.

I had sought God day and night and followed His call to pray for these people in spite of spiraling frustration and anger. I clung to the Scriptures from my world each time fear tore into me. The only thing I had of worth to offer these people was the truth about the One, and I had shared that as best I could.

Still, Nicco had made it clear he had no more use for me and refused to hear more about any One who had more control over his existence than he did.

Mark would never know what happened to me—unless

he found Medea in Lyric and she chose to gloat. My thoughts shifted to the children. Karen and I had planned to make a scrapbook together of her high school years. Who would do that with her now? Who would even venture into her hazardous bedroom to help her gather all her photos and souvenirs?

And Jake. What did the mysterious Restorer signs mean? My own road as a Restorer had been both more difficult and rewarding than I could have imagined. What did the One have planned for my oldest son? I should have done more to prepare him.

Jon and Anne were so young. How would Mark manage? How could I face not being there to see Jon's latest Lego creation? Would they think of me when they walked around the pond after supper? I pictured the color-streaked sky reflecting in still water. Mark's warm and solid arms wrapped around me. The way Anne's curls bounced when she ran ahead of us. Jon's whoop of joy when he caught a frog echoed in my ears.

I'd never again kiss their salty foreheads on a hot summer night as they slept in a tangle of sheets and stuffed animals.

I tasted salt now. Tears poured down my cheeks, wetting my lips as I wiped them away.

I gave up on sleep and pulled aside the narrow pocket door by the sink. Cool water pooled in my palm, refreshing and comforting. I stared at it for a while, then began to wash. I could count my ribs now. They had stopped bringing food again—not that there had ever been much. Weakness manifested itself whenever I stood up. I had to move gradually or sparkling darkness would crowd my vision.

As I had done at least a hundred other times, I tested the door and prowled the room checking for any way of escape. Then I lowered myself onto a chair.

The Rhusicans apparently didn't believe in giving a prisoner a last meal, but I'd treat myself in these hours before dawn. I'd relive my happiest memories in rich detail. Each day of my life had been a gift. My days and hours were in God's hands. If my time was done, I'd thank Him for what He'd given me.

So many images rushed into my mind that it was hard to focus. Finally I picked one shining day to look at. I'd been twenty. The sound was the first part of the memory to flood back.

Guitars thrummed a worship song. People around me clapped and sang. The warm sense of community enveloped me in the tiny but lively campus chapel at Ridge Valley College. Outside the window, trees flounced their fall colors. A gust of wind shook leaves loose to chase each other in spirals. The beginning of my junior year of classes couldn't be more perfect. Classes and practicums, plays and community projects, every day was a banquet of new experiences. God had a plan for my life, and I was squarely in the center of it. Energy and confidence were a hot spring in my soul, bubbling up in unending supply.

The last chorus ended, and the campus pastor pronounced a blessing. Around the chapel, students grabbed their backpacks and started chatting. Waving a greeting to a few girls from my dorm, I made my way down the center aisle. Sunlight pierced the window and touched a man's hair at just the right angle. The blond waves on his downturned head gleamed like gold. But it was the heaviness of his shoulders that stopped me. He looked like a man completely alone—not just in the back row of chairs but in the universe. He stared at the chair in front of him, lost in an expression of sadness that made me ache.

I'd seen him around before but never had any classes with

him. He lived with a group of guys who had an off-campus apartment—one of those budget rooms where busy and broke college men could catch some sleep on a spring-busted couch before diving back into classes and work.

I'd heard rumors he had floated into town one day a few years back and never talked about his past. Whatever he had run from, he looked as if his demons had followed him here.

Maybe he noticed my stillness as the current of other bodies jostled past us and out the door. He looked up.

I was instantly lost in gray-blue eyes. Someone bumped me, and I moved closer. Without my being aware that time had passed, the chapel emptied. The man looked at me quizzically, hiding the despair I'd glimpsed. He probably thought I was nuts. Maybe I was. After all, I needed to go to the library to get started on a term paper. But I couldn't walk away. "Are you all right?" I asked him softly.

His chin lifted. He was about to assure me he was fine and leave me feeling silly for asking. But then his look softened, and he seemed to make a decision. He moved over one chair, gesturing for me to sit down. I eased into the chair beside him and studied his profile as he stared at the cross at the front of the chapel.

"Does He really offer it to anyone?" When he spoke, the voice was deeper and richer than I'd expected. My stomach tingled. I tried to focus on his question.

"Offer what?"

He sighed and rubbed the back of his neck. "The whole thing. Salvation. Forgiveness. Life."

My heart beat faster. I'd shared my faith with cult members who'd serenely waved me away. I'd badgered my freshman-year roommate, whose approach to life was, "Why let God-stuff spoil the fun?" I'd explained Jesus to round-eyed second graders in my Sunday school class. But I'd never seen hunger like this before.

"Yes, of course it's for anyone. That's the point. It's nothing we can earn or deserve."

He looked down at his hands. "Yeah, I understand that part. I've been sitting here week after week trying to figure it out. It's just . . . I'm kind of a different case."

Compassion flooded me. "We all feel that way. We're all sinners. Each of us has felt that the things we did were too horrible—that we must be the one person Christ can't possibly redeem. But He can. He loves you . . ." I was off and running, but he shook his head with a bitter chuckle, and my words trailed away.

"No, that's not what I meant. I'm not sure this offer is for me."

I met his eyes. "It's for every single person on this earth."

The corner of his mouth lifted in a sad smile. "Hence the dilemma." The words were so quiet I could barely make them out, and they didn't make any sense. But I wasn't about to let this end here.

I offered him my hand. "I'm Susan, by the way."

"I'm Mark. Nice to meet you, Susan By-the-way." The teasing light in his eyes chased away his melancholy. My cheeks heated as he held on to my hand. His gaze grew more intense. "You really do know Him, don't you?" He stood up and pulled me to my feet. "Could I buy you a hot chocolate?"

I smiled and nodded. Term papers could wait. We scuffed through bright dried leaves to the student union, where we sipped watery cocoa that burned the roof of my mouth. Nothing had ever tasted so warm and rich to me before. Our words swirled around us, each gust of conversation like different colors of wind-tossed foliage. Even the silences were alive with discovery.

Attraction had flared in both of us that day. While we each could soon catalog the appealing details in the other's appearance, it was the hunger we recognized in each other that filled us with awe. Hunger to know the One who designed us and loved us. Hunger to seek out His purpose for us. I'd never met anyone who devoured the Bible like Mark did. He was able to memorize with an ease that astounded me.

Yet he was also a practical man. He'd landed a job on campus helping the maintenance team and unleashed his gift of fixing things. By the time I met him, he had been hired for freelance building projects by half the professors. Bookcases, decks, play houses—he could create anything. He was also fascinated by the ways things worked. It wasn't enough for him to take an Intro to Computers class. He had to take things apart and have excited conversations with friends about motherboards, poking around the insides of every gizmo he could get his hands on.

In the dismal brightness of my prison in Rhus, I smiled as I thought back to all the times I'd watched Mark bend his head over a project, forehead creased in concentration, a happy light in his eyes, oblivious to anything around him. Tenderness welled up inside me with the memories. I loved him. The secrets he hid from me about his past didn't change that. I would jump at a chance for a twenty-five–cent Styrofoam cup of cocoa shared with him on a bright fall day.

The door hissed open, jolting me from my contemplation. Nicco glared at me from the hall but didn't come in. "Let's go."

I stood up slowly, praying for courage.

Father, if You aren't sending rescue, help me die well.

As we walked down the hall, I looked at all the doors. In this one corridor there were scores of other prisoners. And the building was large. They could be holding hundreds of people. The multiplication of all that suffering broke my heart, and I barely had the strength to keep walking.

"Move. I have more important things to take care of today." Nicco's angry words covered something else. I glanced back at him. His bloodshot eyes darted from side to side, and his fingers twitched in a silent pattern as they hung by his sides.

When we left the building, he gestured me to one of the paths. One part of me soaked in the sight of tall willowy trees and the beauty of the soft gray sky. Another part kept an eye on Nicco. He rubbed a hand over his face and muttered to himself.

He led me to the courtyard where I had first entered Rhus. That day, he had lounged on a stone bench, leaping up to welcome Medea's return. Today there was no languid confidence in him. He looked around as if expecting ghosts to haunt him from the trees.

I was preoccupied with trying to draw strength to face my own death, but even so, his odd behavior piqued my curiosity. "What's wrong?"

His laugh was a bitter, strained sound. "You should know. It's your fault." He turned to me, eyes wild. "You let Him find me." Rage twisted his face, and his shoulders hunched. Then, just as quickly, he backed away a few steps, looking frantically around the courtyard as if he heard something I didn't. He clenched his fists and glared at me. "But I'll fix it. I want you dead." He spat the words with a conviction that let me know exactly how much he wanted that. Then he shifted into a cunning smirk. "But then He might stay. I can't risk it. You brought it here, so you can take it with you."

What was he talking about? Some of his old sneering arrogance returned. He crossed his arms and waited. When I didn't respond, he threw his arm wide and pointed to the stairs that led down into the tunnel. "Go!"

He couldn't mean it, could he? I had given up hope so thoroughly that I stared at him, numb. A warm breath of comprehension thawed some of my confusion. He wanted me to leave. Something about the One had shaken him so much, he wanted me out of Rhus.

I can leave.

I edged a step back. "Wait. Is this another game?" Not that it mattered. Any chance to get away from here was worth taking.

He raked a hand through his hair. "What are you waiting for?" He ran to the top of the stairs. "Just go! Now!" He seemed so out of control, he looked like he might fling himself into the crevice if I didn't leave.

I took a slow breath. Maybe I should try one more time to explain that the One had always known where to find him and wouldn't disappear with me. Maybe if Nicco could grasp the truth, it could change this whole warped culture.

He groaned and pressed the heels of his hands against his forehead. "Medea shouldn't have brought you. Always thinking she could handle things no one else could. But she had to have known." He paced back and forth, muttering, laughing. He was barely touching reality anymore—a rock skipping over waves.

He turned and noticed me again. "Get out!" His voice screeched, and he scampered away from the stairs, leaving me a clear path.

I didn't need an engraved invitation. It might be nobler for me to stay and try to reason with Nicco. Or this might be a trick. But I had expected to die, and now I had a chance to make my way through the tunnel and find my way home. Nothing else mattered.

Hope gave strength to my frail body, and I hurried to the stairs. Three steps down, a picture appeared in my mind and slowed my feet. The building where they kept me. The long hall. All those doors.

God, no. This is my chance. Let me run away.

I worked my way down three more stairs. If I could get away, I could tell someone about all the prisoners here. Someone else could come and save them.

The stirring inside my heart grew. The One had already sent someone to save them.

Haven't I been through enough? I could finally be free of this place. I'm not a Restorer anymore.

But I'd been praying every day for these people, and now the One was prompting me. I couldn't ignore it.

I braced my hands against the cool marble wall beside the stairs and took several slow breaths. Fists clenched, I turned and climbed back up the stairs. Nicco backed away, wild-eyed. "What are you doing? Go away!"

Lord, show me what to do.

"I will." My soothing voice used to work when Anne had slipped into the insanity of a tantrum. Sometimes. Maybe it could also work on insane Rhusicans.

Nicco lurched, as if he planned to push me over the edge. Then he jerked to a stop and backpedaled. He snarled. "What do you want?"

He would do anything to get me away from Rhus. In his twisted mind, I had come to symbolize One that he couldn't control. I braced myself. "The other prisoners. Let them come with me."

His mouth opened and shut but didn't make a sound. He drew himself up, lifted a fist, and took a step toward me. Then he pivoted and paced away, the fist moving to press against his temple. He shook his head from side to side like a dog with a bone caught in its throat. I could almost pity him. Almost.

He froze and looked back at me over his shoulder. A semi-rational gleam lit his eyes. "You promise you'll take them and leave?"

He was too eager. Either the One had gotten under his skin more deeply than I could imagine, or he was like Medea, slipping in and out of lucid thought.

I hesitated. What tricks and traps lay ahead of me? "Yes. Free them all. All of them. I'll take them with me."

He relaxed. A smug smile grew across his face. "Wait here. Or leave. I don't care. I'll bring them." He strode from the courtyard, laughing out loud.

My shrunken stomach knotted. Maybe I should go with him and make sure he kept his word. Of course, if he changed his mind, there wasn't a thing I could do. Besides, I craved my nearness to the tunnel and freedom.

I walked to the edge and stared into the crevice. How would I manage the long hike through the tunnel? Could I convince Nicco to give us some supplies? I paced the courtyard, rubbing my arms.

When Nicco bounded back into sight, his eyes held a mad glint, and I decided not to press my luck.

He skidded to a stop and crossed his arms. "Still here? Well, you can go now." His words dripped with vicious satisfaction.

A stream of thin, dazed captives limped into the courtyard. Dozens of them. Scores. I gave up trying to count. Exhaustion and confusion colored some faces. Others wore vacant stares.

Few even showed interest in their surroundings. Some could barely hobble forward.

"There you go." Nicco waved a careless hand in the air. "We were done with this bunch anyway. You'll save us some trouble if you take them out into the deserts near Shamgar and let them die there." Nicco's earlier agitation had disappeared. He was enjoying himself.

I didn't waste time responding to him. I ran to the closest children, crouched down, and hugged them. "It's all right. We're going home now." I crooned to one little girl until her eyes began to focus. I gently pulled an old woman toward her. "Here, you can help her down the stairs." The woman squinted at me, bewildered, but held the girl's hand when I placed it in hers. I moved along the line, explaining, reassuring. "We're leaving. Be strong a little longer."

Some family members found each other and clung in numb recognition. Most stood mute, staring at the ground. Several dark-haired Hazorites ignored my attempts to talk with them. They skirted around me and hurried past the others to take the stairs. "We should stay together," I called. But they were gone. It was just as well. Shepherding these tattered refugees would be challenging enough.

I approached one woman who was looking around her with at least partial interest. "What's your name?"

"Aiyliss from Rendor clan." She blinked in confusion as she watched the milling bodies in the courtyard. "Most of us are from Rendor."

I scanned the courtyard. More white tunics wandered in from the path. Behind them I saw the vibrant clothes of other Rhusicans. Nicco may have decided it was time to empty their conservatory, but the others might not agree. We needed to get out of here.

"Aiyliss, help me keep everyone moving. Down the stairs and through the tunnel. Just tell them to keep walking as fast as they can. Let's try to pair up some of the stronger ones with anyone too weak to travel." She stared at me, comprehension budding with painful slowness. Then she nodded and moved to help me. Even after I recruited the most alert men and women to help, it was a difficult process. More Rhusicans filed into the courtyard, stood along the sides, and watched in silence.

Every time I glanced their direction, anxiety clawed at me. At any moment, they could grab our minds, force us back. I physically shoved some of the slowest toward the stairs. "Keep moving. Keep moving. You're going to be okay. This way."

The process seemed to take forever, but eventually I was the only prisoner still standing at the top of the stairs. I wasn't entirely sure the whole scene wasn't a Rhusican mind game. I looked at Nicco, wondering if even now he'd stop me from leaving. He just grinned in sour relief.

"Don't come back. And if you happen to meet up with Medea before you die, tell her to bring some stronger guests next time." He sneered in the direction of the stairs. "That bunch wasn't worth the trouble."

Even with freedom calling from the stairs, I hesitated, glancing at the Rhusicans standing behind Nicco. "Why? Why are they letting us go?"

Rage contorted his face. "Our people are dying because of the poison you brought. You and the others who follow the One. The power. The glimpses of Him. We've needed more and more energy to control it once it touched our minds."

I stared at the bright-clad Rhusicans. They were more hollow than the starved prisoners making their way down the stairs. Beauty without substance, empty of anything except satisfying their own whims and creating their own realities.

Nicco stepped close to me and snarled in a whisper, "The older ones have gotten confused. Their minds break apart sooner now."

Compassion flooded me with a tidal surge. I pulled away from Nicco and faced the others, my spine drawing up tall. "There is One who knows you. He understands the skills you have, and the limitations."

Would even one of them listen or understand? If so, all the weeks here would mean something. "You aren't toys and playthings to Him. He cares about you. If you would open your mind to truth, His presence wouldn't be dangerous to you."

The row of men and women watched me, impassive as a shelf of porcelain dolls. Nicco growled and stepped in front of me. "We delve into minds. It gives us strength. We steer others to our will. It's all we have. We'll never give that up."

He had mocked me, tormented me, and dissected my mind as if it were a frog in biology class. But the One filled me with pity for him. "Nicco, I've talked to the One about you. Every day you had me locked up, I asked Him to reveal Himself to you and your people. He's answering. Don't be afraid."

His nostrils flared and he spoke through a tight jaw. "Get out. Now."

A malevolent thread of thought pierced into my mind: He wanted to kill me. He wanted it with a passion beyond lust or greed. Only a thin barrier of fear held him back.

Lord, can I go now?

Inner prompting pushed with the strength of a hand between my shoulder blades. Time to go. I backed toward the cleft in the ground. "May the words of the One burn in your hearts until you know His love." My voice choked. Everything inside me wanted these people to be free, but I'd done what I could. I turned and ran down the stairs. Time to put Rhus behind me and fight to survive the journey ahead.

Chapter Twenty-Nine

JAKE

A hefty Kahlarean soldier leapt over a log and slammed into me.

I hate this.

The realization built while my arm kept swinging. I whacked, dodged, parried, killed, and ran forward to do it all again.

Why had I imagined this would be thrilling and noble? Playing at swords with my dad had been fun. Dreams of being the hero who would free Rendor had given me a warm glow. There was some wonderful symmetry to it all. My grandfather had pushed the Kahlarean army back at Cauldron Falls. My father had to leave his world because of Kahlarean assassins. Now I could be the ultimate champion to save the clans once and for all. Visions had shown me standing at the pass.

But none of this felt the way I'd expected. We might liberate Rendor, but for what? The people were gone. How was I making any difference?

A Kahlarean a few yards away lifted his sword to hack into a guardian who was busy fighting someone else. I charged into him, my shoulder bruising into his breastplate. He hit the ground, and my sword swung through in a strong arc. He died with a shriek. Another sound to haunt my nightmares.

A huge warrior lumbered in my direction. He lifted his weapon, and I was inside his guard before he realized what was happening. More blood. My hands were sticky with it. I fought harder and faster. I wanted this to be over so I could wash my hands.

I was learning to stay alert to the chaos of action all around me. Wade had saved me several times when I was too focused on one enemy and paid no attention to anything else. Now, while I exchanged blows with the next Kahlarean in front of me, I was also able to notice that we were getting closer to the buildings of Rendor. We were in greater danger here. Away from the cover of the trees, we once again became targets for the Kahlarean syncbeams.

Adjusting my hands into a two-fisted grip, I sliced my way past another soldier.

God, why did You forbid long-range weapons to the clans if their enemies are using them? And all You send them is a Restorer? You're doing things the hard way.

As I ran forward, I heard the hum of weapons. Blasts of heat hit the ground around us, though the Kahlareans couldn't target the guardians without hitting their own men, so the stray beams weren't doing much damage.

Okay, maybe it wasn't hopeless after all.

My eyes focused on one of the buildings. Another flash of light erupted. I raced forward. The beam almost found me, but I reached the building and found the soldier first. I made it my job to find the source of each syncbeam and smash the weapon and its operator into the ground.

The fourth time, I misjudged. A syncbeam fired from a

building twenty yards away. I dove forward, but the enemy saw me coming. Razor-edged pain seared across my chest, then whipped back across my legs as my body spun and fell. I heard a strangled scream and realized it had come from my throat. I tried to move, but the fierce fire of the wounds paralyzed me. Someone grabbed my shoulders and tugged. Impossibly, the agony grew worse. My vision blurred, and if I could have gotten breath, I would have screamed again. I clawed my way back toward consciousness. Wade was pulling me out of the line of fire. He dropped me against the side of a building and crouched, sword ready, scanning in all directions. When he was sure there was no immediate danger, he finally turned to me.

Burnt grilled cheese sandwiches. The smell filled my nose. Mom never used enough butter. I could smell the black smoke now. Suddenly, that seemed funny. A fractured chuckle gasped from my lungs; the world went gray.

Wade's worried growl dragged me back. "Jake? Jake, what should I do?"

My face screwed up tight against the throbbing misery of my wounds. Every movement made the agony flare, and I ground my teeth together. Deep breaths. Give it time. The roar of blood pulsing in my ears died down enough that I could hear the sounds of battle still exploding around me.

Healing skin itched and prickled its way across my wounds. The pain dialed back enough for me to open my eyes. Wade's face was smudged with dirt and blood, his round face compressed with worry.

"I'm okay." The lie wheezed out. "Just give me a minute."

He nodded and turned to keep our position protected, but the fight had moved farther into the city, and no one headed our direction.

The healing didn't happen quickly. Willing it to hurry did no good. By the time I could prop myself up, the fighting was far across the city and I could hear the rumble of the river for the first time.

Wade leaned forward, poised, eager to move out again. He looked like a dog straining against his leash.

"I'll be all right now. Go on and help them." I tried to be convincing while clawing myself up the wall to stand.

Wade stared at me, offended. "I'm staying right here until you're ready to move."

I didn't have the energy to argue. Besides, his loyalty warmed me. I stretched my hearing. Which direction had the combat moved? Where could we best rejoin the battle? "Let's circle this far edge of the town and come up behind, from the river."

Wade nodded his approval and waited for me to hobble the direction I'd suggested. "Jake." The sharp reproof made me turn. "Your sword."

My blade lay forgotten in the dust, ugly with gore and dirt. I limped back, embarrassed, and bent over slowly to grab it. The weight almost pulled me back to the ground, but I managed to heft it and straighten. My lurching progress improved as the healing deepened through my body. When the river came into sight, I longed to run straight into the water. But we weren't finished yet.

I glanced around and frowned. "Isn't there supposed to be a waterfall?"

Wade rubbed his beard. "Cauldron Falls is upriver, but it's a long climb."

"But that's where they come from, right? The Kahlareans?"

"The pass is right above the falls. That's where our guardian outpost used to be."

The visions and dreams coalesced in my mind. The clearing. The roar of the waterfalls. Holding off enemies. The pass. That's where I was supposed to be.

I whirled to look at Wade. "I have to go. I'm supposed to defend the pass."

"All right," Wade said slowly. "After we beat them out of the town, you can tell Arland, and we'll send a group that way tomorrow."

Urgency scratched inside my bones. "No. We have to go now."

Wade's limbs locked with the stubborn stance of a bulldog. "You can't run off. At least find Arland. If you turn up missing, he'll waste men searching for you."

He was right. Besides, I'd promised to keep Arland informed. "Fine. Then let's find him." I bit the words out, using all my will not to shout in frustration.

I loped between empty buildings, aiming for the sound of the most conflict. Wade and I ran into a few stray Kahlareans; the dirt on my sword was soon washed away with fresh blood. We also passed dead and wounded guardians. I gritted my teeth and ran on.

We found Arland behind a low wall, planning an assault on a large building that flickered with syncbeam fire. When he saw us running forward in a crouch, the head guardian turned from signaling one of his men. His eyes scanned the singed fabric of my tunic. "Are you all right?"

I nodded. Arland's own wounds had torn open. The side of his shirt was black with oozing blood. "You?"

His grin was feral. "We're making progress." A beam seared over our heads and we ducked lower. Then Arland edged around the corner of the wall to check on the progress of his men.

"I need to head upriver to the Falls."

He whipped his head back toward me. "It's not safe. We need you here."

It was hard to look forceful and determined while crouching behind a wall, but I did my best. "It's a Restorer vision. I'm supposed to be there."

He hissed through his teeth. "Fine. Tomorrow. After we finish here and the men get some rest, we'll head up to the Falls."

Kahlarean soldiers rushed from the building and crossed swords with guardians in the street. The clanking and shrieking grew louder.

"No. I'm going now." I had to shout over the noise.

The anger in Arland's eyes slipped perilously close to hatred. "Jake, don't do this."

Wade braced himself with a hand on my shoulder and leaned toward Arland. "Could be some of the Kahlareans went out the back and are headed to the pass. If one of them gets word across, they'll send reinforcements. It's not a bad idea to seal that up now. I'll go with him."

Arland checked on the battle that was moving still farther into the city. When he turned back, his jaw was set. "Your vision. Are you sure about this?"

"Yes. It's what I've been seeing since I came here. I need to go. Now."

"Fine. But I'm sending some men with you. And I want you reporting back to me by tonight."

Arland glared at Wade, who answered with a sharp nod. The syncbeams had stopped, and we were able to stand. The guardians had taken one more building. Arland vaulted over the low wall and called out to one of the captains as he came out into the street.

"Take some of your men and go with Jake and Wade. Chase down any stragglers and hold the pass." The captain beckoned his men our direction, but at the same time, Ian popped out from behind another house.

"Arland, let me go with him." The head guardian raised an eyebrow, and Ian shrugged. "I owe him. I'll bring my best men and back him up."

Ian's show of support raced through me like the warm fingers of healing had minutes earlier. "Thank you." Ian just looked away.

Arland eyed the progress of another group down the street, but he spared a moment to spear me with his gaze. "When we're done here, I'll send some men to relieve you at the pass. I'm expecting you back before nightfall."

"I'll be here."

Wade led the way back through the deserted streets of Rendor and to the river. He set a brisk pace following the bank. Ian and three of his men followed me. I strained to hear any sounds above the water tumbling over boulders. If there were Kahlareans ahead of us, I couldn't detect them.

When we were well above Rendor, we stopped to indulge in a long drink of cold water. I scrubbed my arms until the skin was red, numb from the icy river. I knew enough not to get my gear and weapons drenched; otherwise I would have plunged all the way into the water. As far as I was concerned, there wasn't enough water to wash away the horrors of the day.

The force of the current churned against boulders, hurtling forward. I stared at the shifting patterns. My life was racing forward now too. After so many weeks of floundering, my reason—my purpose—lay around the next bend.

"Jake." Wade called with the annoying insistence of my

alarm after I'd hit the snooze button one too many times.

The water was incredibly clear. I could count the stones in the eddy near us.

"Jake." A hand thumped onto my shoulder, and I jerked back, confused. Wade's concerned face blurred into focus. "Remember what I told Arland? If any of the Kahlareans are heading for the pass, we need to catch them."

I turned back to watch the water. Clean. Pure. Uncompromising.

A meaty fist clamped around my arm and pulled me to my feet. "You held your own today. Stay focused. You can think about it later." Wade kept his voice low, glancing back to where Ian and his men waited.

"When?" I looked at Wade.

He frowned. "When what?" He clearly thought I was losing it. Maybe I was.

"You keep telling me not to think. When do I get to think?"

Sadness brushed across his face before he could hide it. He forced a grin and cuffed my arm. "Come on, Jake. Let's move."

My limbs dragged. Where was my Restorer strength now? We kept climbing.

"I'll scout into the woods, in case they didn't stay close to the river," Ian called. Wade waved an acknowledgment. I tried to stretch my hearing, and the roar of the waterfall ahead swelled to an unbearable level.

I stopped and closed my eyes, working to focus my hearing in other directions. "That's weird."

Wade planted his sword into the earth and rubbed stiffness from his fingers. "What is?"

"A voice."

"Kahlareans?"

I shook my head. "Sounds like Ian. Who would he be talking to?"

Wade grinned. "Maybe he's talking to the One. You're a good influence."

The voice faded, and I tried to laugh at his joke.

Wade turned to Ian's men. "Go see if he needs help. Meet us up at the outpost."

They cut into the trees, and Wade and I approached the falls alone. We sheathed our swords, freeing our hands for the rough climb. Now that we were moving again, my feeling of urgency returned.

At the top of the falls, we drew our weapons and followed a worn path to a clearing. As soon as I saw the outpost and the sheer rock walls towering near the pass, my heart throbbed. Stronger than déjà vu, a sense of belonging in this place and moment grabbed me. I faced the narrow path where the rock surface created a natural bridge over and across this narrowed section of the river. I expected Kahlarean soldiers to come pouring through like an endless column of ants from a crack in the sidewalk. Nothing stirred.

I swung my sword in a few circles to loosen my arm. "Do you think any of them made it across to get reinforcements?"

Wade shrugged. "Can't say. But we won't let anyone past now, eh, Jake?"

We exchanged grins, and my sense of purpose grew. The Kahlareans weren't going to terrorize our clans anymore. We'd keep their soldiers from fleeing back and reporting that we had retaken Rendor. And we'd fight off anyone who tried to cross from their side.

Wade patrolled the edges of the clearing, peering down the

trails that led here from several directions. I hovered by the pass, staring down the rock corridor looking for a glimpse of anything that moved.

Half an hour later, a crash sounded from beyond the outpost and drew me away from my self-appointed guard duty. Ian burst into the clearing from the side farthest from the river. "We caught one. Wade, my men need your help."

Wade's eyes lit, and he bounded toward the trail Ian had taken. Then he pulled up short.

"It's all right." Ian waved him on. "I'll stay with the boy."

Wade ducked under a branch and headed down the trail.

I turned to watch for any sign of men crossing through the gap over the river, but I threw a glance over my shoulder in Ian's direction. "Thanks for helping."

"I owed you." Ian's low voice darkened.

What was he angry about now? I thought he wanted to help me. And why did Ian leave his men to come and get Wade? Ian was every bit as strong of a fighter and, as a guardian of Rendor clan, had as much authority as Wade to question their captive.

A cold chill crawled from the ground and up my spine. I turned slowly.

Ian met my gaze with hard gray eyes that still reminded me of my dad. Behind him stood four hooded and masked Kahlareans. They had melted into the clearing in perfect silence. Assassins.

My heart pounded with the uneven gait of a lehkan. "Ian, look out!" Why didn't he react?

The Rendor guardian turned to one of the assassins. "He's the one."

"You're sure?" The Kahlarean voice was a breathy whisper.

"Yes. I've seen it myself. You'll pull out of Rendor now? I have your word?"

The bug eyes of the assassin squinted over the cloth that covered the lower half of his face. He was grinning. "You have our gratitude," he said in a throaty murmur. He offered his hand to Ian.

Shock and anger churned in a volatile mix in my stomach. "What are you doing?"

Ian sneered. "I told you that too many people have died because of the Restorers. All they want is to take one captive. Then they'll leave the clans alone." He shrugged. "It's what you're here for, right?" He reached out to grasp the Kahlarean's arm in a warrior's greeting. He didn't notice the flicker of metal in the assassin's left hand.

"No!" I raced forward. Too late.

A compact silver venblade streaked across the short distance and pierced Ian's tunic near his heart. The guardian's eyes widened and he fell backward, twitching as the poison raced through his system.

I swung my weapon in a wild arc, but two of the assassins closed in behind me. One of them bashed a sword against my arm and knocked my blade from my grip. Another reached from behind me to press a curved dagger against my neck. Knobby fingers grabbed a fistful of hair and yanked my head back.

"We'll disable you as much as you like, Restorer," a voice hissed behind me. "But you're coming to Kahlarea. You're ours now."

Chapter Thirty

JAKE

Knife to my throat or not, they weren't taking me without a fight. Fury raced through me with one quick gasp for air, and my muscles tightened.

"Hold!" The command from a familiar voice stopped me. The Kahlareans froze. The assassin's grip loosened enough for me to turn my head.

Arland stormed into the clearing. He spared a glance at Ian's body, and something dark flickered in his eyes but disappeared. "Sorry, Jake. I can't let you do this."

I gaped at him, completely confused.

He strode closer, hands lifted away from his sword hilt. "I know I agreed to Ian's plan, but I can't let you make this sacrifice in my place." He gave me a warning look before turning to the assassins and pasting on a face of devout solemnity. "It's not what the One would want me to do. I'm the Restorer. I'll go with you."

This was crazy. They'd kill him trying to see if he would heal. I couldn't let him do this. "No— "

"I know you wanted to prevent this." His eyes burned into

me and he spoke slowly. "Our people need the Restorer"—he faced the assassins—"but there have been enough deaths. I'll come with you."

Two of the Kahlareans exchanged angry whispers. The one behind me released his grip and stepped toward Arland. "Easy enough to discover the truth."

"Wait!" I leapt forward. Too late again.

The assassin's curved blade sliced across Arland's belly. The head guardian fell to his knees, fresh blood darkening the already saturated tunic. I reached him a second after his gasp of pain and caught him, easing him to the ground.

What kind of stupid plan was this? How could he have offered himself to them? What was he thinking? The Kahlareans watched from a distance, expecting to witness an unnatural recovery, but I focused all my attention on Arland. "Why?" The word tore from my throat.

The corner of his mouth quirked upward. Then his face contorted in a grimace. He drew a rough and wheezing breath. One hand pulled my head closer. "They'll want you alive. Fight them, Jake." The words were barely audible.

I couldn't pull my gaze away. He squinted with pain. When his eyes opened again, they were clouding. My grip on his shoulders tightened. I wanted to shake life back into him.

God, heal him! Do something.

Arland's body arched. He struggled to control the pain and focused on me with all the power of a leader of men giving his last command. "I've seen enough Restorers come and go." He gasped and fought to get the words out. The next words were whispered for me alone but were every bit as strong as a shout. "Stay around for more than one battle."

He was dying. My reluctant ally, the leader of the guardians.

I wanted to scream, make time stop, make this not be real. His eyes held me, demanding an answer.

I leaned closer. "I promise."

His hand lifted, and I grasped it. He guided it to rest over his sword hilt. One more grimace flashed across his face. Could have been pain, or a triumphant grin. "Fight them, Jake." Then he closed his eyes.

Behind me, one of the assassins whispered to his colleague, "Is he healing?"

"I didn't try for a mortal wound. He must have already been damaged." They studied my friend's body like he was a formaldehyde-soaked cat in biology class.

Rage erased conscious thought. My hand closed over Arland's sword, and I drew it in one smooth movement, lifting from my crouch and swinging it wide. I took out one Kahlarean with the first swing.

The others hissed and fell back.

A roar sprang from my throat, and I charged straight for one who wielded a drawn sword. I engaged him, and our swords crashed and scraped. I circled to keep from turning my back on the other two. Speed was my only chance.

With reckless fury, I knocked aside my opponent's blade and lunged forward. The move left me open, but I didn't care. I barely felt his sword score my leg as I moved in tight and killed him.

I shoved his body aside and faced the last two elite killers, one of whom had drawn a sword. I met his downward swing, instincts reacting with no time to spare. I countered strike after strike, looking for an opening and worrying about the second assassin who had drifted out of my sight line.

Every bit of training from the guardian tower months ago,

each move I'd learned from my dad, every new trick I'd picked up from Arland—it all surged from my memory to serve me now. The assassin seemed to move in slow motion. His blade arced in a lateral swing, and I blocked, spun, and sliced deep into his sword arm. He fell back, and I charged forward to finish him.

As my feet carried me forward, something sharp pricked my left shoulder. Ignoring it, I stormed forward and managed to kill my opponent in a few more clumsy strokes.

I tossed back my sweat-soaked hair. My dad would have scolded me on my lack of finesse, but hey, it worked. I felt a grim satisfaction and none of the repulsion I'd labored under during the morning's attack on Rendor.

Now I could spare a second to turn.

The last assassin had grabbed a sword from one of the dead Kahlareans and stood with eerie stillness, watching me. My shoulder throbbed, and I craned my head to check it. Silver gleamed from the narrow venblade wedged deep into my flesh.

My breathing kicked into frantic panting. I passed my sword over to my left hand so I could reach back to tug the dagger free. It fell from my nerveless fingers even as the sword slipped from my hand.

The assassin kept his distance, allowing his poison to do all the work. He would wait until I was completely paralyzed and then drag me away.

I stumbled to pick up Arland's sword from the dust at my feet. His lifeless body shouted silently to me from its crumpled shape across the clearing. He had finally let himself believe in a new Restorer for his people. He had given his life so that I could defend the clans. I wouldn't let him down.

Months ago—it felt like lifetimes ago—I had raised a can

of soda in our kitchen on Ridgeview Drive and toasted, "To those who serve the One."

On legs clumsy with creeping paralysis, I ran at the last assassin. "For the One!" I shouted the words, my throat raw with anguish and determination. He raised his sword to meet mine, his oversized eyes bulging. For precious seconds, sheer will held back the deadening toxin in my bloodstream.

It was long enough. If my earlier sword fighting was less than elegant, now it must have appeared comic. I drew wide, frantic curves through the air. The assassin was forced to block. We locked blades, and I squeezed upward, trapping his guard against mine and forcing our bodies close. I snarled into his face with my last bit of strength.

I released my sword.

His eyes squinted in a grin as he assumed my right hand was succumbing. I let him believe it and doubled over. My hand found my boot knife, safe in the sheath against my right ankle.

It was in my palm and thrusting up into the Kahlarean's chest almost of its own volition. I don't know where the strength came from, but the dagger did its work.

The hooded assassin clawed at the handle and fell back. My own body sank to the ground like melting wax.

I had a few seconds to relish my victory. I'd done it. The assassins were dead. Arland's sacrifice wouldn't be useless. I'd stopped them from taking the Restorer.

Paralysis advanced from my limbs toward my chest. Terror took over when my lungs refused to obey my demand to breathe. Gray shards of darkness jammed into my vision from all directions. A metallic tang filled my mouth like the aftertaste of penicillin.

God, don't let any more of them come until I'm awake.

My body died by inches, and I felt it happen with hideous awareness—until the darkness won.

Chapter Thirty-One

JAKE

"Is he alive?" A soft voice tickled my consciousness.

Oh, Lord, don't let it be more Kahlareans.

I struggled to force my eyes open. A guardian stood nearby, but he wasn't looking at my body. He was speaking to one of our men who crouched beside Arland.

I took a shuddering breath and held it, waiting.

The guardian's angry curse gave me the answer.

I moaned.

Two dirty, bearded faces soon hovered over me. "Jake? What happened?"

I tried to shift, but my limbs still carried the frightening numbness of circulation pinched off.

My lips moved. I shaped my next moan into words. "Help me."

One of the men knelt down next to me. "What can we do?"

It was getting easier to talk. I told my head to lift and had slight success. "Arland. Get me over to him. Hurry."

I wouldn't give up hope. It had happened before. Kieran

had died defending my mom. Then the One brought him back as the new Restorer. The men dragged me closer to Arland and propped me up. This time my hand obeyed my command, and I was able to reach out and rest it over Arland's heart, though I still couldn't feel the rough wet fabric beneath my fingers.

I dropped my head.

Lord, he'd be a much better Restorer than I ever would. I know that You couldn't have meant for him to die. The guardians need him. I did what You asked. I told the songkeepers about the fake Records, and I led the men in saving Rendor. Take the signs away from me. Give them to him. Bring him back.

With a deep sigh, I raised my chin and opened my eyes, fully expecting color to wash across Arland's face. My own body continued to restore, but Arland was as pale as a Kahlarean and as lifeless as the other corpses around the clearing.

I lifted my face higher, staring past overhanging pine branches and up to the thick gray sky. Desperation wrenched a cry from my soul. "Heal him!"

The two guardians near me edged back a few steps and exchanged a look. For the first time, I noticed several other men had been patrolling the clearing. They stopped and turned in our direction. I ignored them all.

My limbs functioning once again, I grabbed Arland's shoulders. "You can't go. You can't. It's not supposed to be like this." I closed my eyes and prayed again.

Finally, a guardian pried my fingers free and pulled me away. "Jake, what happened here?"

I forced myself to focus. They needed an explanation. The man helped me to my feet, and I gave him a terse summary of Ian's treachery and my battle with the assassins. I wanted to throw myself over Arland and cry like a little kid, but when I looked at him again, resolve hardened in my muscles like cooling steel. "Send two of the men to search for Wade. Ian lured him away. Find out what happened."

An older guardian, with gray streaking his beard, quickly signaled to his men, then turned back to me. "Once Arland knew we had things wrapped up in Rendor, he told us to gather supplies and come provide backup for you at the outpost. He set out ahead, and we never caught up to him. Do you think he suspected there'd be trouble?"

Grief battered my attempts to stay strong. "I don't know. I don't think he could have imagined that Ian would be planning to give me to the Kahlareans. But Arland saved my life. He distracted the assassins long enough to give me a chance." My throat felt thick, and for a second I wondered if the venblade's poison was flaring up again.

The old guardian stared at me. "What do we do now?"

Why was he asking me? I didn't want to have to make decisions. I wanted to curl up in a ball. I ground my teeth together.

The two men returned, one of them supporting Wade, who stumbled into the clearing and looked at the carnage in a daze. "They ambushed me." He pressed his hand against the back of his head. "Something crashed into the back of my head, and they must have thought I was dead. Jake, I'm sorry."

I waved that aside. "Any sign of Ian's men?"

The other guardian shook his head.

I brushed the back of my hand across my forehead, feeling the sensation of damp skin. The numbness was wearing off. "I don't know if they were in it with Ian or if he just lured them away." I stared at Ian's body and fought the urge to kick him.

No time for tantrums. The men had lost their head

guardian, and there was still a lot to take care of. My mind sharpened. "Okay, Wade and I will head back down and make sure everything is secure in Rendor. You men stay here and don't let anything that moves cross that gap. I'll send up more men before dark, and we'll leave a dozen to replace you all tomorrow."

Wade rubbed the back of his head. "And tomorrow?"

I gave him a level look. "We have one more job to do. We're taking the men and heading to Lyric."

The long hike back down to Rendor gave me time to plan. Wade dogged my steps but didn't attempt any of his usual genial conversation. I tried to reassure him that he hadn't failed in his role as my protector. No one could have anticipated Ian's plan. Nothing I said seemed to help. His inability to protect me, plus the death of his captain, had crushed any playful energy out of him for the moment.

In contrast, my various wounds healed and the poison left my system. I had plenty of energy—and resolve.

When we reached the city, we found that the men had already established a base camp in several large central buildings. "Wade, I need to speak with the captains. Will you find them?"

He nodded, eager to do something helpful.

"Oh, and we need to pick six of the most reliable men in the guardians to send up to the outpost." I rubbed my shoulder. It felt stiff. Maybe it was just tension.

Wade rattled off names and clans of several men. I nodded. "Fine. Whatever."

Word spread that we were back, and the captains gathered

in no time. Many of the other men hovered nearby as well. Let them listen. This affected them all.

No sense easing into the news. "Arland was killed by Kahlarean assassins. He gave his life to distract them enough to give me a chance."

The men had seen so much horror they almost couldn't absorb this added loss. They stared at me with battle-stained faces, expressions numb like they'd all been stabbed with venblades.

Wade stepped up beside me. "Ian made a deal with the Kahlareans—he betrayed Jake."

That stirred grunts of shock and disbelief. I lifted a hand. "I understand his reasons. He knew that the Kahlareans had killed others in their obsession to capture a Restorer, ever since the time of Mikkel. He thought he could keep the clans safe if he turned me over to them. In his mind it was a fair trade."

"What happened to the assassins?"

Wade puffed out his chest. "Jake killed them. All four of them."

Eyes widened, and even some of the oldest and grimmest of the guardian captains nodded.

I'd finally earned their respect, but I had more important issues to focus on. "Ian thought his plan could protect the clans. Cameron thought surrendering Rendor to Kahlarea would protect the clans. He thinks forbidden weapons will help us keep up with our enemies. He's wrong. The One is our protector. Not schemes, not deals, not new weapons."

Power surged through my words as it had in the clearing above Braide Wood. I should have been more nervous addressing the leaders of the guardians. They hadn't been impressed with me in the past, nor was losing their very capable leader because of me likely to change their minds.

Yet they hung on every word, and I knew they would follow me.

"We've regained Rendor because the One was with us. Now it's time to find out what Medea did with all the clan who were still living here. Tomorrow I'm going to Lyric. Are you with me?"

"The Restorer!" called a reedy voice from behind a group of men. It was the young messenger I had helped earlier.

"The Restorer!" the rest of the men echoed in a deep shout.

I drew the captains in closer and sketched out my plans. Reinforcements needed to be sent up the pass. Wade had found four of the six men he recommended. Of the others, one had died in a syncbeam blast, the other was crippled by a sword wound to the leg. A captain from Blue Knoll suggested a few other men, and Wade nodded and went off to send them on their way.

"We also need to send four men to carry down the two bodies." I was mentally ticking off things we had to do before nightfall.

"Two?" one of the men asked. His snarl told me he'd just as soon leave Ian's body to the bears and ground-crawlers.

"You heard me. Arland *and* Ian. We'll have the funeral at first light. For them and the others who fell today."

The captains filled me in on what they'd already set up. One building was converted to a makeshift healer's lodge, although we didn't have any healers with us. The messenger offered to head to the nearest village to find one. I sent him on his way but told him to keep our victory a secret for now. The next few days would be dangerous enough. Secrecy gave us an edge.

Several of the men from Rendor volunteered to stay and

guard their reclaimed city. It took some hard math to be sure we'd have enough men left to patrol the pass at the falls and hold the city in case Cameron's guards followed us or Kahlareans who'd escaped the battle regrouped.

With casualties and the division of our troops, we were left with about forty men to march on to Lyric. "And the lehkan troops will reach the plains outside Rendor by tomorrow," the Blue Knoll captain said.

I brightened at that reminder. We finished making plans for the next day, and the captains scattered to continue their work.

"Jake, this way." Wade had been busy while I met with the captains. He'd found an empty house near the buildings where the rest of the guardians were camped. I stumbled after him, weak with sudden exhaustion. He slapped an encouraging paw against my back and nearly knocked me over. "I found your gear. They've moved all the supplies up from the transport station. I figured you'd want to change."

I looked down at my tunic. Syncbeam burns, blood, and dirt covered the fabric. I managed a grin. "Now why would you think that?"

Wade steered me to a washroom down the hall and left me in peace.

Running water. I let it pour over my hands: clear, moving forward, like the river. It mesmerized me.

Until something thumped against the door. "Jake, I'm fixing us some supper. You almost done?" Wade bellowed loudly enough to pull me out of my fugue.

"Yeah. Be right there." I cleaned up and hurried out to the common room.

Wade shoved a mug of clavo into my hands, spicy enough to make me sneeze. It had cooled, so I guzzled it to the last drop and realized I was hungry. The thought surprised me. It felt disrespectful to have a normal appetite after this day of violence and loss. But Wade was digging in, so I did too. I hadn't eaten breakfast — way too on edge. We'd fought nonstop since then. My body had healed from grave wounds more than once. I was starving.

After my third helping of stew, Wade raised his eyebrows but didn't say anything.

Finally, I leaned my elbows on the table and relaxed. The room seemed to be shifting slightly. It was like getting off a wild ride at the amusement park. For the first few steps afterward, the whole earth wobbled. Now that I wasn't fighting, hiking, or making speeches, I noticed how off-center everything seemed.

I wrinkled my forehead. If I concentrated really hard, everything would stop moving for a few seconds.

"Wade, why did the men listen to my plans and agree to follow me?"

He tilted his chair back and gave me a genuine smile. "Jake, anyone could see it."

"See what?"

"That the One is with you. They know you're the Restorer now, even if you weren't confirmed by the Council. You fought with them today. You convinced us all to come here. We won a battle we shouldn't have been able to win. Of course they'll follow you."

He said some more things, but the tabletop had edged closer to me. It looked comfortable; I rested my forehead against it for just a second. From a distance, I heard Wade's low chuckle. "I guess even Restorers need sleep, eh?"

It took superhuman effort to stagger into a side bedroom and collapse onto a pallet. Wade called from the hallway, "You can sleep. I've arranged for a watch."

A watch? Images of a Timex floated through my mind. I smirked at the stray thought. Just before I sank all the way into sleep, I saw Arland's face, heard his words: "Stay around for more than one battle."

I flopped onto my stomach. "I promise," I whispered, my cheek squashed into the pallet.

Chapter Thirty-Two

JAKE

The captains agreed that we should approach Lyric together. Instead of hopscotching on transports, we took several days to hike, with the lehkan regiment riding all around us at a slow pace. The remaining men had time to coalesce into new groups. We restocked our supplies as we made our way through one village, and even picked up a few more lehkan.

The worst of the wounded had remained in Rendor. Those with minor injuries benefited from this time to mend. Weapons were sharpened, alliances reinforced. Wade commandeered a lehkan for my use, and I got a little better at managing the skittish creature. The captains had wholeheartedly endorsed most of my plans, but when I told them I wanted to keep the fact that I was a Restorer a secret a little longer, they balked.

I wasn't worried about my safety; I was no longer shy about revealing my role. But we didn't know the situation in Lyric, and having an ace up my sleeve felt like good strategy. They finally agreed.

The extra days also gave me time to thrash over some things with the One. I followed Wade's advice to "not think" for as long as possible but eventually had to confront everything that had happened. Yes, we had taken Rendor, I had survived, and the One's power had poured through me when needed. But I had nightmares about the men I'd killed.

And Arland was dead. When I'd wake in a cold sweat, I'd hear his last words: *Stay around for more than one battle.* It was on me to make sure I kept my promise to him.

One night, when Wade was snoring, I slipped away from our campsite to pray. It was the only time I could get out from under the shadow of my dogged protector.

"I know what I'm supposed to say." Even though my voice was soft, the words were harsh and wrenched from deep in my gut. "I'm supposed to thank You for doing what You promised—for having a plan, for being in charge. But I want to say something else." I stopped myself. How could I rage against the One who had restored life to me over and over?

Tell Me.

The invitation was gentle and so clear it was almost audible. I huffed and ducked my head with a grin. He knew what I was feeling anyway. No need to hide behind politeness.

"Okay, You know I've always wanted to make a difference. And when I got to know You, I figured You were the one who put those dreams in me. I wanted to be a knight and battle dragons and lead an army and right wrongs. My picture of what it would be like was silly, but I really wanted to serve You. So was I wrong? Have I completely blown it? Was it all stupid pride to think I could do something important for You?"

It's all important to Me, Jake. You followed when you thought you understood the path. Now you know more about the cost. Will you still follow?

The words pulled me up short. Was He really offering me a choice? Some choice. Sure, when I agreed to follow Him, I didn't really understand all it would involve. But now that I did, could I really walk away?

"Of course I still want to follow You." Then my eyes stung, and I squeezed them tight. "But did Arland have to die? The people need a strong leader. What are You going to do?"

His answer came with startling clarity and left me so shaken that I stumbled back to my blanket in the camp. I lay awake staring up at the black sky for most of the night. I composed another song in my head. Not one I'd ever share. The people here wouldn't understand some of the references. But it helped me get through the night.

Holy One,
Maker of all that is,
Hold me close
When darkness seeks to bury me;
Keep me safe in You.

Holy One,
You who set the stars in place,
Guide my path as You guide theirs;
Never let me stray too far
From Your way.

Holy One,
Bring light into my heart.
See the torment chaining me
To the wall of my own sin.

Set me free
Teach me how to hope again.

Though the world has wounded me,
You have never failed.

The next night, we made camp close to Lyric. Evon, the young messenger, had run ahead to gather all the information he could. He rejoined us and sat with Wade and me around a heat trivet and gratefully wolfed down the boiled caradoc in our bowl.

"Sounds like things in the capital are very unstable." He wiped gravy off his chin with his sleeve. "There are whispers that the king is crazy. He stormed into the worship tower one day and shouted all kinds of incoherent things until some of his guards talked him into leaving. And the whole city is in chaos. No one knows for sure who is in charge. The transtechs have stopped working on all the projects the king had them doing. Some have left Lyric, and others are stirring up trouble. The songkeepers have gathered and want to reinstate the end-of-season Feast day, but the king isn't allowing them to use the worship tower. There's been lots of confusion about old Records and new Records."

He shrugged. "I couldn't find out for sure how strong the king's guard is, but everyone in the city is still afraid to cross them."

I rubbed my chin. Wisps of beard were filling out on my face. I hadn't shaved in weeks. "Okay, so did you find out anything about Medea? Is she still alive? Is she still in Lyric?"

Evon hunched down into his cloak and twisted the edge of it between his fingers. "Sorry, no one knew anything." He looked up at me. "I've been trained to memorize and deliver messages, not spy." His gaze dropped to the pine needles scattered on the ground. "I did the best I could."

Poor kid. In over his head. Just like me. "You did great. This will help a lot."

He answered a few more questions, then hurried off to settle his blankets among a group of young guardians. My fingers drummed nervous patterns against my leg.

"Jake?" Wade mirrored my worried frown.

I yawned. "Let's get some sleep. Tomorrow's a big day."

Wade didn't buy it. "Will it be a problem for you if she's still there?"

I stared at my boots. Even thinking about her made my stomach clench. "I don't know. But if she gets me under her power again, do me a favor?"

"What?"

I launched to my feet. "Kill me yourself."

The next morning, we approached the main entry tunnel of Lyric. I rode at the front of the guardian army, sword at my side. As the scalloped white walls rose up before us, I glanced back. I had a moment to appreciate the irony. Here I was, riding at the head of an army. No shining armor or white charger. My lehkan was a far cry from the regal mounts in my childhood books. But I did have a few dragons yet to slay.

As we drew closer, a sound rose on the morning air. Voices raised in cheers. I craned my neck and looked up. Lining the top edge of the three-story-high wall were men, women, and children of Lyric. Some waved bright cloth. All were shouting.

I nudged my mount over toward Evon. The young messenger tilted his head away. "I didn't let anyone know about you being . . . you know. But I may have mentioned that we saved Rendor." He glanced at me, biting his lip.

All around me, battle-weary men revived. Cavalry sat taller in their saddles. Guardians who had been banished and hunted and betrayed by the people they served lifted their chins, absorbing thanks that were long overdue.

A slow grin tugged my lips until it stretched so wide my face hurt. The cheering became a chant. "Jake! Jake! Jake!"

Evon edged farther from me, his neck turning red. "I kind of told them we won because you led us."

The loud welcome lit the faces of the men. How could I be angry at the boy? They needed this.

Then a rust-clad figure with slick black hair stepped into place over the arching entryway. The cheers choked off and the air became silent, except for the snorts of lehkan and jingle of tack.

"The king thanks you for carrying out his plan and freeing Rendor." Cameron's voice boomed and he flashed a smug smile.

Didn't he know how hokey he sounded, referring to himself in the third person?

"Lyric is dealing with . . . unrest, so the guardian army must remain outside the walls. But Jake, you may come in. The king is eager for a report from his son and heir!"

He shouted the last words and turned to the citizens closest to him along the wall. A few people attempted a halfhearted cheer, which quickly fizzled out.

"Don't go in there alone," Wade growled from behind me.

I swung my leg over and hopped down from my lehkan. I gave Wade a grim smile. "Don't worry. I won't be alone."

Before he could argue, I marched through the tunnel. The

king's guard at the far end stepped aside and I entered the central courtyard of Lyric. Two other guards in rust tunics and black vests flanked me as I strode toward the old Council offices. "Thanks, guys, but I know the way."

Their stoic faces didn't flinch. After escorting me to the familiar door, they took up position in the hall.

A dark chill ran through me as I stepped into Cameron's office. Weapons still decorated one wall, and tapestries another. I prowled around the onyx-topped desk and peered through the door into his inner office. The room was empty. At least Medea wasn't lurking nearby. I slid my sword a few inches out of my sheath and back again several times, testing its readiness.

Cameron entered the room like the tornado-in-a-bottle I made for the sixth-grade science fair. Starched tunic, arrogant posture, and rigid face couldn't completely hide the storm churning inside of him.

"So I send you for the healer and you disappear. And now you're back." He sneered.

"What happened to Medea?" Best to know what I was going to be up against.

His bitter laugh leaked venom. "Your concern is so thoughtful. We won't have to worry about her anymore." Regret chased across his face, but then he took a deep breath and smiled with all the teeth and false warmth of a politician. "So you've returned to take your place beside me. Come and sit down." He waved a hand toward the chair behind his desk.

I didn't move.

He leaned against the edge of his desk and crossed his arms. "You know, I was going to defeat the Kahlareans once all the weapons were ready. You didn't need to jump ahead of my plan. But since you succeeded, we won't hold it against you." His smirk was almost genuine. "The people love you—the young, reckless hero."

He bent forward from the waist, and his eyes darted around as though he were sharing a conspiracy with me. "You know, I've had a few problems with the changes I've been making." He lounged back again. "But with you here, they'll fall into line. You'll tell the clans to stop clinging to the old Records and to follow me. Together we'll push back the foreign threats for good."

Was he nuts? He sounded like he believed his own rhetoric. I stepped closer and glared straight into his face. "No."

His dark eyebrows drew together. "Jake, I'm giving you a rare opportunity here."

His reptilian stare used to frighten me. Not anymore. "Cameron, you nearly destroyed the People of the Verses. It stops now. The Council will be reinstated, and the worship tower will be opened to the songkeepers and the people again."

One hand strayed behind him, reaching for something on his desk. He smiled and grabbed my shoulder with one hand. I didn't react fast enough.

A sharp pain pierced my stomach. I shoved Cameron away and pulled the small weapon free. A venblade.

I sighed. This was getting old. And now Wade would need to find me another new tunic.

"Cameron, there's one thing I forgot to tell you."

The smug grin on his face faltered slightly, but he recovered. "What's that?"

I tossed the small dagger across the room. It was barely affecting me. Maybe I was building up an immunity. I stood tall. "I'm the Restorer."

Cameron turned grayish-white, the shade of old sweat socks.

I slugged him hard with a right hook, and his eyes closed. Man, that felt good.

He fell back against his desk, and the door of the office burst open.

I turned to the guards, rubbing my stinging knuckles. "The king just attempted to murder me. Take him to the guardian tower and lock him up. And send word to all the chief councilmembers still in Lyric. We're calling a Council session. Now."

Their eyes took in my bloody tunic, the sword at my side, and Cameron sprawled across the desk.

A wedge of doubt jammed against my confidence. *What if they throw me in a cell instead?*

But they'd seen Lyric fall apart under Cameron and heard the One's authority in my voice. They obeyed without a word.

As soon as the door shut, I doubled over, clutching for the edge of the desk. Okay, so maybe I wasn't completely immune. Numbness began to creep through my muscles again. My lungs spasmed for air. I should have driven the venblade into Cameron instead of just having him locked up. Then the room went fuzzy, like a television with bad reception. Someone pulled the plug, and the screen went blank.

When I woke up, Wade's face scowled down at me. "You've got to quit doing this, Jake."

I laughed, but that hurt too much and I started coughing. When I caught my breath, I looked up at him again. "So how did you get in here?"

Wade helped me to my feet. "The king's guard decided to let us in. We were ready to show them how real guardians do battle. Then they got word the king had gone mad and tried to kill the hero of Rendor. They didn't have the stomach for a fight." He sounded disappointed.

Hadn't he had enough fighting for one week? I hid a grin.

As the aftertaste of poison in my system faded, pure joy surged through me. The guardians were back inside Lyric. Medea was dead. Cameron had been stopped.

Wade looked around the grim office. "So what next?"

My mood sobered. "We still have to find out what Medea did with the families from Rendor. Let's go talk to Cameron."

That interview was as frustrating as I should have expected. Cameron wouldn't say a word, even when Wade cracked his knuckles and offered to help me persuade him. I pulled Wade out of the cell and made sure that several of the guardians were left to watch Cameron. As I left the prison area, a sudden flurry of activity assaulted me like a bunch of rabid pigeons flapping in my face. Councilmembers, songkeepers, transtechs—everyone had questions, needed reassurance, demanded information. Wade helped me field some of the early decisions. The rest could wait until the afternoon, when the Council met. Wade finally drew me away from the clamor, and we retreated to the wall near the city entrance. Climbing the stairs got us away from the chaos of a city unsure whether to celebrate or panic.

I leaned on the wall and looked out at the berms between the city and the transport station. "Wade, what kind of victory is this? We've got to find the Rendor families. I don't know what to do next."

Wade gave a dark chuckle. "If Cameron knows what Medea

did with them, he'll tell us eventually."

I wasn't so sure. Cameron worshiped power. And the only power he had left was in his secrets. I pushed my hair back and stared at the road outside the city.

Something moved in the far distance. A pale shape hovered at the edge of the hill, where the road curved toward town. "Wade, what's that?"

He squinted. "I don't see anything. Wait. There *is* something moving out there." He stumbled back a step. His voice dropped to a terrified whisper. "Messengers of the One, it's the Shades of Shamgar."

I'd never heard that ghost story, but whatever was approaching did look like something from the grave. Pale wraiths, all dressed in white, moved with slow, uneven gaits. A creepy chill gripped me. "Zombies." I clutched the edge of the marble wall and tried to breathe.

As I stared, my focus telescoped. They weren't the specters from horror films that I had thought. They were pale, horribly thin, limping people. And at the front of the ragged column was a lady with straight brown hair, her arm around the shoulders of a young girl.

Shock, confusion, and wonder raced through me. "Wade . . ."

He edged back toward the wall to stand beside me. I leaned forward. "I can't believe it." I grabbed Wade's arm and gave a glad shout. "It's my mom!"

Chapter Thirty-Three

JAKE

We vaulted down the steps and raced through the tunnel. My feet tore up the pavement. My mom lifted weary eyes and squinted at me. "Jake?" Then a smile lit her whole face. "It's you? Where's your dad?"

I hugged her. She was so thin I held back on the fierceness of my grip, afraid I would bruise her. "The portal didn't let him through. He's still at home. Where have you been? I thought you'd made it back to the attic by now."

Tears washed down her cheeks, and I sniffed, fighting back the moisture in my own eyes. Must be allergic to something in the air. I glanced behind her. "Who are all these people?"

"Rendor clan," she said softly.

She stepped back, giving me the adoring look only a mom can give. A fan club of one. Some days her pride in me made me feel embarrassed. Today it was exactly what I needed. Questions flew between us as we limped into the city. I held her arm to support her and noticed she seemed shorter than I had remembered.

The Council session brought some sense of order to the impossible events of the day. My mom looked all done in but insisted on addressing the Council and telling them what she'd learned in Rhus.

She hurried through the tale of their harrowing hike out of the tunnel, across the Pebbled Desert, around the clay pits of Shamgar, and finally back to Lyric. Some of the Rendor clan were skilled enough hunters to get them a little food. One of the banished clan members had knowledge of the path through the dangerous clay pits. Afternoon rain gave them much-needed water, which they sucked from their tunics until they reached a stream.

The lines in her face hinted at all the things she wasn't saying. I determined to get more of the story from her later.

The refugees were taken in and cared for with all the hospitality the city used to be famous for. My own declaration to the Council that I was the new Restorer was almost anticlimactic.

My mom left to get some food and rest while the Council wrangled for a while in their incomprehensible way, working out details for how to restore order to the clans. I stuck around, sprawled in a chair in the Rendor balcony, determined to make sure they started making things right.

The best part of the day was the hurriedly arranged worship gathering in the tower. After the rains, the call went out for everyone to gather. Music filled the huge room. For the first time in several seasons, a cloud of mist coalesced above the worshiper's heads and settled on us all like a benediction. I fell to my knees as images from the past days galloped through my mind. I'd been terrified when I found myself alone in the grove by the portal. So much had happened since then: journeys, intrigue, battles, betrayal. And I'd lost count of my injuries and how many times I'd died and recovered.

I'd been craving this adventure—bursting with reckless determination to make a difference. I hadn't had a clue how hard serving the One could be. Well, serving Him wasn't so bad. It was the people. Serving them, leading them. That's the part that was really rough.

An invisible hand rested on my shoulder. *Well done.* The voice of the One was familiar and warm, the words simple.

But they stirred inside like a gust of wind kicking up fall leaves. He was happy with me. That knowledge was all I needed.

At some point, the music and singing faded to holy quiet, but the stirring inside me built. I stood and looked up through the mist, toward the windows towering far above. Forgetting the throngs of people in the tower, the song I'd begun composing on my first day through the portal welled up from a place deep inside my marrow:

In the morning light, alone
May this tower always stand,
A tribute to Your guidance
And the comfort of Your hand.

I'll take the path You show me
Though it's dark beneath my feet.
Give me strength to walk this trail
'Til Your purpose is complete.

When the journey trips and cripples,
I give my wounds to You.
Lead me back to where Your songs
Drown the voices yet untrue.

Hope is born to find the way
Though early dreams grow hollow;
Your light will guide me forward,
Whenever faith will follow.

One of the songkeepers repeated the last verse after me. As he sang it again, the whole gathering joined, and I felt the power of the One's love draw a response of deep commitment from each soul in the tower.

After the notes faded, another songkeeper called out a last prayer, and people began trailing out through the eight arching entryways. My mom was still kneeling on the floor. She had her hands over her face, and when she moved them away, her skin was wet with tears. Man, she cried a lot. I helped her to her feet, and she grabbed me in a tight hug. I patted her back awkwardly, not knowing what to say.

The songkeepers made their way down from the dais, and a slim blonde form caught my eye. "Linette!" I broke away from Mom and headed toward her.

Linette turned, and her face glowed as I stumbled to a clumsy halt near her. She threw her arms around me, and my ears grew hot. "Jake, it's wonderful to see you. I heard that the Council officially recognized you as the new Restorer." She pulled away and looked past me, smile equally wide. "Susan, how are you?"

My mom hugged her. "I thought you were helping Kieran in Sidian."

She nodded. "I am. I just came to bring Tara the news. Tristan and Kendra had the baby." Her voice went up in pitch, the way girls' voices do when they talk about babies. "It's a girl, Emmi, and she is so amazing. She has Kendra's dark hair but Tristan's jaw. And the sweetest little nose."

Mom and Linette jabbered some more. Women sure get excited about babies.

Linette's giggle was an even more amazing sound than her singing. I stood nearby, hoping she'd do it again.

"Is Tara here in Lyric?" Mom asked.

"No. After I brought her the news, Lukyan asked me to come here to meet with the songkeepers. He thought they might need a little encouragement to take up their role again." Her face sobered. "They feel a lot of shame for letting things get as far as they did."

My mom smiled at me. "But things are back on track now." She reached up to smooth my hair, and I ducked aside. It made her laugh. "Well, Jake and I need to be going now. I want to get back to the portal before it gets dark. Mark must be worried sick."

I froze. I'd been dreading this moment. "Mom, we need to talk." I glanced apologetically at Linette. She gave Mom one last hug and promised to convey her love to everyone when she headed back to Hazor. Then she walked away to greet Wade. They strolled from the tower, arm in arm, and a wave of irritation swept over me.

My mom touched my arm. "Jake?"

Dark circles ringed Mom's eyes, and even with a good meal and a nap, she looked frail. This was going to be hard. "Mom, I'm not going back home with you. Not right now."

She stiffened and turned a more transparent shade of white. "Jake, you can't be serious. You don't belong here. It's got to be some of Medea's control in your thoughts. Remember? It happened before. She and Cameron wanted you to stay here, so it can't be the right thing to do."

She was talking faster and faster, as if by sheer weight of

words she could change my mind.

I took her hand and waited for her to slow down. "Mom, I understand why you'd think that, but I made a promise to Arland."

She held my hand in a death grip as she listened.

"When I came here, Arland was leading the guardians. They were all confused and angry. Even though you and Kieran had each saved the clans when you were the Restorer, they felt forsaken. Arland said they need a Restorer to stick around for more than one battle."

"But Jake—"

I patted her hand and made a hushing sound. "Let me finish."

My eyes pleaded with her to listen. When I was growing up, she'd always been pretty good at letting me have my say before pronouncing her answer of "no." The memory made me smile gently. I didn't want to hurt her. I had to get her to understand.

"After Arland died, I asked the One what He was going to do about giving the people a leader." How to explain what I had heard that night outside our campsite? I shifted gears. "Mom, have you ever heard the One tell you something? I mean, heard Him in your heart?"

Her eyes were wide and red-rimmed, but she nodded. "Of course. But Jake, you have to be careful about that."

"I know, I know. It would be easy for me to convince myself that eating pizza all day long was a great plan and that God told me to do it."

I was rewarded with a tight smile from her. She sniffed and rubbed her eyes.

"But this isn't like that. Mom, I heard Him. It's the clearest thing I've ever known in my life. It's not a delusion. It's what the One asked me to do. He wants me to serve Him here."

Watching her face was like rifling pages of a book. She tried on the thought, fought it, tested it again. When she closed her eyes, I knew she was asking the One to confirm it in her own heart.

When her shoulders drooped, I knew He had.

Her eyes popped open and she dropped my hand to grab my shoulders. "But you can't just disappear from our world! How will we explain it?" She was talking fast again, but with less conviction.

"I was going off to college anyway. You can just let people think that's where I am."

"Are you crazy? What about Christmas? What will I tell your grandma? Or your friends who call wanting to get your phone number?"

I'd already gone over these objections with the One, during the hours of hiking toward Lyric.

"It's going to be okay. The time passes differently anyway. I could stay here a few seasons and come back to find out only a day has gone by for you guys. And you can come through anytime you want to check on me—if the portal lets you."

I scratched my head. I still wasn't sure how the thing worked.

She turned away, her arms wrapped around her waist. I almost missed her quiet words. "What will I tell your dad?"

I didn't know what to do.

God, help me comfort her. Help her know this is a good thing.

I stepped closer and put one arm around her shoulders. "You know how Dad is all intense about how he deserted his people by staying in our world?"

She nodded, her face softening the way it did when she thought of him.

"Well, I think maybe this will feel like the right thing to him. Kind of a balance. He can't come back anymore, but he can give his son to the clans."

"But we don't understand everything about the portal." Her words were coming more slowly now. She gave a deep sigh. "What if I can't come back through? What if you can't get back to us when you're ready to?"

"Mom, there's a lot we'll never understand about the portal, but that's not what we're putting our trust in. If the One wants me here right now, He'll take care of me. If He wants me to go home, He'll make a way. That's who we need to trust."

Listen to me—preaching to my mom. I expected her to roll her eyes.

Instead, she gave me a teary smile. She pulled my head closer and rested her forehead against mine. "Go with the One," she whispered.

Now my own eyes filled, and I let the tears fall. "I will."

We walked slowly out to the courtyard. Mom's gaze drank in the surroundings with the sense of someone saying her good-byes. Wade hadn't gone far, as he was reluctant to let me out of his sight. He gave a deep belly laugh in answer to something Linette was telling him. I frowned.

They saw us and hurried over. My mom started asking Wade to look out for me. She was winding up for a long lecture, so I took the opportunity to pull Linette aside.

"Do you have to go back to Hazor?" I blurted out.

She blinked a few times. "Why?"

I swallowed and rubbed sweaty palms along my pant legs. "The One has asked me to stay—to lead the people here in Lyric. I just thought . . . well, I could use your help."

She tilted her head, her eyes warm. "Oh, Jake, I'm so glad you'll be staying here. Kieran will be so relieved that there's a Restorer keeping the clans safe. It's been driving him crazy, not being able to come and fix things."

Her enthusiasm for my calling flooded me with hope.

Then she smiled gently. "But I can't stay. I promised to help Kieran. He needs me."

"But he's not the Restorer anymore." *Great, Jake. That sounded like a whiny kid.*

Her eyes clouded. "I know. But it's where I belong."

I wasn't sure exactly what she meant by that. Did she mean as a songkeeper, or something more? My stomach twisted as I tried to sort that out, and she turned away. She gave my mom one last hug and then disappeared down a side street. Wade and I watched her leave and sighed in unison. I ignored my mom's sympathetic glance.

Wade and I walked with my mom to the portal, so quiet that we could hear our feet squish against the moss. When we reached the grove, she didn't start bawling like I'd feared. She pulled herself up tall and gave me a soft smile and one last hug. She was a brave woman, even if she was my mom. Then she stepped between two narrow trees, through the ripple of energy that no one else seemed to see, and disappeared.

I was doing the right thing.

But my steps rang hollow on the walk back to Lyric. I could have gone through with her. Back to sunlight and stars, cell phones and books, pizza and soda. Back to my family.

When we entered the city, my feet aimed straight back to the worship tower.

Wade stayed back near the entry while I hurried to the center of the tower and dropped to one knee. Hand on my sword hilt and head bowed, I turned my thoughts to my Chief Guardian. "Sorry for being so thick, but could You just tell me one more time? Are You sure You want me here? I'm going to need some directions. The songkeepers are still sorting out how to undo the damage from the fake Records. The Council does nothing but argue. The Kahlareans are probably going to keep trying to get across the River Borders."

Cool moist air swirled around me, a gathering mist that carried reassurance and enough strength to fill my bones. The Voice spoke, with a tone of confidence and wild joy. His words would carry me for all the seasons of work ahead. They were the only words I needed.

Jake, follow Me.

Chapter Thirty-Four

SUSAN

Dust motes sparkled in the quiet attic. Late afternoon sun angled in from the low west window, blinding me with its brilliance. Without a thick gray atmosphere obscuring any glimpse into the cosmos, the light looked golden. I took a deep breath and waited for vertigo to pass.

Home. I'd made it back. The familiar bits and bobbles of our suburban life smiled at me from under the eaves.

Another shaky breath and I turned in a full circle. Alone. Somehow I'd expected Mark to be waiting—standing guard by the stones.

My relief sagged under the weight of sudden anxiety. How much time had passed? Was Mark all right? What had happened to him while I'd been gone?

The pull-down stairs unfolded into our back hallway. At least Mark hadn't shut the trapdoor.

I worked my way down the narrow treads and stopped to listen. The house felt quiet. Too quiet.

Father, let him be all right. Please, please, please. If he managed to get through to Lyric somehow and we never found each other—

Something clattered from the direction of the kitchen. A voice murmured. The ache to be back in Mark's arms rolled over me. I ran through the living room and into the kitchen.

I skidded to a stop in the doorway, hands grabbing the frame for support.

Mark sat at the kitchen table, chasing a piece of spaghetti around a freezer-meal tray with a fork. The bruises on his face were less swollen but still colorful. "Yeah, have Murray handle that account. No, I don't know when I'll be in." He snapped his cell phone shut and tossed it on the table. He shoved his plate aside and rested his forehead against his fists.

"Oh, God, bring her back." The groaning prayer that wrenched from him would stay with me forever.

Then he must have sensed my presence in the doorway.

"Susan!" He was an explosion of movement. I'd never seen him move that fast before, even when crossing swords with Hazorites. He knocked over a kitchen chair in his dash to meet me. "Thank the One."

His arms nearly crushed me.

Nothing had ever felt as wonderful.

He held me out and stared, scanning me. First, like a warrior assessing battle damage. Next, as my best friend, reading a glimpse of my experiences through the clues in my face and body. Finally, he took in every inch of me with the hunger of a lover.

My skin flushed, and I flung myself back into him for another hug. "I'm home."

He gave a joyous bark of laughter. "Yes, I see that. Where's Jake?"

I froze. "I'll explain in a minute." I dropped my voice to a whisper. "How much time has gone by? Are the kids—?"

"A few days. Karen's still on her band tour, and the other kids are at camp. I'm"—he cleared his throat—"alone."

I'd already seen his desperation when he'd slumped at the table. Now I heard its dissonance rattle in his throat. I'd been in a miserable prison in Rhus, but he'd been tortured every bit as much as he waited and worried.

A few days? My head spun. A slow breath drew in the scent of garlic from Mark's microwave dinner. A few dishes cluttered the sink, and take-out bags were wadded on the counter. Mark's whiskers scraped against my skin as he nuzzled me. His shirt was rumpled. I touched a cut over his eye. Even multicolored with bruises, he was beautiful.

His fingers dug into my arms. "What happened? How did you get away from Medea and Cameron? I tried to go through a hundred times and the portal didn't work. Did Jake find you? Where is he?"

I sank into a chair. The silence pulled taut. Mark didn't move. My fingers traced wood patterns on the table while I struggled to squeeze the words out. "He's staying for a while."

It took three mugs of spice tea—the closest thing to clavo I'd been able to find in our world—to fill him in on everything that had happened. I loved him too much to tell him everything Nicco had done to my mind.

"You're so pale." He touched the scar on my face, then kissed it softly. "And thin. You're not telling me everything."

I'd never been good at hiding things from him, so I opted for distraction. "Jake led the guardians and got the Kahlareans out of Rendor. And he defeated Cameron."

Mark swelled with pride as I told him about Jake's adventures. Finally, I summoned the courage to explain Jake's decision to stay.

My husband raked a hand through his hair and paced a rut into our living room carpet. He argued, complained, and decreed that it was a bad idea.

Once he got that out of his system, we went over his objections and struggles one by one, and he calmed down. As Jake had predicted, Mark found symmetry in our son's decision. On some level, he could accept it. And maybe he knew that if he kept ranting about it, my own compartmentalized pain would break out again. For my sake, he sat down and took a deep breath. "I'm sure he'll be fine. You couldn't drag him back. If the One wants him there . . ." He sighed with the pain of being separated from both his world and his son. For a man who thrived on fixing things, there was no crueler challenge than to know that those he loved were facing battles where he couldn't help.

He picked up my hand and outlined a circle in my palm. Then his hands traveled to my face, and he stroked back strands of my lank hair.

I probably looked terrible with the shapeless, rough-woven tunic that someone in Lyric had given me, skin sallow from weeks of imprisonment, not to mention the new scar on my face.

I pulled away. "I need a bath."

He frowned. "I'm not letting you out of my sight."

"And I'm hungry. Are there any microwave dinners left? That spaghetti smelled good."

He held my chin. "All right. I'll heat up some supper for you and let you get changed. But make it quick, okay?"

Warmth curled up under my heart and purred.

In the shower, I used some of Karen's best conditioner. I would have preferred to soak for an hour in a froth of bubbles, but I didn't like being away from Mark for long, either. After I blissfully slipped into my favorite jeans and T-shirt and wolfed down two servings of spaghetti, Mark and I snuggled on the couch. He filled me in on his difficulties during the past few days. He'd nursed broken ribs, fended off my mom's questions about why I hadn't returned her calls, and told Harvey that Jake couldn't come in to work.

I rested my face against Mark's shoulder. "You're taking Jake's news pretty well."

He shrugged and my cheek rose and fell. "You're here. I'm concentrating on that. Do you know how scared I was that you'd never come back?" His voice sounded thick, and his chest moved unevenly. "I prayed for you every minute."

A shudder ran through me as I remembered the bleak room in Rhus. "I needed it." I reached up to twirl one of Mark's curls around my finger. "So how long should we wait before we check on Jake?"

He batted my hand away and grabbed my face for a quick kiss. "I don't want you going back there."

I leaned back a few inches. "But if you can't go through the portal anymore, I'll have to. Unless Jake comes back himself. And if he doesn't, I'll have to go find out what's happening."

Mark sighed. "All right, I do have a few thoughts about that. Maybe I can reprogram the portal stones so they'll work for me again."

I grabbed a throw pillow and slammed it into the top of his head. "Are you nuts?"

Mark plucked the pillow from my grip and tossed it across the room. He smiled into my indignation and melted it. "I'm just saying we might have some options." Then he sobered. "Besides, I'm not letting you go back there alone." His fingers stroked the side of my face and burrowed into my still-damp hair.

I let him draw me close, smelling the faint touch of Ivory soap on his skin. My fingertips brushed over the afternoon stubble on his jaw. "How about if we agree to try the portal in one month. That could be years over there. Or minutes. But we should at least check."

"It's a deal." He settled deeper into the couch. "It's funny."

"Hmmm?"

"Jake's eighteen."

I wasn't sure what he was getting at. "Um-hum?"

Mark stared out the living room window. "That's how old I was when I came here. And it turned out pretty well for me." He turned his crooked grin in my direction.

I stared into his blue-gray eyes and savored the feeling of being loved—loved enough to leave a whole world behind. Then my eyes drifted past him. I could just see the corner of the dining room from this angle.

"Mark!" I jumped to my feet and scampered to the doorway, then looked back at him in shock.

He lounged back on the couch and gave me a lazy smile.

He'd repaired the smashed doors of the china cabinet earlier in the summer, but the bare shelves had been a reminder of everything that had been broken. We'd existed in a storm of tension since Cameron and Medea's invasion and never made time to rebuild our collection of teacups.

Now one Delft cup perched on a blue and white saucer.

Mark hefted himself off the couch and came to put an arm around me. "It's just a start. I found it online. I needed to do something while I was waiting. There should be some good yard sales next weekend. We can find some more together."

Tears stung my eyes and I couldn't speak.

"Do you like it?" His voice turned worried.

We'd collected antique teacups, and a lot more, in our twenty years together. I wondered what new things we'd discover in the next twenty.

"I love it," I said softly and buried myself into his arms.

etc.

bonus content includes:

- Reader's Guide
- Glossary
- Map
- "Jake's Song"
- About the Author

Reader's Guide

1. Jake is eighteen and preparing to leave for college. How does his stage of life affect his response to the idea of being a Restorer? How does his initial reaction differ from Susan's or Kieran's? Do you identify with any of his traits?
2. In *The Restorer*, Susan's role was loosely inspired by the Old Testament character of Deborah. In *The Restorer's Son*, Kieran's story had some parallels to Gideon, as well as to Jacob and even Jonah. What Old Testament imagery did you notice in this story? In Jake as the youthful songwriter/leader? In Susan leading out captives? Other threads?
3. Jake is eager to heed the One's call to follow, until he confronts betrayal, confusion, and his own failures. Then he decides to quit and go home. What incidents in your life have shaken your faith and your determination to follow the One? How does Jake change as the story progresses?
4. Susan has a dark journey in this story. What do you think the Rhusicans might symbolize? Are there any circumstances in your life that remind you of the bare room where Susan is imprisoned?

5. What impact do you think Susan has in Rhus? Was she powerless? Did you see hints of purpose that the One might have had for her time there: for the other captives? For the Rhusicans? For Susan herself?
6. In *The Restorer's Journey*, we met several new characters who played prominent roles. What did you think of Nicco? Ian? Arland? What were their goals, desires, and drives? Did they change during the course of the story?
7. What key themes did you unwrap in this story? Were any similar to the themes from the first two books? Different? How?
8. Did you agree with Jake's decision at the end of the book? Why or why not? What do you think will happen to his family in our world? What problems will Jake face among the People of the Verses?

Glossary

caradoc: Docile herd animal with soft, shedding coat that is used for creating cloth.

clans: The People of the Verses comprise twelve original clans: Lyric, Braide Wood, Rendor, Shamgar, Corros Fields, Blue Knoll, Ferntwine, Terramin, Sandor, Taborn, and the returned "lost clans" of Kalem and Radella.

clavo: Spicy tea with a rich flavor and near-healing properties; favorite hot beverage of the clans; usually brewed in a wide wooden bowl over a heat trivet and ladled into mugs.

clay fields: Flat, deserted lands near Shamgar, with treacherous pits of bubbling liquid concrete that have been known to trap and swallow animals and humans who stumble into them.

conservatory: The building where Rhusicans house their captives and practice their skills of delving into and manipulating minds and shaping realities.

Council: Governing body of the People of the Verses, comprising chosen representatives from each tribe; meets in Lyric and makes decisions that affect all the tribes.

first-years: Men and women in the first year of guardian training; usually about eighteen years old.

ground-crawlers: Ten times the size of a North American earthworm, these burrowers come out only at night. Their skin is toxic to anything they touch, causing acidic burns to animals and humans.

guardian: Member of any clan who trains for military/protector role, which includes serving the Council and the people, training for and engaging in battle, and patrolling the borders.

Hazor: Nation across the mountain border of the People's clans. Hazorites worship the hill-gods and have been known to sacrifice their children to those gods, though the practice is currently forbidden, due to the efforts of a Restorer who promised to serve the people of Hazor in exchange for the safety of the clans. Their king, Zarek, rules from the capital, Sidian.

healer: A person skilled in treating illness and injuries with electronic diagnostic devices as well as herbal remedies. Most villages have their own healers, but near Braide Wood there is a lodge where especially difficult cases from all the clans are handled.

heat trivet: Flat panels or tiles that glow with heat or light. Various sizes are used to provide surfaces for cooking and illumination. They are a smaller version of the technology used to create the light walls common in homes.

house protector: One who takes a formal vow to defend another's person and family (household) with his or her life.

Kahlarea: Nation across the river that borders one side of the People's lands. Kahlareans are pale with bulbous eyes, and their assassins are feared everywhere for their stealth and ability to hide and appear from nowhere.

king's guard: After Cameron took control of the clans and disbanded the Council, he changed the elite Council Guard into his own private cadre.

lehkan: Animals used for riding. They look similar to elk, with fierce antlers and soft llama-like fur. They are ridden under saddle and guided by leg commands.

light cube: Small handheld incandescent light source that can be set to overload and disintegrate everything it touches; has been used to cremate bodies.

Lyric: Central city of the tribes. The Lyric tower is the place where the One meets with the People in an especially tangible way. Lyric's walls are white and form a scalloped pattern as they encircle the city.

magchip: Renewable energy source for a variety of technologies.

messenger: Because the clans and the surrounding nations don't have a written language, messengers memorize information to take from place to place. Messengers are typically young, agile, and fast.

Morsal Plains: Farmland near Braide Wood; site of a major battle with Hazor during the time of Susan the Restorer.

People of the Verses: The collection of tribes who worship the One. They pass down the Verses to their children through daily recitations.

portal stones: Fist-sized round, smooth objects with hidden technology. When three are aligned correctly and activated, they create a portal between the world of the People of the Verses and our world.

Records: A sacred recording of the Verses in their original form, spoken by the One. Each clan has one, which the clan's eldest songkeeper plays on end-of-season Feast days.

Restorer: A leader, traditionally a guardian, sent by the One to save His people. Once called by the One for this role, the Restorer develops heightened senses and gifts of various kinds and heals rapidly from most injuries.

Rhusican: A person from Rhus, a nearby nation; usually attractive, with reddish-gold hair and vibrant aqua or green eyes. Rhusicans have the ability to read and affect minds and to plant poison in people's thoughts that can influence their behavior and even cause death.

rizzid: Venomous, lizard-shaped creature muddy red in color and covered with fur; climbs walls and has rows of sharp teeth.

scrambler: A device used to deactivate magnetic locks.

season: The time it takes grain to go through one full cycle of planting, growth, and harvesting; there are six seasons each year.

Sidian: The capital city of Hazor. A center of commerce and home to Zarek's palace, the prisons, and the location of the primary hill-god shrine.

songkeeper: A person who leads worship, composes songs, encourages people, and promotes the faith life of the People.

syncbeam: Long-range, focused energy beam used as a weapon.

transtech: A person skilled in designing and repairing the wide variety of technology used by the clans.

transport: Automated vehicles of various sizes that follow programmed routes between and within cities; long, sleek, silver, with curved doors that slide up into the roof.

venblade: Small dagger used by Kahlarean assassins; reservoir in the handle injects poison into the blade to cause paralysis in the victim.

Verses: Holy account of the People's history, laws, and promises about Restorers and the coming Deliverer, given directly by the One. The Records contain an audible version of the original directives from the One; however, the Verses are still a living tradition, and the One guides each generation of songkeepers in adding the next section of history. These additional sections of the Verses are not in the Records but are equally unchanging and sacred and passed down by vigilant oral tradition.

worship tower: Sometimes referred to as "the tower"; the tallest, most central tower in Lyric, made of white stone. Large arched entries face outward in eight directions. The entire roof is formed of skylights, and a platform in the middle of the tower rises and rotates during worship gatherings.

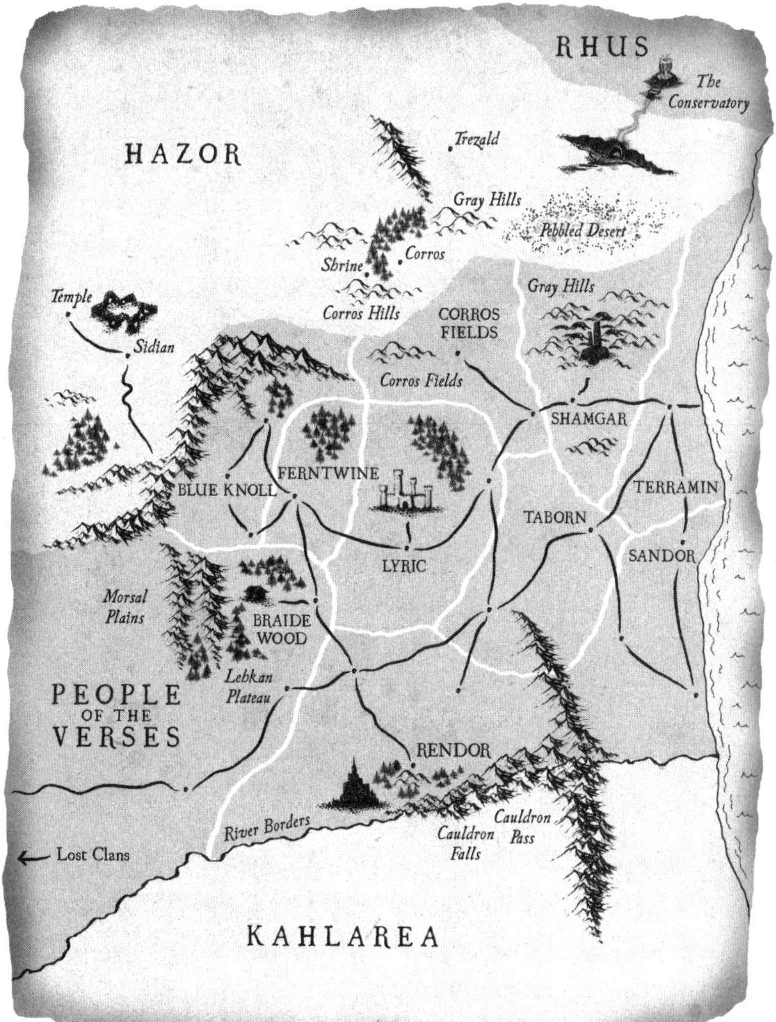
RHUS
The Conservatory
HAZOR
Trezald
Gray Hills
Pebbled Desert
Shrine
Corros
Temple
Corros Hills
CORROS FIELDS
Gray Hills
Sidian
Corros Fields
SHAMGAR
FERNTWINE
BLUE KNOLL
TERRAMIN
TABORN
SANDOR
LYRIC
Morsal Plains
BRAIDE WOOD
Lebkan Plateau
PEOPLE OF THE VERSES
RENDOR
River Borders
Cauldron Falls
Cauldron Pass
Lost Clans
KAHLAREA

Jake's Song

Words by Sharon Hinck
Music by Joel Hinck

Slowly ♩ = 68

C G Am F C G Em7
1.In the mor-ning light, a lone May this tow-er al-ways stand,
2.I'll take the path You show me Though it's dark be-neath my feet.
C Am C F G 1. C F
A trib-ute to Your guid- ance And the com-fort of Your hand.
Give me strength to walk this trail 'Til Your pur-pose is com-
2. C Em A D A Bm G
plete.
3.When the jour-ney trips and crip- ples,
4.Hope is born to find the way
D A F#m7 D Bm
I give my wounds to You. Lead me back to where Your songs
Though ear-ly dreams grow hol - low; Your light will guide me for - ward,
D G A 1. D G 2. D
Drown the voi-ces yet un - true.
When-ev - er faith will fol - low.

etc.

About the Author

SHARON HINCK holds a BA in education, and she earned an MA in communication from Regent University in 1986. She spent ten years as the artistic director of a Christian performing arts group, CrossCurrent. That ministry included three short-term mission trips to Hong Kong. She has been a church youth worker, a choreographer and ballet teacher, a homeschool mom, a church organist, and a bookstore clerk. One day she'll figure out what to be when she grows up, but in the meantime, she's pouring her imagination into writing. Her stories focus on characters who confront the challenges of a life of faith. She's published dozens of articles in magazines and book compilations, and released her first novel, *The Secret Life of Becky Miller* (Bethany House), in 2006. In April 2007, she was named "Writer of the Year" at the Mount Hermon Christian Writers Conference.

When she isn't wrestling with words, Sharon enjoys speaking at conferences and retreats. She and her family make their home in Minnesota. She loves to hear from readers, so send a message through the portal into her writing attic on the "Contact Sharon" page of her website, www.sharonhinck.com.